THE FALLING MACHINE

The

SOCIETY OF STEAM

BOOK ONE

THE FALLING MACHINE

ANDREW P. MAYER

an imprint of Prometheus Books
Amherst, NY

Published 2011 by Pyr®, an imprint of Prometheus Books

Inquiries should be addressed to
Pyr
59 John Glenn Drive
Amherst, New York 14228–2119
VOICE: 716–691–0133
FAX: 716–691–0137
WWW.PYRSF.COM

15 14 13 12 11   5 4 3 2

Library of Congress Cataloging-in-Publication Data

Mayer, Andrew P.
The falling machine / by Andrew P. Mayer.
p. cm. — (Society of steam ; bk. 1)
ISBN 978–1–61614–375–6 (pbk.)
ISBN 978–1–61614–376–3 (e-book)
1. Steampunk fiction. I. Title.

PS3613.A9548F36 2011
813'.6—dc22

2011001709

Printed in the United States of America

For Hans Mayer, my father,
who never let adversity limit his passion for discovery

Chapter 1

Wonders of the World

"Life is short, yet it is the nature of man to make it move faster all the time." Sir Dennis Darby punctuated his pronouncement with a firm smack of the silver tip of his cane against the concrete underneath his feet.

Sarah and Nathaniel stood nearby, looking up at the old man, quietly and respectfully waiting for him to continue, but before he could say another word his intended dramatic pause was broken by a long, throaty groan rising up from behind them.

Just below them, the Automaton had begun to slowly and methodically spin the massive wooden spool with his left hand. The wheel was five feet across, with a thick iron post running up through the center of it. Viscous black grease oozed up from where the pole made contact with a metal collar that held it in place, and the noise vanished.

"Tom," Darby said, addressing the mechanical man, "are you bored?"

The Automaton lowered his arm. "I can stop if you'd like . . . Sir Dennis." His sentence sounded like a song, and each word was spoken as a single separate note—high and smooth—with just a hint of a rasp from the metal whistles and reeds that played together to create his voice.

"I just wanted to make sure you were paying attention," Darby continued. "It's far beyond even your impressive abilities to halt the march of progress." The old man smiled and looked down at his creation. It was a rare expression on his usually stern face. "No, my dear Tom, humanity will always strive to learn more, rise higher, and go faster. And one day people will look back to this year of eighteen hundred and eighty and imagine that we were a primitive and ignorant people, just as we do now to those who came before us." The widening grin pushed his sharp features and graying muttonchops out to the sides in a way that was slightly unsettling. "But that is the price of progress, as we forge ahead to make the lives of our descendants better than our own." Darby had been wearing a version of his current look of childlike wonder almost from the first moment the four of them had set foot onto the Brooklyn side of the bridge construction site.

They had all dressed up for the trip, as it was intended to be a formal outing. Both of the men wore full suits, with vests, jackets, and hats, as well as long overcoats to protect them against the winter cold. The Professor's greatcoat was made of sensible black wool, while young Nathaniel's was far fancier. His lapels and cuffs were trimmed with the same rich, black beaver fur that lined the jacket's interior. Ebony silk top hats rested snugly on their heads.

The two gentlemen were also of similar height and build—six feet tall and slim—but Nathaniel had the athletic demeanor of a young man, while Darby's frame was looser and slightly hunched, his age having drained away the vitality of youth.

The Automaton stood at five feet, six inches exactly. He was dressed in a similar fashion to the men, but with only a jacket wrapped around his long cylindrical frame. He had no need of an overcoat, despite a temperature that was only being held a notch above freezing by the light of the morning sun.

The mechanical man's face and neck were completely unbound by leather or cloth, showing a series of tubes and metal shafts that connected his head and body. His delicate features were lovingly painted onto a smooth porcelain mask: the eyes were bright blue, and his lips had the same mysterious hint of a smile as the *Mona Lisa*. The back of his head was a skull-shaped slab of solid brass, and a delicate ribbon of steam drifted lazily out from a valve at the back of his neck.

The Professor's voice grew louder, as it usually did when he was becoming entranced by his own words, "And you Tom, you are *my* response to that most human urge—mankind's never-ending desire to bring light to the dark boundary of the unknown.

"And even standing in the shadow of this modern-day marvel," he said, pointing up to the massive tower, "you are still an object of wonder." Darby swept his arm across the vista of stone and wire that stretched out in front of them as if he were unveiling it for the very first time. "Even compared to the Brooklyn Bridge."

Rising up and out from the anchorage where they were standing were two cables of twisted steel, each one as thick as a man, heading from the shore and out over the water. They rose up and over the top of a stone tower standing almost three hundred feet tall and then dropped back down, crossing the East River to another tower of the same height that sat just off the edge of Manhattan Island. The building of the road that would eventually connect the two cities had only just been started, and the cables hung expectantly above the water, ready to bear their load.

"The greatest wonder of the modern world," Darby said, and then winked at the girl, "even if it isn't quite finished yet."

Sarah smiled and clapped, the effect muffled by her gloves. "It's gorgeous, Professor." She moved forward with the layers of her ruffled blue skirt rustling and swaying with every step. "Thank you so much for bringing us out here so we could see it." Her matching fur cape was wrapped around her tightly enough that the rigid feminine curve of her bodice could be seen underneath it. The blonde curls of her hair had been pulled back and piled up into a severe bun. Pinned to the top of it was a navy-blue bonnet, the fashionable veil coming down to just above her eyes. But underneath all the structure that had been built to support and define the modern woman of 1880, a natural aura of relaxed strength and beauty still shone through.

Trying not to stare at Sarah, Nathaniel squinted his eyes even more than usual as he turned his gaze to the bridge, tipping his head so far back that his hat seemed poised to slide off. "Do you think something so big will actually hold up, Professor?"

"Of course it will." Darby nodded firmly, some of his usual intensity returning to his face as he did so. "The principles behind it are quite sound. A large-scale structure such as this simply requires a rigorous application of math, human ingenuity, and hard work. A bridge is the culmination of all those things."

The Professor took a deep breath, filling his lungs completely and then holding it for a moment before speaking. "All right, everyone, are we ready for an adventure?" He lifted up his cane and pointed the metal tip toward the wooden platform that acted as the entrance to the walkway. It seemed far less sound than the concrete and stone edifice underneath their feet.

Sarah looked over at him. "I've already had my fair share, Sir Dennis." Then she gave him a brave wink and a smile. "But I'm always game for more!" She knew that her father would have frowned on her flirtatious attitude, but she and Sir Dennis had often shared such moments over the last few years.

Inclined to tomboyish behavior as a girl, her early teens had been a time of rude awakening, divorcing her from the casual company of boys and men in ways she still found frustrating and unfair. It only took a glance in a mirror to remind her that she had been gifted with a beauty that had forever stolen away an innocent connection with the opposite sex, and she was still struggling to understand the power of it.

From her mother she had inherited all the best Harrington family traits: long blonde hair, an upturned nose, and sparkling green eyes. And enough men had become hypnotized by her lips while she spoke that she knew she had been given her father's full mouth. She was grateful for it. Even though her suitors often ignored the words that came out of it, at least it kept their eyes on her face, which was a higher level of attention than her fuller-figured friends often received.

Nathaniel stepped up behind her. "It's windy up there, Sarah. Are you sure you're up to it?"

She turned her head and looked back at him over her shoulder. "I'm not the delicate flower you seem to think I am, Nathan." The words came out in a colder tone than she had intended. Much to her father's chagrin, she had also inherited the quick Stanton temperament, and her sharp words often surprised her as much as it did everyone else.

She marched to the end of the anchorage, heading toward the steps that led up to the walkway as fast as the complicated layers of her dress would allow. Just beyond them, the rickety trail of wood and wire stretched off into the distance, almost parallel to the massive cables as it arced up toward the closest tower. "I'll be fine," she said to herself as much as anyone else.

Nathaniel frowned slightly, giving his already-sullen features an even grimmer look. At twenty-two he was still a young man, and some women found his brooding attractive. It clearly had the opposite effect on Sarah. But his dark moods were a part of his passionate nature, and not something that he felt a great need to control. "I suppose we're *all* going up there—the whole damn circus." He lifted up his top hat and swept his black hair back over his head, then pulled it down tightly and started to follow after her.

Dennis Darby stopped him, clamping a hand down onto Nathaniel's shoulder and giving it a squeeze. "Is there need for such language?" He turned back to the Automaton, still entranced by the large wooden wheel. "Now come along, Tom."

The metal man let go of the empty spool that he had been toying with and strode forward in a smooth, gliding motion. It was, as always, the mathematically perfect arc of his movements that made his inhumanity so obvious. "We are part of a . . . circus? Does that make me . . . the acrobat, or . . . the clown?"

"You're the side show," Nathaniel grumbled. Pulling a silver flask from his jacket pocket, he undid the cap with a quick twist and knocked back a swig.

Ignoring Nathaniel's activities, Darby scanned his eyes over the machine-man, glanced up at the wooden footbridge, and then shook his head. "I'm a little worried about your weight up there, Tom. I think you're going to need to drop some ballast first."

"What if there's trouble?" asked Tom.

"At this moment I'm more worried about the strength of those wooden slats you'll be walking on then any potential villainy, especially with all that equipment we've loaded inside you. It wouldn't do to have you plunging into the river." He tapped his cane against the metal man's chest. "Dropping those armor plates should do the trick."

Tom nodded his head in another perfectly smooth curve. He unbuttoned his brocade vest, then the pleated shirt underneath, his leather-gloved fingers moving slowly and deliberately. The tiny curls of steam that rose up from his wrists as he worked were quickly consumed by the winter breeze.

He opened his shirt to reveal a pair of broad brass breastplates underneath. Each one was sculpted into an idealized form of the impossibly perfect contoured muscles of a Greek god. There was a loud click as he twisted the first one free from the metal snaps holding it in place. It lifted upward and off, revealing rows of cogs spinning away underneath. He placed it down onto the rough wooden planking. If exposing himself had an emotional impact on Tom, it was impossible to read from the painted-on features of the porcelain mask that acted as his face.

Nathaniel stared at him for a few seconds. There was a slight sneer on his lips as he watched the Automaton remove the second brass plate and place it on top of the first with a dull clank.

Sarah, standing one step from the top of the stairs, had also found herself unable to tear her eyes away. As Tom began to rebutton his clothes, she shook her head as if waking up from a trance. Looking for something else to rest her eyes on, she caught a glimpse of the large sign that stood at the entrance to the walkway in front of them. She read it out loud, for Tom's benefit: "'Safe for Only Twenty-Five Men at One Time. Do Not Walk Close Together, Run, Jump, or Trot. Break Step!'" She let out a nervous laugh. "Sounds a bit menacing."

"Wise words, those," said a stranger's voice. The words were spoken in a deep Irish brogue that contained both a lilt and a rumble. "Any way you read it, though, yer gonna want to step carefully up there." By the way he was dressed, the speaker was clearly a member of the working crew, his nose and cheeks bright red from the breeze. The thick cloth coat he wore was threadbare at the hem and cuffs, and he pulled it tightly around his barrel frame to keep out the cold of the early January morning. The slouching circle of the kepi cap that rested on the top of his head was a leftover from the Civil War, although all the military insignia had been stripped off of it a long time ago. "The wind's not too bad today, though." His face was broad and round, with a set of thick red-and-gray muttonchops that traveled from ear to chin. His skin was ruddy and rough, placing him clearly in his late forties or early fifties. "Not as bad as some days, anyway."

Darby extended a hand. "And you would be, sir?"

"Barry Moloney. One of the foremen here at the Brooklyn Bridge, and yer official tour guide on this fine Sunday." He doffed his hat, then took the offered hand and gave the old scientist a single quick shake. His gloved paw enfolded the Professor's hand almost completely. "Mrs. Roebling told me to meet you over here and give you the run of the place. She said to give you her apologies, and let you know that she and her husband will meet with you back at her house once you've finished your work at the top of the tower."

Sarah beamed. "You see that, Nathan? There's a woman in charge. We're not all as incapable of critical thought as you seem to think we are."

The Irishman smiled. "Well, she does give the orders. But it's her husband, Mr. Washington, who writes them down first. Poor man got the sickness down in the Caissons, and now he can barely move." He looked at Sarah squarely in the eyes. "Yer not one of them suffergettes, are you?"

"Not officially," She thrust out a white-gloved hand. "My name is Sarah Stanton, Mr. Moloney. Pleased to meet you."

He shook her hand firmly and stared straight into her eyes. "That's a good grip, Miss Stanton." The Irishman smiled over at Nathan. "Rope that lass quick, boy, or she'll marry the first man that tames her fire."

Nathaniel replied with a sniff. "This 'lass' is the daughter of Alexander Stanton—the Industrialist—one of the most powerful and respected men in all of New York City, and a founding member of the Paragons. I'd ask that you treat her, and me, with a little more respect."

For a moment the easy smile vanished from the Irishman's face to be replaced by something darker. "All right, young sir, didn't mean to offend. I'm just here to help you and yers safely up to the top of the tower and . . ." His word's trailed off as he saw Tom for the first time. "Good Lord!"

Darby nodded to the metal man. "Go ahead and introduce yourself, Tom."

The mechanical man finished closing the last button of his jacket, then strode forward and held out his hand. Even under the black leather glove the large round lumps at the knuckles clearly revealed that it wasn't a human appendage underneath. "I am called the Automaton, . . . Mr. Moloney. I'm very glad to meet you."

"Are you now?" Moloney grasped the offered hand gingerly, then pumped Tom's arm quickly up and down. He glanced over his shoulder at Darby. "Does he think he's alive?"

"What Tom thinks or doesn't think is still a matter of some great debate," the Professor replied. "Most people would say that if he is able to reason then he must be alive. Having both created him and taught him, I'd like to think that's so. At any rate, I'd ask that you treat him with the same respect you'd give me."

"*Cogito, ergo sum*, . . . Mr. Moloney," the Automaton said.

Barry let go of Tom's hand and then walked away from the group to a pile of tools that sat nearby. "Now I've met a metal man. . . . That'll be something to tell the wife, anyway."

Darby continued to talk, behind him. "I have some experiments I'd like to run once we reach the top of the tower."

"We've both got a job to do today." The Irishman pulled up his large pack, constructed from what appeared to be brass and canvas, and slung it over his back. He wobbled slightly as he heaved it up over his shoulders and buckled its thick leather strap tightly across his chest.

"What's in the pack, Mr. Moloney?" Sir Dennis asked. "Perhaps my mechanical friend here can carry it for you."

"Thanks sir, but no. These are tools for tomorrow's first shift. I'll be killing two birds with one stone by taking them up to the top of the tower with us." Moloney walked up to the steps and dropped the rope from the front of the walkway. "Now watch yerrselves. That footbridge is safe, but it can be a bit treacherous if you haven't been up it before."

The path was constructed from a series of wooden planks four feet across, each suspended from the metal wire strung between the tower and the anchorage. It was a tiny suspension bridge built to aid in the construction of its bigger brother.

The Irishman waved them forward. "All right then, up we go. Keep one hand on the cable at all times, and take it slow. If you watch each and every step you take, you'll be fine."

With their first step out from the anchorage and onto the footbridge they were already high above the buildings below. "I'd say there's nothing to be scared of, but a bit of fear will do you good up here."

Sarah and Nathan moved quickly forward, each of them trying to move a little faster than the other, clearly attempting to show the other how fearless and resolute they were.

Darby was more obviously hesitant. After he had walked out and up a hundred feet, a gust of winter wind whipped up around them. The old man's hands instinctively grabbed for his hat, and the walkway swayed beneath his feet as he did so. With one hand already on the wire railing, his other grabbed for it as well, and he dropped his cane. It bounced once, and then began to roll toward the edge of oblivion.

Tom moved forward suddenly and smoothly. Sliding past his creator, he scooped up the stick before it could fall over the edge. His shifting weight rocked the bridge even more.

With his fingers tightly gripping the thin wire, Darby closed his eyes, shook his head, and waited for the world to steady itself. "I've never been much of one for heights, I'm afraid," he said to no one in particular. "It's a poor trait for a man who has engineered so many devices designed to pierce the sky."

Tom came up behind him. "Don't worry . . . Sir Dennis. I have your . . . cane."

"Hold onto it, Tom," Darby said, and then took another long deep breath. He slowly released it as he counted to ten. Over the last decade he had developed an advanced breathing regimen with a specific pattern of inhalation for almost every occasion. His book based on his theories about the different ways that oxygen could be used to reinvigorate the body had sold quite well. It described a technique that he believed would allow a man to stay healthy and whole for a hundred years or more. Darby puffed out the air in his lungs with a final *Breath of Courage*. "Thank you, Tom. I'll be fine in a moment."

Barry walked back to the two of them. "You and that machine doing all right? The lad and the girl are almost up to the top."

Darby followed his gaze upward to see them, and then reeled slightly. "We'll be fine, sir, just fine. Tom is simply looking after me, and I'm afraid it's been quite a while since I've had their youthful vigor."

Moloney flashed him another smile and then tipped his head in their direction. "You just take yer time, Sir Dennis. I wouldn't want to be the man they said was responsible for the fall of a fine genius like yerself."

Darby took another deep breath, held it quietly for five seconds, and then followed it with a resolute step forward. "Let's go, Mr. Moloney. I'm sure I'll be much steadier once we've made it to the top." But by the time he reached the tower Darby had gone white as a sheet. He sighed heavily as he stepped off the wooden bridge and onto the relative security of the flat stone platform.

The area at the top was wide open, and free of any obstacles except for a few tall wooden cranes. They were still used to bring materials up and down the sides of the bridge, although the main work of laying the wire over the towers had been completed over a year ago. Only the capstones had yet to be put in place, allowing the wire to settle while the road was hung.

Nathan and Sarah had reached the top well ahead of Sir Dennis, and they were already arguing as he arrived. Her voice grew from a whisper to a controlled shout. "Two years ago they voted on giving women the right to vote in the United States Congress!"

Nathan frowned and let out a harrumph. "Which it failed to pass. Which it will *always* fail to pass," he continued, waving a finger at her. "And that's because once a woman is married it's the job of the husband to decide what's best for his family, the country, and his *wife*."

She placed her hands on her hips. It was a provocative move in every sense of the word. "Well, I can think for myself, Nathaniel. Should a thinking woman simply exist at the whim of any man who takes a fancy to her?"

The young man pondered her question for a moment. "It clearly isn't good for *anyone* if pretty girls spend their days worrying about money and politics."

"Well I can promise you, Nathaniel Winthorp, with that attitude you will never need to worry about making those decisions for me."

He frowned, realizing that he'd gone too far. "I'm sorry, Sarah." His tone was measured, but clearly angry.

Darby clucked his tongue loudly, grabbing their attention. "That's quite enough from both of you. I won't have this morning ruined by two bickering children." He rested his hand on Tom's shoulder. "We've been given an opportunity to see the world from an incredible vantage point that few people will ever experience, and I fully expect us *all* to appreciate it." Scolding them had already put some color back into his cheeks.

Sarah walked over to him. "I'm sorry, Professor. Of course you're correct." She took a look around her, and her eyes widened as she turned her head. They were high above New York, with a clear view of the city for miles around. Just across the river, the shore of Manhattan was encrusted with docks stuffed to bursting with ships of different shapes and sizes.

Beyond them the city of New York was laid out in a well-ordered maze of streets. In contrast the buildings that defined them were completely random: a jumble of wooden and brick structures of different heights and sizes. The steam and smoke poured into the air from thousands of chimneys—proof that this city no longer slept, and barely even rested on a Sunday. Only the steeple of the Trinity Church on the lower part of the island managed to clearly rise above the riot of human industry, and now they were looking down on it.

Directly below them the East River was crowded with boat traffic. Most of the ships were still the tall-sailed schooners that had transported men and goods from one end of the planet to the other for the past two centuries. But gliding in between them were modern paddleboats and steamers that seemed well on their way to utterly replacing the age of sail with one of steam, with the billowing gray clouds of vapor rising up from their stacks mirroring the city itself.

Sarah grabbed the Professor's arm. "It's truly marvelous, Sir Dennis. It's hard not to feel a bit godlike standing above the world like this."

"Seeing this humbles me," Darby countered. "It makes me realize just how many men there are in the world, and what they have managed to create." He walked over to his metal creation and removed his top hat. "Deploy the camera if you would, Tom."

Tom walked up to the edge of the tower and then eased his right leg backward. The knee bent at an unnatural angle until it was fully reversed. As he leaned down, his arms extended out on brass rods, reaching down until his hands were flat on the ground.

With his body firmly planted, his porcelain face mask pulled free of the rest of his metal skull and slid downward, revealing the interior of his head to be three brass ovals held apart by metal shafts springing up from his neck. The series of pipe whistles that he used to speak were visible now, along with a camera lens that sat in the center of his forehead.

"That's a wee bit disturbing," said Mr. Moloney. "How does he see with his face off like that?"

"Tom has a variety of cartridges that I can place into his head. Each one changes how he interacts and samples the environment around him." Darby's tone had slipped naturally into a teacher's cadence—firm and slightly superior. "So, while he has many ways of understanding the world, 'seeing' isn't actually one of them."

"What's that mean?" asked Barry.

Nathaniel chimed in. "It means that the only reason he *has* a face is so there's something to talk to. But he doesn't actually have any genuine human features. No eyes, nose, mouth . . . or soul."

"But," Darby said loudly, cutting the young man off, "his sense of hearing is something quite extraordinary. It allows him to perceive things around him in ways we do not."

The Irishman peered a little closer. "Like a bat then . . ."

"Something like that," Darby replied, "except he can hear with his entire body, and not just his head." The inventor turned back to his creation. "I'd like a complete set of photographs, if you would, Tom. And then collect the air samples that we discussed previously."

"Of course . . . Sir Dennis."

"And we're going to be up here for a little bit, so I don't want any more arguing." He turned to the Irishman. He had slipped off his rucksack and was squatting over it, fiddling with something inside. "Perhaps, if Mr. Moloney here would be so kind, he could tell us about some of his experiences in the construction of this marvel."

Looking back over his shoulder, Moloney nodded. "If you can give me just a few moments, Sir Dennis, I'm sure I'll be able to tell all of you a few things that you might find quite surprising."

Nathaniel moved closer to the Professor and tapped his shoulder. "If you have a moment, Sir Dennis—I wanted to ask you about the matter of the improvements to my flying harness."

Darby frowned. "This is hardly the appropriate time or place to bring that up, Nathaniel. I'm still working on perfecting some of those ideas that we've discussed." He rubbed his gloved hands together against the cold. "Certainly it would make sense if a way could be found to make the Turbine suit both lighter and stronger. In fact, I've already made a prototype that replaces the main engine, and updates some of the previously stiff elements using some of the same principles of tension and suspension being used on this bridge. It needs testing, but . . ."

Sarah's voice cut through his speech. "Professor, look. . . . Is that a balloon on the horizon?"

Darby peered up and looked out across the skyline where she was pointing. "I believe you're right, my dear." A small black circle floated high above the river.

"It must be a hardy soul who would brave the skies in a wicker basket on a cold winter morning like this." Darby tucked his cane under his arm and reached into the pocket of his coat to pull out a small, leather-bound box. As he opened the lid, a pair of lenses slid up along thin metal rails and locked into place with a satisfying snap. With a quick flick of his wrist the eyepieces extended out into two telescopes. He put the back of the box up to his eyes. "Most peculiar. . . . It's larger than it first appears. The gondola is almost like a boat. . . . It also seems to have a propeller attached. . . . But what powers it? And who designed it?"

Nathaniel tapped his shoulder. "Sir Dennis? If we might, I'd like to continue our conversation."

"What?" The Professor lowered the device and shook his head slightly before gazing back. "Not now, Nathaniel! You're standing at the top of the world—enjoy it!" He compacted the lenses by pressing them back into their case. "Come by the Aereodrome when we're back at the mansion and I'll show you what I've put together." He slid the box back into his pocket.

Sarah's voice rang out urgently. "Professor—"

Nathaniel cut her off with an impatient growl. "Not *now*, Sarah. Can't you see we're talking about something important?"

"Oh, she knows it, lad," Barry said. "But I think she's referring to me, and I'd like yer attention as well."

The two men turned to look at the Irishman. A metal frame was lashed around his upper body. It was a complicated affair made of brass pipes, springs, and gears, all held together by a leather harness and straps pulled tight enough to dig into the cloth of his coat. But the most noticeable items were the two steel cages around his arms; each one holding in place a short harpoon tipped with a shining barb that sprouted out a foot from the end of it.

The Professor's voice was calm and even as he gave the command: "Tom, fire the emergency rocket."

A brass hatch in the Automaton's shoulder popped open, ripping through the fabric of his jacket. A cloud of white smoke sprayed up from the hole, followed by a small rocket flying up and out of him. In an instant it rose a hundred feet into the air above them and then exploded with a green phosphorous glow that burned like a tiny second sun in the New York City sky.

"Neat trick, metal man," Moloney exclaimed as he leaned back. Two long rods were attached to the back of the harness. When they touched the ground he braced himself against them. "But it won't save you." He put his right leg up against the Automaton and gave him a solid shove. One of Tom's gloved hands scrabbled against the stone as he tumbled, but with his legs bent backward he couldn't find any purchase against the granite. The mechanical man teetered on the edge for a moment; then his momentum carried him over and he disappeared from sight.

Darby bolted to where the Automaton had disappeared. "No!" He turned back to look at the Irishman. "What have you done?" Nathaniel knelt next to the Professor and held him back from the precipice.

Moloney nodded. "Removed a threat, Sir Dennis. . . . But that's not my main job here today."

Nathaniel jerked forward threateningly. "Who are you, really?"

"Easy now." The Irishman smiled broadly through his red whiskers. "You've probably figured out that I'm not Moloney the foreman. But you can call me the Bomb Lance."

Chapter 2

Over the Edge

The shock on Sir Dennis's face transformed into anger. "Whatever it is you want, sir, you won't get it from me."

Sarah had quietly edged up behind the Irishman. Keeping his eyes, and weapons, locked on the two men in front of him, he only moved his head slightly to the left to acknowledge her. Get with the others, lass, before you force me to do something unpleasant to yer friends." He prodded her slightly as she walked around him toward Nathaniel. "I would have guessed that the Industrialist's daughter had a bit of her father's courage, but being a fool will only get someone hurt."

Darby raised his cane and shook it. "Don't threaten her, villain! The Paragons will put a stop to you!"

"Oh, I'm counting on it." He took a step back. "I'm not alone, Sir Dennis, just the first." He thrust out his lance toward the old man. "Now let's have that key from around yer neck."

"How . . . ?" There was an obvious tone of shock and surprise in the Professor's voice that he tried to hide in his next word. "Key?"

"No need to pretend." The Bomb Lance waved Darby forward with his right harpoon. When he was close enough, the Irishman hooked the front of the Professor's starched white shirt on one of his barbs and ripped it open. He nudged the ascot aside, revealing a dull, gray metal key hanging around the Professor's neck. "Take it off and hand it to me."

"It's nothing you'd want—a keepsake," the Professor protested. He picked it up and showed it to him. "It's lead, not even brass. It couldn't possibly have any value to you."

"I'm not the one who wants it. I'm just the man getting it for him." The

Bomb Lance pressed the barbed end of his harpoon into the Professor's chest with just enough force to break the skin. "Now hand it over."

Darby unbuttoned his overcoat, then reached his hands around behind his neck and undid the clasp that held the key in place. He dropped it into the open palm just underneath the harpoon pressing into his flesh. "You have no idea what that is, do you?"

"Don't know, and don't care." The Bomb Lance held it up for a moment. "But I'll agree it doesn't look like much." He took three steps back. "Just so you can rest easy, I'll tell you that I'm going to let the girl live. She gets to tell her father and the rest of the Paragons that the Children of Eschaton are coming, and there's not a damn thing they can do to stop us."

There was an audible "clack" as the metal rods locked into place behind him. Black smoke coughed out from behind his right elbow as the harpoon fired. The bolt plunged through the side of Sir Dennis's chest, the momentum spinning him around and throwing him backward at the same time. As he began to fall, the energy from the attack carried him over the edge of the tower, and he vanished. "No!" Nathaniel shouted as he leapt toward the Professor, but there was no hope of rescuing him.

The Irishman let out a rasping laugh. "And that's what a Bomb Lance can do to a man."

Nathaniel spun around to face him. "You piece of Irish filth! I'll kill you!"

"Now now, don't judge the whole country by me," the Bomb Lance said. "It was good Irishmen what built the tower yer standing on!"

Sarah's voice was soft, measured, and almost without emotion. "But you're not a good man, are you?"

The Bomb Lance looked over at her and sighed. "Not anymore, lassie, no. I haven't been *good* for quite a long time." Keeping the left harpoon pointed at Nathaniel, he lifted his right arm straight up over his head. The wheels and wires attached to the frame slid around as he did so, pulling up one of the small harpoons resting in a bandolier on his back into the frame on his upper arm. "I was never good enough for the people in yer world anyway."

He lowered the arm straight down from the shoulder with a single sharp movement, and a fresh harpoon slid down and snapped into place. Once again he had two of the barbed spikes facing them. His face softened for a moment, as if he was having a pleasant memory. "But the Children of Eschaton aim to change all that: who's up, who's down . . ." The edges of his lips curled up in a dark grin. "And once that's done, we'll see about what it really means to be good or bad."

Nathaniel took a defiant step forward. "You've just murdered in cold blood one of the greatest minds the world has ever known!" Then he took another step, bringing the two men within a few feet of each other. "Why?"

The Irishman clenched his jaw, bristling at the question, and then brought the harpoon up to bear on Nathan's head. "I don't need any more reason to kill a man than that he's in my way." He swung his left arm like a club, slamming it into Nathaniel's head. "But I have a better one for you." He hit Nathan again as he reeled from the first blow. The boy dropped to the ground, the wind catching his hat as it came off his head. It rose up in the air for a moment before tumbling into the river below. The Irishman looked down at Nathaniel with contempt. "You're a rich, pompous prick." He aimed his left harpoon down at Nathaniel and fired. The barb shot straight through Nathan's thigh, making a deep ping as it sank into the granite below. The young man screamed. Blood began to pool beneath the trapped leg, steaming in the cold winter air.

The Bomb Lance turned toward Sarah and pointed a harpoon straight at her chest. "As I told Sir Dennis, lovely girl, I'm going to let you live. But I need you to give the Paragons a message."

A tear rolled down her cheek. "They'll kill you for this."

"That's as may be, but it's not yer business, and it's not right now. I just need for you to tell them that the Eschaton is coming. Can you do that for me?"

Sarah pressed her lips together.

He poked her slightly with the tip of the harpoon. "You just say yes, and we're all done here."

"Wait." She lifted up her left hand and bowed her head slightly.

"Wait for what? Your Professor and his machine are dead. And yer boyfriend is going to bleed to death if you don't do something."

"Wait for that," she said, as the Automaton's arm slammed into the side of the Bomb Lance's head. When he fell to the granite he was unconscious.

She looked at Tom and gave him an order. "You must help Nathaniel." He stepped forward, and she saw the crumpled form behind him.

She ran toward Darby. "Professor!" The harpoon was still in him, hanging out of his chest. Tom had managed to catch him, interrupting his fall from the tower, but the jolt had made the wound far worse. He looked up at Sarah and tried to smile as she ran toward him, but the blood-flecked grimace he produced was terrifying.

Tom kneeled down by Nathaniel's side, wrapped his hand gently around the shaft of the spear, and pulled slightly. Nathan screamed as it moved. "Stop it! Just stop!" he gasped out.

"The . . . harpoon has penetrated your . . . leg and lodged into the . . . stone. It will need to be removed." Tom made a fist with his right hand. The wrist bent all the way back until his fingers were flush against the top of his arm. With his left hand he reached under his shirt and into the clockworks of his stomach. When he pulled it out again he held a small saw-blade between his fingers.

"What are you . . . ?" Nathan tried to get up on his elbows. "Aaah. Haaaah!" The pain from the metal shaft rubbing against his bone dropped him back to the ground.

Two small poles extended up from Tom's right wrist, and the blade snapped into the eyeholes at the top of them with a firm click. A gear rose up from underneath and engaged with another one on the side of the blade. It spun with a high-pitched whine. Nathan's eyes grew wide. "Stay the hell away from me!"

"Lie back, please." Gripping the harpoon with his left hand, Tom pressed the spinning saw into the iron shaft. A jet of steam blew out from the back of Tom's neck, and a shower of sparks arced out as metal touched metal.

Sarah put the Professor's head on her lap and stroked his hair with her hands. His hat had been lost in the fall. "You're going to be okay, Sir Dennis. Tom will be here in a minute."

Darby's voice was faint. "He's not a surgeon, my dear. But even if he were, I think my wound is clearly fatal."

She moved her hands hesitantly toward the bloody gash, then pulled them away. "Don't say that!"

He tried to smile. "It'll be all right, I think. But I'll need you to be strong for me."

"You can't die!" She bent down and gave his forehead a kiss. There were tears in her eyes. "I think I've been falling in love with you, Professor—perhaps for quite some time."

He looked up at her. "You have no idea how flattered I am to hear those words coming from those delightful lips of yours, my dear. But I'm also—" He coughed. There was blood on his mouth. "—three times your age. No matter what you might feel for me, that was never meant to be."

"No!" She looked upward, and tears continued to roll down her face. "You're going to live!"

"Wishing won't make it so. But I need to speak to Tom before I go. And I need you to—" He coughed again. It sounded worse this time. "—help him, Sarah. If you do care for me, then you'll find the best parts of me are inside of him. It will take time for Tom to discover what he is capable of, and he'll need your assistance to find out. "

When she opened her mouth to reply, she was cut off by a scream from behind them. She turned to see the Automaton lifting Nathan's leg free from the cut end of the harpoon. The young man's eye caught hers, and he called out her name. "Sarah!"

She quickly stood up. "Tom, come here. We need you."

Nathaniel whimpered slightly as Tom pulled off his coat and wound it around the wound. "Please try to relax." Having completed his crude bandaging, he walked over to Sir Dennis.

Tom stood above the Professor, Sarah by his side. "You are badly hurt . . . sir." He held up the saw-blade. It was slightly scorched. "I should remove the . . . harpoon."

Darby shook his head. "Far too late for that. Now come down here so I can speak with you."

The Automaton folded his legs, collapsing down into a squat. "How can I save your life, Sir . . . Dennis?"

"You can't, Tom." He reached up and took his left hand. "But, I need you to retrieve the Alpha Element from that Irishman if you can. Second, I want you to find the new body I was building for you in the laboratory. It's not complete, but once you're in it you'll be able to finish the work yourself." His grip tightened for a moment, and then his hand fell away. "Sarah will help you."

Tom reached down to grasp his fingers. "Sir . . . Dennis, I can . . ."

"You have the potential to become much more than you already are, but it won't be easy." He started coughing again. The blood on his skin was brighter now, and there was a wet rasp coming from his lungs as he fought to draw in another breath of air. "When dark times come it is men of honor who must lead us back to the light of reason."

"But, I am not a . . . man."

"No. But you can be . . . the light." He looked up at the Automaton and smiled. Then Sir Dennis's eyes grew wide as he struggled to inhale again and couldn't draw a breath. "I . . . I . . . I . . ." The words vanished into tiny gurgles as blood replaced the remaining air in his lungs. He closed his eyes, shuddered, and then sagged as the life left his body.

"Sir . . . Dennis?" Tom held him for a few moments, and then lowered his creator's lifeless body down onto the cold stone.

Chapter 3

Wireworks

Sarah heard a grunt rise up from the Bomb Lance's prone form as she walked toward him. When she got close, she pressed the tip of her black boot up against the Irishman's shoulder and pushed him. He shifted over, rolling back the moment she stopped. Sarah lifted up her skirts slightly, swung her boot back, and then gave a good solid kick to the man's ribs. He groaned loudly.

Frowning, she put her heel against the brass frame he wore and gave it a hard shove. "Roll, damn you!" she yelled, and gave him another shove. He spun over onto his back while she stumbled in the other direction. "You're going off this tower!"

Swimming back to consciousness, the Irishman used the harness to block her foot as she attempted another kick. "That'll be enough of that," he said in a drowsy slur. He hooked her leg with his arm and pulled her down in a flurry of skirts and ruffles. "I'm not supposed to hurt you. . . ."

Down on the ground, Sarah's feet flailed until one of them connected with his chin. He batted back at her with his brass-clad arm, knocking her legs away before she could hit him again. He was clearly awake now. "But you do that again, lass, and I'll skewer you."

There was blood in his eyes from where he had been beaten down by the Automaton, and he tried to wipe it away. The polished iron barb at the end of his arm glittered as he brought his arm up to his face. He switched to his left.

When he looked up, the Automaton was moving toward him, the sawn-off end of a harpoon in his hand. The Bomb Lance held up his right arm and fired. The metal tore cleanly through the right side of Tom's chest until the wooden peg at the end caught in the armature, spinning the machine-man around and throwing him down to the ground.

The Irishman rose to his feet and took a moment to survey the scene. He nodded approvingly to himself. "Good enough for a day's work." He ran toward the foot bridge and sprinted onto it, heading back toward the anchorage.

Sarah knelt down next to the Automaton. "Tom, are you all right?"

He tugged at the harpoon. "It appears to be stuck." He wiggled it back and forth a few times and then pulled on it again. It came free, catching a steel spring and uncoiling a ribbon of metal as he pulled it out of him. "I am going to stop him. Please help . . . Nathaniel."

Rising up, harpoon still in his hand, Tom walked to the edge of the footbridge. The Bomb Lance was fifteen yards away, moving as quickly as he could back to the anchorage, but forced to flee from them in a straight line. Tom flung the man's weapon back at him.

Out on the wooden path the Irishman slowed his run, then came to a stop as fast as he dared. As he was plucking out his handkerchief from his jacket pocket to try to wipe away the blood, there was a crashing sound. One of his harpoons had smashed through the slatted boards a few feet in front of him. He turned to see the metal man standing at the edge of the bridge tower. The Automaton dropped into a sprint and headed toward him.

Sarah watched Tom go and then turned back to Nathaniel. He was grimacing as he tried to use the arms of his jacket to stanch the wound. "It's not a mop," she said sternly. Sitting down next to him she grabbed the coat from his hand and tore a long strip from the sleeve.

"Finally, you notice *I'm* in trouble," he replied through gritted teeth.

She stopped what she was doing and stared at him. "Look at me." He refused to make eye contact. "Look at me, Nathaniel!"

Responding to the urgency in her voice he turned to see that there were fresh tears in her eyes. "What is it?"

Her face was a mask of anger. She pointed at the body a few yards away. "He's dead, Nathaniel. That's Sir Dennis Darby's dead body lying not ten feet away from us, and you want to cry to me about the fact you were ignored while he died." She roughly pulled up his leg, and began winding the cloth strip around it. "I won't have it!"

"Ow! Sarah, I . . ." She stopped, and he stared into her eyes for a moment.

Then he turned away, reaching into his jacket pocket to pull out his flask. Sarah frowned, but said nothing as she continued to work on his leg.

The Automaton and the Bomb Lance were both at a full run when the Irishman reached the end of the footbridge. Tom was twenty yards away, but closing at a good pace. The Irishman lifted his arms into the air. The harness responded and reloaded both arms. He aimed them at his opponent and leaned back into the supports on the back of his harness. "Where there's a will, there's a way," he muttered out loud.

"Platitudes won't save you, Murphy." The voice came from behind him, wrapped in a Western drawl and a blast of tobacco smoke. The Bomb Lance turned to see a man in a ten-gallon hat and oiled duster standing behind him. "But Doc Dynamite is here to rescue your Catholic ass anyway." The man lit the stick of explosive in his hand from the cigar in his mouth and then threw it out onto the footbridge.

"So you *finally* decide to arrive," said the Bomb Lance. "You were supposed to—" The Texan grabbed the edge of the Bomb Lance's brass frame and used it to fling him down the stairs. He jumped after him as the dynamite exploded with a deafening bang. A rush of air and smoke blew over their heads. The Bomb Lance rolled over to look at him. "You were supposed to be here an hour ago." He stood up and checked that his frame was still in working order.

Doc Dynamite's features were so rugged and leathery that it seemed impossible to tell whether he appeared to look old for thirty or was a young-looking man twice that age. But he had an easy smile and blue eyes that would have seemed almost friendly if not for the scar that traveled across his face from the left side of his forehead to the right of his chin. He wore a plain striped shirt, a worsted cloth jacket, and a bandana around his neck, with a faded yellow duster over everything. His denim jeans were tucked into a pair of red cowboy boots with two large yellow letter "D"s stitched onto each one. "Tell it to the frog. He could barely get that contraption of his up into the air." He pointed behind him, where the balloon sat parked on the roadway thirty yards behind them, belching black smoke from large engines on either side. "The decrepit Frenchy kept bitching about how the cold made everything impossible to do."

He reached into the pocket of his jacket and handed the Irishman a bandana. "Look atcha. You're a mess." He winked at him. "Even for a Mick."

"It's good to see you, too, Jay, now the job's almost done." He wiped away some of the blood. "'Almost' being the main word in that sentence there."

He stood up. "Now let's see if my little friend solved your problem, because someone shot up a rocket, and the rest a' the Paragons are on their way."

They walked up the steps in time to watch the severed end of the footbridge slide away from the bridge frame and land with a distant crash into the construction yard below. The other end was still attached to the tower above them, and the remains dangled straight down toward the river.

The Bomb Lance wiped his eyes again and then peered down over the edge of the anchorage. "Looks like we destroyed the damn thing."

"I don't think so, partner," the Texan replied. He had pulled out another stick of dynamite from inside his duster and was using it to point over to the left side of the bridge. The Automaton balanced on top of the suspension wire.

"Well I'll be damned." The Bomb Lance held up his left arm, aimed his harpoon, and fired. Tom moved a few steps down the cable toward them and the harpoon sailed harmlessly past him.

The Irishman grimaced as he watched his attack miss.

"I'm going to reckon that there is the famous Automaton," the Texan said as he grabbed the Bomb Lance's right arm. Pulling out a roll of gauze from his coat pocket, he used it to bind a stick of dynamite to the harpoon, tying it in place with surprising grace. "Too bad we're going to have to blow him to hell. I've always wanted to see what that thing looked like up close."

"That must be a damn shame for you, cowboy, missing out like that." The Bomb Lance pumped his arm again, and then held it up to fire.

"Just try and get it somewhere near him," Doc Dynamite instructed, drawing deeply on his cigar and making the ember glow bright red. "And it's a short fuse," he said as he touched it to the paper, "so fire fast."

The harpoon wobbled as it flew, and the Automaton was clearly going to dodge it easily. When it exploded, the Texan let out a war whoop followed by a "Kaboom!"

The concussion shredded Tom's clothes and threw him off the cable. As he fell, his arm snapped out to snag one of the vertical supporting wires that dangled down, waiting to be connected to the roadbed that had yet to be built. The leather glove covering his hand shredded and burned as his momentum was violently redirected. For a moment he almost seemed to be floating in the air; then he swung his other arm around and grabbed the wire with both hands. He swung slowly back and forth as he climbed back up.

The Bomb Lance shook his head. "I don't believe it. Nothing kills that thing."

"That's because it ain't alive. Now stop flapping those Irish lips and get another spear ready." He held up the dynamite. "We'll blow him up for sure this time."

The Automaton clamped one hand over the other until he reached the main cable. He hefted himself up onto the main cable as the second dynamite-tipped harpoon flew toward him.

This time he ran down the cable, letting it explode behind him. The force of the blast ripped away the remains of his jacket and shirt, revealing the rows of clockwork cogs underneath. He rose up into the air slightly, and for a moment Tom seemed to be almost skating down the thick wire, the energy of the blast propelling him forward.

As he reached the end of the cable and was about to step onto the anchorage, a harpoon slammed directly into his torso, halting his movement. An instant later a second spear found a weaker spot and tore straight through him, pulling out some of the gears and wires from his body as it exited through his back. As he began to slide off the wire, the Automaton threw himself into the air. His graceful landing was interrupted by a stick of dynamite that exploded underneath him, throwing him back into the air. He landed flat on his back, his brass frame smacking into the stone of the anchorage with a clang.

Doc Dynamite and the Bomb Lance were standing only ten feet away. "I think we broke the bronco, Murphy." The Texan said it with a note of triumph in his voice.

"Why don't you toss one more of those bombs of yours at him to make sure, if you don't mind."

"It's called dynamite, and we're too close." The cowboy pulled out another stick, lit it, and casually chucked it. "We'd best run."

They headed down the road toward the balloon, and the Automaton jerked up behind them. His porcelain faceplate had been shattered and blackened by the blast, and it was clear by the way he twitched as he tried to move that the explosions had done something unpleasant to his mechanisms. His arm reached out and grabbed the dynamite stick, then hurled it back toward the other two men. It exploded in midair as it sailed toward them. The force of the blast knocked both men to the ground, smacking the air out of their lungs, leaving them gasping and coughing.

The Automaton stepped out of the smoke, standing only a few feet away from the Bomb Lance. "You will give me the . . . key."

The Irishman got up to his knees and pointed his right arm at Tom. The Automaton grabbed the spear and twisted, then yanked the harpoon completely out of the frame. There was a popping sound as the metal wires tore free from tension, then a plink as they snapped. He threw the harpoon and a chunk of the frame over the edge of the anchorage.

"No more of that." He stepped on the Irishman's chest and leaned forward, letting his considerable weight keep the air from coming back into his lungs. "I want the key."

The Irishman fumbled for his pockets, but couldn't get more than his fingertips into them. "I can't reach . . ."

The Automaton grabbed onto the man's elbow with one hand and used the other to tear the rest of the frame completely off of his right arm. His hand no longer encumbered, the Bomb Lance dug down into his pocket and produced the key.

"Thank you." Tom reached out to grab it and then jerked back as three bullets from Doc Dynamite's gun tore the rest of his face away. The glass lens of the camera underneath shattered. "How d'ya like the taste of lead, you hunk a' junk?"

Tom staggered for a moment and then lunged at the Texan, leading with his fist. It wiped away the Texan's smile as it cracked into his jaw.

Doc Dynamite tried to roll with the blow, but it was far too late. He tried to talk, and screamed, "Ooo oke my od am ace!" The Automaton tried to attack again, but failed to connect as a harpoon smashed into him. The impact was much weaker than the previous shots had been, but it was still enough to knock him down. The Bomb Lance's last shot had also been the final one for his frame, and the remaining tension wires escaped their bondage, hanging slack from his shoulders and arms.

Doc Dynamite reached into his coat, but the Irishman grabbed him and yanked him down the road. "At eh ell?"

"We need to go, you idiot! The Paragons are here!"

Realization dawned on Doc Dynamite's broken face as he saw a figure coming toward them from the far side of the anchorage with a gun in his right hand. The two of them turned and ran as the bullets whizzed by.

The man shooting at them was clearly someone who wanted to be seen. His royal-blue jacket and bright red vest were both cut entirely from thick leather. The heavily padded shoulders over his well-developed frame gave him an imposing silhouette. A blue leather mask covered his face down to the bridge of his nose in front, and the rest of his head and neck in back. Securely attached to the top of his head was a red, white, and blue top hat, a steady cloud of steam rising up from it like a chimney.

In his left hand he held a large steel shield emblazoned with the symbol of a gear, and in his right was a gun that connected to both a bandolier of bullets that circled his forearm and a small brass pipe that ran to a pressure canister on his back. With each shot steam blasted out of the gun, propelling the bullet and loading another one into the chamber simultaneously.

Reaching into his duster as he ran, the Texan pulled out a short stick of explosive that was colored blue instead of the usual red. He lit it and dropped it onto the road. A second later it exploded into a curtain of smoke that completely hid the two men from their pursuer.

The masked man stopped running when he reached the Automaton, and fired a few more desperate shots into the smoke cloud. "Where's my daughter?" he yelled at the metal man.

The Automaton attempted to reply, but something in his throat had been damaged from the abuse he had just received. "The t-t-t-top of the t-t-t-ower."

Sticking his gun into its holster, he knelt down and grabbed Tom by the shoulders. "Is she all right?"

The Automaton nodded yes. "She is o-k-k-k-kay."

Standing up, the Industrialist saw a black balloon rising up out of the smoke. The large propellers on either side of the gondola pushed it up and away from the bridge, and it headed deeper into Brooklyn.

His gloved hand hovered over his gun for a moment and then relaxed. The Automaton rose up behind him. His movements were jerky, and for an instant it seemed as if he would topple back to the ground. Finding his balance, he reached up to his head, and pressed a finger into his throat. "Those men killed . . . Sir Dennis."

"Damn it to hell!" The Industrialist lifted his gun and fired shot after shot at the balloon until it was nothing more than a dot in the sky.

Chapter 4

Hallowed Halls

Sarah Stanton let out a loud and unladylike grunt as she tugged at the ornate brass handle. There were two of them, each connected to a massive slab of bronze ten feet wide and sixteen feet tall, and no matter how hard she tried, they were as immovable as the granite that surrounded them.

"Definitely locked," she said, and let go. Gasping in her corset she took a moment to compose herself, looking up while she caught her breath at the reliefs that had been cast onto the metal. The dim, dirty glow from the cloudy February day illuminated scenes from ancient mythology in the tarnished bronze: illustrations of powerful Greco-Roman deities locked in mortal combat against foul monsters. The swords, shields, and lightning bolts of the gods were arrayed against the fangs, claws, and serpent hair of evil creatures hell-bent on destroying the world.

The expressions on the gods' immortal faces were intense and grim. As Sarah stared into their metal world, the images seemed to mock her inability to simply open the door. The message of the battling was suddenly clear: mortals should not enter into the world that lay behind these doors unless they had the strength to defeat evil beyond imagining.

Tired of the scorn of the gods, Sarah turned away and looked down onto the hustle and bustle of the street traffic rolling down Fifth Avenue on a chilly Friday afternoon.

She smiled to herself and rolled her eyes at her foolishness. She may not have been a Paragon, but she knew at least one way to outsmart the gods. . . . If the front doors had been locked it meant there would only be minimal staff on duty inside, and she knew another way in.

After Alexander Stanton had been forced to reveal to the world he was actually the hero the world knew as the Industrialist, he had told Sarah the story of "the first Paragon." His name was Prometheus, one of the Titans, and he had bravely stolen fire from Mount Olympus, bringing the precious gift down to man so that they could chase away the cold and the night.

When he discovered what Prometheus had done, Zeus condemned the disobedient god to be punished for all eternity. Chained to a rock, the firebringer's liver would be eaten by a vulture every day, and then regrow each night, until the end of time.

But even Zeus could not steal back the fire. Humanity would be able to keep its gift. Her father had told her that, if he could have, he would have used his powers to kill the bird and break the Titan free from his chains. But since he was just a man, he would follow in the footsteps of Prometheus, bringing the light of knowledge to mankind, no matter what the consequences or the cost.

A few years later, when she had first seen the images for the front doors to the Hall of Paragons sketched out on parchment in her father's office, she had asked him if he found it ironic that Prometheus remained bound and tortured, while Zeus rode in his chariot high above, throwing mighty thunderbolts down to Earth.

He had scowled at her and told her to leave, something he only did when either she or her mother were being what he considered "far too clever for your own good."

Shivering from the chill, Sarah stepped down the Italian marble staircase that swept down to the street from between the two massive granite columns that flanked the entrance. She made a sharp left when she reached the cement sidewalk and started walking up Fifth Avenue. The front of the Hall filled almost a third of the block between 49th and 50th Streets. Having been constructed as a modern-day version of the great buildings of Rome, it had for the last six years been the biggest structure on Fifth Avenue, adding a counterpoint to the soaring gothic towers of St. Patrick's Cathedral just down the avenue.

The building was every bit the mysterious and impenetrable fortress that it had been designed to be. The imposing bronze doors were only the first of many formidable challenges faced by any enemy who might wish to enter and hurt the Paragons in their home.

Although that hadn't stopped everyone—a good portion of the northwest corner of the building had been shattered when the Steam Hammer had attempted to undermine the Hall's foundations and found himself crushed under ten tons of stone.

She could still see the cemented cracks, and the slightly whiter rock that had been brought in to replace what had been destroyed.

But the building still stood, and the villain remained down below there somewhere, surrounded by walls that he would never be able to break.

So far the only nonmembers who had ever actually made it inside were invited guests, and most of them never got farther than the foyer.

And for most of them it was enough. The grand entry hall was the great showpiece of the building, designed to inspire awe in those lucky enough to see it. Built around a 500-square-foot red-marble floor, it was capped off with a vaulted ceiling that floated three stories above on two rows of massive Roman columns.

On the walls were enormous frescoes that stretched up the full height. And unlike the classic mythology used on the front doors, these color renderings depicted the actual likenesses of the individual members of the Paragons, portraying them as if they were the gods themselves, looking down into the room from the sky above.

Sarah had never been shy about letting people know that she thought these images of her father and the other all-too-mortal Paragons shooting bolts of lightning, fire, and steam from their hands were comical, to say the least. Sir Dennis had even admitted to her that he felt a bit ashamed when he saw a perfectly idealized version of himself staring back down at him from so high above. And now that he was dead, the mythical man was the only one who remained.

Reaching the corner of the building, Sarah turned left and slipped down the slim alley that traveled along the north side. The six-foot-wide corridor was clean, but gloomy, and few people even noticed its existence. It was simply there, one of many hundreds of odd little spaces in the ever-growing metropolis of New York that went ignored. But Sarah had always thought the unnoticed was far more interesting than the ostentatious.

The side of the hall that faced the alley was a massive wall of featureless stone blocks. Wide metal doors were cut into the side of them at regular intervals, allowing supplies to be loaded into the buildings. If Sarah had ever been intent on breaking into the building by force, it seemed to her that this would be a far more logical place to make an attempt. But perhaps whatever megalomania it was that convinced a man to put on a costume and name himself after an animal or an object would also prohibit him from trying something as subtle as looking for a weaker door.

To Sarah this simple alley was a romantic place, and she had often gotten "lost" there when her father had brought her to the construction site. No matter how much her father admonished them afterward, the workers were always lenient with her and Nathaniel, allowing the children free rein to explore the unfinished halls while her father was off doing his business of running his railroad or saving the world from another ridiculous villain with delusions of grandeur.

The time she'd spent running through empty rooms and half-finished hallways had given her knowledge of the building that was beyond most of the Paragons.

Sarah stepped down into a stairwell that ran parallel to the wall. Ten steps took her down five feet below the ground. The door that stood locked in place at the bottom was a flat sheet of bronze with no handle. The only break in its otherwise featureless surface was a small hole about the size of a nickel where a knob would be on a normal door.

Sarah snapped open her reticule. The bag was small, and it only took her a moment to find what she was looking for and draw it out. The key was four inches long, and the entire piece was ornately designed so that it appeared to be a stylized letter "P" with a blank stem where the teeth would normally be. Like most things associated with the Hall, the gaudy exterior hid something far more complicated underneath.

She slipped the key into the door slot and then simply held it there. The door hummed for a moment, followed by a heavy thunk as something hidden beneath the metal sank into place. The key disappeared, and a few moments later the door released, swinging inward just a few inches. Sarah pushed it open the rest of the way and stepped inside, escaping from the cold of the winter day into the relative warmth of the building's interior. She closed the door, cutting off the gray daylight and leaving only a dim gloom broken by the glow of the pilot lights from the gas lamps on the walls. Her key was poking out from the inside, the mechanism inside the door having flipped it over as it passed through. She pulled it out and slipped it back into her purse.

Grabbing a small brass lever on the wall to the left of the door, she pushed it down until it came to rest with a small click. Hidden machinery clanked audibly behind the wall. There was a hiss, and then a pop as the gaslights flared to full brightness behind their reflectors. They lit a cramped stairwell.

Sarah climbed to the top and reached a landing with two doors—one directly in front of her, and another to her left that she opened and stepped into. Inside was a cramped supply closet that was utterly free of the exotic weapons or colorful costumes that people often assumed must be stored everywhere. Instead there were simply rows of wooden shelves containing ink, pencils, pen nibs, cleaning supplies, and all the other mundane and sundry items needed for the care and maintenance of the Hall.

Sarah pulled off her winter coat and gloves, folded them neatly, and placed them up on the highest shelf she could reach inside the closet. She slipped her hand behind one of the dusty boxes of paper and pulled out a large brown-paper envelope from the back. Inside it was a pair of beaded slippers. She sat down and pulled off her winter boots, replacing them with the footwear she had just found.

Stepping out of the closet, she closed the door and put her ear up to the other door. "No one out here," she whispered to herself, hoping it was true, and cracked it open.

Sarah almost glided as she moved down the rust-colored marble floors of the main corridor in her slippers. She looked around constantly, still not sure that one of the building staff wouldn't run into her. In normal times that wouldn't have earned her more than a reprimand, but since the death of Sir Dennis she had been told by her father in no uncertain terms that she was to stay out of the building, and she had a destination that she could only reach if no one knew she was here.

She made a right, heading down another long corridor. It was dimly lit, the gas lamps burning low. The yellow light reflecting off the red stone gave everything a dull orange glow, as if morning were just over the horizon.

She heard what was clearly her father's voice echoing from in front of her. "Damn," she whispered. Her path would take her past the main conference room, and it sounded like the Industrialist was inside of it, making one of his famously long-winded speeches, although she couldn't make out any of the words.

In the almost four weeks since Sir Dennis Darby's death Sarah had seen her father only infrequently, and she had only really spoken with him once. Darby's funeral had been held in Central Park, exactly one week after "the bridge incident," which was what everyone in polite society had taken to calling the murder. The papers had given the event much more lurid names, "Darby's Downfall" being the one she found most distasteful, for a number of reasons.

The ceremony had been simple and short, the way that the old man had requested. Still, there were tens of thousands of fashionable New Yorkers who had made the trek northward to pay their final respects to the fallen genius. He was a beloved man, but Sarah was convinced that most of the mourners simply wanted a chance to take a closer look at the Paragons without having to expose themselves to the deadly dangers that normally came with being a bystander when the heroes went into action.

Each of the other heroes had given a short eulogy, describing what it was that the Professor had meant to each of them. Nathaniel's had been the longest—an emotional ode to the man he called his "spiritual father." She supposed it was supposed to be an epic poem, heroically describing how the Professor had struggled against death while only a few feet away from him the mighty Turbine bravely faced the Bomb Lance's harpoons until finally one of them had speared his leg and bound him to the "granite spire" of the still-unfinished Brooklyn Bridge.

Like everything involving the Paragons, the official account had little relationship to the messy ambiguity of the events as they had actually occurred. They had also completely removed any mention of Nathaniel's unconscious form being lowered down from the tower in a basket like so much fish. Sarah had mentioned to her father that she was concerned that Nathaniel's need to protect his reputation would diminish the chances of tracking down the man who had murdered Professor Darby. He had scoffed at the suggestion and told her that the only truth in history was what people could read between the lines. "The truth is that the average man doesn't have the capacity to understand the boring details, or the moral capacity to understand what they meant if he did." Sarah replied that she thought that the world could use a strong dose of the truth every now and again.

Her father had been the final speaker at the funeral, delivering a patented Stanton droner. It recounted, in detail, the mythic founding of the Society of Paragons, including his early days as the Industrialist, and how he was unable to capture a black-hearted villain called "the Lightning Rod" who was using bolts of electricity to "slay every man who ignored his genius."

He had tracked the maniacal master of electricity to the Darby mansion, where he was hoping to steal some of the Professor's amazing devices and use them for nefarious purposes.

But the Industrialist found Darby first and took possession of an invention called the "grounding shroud." Using it, he was able to siphon off the villain's electrical energy field and claim the day in the name of the Paragons.

Seeing the potential in combining his skills with the clearly superior intellect of Sir Dennis, the Industrialist proposed that they work together, creating an organization dedicated to "protecting those who cannot protect themselves."

"And the rest," he concluded, "is history."

The audience had cheered wildly at the end of his story, as they always did whenever they got a chance to see the Paragons in the flesh. Sarah knew that the truth was, once again, far more nuanced than the simplified fairy tale he told the adoring masses.

It was her father, not the Lighting Rod, who had broken into Sir Dennis's mansion, hoping to find some technology to use to stop a villain who had given him nothing but trouble and bad press. In particular, Alexander Stanton was looking to grab an electrical dampening device that Darby had shown at the scientific exposition the year before, an event that the Stanton Railroad Company had funded.

When Darby had found out that his home had been vandalized he was furious, especially considering that Alexander Stanton had gained a growing reputation for not giving credit where it was due.

Ultimately Darby had been "convinced" to join forces with her father only after being given a considerable sum of money to help with his research, along with a promise that any future profits they made in their fight against crime would be given to a foundation dedicated to sharing those inventions with all mankind. In the years since, not a single dollar had been given to charity. According to her father's accountants the operating costs of the Paragons were far greater than any money made by their inventions.

That funeral had also been the last time she had seen Tom. On the outside he appeared to be back to normal, as if the damage he had taken from the battle at the bridge had been completely repaired. His mask had been replaced with a freshly painted one, and he had been given a new suit and gloves. But when he moved it was obvious that it was all a façade. He had a profound limp, as if something deep inside of him was broken, and his right arm swung free. His part in the incident had been removed entirely from the official story, and he was not allowed to speak at the funeral, although a great cheer went up when he was introduced to the crowd by her father as "Darby's greatest creation."

Ahead of her the massive doors leading to the conference chamber were wide open. She slowed her pace and crept along the wall on the same side of the corridor as the entrance.

She could make out her father's words clearly now: ". . . will read to you Sir Dennis Darby's final wishes," he said. "But before I do, I must emphasize that no matter what words this document contains, the Paragons will move forward in a manner that *we* decide is best.

"As our leader, Sir Dennis acted as our visionary, his incorruptible heart providing us with determination and direction. But if we are to follow his dream and move humanity forward toward a greater tomorrow, we cannot blindly follow his wishes from beyond the grave. No matter how great a thinker the man may have been during his life, the world is constantly changing. While his demise is a tragedy, it is the cycle of life and death that powers the engine of progress."

"Pish," Sarah said, realizing that she had said the phrase out loud only when the sound of it reached her ears. Sarah pressed a hand to her lips and leaned her back against the wall outside the door. She slowly let herself slide to the floor as she listened to her father's words, the same way that she had done so many times as a little girl.

"Now," her father continued, "these are the final words of our fallen leader, Sir Dennis Darby."

"'Dear friends,'" he began, "'if you are hearing these words then I have passed on from this world and into the next.'" Stanton paused for a moment to cough slightly. "'Do not mourn me too greatly. Those of you who knew me well will be comforted by the fact that even as I write this document I have already lived a life so full of discovery and accomplishment that it would satisfy any ten men. And so I can ask for no more, although I am hopeful that I still have a great deal more of life left to live. I do not wish to die. Nor, do I imagine, would anyone who cares as deeply about the future as I do.

"'I still spend each and every day in a state of constant amazement at the new things that we are discovering, and go to sleep each night with greatest anticipation of what we will learn tomorrow.

"'But our days on this world are numbered from the moment we are born, and the most that any of us can hope for is that when they have ended, we will have left this world nobly, and with our good name intact.

"'I have spent my time on this planet in pursuit of a dream of a better life for all mankind, helping humanity find dominion over that which would bring men misery or harm. I have used the power and possibilities of science to fight back against the petty desires that cause conflict and death. I have done all this so that we may strive to use our intelligence to become so much more than the simple, dangerous creatures we are now.

"'Some claim that we have already reached the zenith of human ingenuity, but I believe that we have only just begun to see the marvels that—'"

Her Father's voice was cut short by two words: "Yah, yah." The new speaker had a clearly recognizable German accent. "It is obvious zat Darby had *everybody's* best vishes in mind. Aber, I have had been lectured by der ghost of zis man too much already over zis last week." Sarah shuffled herself closer to the door. The entrance was cut through a wall of granite four feet thick, and she was able to peer directly into the room through the crack between the open door and its frame. She saw the portly form of Helmut Grüsser, the Submersible. He was wearing his dress costume to the table, an outfit intended to evoke the Paragon's grandeur without the ungainly complexity that came with the armor and devices that they lugged into action with them.

In the Submersible's case it was a cloth jacket. The baggy fabric was gathered at his elbows and knees, and was supposed to suggest the diving suit he wore when commanding his amphibious vehicle. On each of his shoulders was an oversized brass epaulet with tassels made from golden thread. Nathan had once described them as "Grüsser's broken broom heads from his days as a janitor in the navy." It wasn't the kind of joke you would ever make to the man's face.

The Prussian had once been a high-ranking naval officer, clearly on track to become an admiral. But rumors swirled about an incident with a young officer's wife that had ended his military career in scandal and disgrace. And if the stories had followed him all the way to New York it was hard to imagine that there wasn't at least some truth to them. But he was also a well-respected member of the Paragons, and seemed to have avoided repeating whatever mistakes it was that he had made on the other side of the Atlantic. "Perhaps ve can hear vat Darby's vishes are mitout having to zit through ze whole thing." The heavy accent was spit out with a staccato bluster from underneath his waxed mustache. "Und zose who still vish to can read every magical verd of vat he had to say for zemselves." It would have been comical if not for his casual disrespect of Darby's final words.

When the Submersible had first joined the Paragons her father had taken a shine to the rotund Prussian, and for a short while they had been best of friends. Her father had often brought Grüsser over to the house, and after dinner they would spend hours discussing military strategies, historical and imaginary.

But Sarah, still a girl at the time, had disliked Grüsser from the first moment she met him. Something about the man reminded her of a troll, and there was no proof that he wouldn't actually eat a child given the chance.

And then, just about the time the rumors began to circulate among the staff, his visits to the mansion ceased completely. Nothing was said, but Grüsser was no longer mentioned by her father, except that a few times her father warned her that "the German" wasn't the kind of man that it was safe for her to be around alone.

During those few occasions where she had been forced to interact with him socially, she had found Grüsser's leering smiles and forced compliments most unpleasant. His eyes would rove up, down, and across her figure as they spoke, and it sent shivers down her spine. There was clearly something not right about the man. "Vat I am more conzerned viz is Darby's requests fur der future of der Paragons," he said.

"Excuse me," said another voice, breaking into the conversation. She couldn't see him, but the Sleuth's English accent was easily recognizable, even if she had never heard his polished tones being used in such a commanding and penetrating manner as they were right now. "But these are the final words to us from the man who was responsible for the founding of this organization." There was also an undercurrent of reprimand and condescension, and in her head Sarah applauded him for it. "I think that the Industrialist deserves our full attention, as does the memory of Sir Dennis. I doubt that simply reading off his wishes like a grocery list would give us the full benefit of his wisdom, even if we do decide to go against his final requests."

To Sarah, Peter Wickham seemed to be the opposite of the rotund German in every way. He was trim instead of fat, honestly standoffish instead of falsely close, prim and proper instead of ostentatious and gross. He had also always been kind to her, even if he didn't seem to pay her much attention. As a game she would sometimes stare directly at him, seeing how long it would take him to realize that someone was watching him with the same degree of intensity he usually gave everyone else. Sarah had never managed to count to ten before his gaze caught hers.

From her hidden vantage point she could see Helmut Grüsser nodding primly at the Englishman. "Of course, my dear Vickham. I have nozink but der greatest respect for our departed leader. . . ."

The Industrialist cut him off. "Then you'll allow me to continue." There was a moment of strained silence, and then the Submersible relented. "Ja, of course." He gave a prim salute. "I apologize."

Stanton cleared his throat and then continued to read. "'I believe that we have only begun to see the possibilities of a future that will forever improve the lives of every man, woman, and child on this planet. There are new inventions that will, one day soon, allow even the most wretched man to live like a king, and for no child to go to bed hungry at night.'"

Her father stopped reading for a moment, his long pause clearly meant to offer an opportunity for anyone to dare to speak up.

When there were no more outbursts or interruptions he continued. "'In my mind this is the true purpose of the Society of Paragons. We are the protectors and stewards of that future; parents of a tomorrow that we will never see. It is a world that will be beyond our ability to imagine it, even if it is built from our dreams.'"

Sarah smiled to herself as she listened, and then suddenly shook her head. She had already risked too much by sitting there listening to Darby's last words.

She shimmied herself away from the door. Now all she needed was some way to get past the doors without being noticed. There was no other way to get to where she wanted to go, and she knew from firsthand experience that all the men in that room were experts at ignoring women when they were discussing Paragon business.

Dragging herself across the corridor, she did her best to try to squeeze herself into the shadows that hugged the bottom of the wall.

As she moved past the door she could see her father standing directly in front of her behind the massive granite table, his eyes fixed on the document he was reading. If he even so much as glanced up he would discover his daughter squirming across the floor like a salamander. Her heart was pounding in her chest, and every breath she took sounded like thunder.

Next to Alexander, Nathaniel was absentmindedly staring at his nails, clearly deciding which one would be the best for chewing. His eyes flicked up, and Sarah froze. He was staring straight at her, and for a moment she thought that it was all over. There was no way he could have not seen her. A numb feeling clutched at her heart, and her skin went cold.

She would be in such terrible trouble. When would she ever learn?

And then his eyes turned back to her father and settled back to his nails.

Sarah quickly pulled herself out of the view of the open door with no obvious shouts of alarm or other signs of detection.

What if Nathaniel had seen her and decided to *let* her escape? But he never would do any such a thing. His loyalty to the Paragons was far greater than any amorous feelings he might have for her.

Safely out of sight, she took a few moments to gather her composure and then stood up. But she had just managed to tempt fate and win, and she wasn't going to try it again. Soon the sound of her father's voice once again returned to a confused muddle in the distance.

Sarah had managed to sneak past the world-famous Paragons, and she couldn't help feeling very pleased about it.

She turned right, stepping from the main corridor into a smaller side hall. The polished granite walls were gone, replaced with a combination of rough plaster walls and white stone. The ceilings here were lower as well, and the gas lamps were stationed fewer and farther between. The light was murky here, like an endless twilight in a smoke-filled sky.

Taking another step, she came to the top of a twisting stairwell that descended into darkness. Without stopping she grabbed the railing and headed down.

By the time she reached the bottom it was pitch black, and while the end of the railing told her that she had reached flat ground, Sarah still tapped her foot out on the floor in front of her to make absolutely sure that no more stairs were hiding in wait.

Finding none, she put her hand flat against the wall and stepped blindly forward. After a few feet her trailing hand crossed the bump of an igniter switch. For a moment she considered the idea of pressing it and banishing the darkness. It was a comforting thought—she had no idea what hidden dangers lurked in the darkness, real or imagined. But it had been ages since she had been down here alone, and Sarah couldn't remember which lamps were controlled by what switch. While she was sure it would light up the hallway ahead of her, it was equally likely it might illuminate the stairwell behind her as well. She didn't need a curious staff member investigating the lower levels—especially now, when she was so close.

Groping through the blackness, she reached the end of the hall and turned to the right. Sarah gasped as her left foot found empty air, then landed heavily on a step. She had forgotten about this second descent, and her slipper lived up to its name as it shot out from underneath her, sending her pitching backward.

Her left hand found the railing by instinct, painfully yanking on her shoulder as she simultaneously fell and tried to pull herself up. Meanwhile her right foot had managed to find some purchase on the next step, saving her from a fall. She felt a sharp heat rise up from the bones of her ankle as it smacked into the stone.

Managing to regain her balance, Sarah whispered a prayer to herself as she stood upright. Lifting up her right foot she swiveled it around. The pain quickly subsided, and it seemed as if none of the damage was permanent.

Ten feet beyond the bottom of the steps her hand found the cold, flat iron of what she knew was the door she had been looking for.

She reached into her bag and pulled out another key. This one was much smaller than the one that she had used to unlock the entrance, but no less mysterious and ornate. Although she couldn't see them, her fingers felt the ridges of strange metals that had been inlaid into the teeth at one end, and the wire that had been tightly wrapped around the flat head of the key at the other.

Starting near the top, Sarah slowly swiped her hand back and forth across the door's smooth surface until she found the keyhole. She slipped the key into place, and the door began to vibrate with an audible hum, the metal in her hand becoming instantly warmer.

She twisted the key around in a full circle, and from somewhere inside the frame a mechanism shifted, letting out a heavy clunk. There was a slow scraping sound from inside as bolts released themselves from the frame.

When the process was complete, the door swung open in an easy arc. It wasn't until she exhaled loudly into the darkness that Sarah realized she had been holding her breath the entire time.

Putting the key back into her bag, she stepped through and groped along the wall with her hand until she found the familiar round shape of one of Darby's gas igniter switches.

When she twisted it, what came to life was not the flickering yellow light she expected, but a white, almost glaring illumination. Unlike the gas lamps, which mostly spread their light upward, the incandescent globes illuminated cleanly in all directions, revealing a low-ceilinged chamber carved into granite rock, over a room filled with a series of small worktables.

She let out a small laugh as her eyes adjusted. The glowing spheres were cut into the walls, with a filament glowing so brightly inside of each one that they left marks in her vision when she looked away.

While Thomas Edison, over in Princeton, had been loudly proclaiming for years that he was on the verge of discovering a practical electric bulb, Sir Dennis had completed the same invention under the streets of Manhattan, and bothered to tell no one.

The laboratory was thirty feet wide, and stretched out in front of her for twice that distance until it reached a massive door at the far end. It looked like something out of medieval history—a gateway fit for a fortress.

It was made from massive wooden planks strapped together with bands of iron, and in front of it a series of thick brass bars rose up from the floor and disappeared into the ceiling. There was even an open slot in the floor a few feet in front of it, as if someone had attempted to construct a miniature moat.

Although Sarah had been in this part of the laboratory a number of times before, she had never gone beyond that door, or even seen it open.

Her eyes went wide when she realized that on the left wall, laid out flat on a steel slab, was the Automaton. A set of six of the electric lights had been placed all around him, and he seemed like a mechanical angel bathed in their brilliant glow.

The mechanical man had been completely stripped. The plates that usually covered his body were removed and neatly stacked on a nearby table, leaving his insides clearly visible. Rows of meshed cogs slowly rotated, glinting as the lights reflected against the serrated edges of the turning gears.

As she walked up to him, Sarah could see that Tom's arms and legs had been shackled to the surface of a steel slab. Close up it was clear that no one had bothered to make any real attempt to repair him beyond his new face. His right arm was still damaged, with the rods scorched and bent from the dynamite.

Almost without thinking Sarah pulled out her handkerchief and gently began to try to polish the soot off of his damaged arm, but it was tattooed into the metal.

In the quiet of the laboratory she could hear the rhythmic ticking that came from his heart, a brass sphere in the center of his chest. It was suspended inside a metal cage in the middle of his body. Gear-tipped rods sprang out from it in every direction, their teeth resting against a series of larger cogs in his chest. Those, in turn, moved the other cylinders, gears, and rods spreading out across his body.

A pipe on the right side of the heart let out an occasional hiss as a rotating gear pulled open a spring-loaded cap at its end and released a small puff of steam into the air. Underneath was a large bolt with a wing nut at the end of it.

The heart of the Automaton was the one piece of his anatomy that Professor Darby had gone to great pains to point out to Sarah when he had first invited her down into the lab. "This," he had told her, pointing out the device, "is everything that makes the Automaton what he is. Inside of it is something that I call the 'perfect gear.'"

"But however does it work?" she had asked him.

Darby had given her a look, one that she had never seen him make at any other time in all the years that she knew him. It was a boyish grin, and for a moment she could see him as he was when he was thirty years younger—a clever young man still facing a world full of secrets to uncover. Then he rolled his eyes. "I have some thoughts, of course, but I don't actually know."

Resting her hand against the cage, she could feel the rhythmic pulse of the machinery as it turned inside of the Automaton. She felt the stinging squeeze of tears as the memories and emotions of the loss of Darby welled up inside of her.

"Miss . . . Stanton," came the words in the Automaton's singsong tones, "is that you?"

She jumped back slightly. Somehow she had convinced herself that the machine man had been unconscious, even if he was never truly "conscious" to begin with. "Tom?" Her throat felt thick, and the words came out slightly choked. "It's Sarah!" She took a moment to swallow and try to clear her voice. "I'm here. How are you?"

"It's good to speak with you Miss . . . Stanton. It has been a few days since I have had a visitor." At least someone had bothered to repair his ability to speak. She supposed that was the minimal work needed to make Tom presentable for the funeral.

She reached over and began to pull out the long pins from his shackles. "What have they done to you, Tom?"

The Automaton tried to lift himself up, but was trapped by the restraints. Sarah opened them easily, and Tom folded himself up until he was eye to eye with her. The harsh glow from one of the electric bulbs shone down directly into his chest, turning his torso into a mosaic of spinning light and shadows that somehow made his injuries look much, much worse. "They have *done* nothing. I was simply told to wait down here until the . . . Paragons decided what it is they should do with me."

"Strapped to a table? Alone and broken in the dark? That's monstrous." She popped open the leg restraints. "Why don't you stand up?"

Tom began to try to move his legs. From somewhere deep inside of him came an unfriendly grinding followed by a dangerous-sounding metallic ping.

Sarah put her hand on his arm and tried to help, but it felt as if she were attempting to provide aid to a boulder. "Does it hurt?"

"I do not, I think, feel pain in the same way that you do, Miss . . . Stanton. It is simply uncomfortable."

She touched his chest near his shoulder where the harpoon had pierced him, and the touch dislodged a small tin box that had once held a spring. It bounced noisily across the floor. "I'm sorry, Tom! What can I do to help you?"

"No apology is necessary. I am fully capable of self-repair given the right materials."

Sarah's eyes widened. "Did someone tell you *not* to fix yourself?"

"Yes. The order was given to me by your . . . father."

The anger rose up inside of her, and she clenched her hand into a fist. "This is unconscionable! I demand you repair yourself immediately!"

"I will need supplies. Perhaps you can open those?" He pointed at the sliding doors of the cabinet next to the table.

Then she heard another voice. "Let's think on that for a moment, shall we?" It sent a shock through her that made her jump. "I'm not sure that going directly against your father's wishes would be the best course of action at the present time, Miss Stanton." The voice was male, clearly older, and spoke with a commanding British accent.

Sarah spun around, then immediately took a small step back. Dressed in his full costume, and standing only a few feet away, the Sleuth was an intimidating figure. A black mask covered his face from the forehead down to the tip of his nose. The molded leather was shaped to give the appearance of a deeply furrowed brow, like a man eternally in concentration.

Hanging from the bottom of the mask was a thin curtain of black leather that obscured the rest of Wickham's face. Whatever menace that it might have projected was mitigated by the thick gray hairs that sprung out from the back of his head.

The rest of the Sleuth's outfit was striking in its quality and detail, although it took Sarah a moment to tear her gaze away from the eyeless face.

He wore a black leather greatcoat over a wool vest stitched with a pattern of magnifying glasses in silver brocade. Underneath it all was a simple charcoal-gray shirt. His pants were a pair of gray-and-black striped breeches that accentuated his long, lean legs. Pointed boots rose up to meet them.

"I'm sorry if I startled you, Miss Stanton." He pulled the mask down and let it hang around his neck. Underneath, the face was as long and sharp as the rest of him, the skin stretched tight around the skull, steel-gray eyes looking out from deep sockets. "I certainly didn't mean to."

"If you don't want to scare people, then why would you wear such a frightening mask?" she asked him, putting her hand to her chest. She felt the rapid beating of her heart underneath it.

"Well, it *is* good to startle your *enemies*, my dear." Wickham smiled. "Striking terror into their hearts and all that."

Tom managed to rise up a little farther and spoke. "It is good to hear your voice Master . . . Wickham."

A sudden realization struck Sarah. "How did you know I was here?"

He let out a soft chuckle. There were rumors that the Sleuth had been quite the charmer when he was a younger man, and even though it was clear those days were long behind him, she could see the rakish youngster peeking out through the practiced veneer of the calm, collected elder. "It wasn't much of a mystery for me to notice a young lady sliding her bustle down a hallway, even if she was doing her level best to do it quietly."

Sarah felt a stab of panic rise up through her. "The others?"

He shook his head. "No worries, Miss Stanton. I am the only one who knows of your current adventures in the Hall of Paragons. Uncovering things that are trying to stay hidden is my specialty, after all." He took a look down at the Automaton, peering into his body where the light shone through. "The other Paragons express their considerable power using far more . . . direct means." He slipped a magnifying glass from a hidden pocket inside his coat and focused it over Tom's shoulder, where the tin box had been before Sarah dislodged it. "I excused myself and left them to listen to the final words of our fallen leader. I'm sure they'll find them most upsetting."

Sarah closed her eyes. "Thank you for not saying anything."

He reached a hand down into Tom's torso. "Don't give me your gratitude yet, Miss Stanton."

Sarah felt a second tingle of fear run through her. "You wouldn't tell. . . . I mean, there's no reason to . . ."

He carefully and slowly pulled out his hand. A small cog, badly scored and bent, was trapped between his middle and index fingers. "There are some questions that need to be answered before I can safely say I'm willing to keep your secrets." He pointed across the room toward the doors. "Follow me, both of you."

The grinding started up again as Tom rose, but this time he was able to move off the table. He took a tentative step forward, swaying dangerously before planting his next foot on the ground.

The Sleuth nodded approvingly. "Simply creating a machine capable of mimicking human locomotion is an astounding feat, and yet Sir Dennis managed to build one that could mimic the mind of a man as well."

With each step Tom took, he seemed to teeter on the edge of disaster, but he managed to place the alternate foot down without falling. Sarah held out her arm. "Thank you, Miss . . . Stanton, but you cannot carry my weight, and I am afraid you will unbalance me if you try."

She let go of Tom, but stayed by his side as she spoke to Wickham. "Is it possible to simply 'mimic' thought?" she asked him. "Can something pretend to think and not be thinking?"

He pondered it for a moment, and then smiled. "I'm afraid that uncovering the answers to those kinds of esoteric philosophical questions is quite outside the realms of my expertise."

The Sleuth strode toward the dark end of the chamber, his long legs giving him a gait that neither Sarah nor the broken Automaton could match. "My world is built from facts and the deductions I can make from them." He turned his head and spoke loudly over his shoulder to them as he walked.

"And currently it is one that is almost overwhelmed by a number of mysteries that have been much on my mind since the tragedy at the bridge."

"Could you slow down, please?" Sarah asked him.

"Of course." But his actual gait seemed to remain the same.

"Tom," the Sleuth said. "First question: who was responsible for the death of Dennis Darby?"

Tom's voice rang out. "The . . . Bomb Lance."

"For his *physical* murder, yes. No question there." The Sleuth stopped at the massive gate and waited for the others to catch up. "But that's not the same as having a genuine reason to kill a man."

Sarah tottered on her heels as she came to a stop. "He wanted the key."

"Clearly that. And, unfortunately for all of us, he got it."

"But why was it so important?" Sarah asked him. "What does it unlock?"

"Dennis had a penchant for complicated metaphors. Men, machines . . ." He tapped his hand against the clasp holding the sliding doors together. "Keys, locks . . ." The Sleuth let his words trail off and regarded Sarah silently, wrapping his long fingers around his chin.

She looked straight up at him. "You said you had some questions for me."

"You understand, Sarah, that if I were to tell the others that you were down here it would never be for reasons of malice."

Sarah felt a familiar queasiness rising up from her stomach. "I suppose it would be for my own good. . . ."

"Yes," he replied. "That *would* be the reason."

"If you were a young woman in this world, Mr. Wickham," Sarah said with a slight sharpness in her voice, "I'm afraid that you'd end up hearing that phrase all too often. At some point I began to realize my 'own good' is an easy excuse that people use when they're telling you what to do."

"I understand. If it makes you feel any better, it's something they say to young men as well, especially when you're the type who dresses up in costumes and gallivants across the city during the night."

"I can see how that might frighten the horses," Sarah replied.

He tapped a finger against his cheek and grinned. "Sometimes you truly are your father's daughter."

"I'll take that as a compliment."

The Sleuth pointed at the gate. "If, Miss Stanton, I open this door and show you what lies beyond it, you will become *involved*—irrevocably and absolutely. I will try to protect you from harm, but since I'm not sure exactly what is going on here, I can't promise you that you won't be entering a world of danger beyond my ability to keep you safe."

Her mind flashed back to the brass reliefs on the front door: poor Prometheus tied to his rock as the gods went about the business of war. "The world of the Paragons . . ." she said slowly to herself. "But I'm the daughter of the Industrialist."

"Yes, you are. The fact that you came this far on your own makes it obvious that your father has already allowed you to become involved to a greater degree than he should have. But there is still a great deal you don't know, and that ignorance may give you a modicum of safety. And if not safety, then at least some comfort." His face was very stern, his forehead now furrowed into ridges very similar to those on his mask. "So I have two questions for you."

Sarah nodded.

"Firstly, are you sure this is what you really want? I'm well acquainted with the satisfaction that comes from discovery. But I want you to understand that there are often unintended consequences and responsibilities that also come with knowledge." He paused and looked directly into her eyes. "This won't be a game any longer, so I want you to be sure."

Sarah pondered for a moment. Even growing up as a child of privilege in New York City, it was impossible to be ignorant of the fact that most people in the world lived much sadder and more desperate lives than she had ever known. And while some might claim that it was destiny that put you into your circumstances, Sarah had always believed that it was mostly luck that had given her the life she'd lived. And yet she had always been determined to not let that hold her back.

She heard herself saying the words before she had even decided she believed them. "I . . . I am, Mr. Wickham."

He nodded solemnly and then continued. "Secondly, showing you what is behind this door means that I am about to break a number of sacred oaths.

So, even as I am keeping your secrets I will now be asking you to keep mine. Can I trust you, Sarah Stanton? Are you someone of honor, integrity, truth, and righteousness?"

As she heard him speaking the words a jolt of recognition struck her. They were part of the oath that every Paragon took when they became a member. "I swear to fight for honor, integrity, truth, and righteousness," She had heard her father say them many times over the years as he had inducted new members into the Society.

"and that you will use the secrets and powers of the Paragons to protect those who cannot protect themselves," Wickham continued, completing the oath.

"I . . . I will!" she stammered back.

He took her hands in his. They were surprisingly smooth and cool. "I can't make you a Paragon, Sarah. But I can ask you to live up to Sir Dennis's ideals. In the end I think that may be worth a great deal more."

"I'll do my best, for you . . . and for Sir Dennis!"

"That's my girl." He held onto her hand for another moment, his eyes locked onto hers. Sarah felt mesmerized. "If things should go bad, remember that an oath isn't just something you say—it's a promise you make to yourself so that you'll have something to rely on in those dark moments when you think you have nothing at all."

"I understand."

"I truly pray that you never have to."

Chapter 5

Powerful Devils

Wickham kneeled down for a second, fumbling at something around his neck. When he placed it into the keyhole there were a series of rhythmic snapping sounds as the vertical brass rods that barred the door rose rapidly up into the ceiling, one after another.

"You may want to keep out of the way." The old man put his hand on her shoulder and had her take a few steps back. After the last of the rods had disappeared, the door lurched forward as if it had been shoved by the hand of a giant.

Poised over the slot in the ground, the gate began to sink down into the floor. Sarah looked over the top of it as it descended and peered into darkness beyond, but only a few feet from where they stood the gloom gave way to total blackness.

It took almost a minute for the gate to disappear entirely. Only after the top of it was completely even with the floor did Wickham step through. He took a few steps, then reached out to the wall and dialed a switch. Along the ceiling in front of them two gas lamps clicked, then flared to life, followed by dozens more, one after another, the brightness moving out into the room ahead of them until a huge metal chandelier on the ceiling flared to life, the polished reflector behind it sending light down into the room.

As her eyes adjusted Sarah realized that they were standing behind a metal railing. The roof of the room continued out at the same level from where they were standing, but the floor was forty feet below.

She looked down and saw that just beyond it a cavern stretched out in front of them with machines the size of locomotives and larger spread out across it like the discarded toys of a giant child.

The Sleuth started walking down a cement stairwell that had been built along the sheer wall. "Darby was no threat to anyone, physically speaking. Anything he had could simply be taken from him. Question: why murder him?"

Sarah tried to ponder Wickham's query as she followed him down. But as she did so the images of Darby's death confronted her again in her mind's eye. "It's not . . ." She remembered the sound of the harpoon, the horrible wound, the blood, and the look of anguish on the Professor's face as he tried to calmly face his own death. "Maybe he just . . ."

"The Bomb Lance told you that he would let you live in order to send us his message, which, conversely, also means that he must have come there with the intent to kill everyone else. If we can figure the reason for the slaughter, it should—logically—lead us to who wanted him *dead*."

Sarah was unhappy with the coldness of the Sleuth's tone. He was reducing the lives of men down to cold hard facts, but she let it pass without comment. She had never been the kind of woman to back down to a man simply because he was showing passion or anger. She wasn't going to let a lack of emotion scare her, either. "I've been thinking about that myself, and I have a theory."

He stopped and turned his head around to face her. "Do you, my dear?" he said, cocking up his left eyebrow at her. "What is it?"

"That whatever it was they stole from him, they wanted to make sure that he could never make another one. No new body for Tom, no more flying suits for Nathaniel, or machines for any of the other Paragons."

A screeching noise rose up from behind them, metal against metal. Sarah turned to look and saw Tom's hands grinding down against the railing as he used it for support. The descent was clearly difficult for his broken body.

Wickham made a face that seemed halfway between sadness and disgust, and then let it vanish as he turned back to Sarah. "That's very good, Miss Stanton—very logical. I agree that must be a part of it."

While there were a number of large machines all around them, the object they were walking to was huge—even in comparison to all the rest. Two massive frames of iron stood on either side, each made from two pillars rising up three stories from the floor to meet at a point at the top. Held up by an axle in bewteen these enormous A-frames was a flywheel so large that it sank down into a cement-lined pit in the earth between them. And rising up on either side were two great pistons, each topped with a massive slab of curved metal suspended in the air at the top of the structure, hanging motionless as they waited for the power that would send them into motion.

A set of wrought-iron stairs on the left side led up to a walkway suspended twenty feet in the air that ringed the entire machine. For all its massive size and weight there was something about its design that made it look almost ethereal, like a skeleton of an industrial beast

It was also familiar. Sarah had seen a machine like it four years ago when her father had taken her to the Centennial Exposition in Philadelphia. It was called a Corliss engine, and it had been one of the stars of the show—a modern marvel of efficient steam power. The engine had provided electric current for the entire exhibition, bringing to life a variety of industrial machines that were used for producing screws and the like. This version was clearly Darby's attempt to improve on that original design, and she could only imagine what it was capable of.

The old man pointed over to another object standing several yards away. "And do you have any idea what that is?" It was a sturdy-looking iron box fifteen feet long and seven feet high. Clustered around the far end were four tall tanks that looked a bit like mourners hunched over the end of a coffin.

Out from the top of each tank a straight metal pipe rose upward. After a few feet the pips angled together into a single tube that then made a hard right angle when it reached the ceiling. Steel fasteners held it fast to the roof as it snaked from one side of the cavern to the other, until it finally dropped down straight into the middle of Darby's Corliss engine. "Do they collect energy from the engine?"

Tom reached the bottom step. "They do the opposite," he said. "That box is the . . . fortified steam generator."

"Just so." The Sleuth pushed forward. "Follow me, Miss Stanton, and pay close attention. I'm about to reveal one of the Paragon's most closely guarded secrets."

As a child Sarah had often been reminded that "curiosity killed the cat," usually after being found somewhere she didn't belong, or after returning home with dirt smeared across one of her dresses. She could hear her father saying the words to her now using the stern voice he reserved for expressing disappointment.

Of course he wasn't the only person who compared her sense of inquisitiveness with that of a deceased feline. Nathaniel had often reprimanded her for sticking her nose into places it didn't belong, warning her that one day it was going to get bitten off.

But knowing a rule and following it were very different things, and although Sarah had known that Nathaniel and her father would be *very* displeased with her current actions, she was not going to miss the opportunity to help the Sleuth unravel a mystery. And clearly, whatever this machine in front of her actually did, it was well worth knowing more about if it truly was a "guarded secret."

Up close the apparent simplicity of the design of the box was revealed to be a by-product of the surprising amount of strength built into it. The entire exterior was constructed from flat sheets of thick boiler-plate iron, held together with quarter-inch rivets. Cut into its surface at regular intervals were a series of small glass portholes. Each one was covered with a sliding brass plate held in position by a pin and a wing nut, allowing it to rotate down once the nut was loosened. She found one that was already hanging on its hinge, and peered inside. The smoked-glass plug was at least an inch thick, and she could see nothing through it. She turned her head and looked up at the Sleuth. "A steam engine?"

Tom replied, "It is not, technically, an . . . engine. A . . . boiler would be more precise."

She looked over the machine again. "Then I'm afraid I'm confused." She pressed her hand up against it and felt the cool metal. "There's no firebox."

Tom, limping his way across the floor, managed to catch up with them. Wickham pointed at the metal man as he drew closer. "Tom has no flame inside of him either, but somehow he manages to find the power he needs to move."

She supposed at some point she must have wondered what it was that gave Tom his power. She had taken to assuming it was some kind of spring wound up inside of him, although she had never been told that was true, nor seen anything to support that theory. Exposed to the light of reason the idea of the Automaton being a man-sized wind-up toy suddenly seemed ridiculous. "Then I'm afraid I don't understand."

The Sleuth nodded, then smiled. "Perhaps it will become clear when I show you how the machine works."

Pulling off his right glove, he used his bare hand to slip open the second button down on his gray shirt. He reached under his tie with his left hand and pulled out a dull metal key on a chain. "Does this look familiar to you, Sarah?"

She stared at it for a moment; then her eyes went wide with recognition. "That's the key! The same one Sir Dennis was wearing! But . . . the Bomb Lance stole it!" She reached her hand up toward it and then drew it back. "If you have it, then . . ."

"I did nothing sinister to get this, I can assure you. It is simply a copy of the other." He pushed open a small clasp and slipped it off. "One of only three that exist in the world." He put his ungloved hand on her shoulder. "And I must trust that you will let no one else know that I have it." The intimacy of the request felt almost . . . fatherly, although her own father rarely ever took her into his confidence. When Alexander Stanton wanted something from someone it was expressed as a statement, never an inquiry.

Wickham lowered his gaze to catch her eyes. "I hope you understand the magnitude of what I'm telling you."

Realizing that she had been lost in her thoughts, she quickly glanced up at him and nodded. "Of course, Mr. Wickham! I'll guard your secrets with my life." As the words came out of her mouth Sarah felt like a character from one of the boys' adventure magazines that she had "borrowed" from Nathaniel when they were growing up. She had suddenly become young Jim Hawkins heading off to Treasure Island with a map in his hand. "But why did he want that iron key? What does it open?"

He held the dull metal closer to her, his index finger and thumb wrapped around the ornate metal head. "Not iron my dear: lead."

She looked closer. "Another one of Dr. Darby's magical door openers?"

"What would lead you to that conclusion, my dear?"

"Lead is too soft for a normal key. It would twist apart the first time you tried to use it."

"Just so." Grabbing the top of the blade end he tugged upward. The lead covering slid away, revealing a slim rod of a brighter metal underneath. It gleamed brightly, but Sarah realized it wasn't a reflection. The key cast out an unearthly light of its own.

She stared at, mesmerized. "It's like a mirror. . . ."

The Automaton was standing next to her now, and his voice surprised her. "Please . . . Sir Wickham. The exposed metal can be dangerous."

He slid the lead cap back onto it and handed it to the metal man. "Place it into the machine, Tom, if you would be so kind. We're going to give Sarah a demonstration."

Tom took the key and nodded.

Sarah pursed her lips. "I have more questions now than when we started."

"Have patience, my dear. The lion's share of solving a mystery is piling up questions until there can only be a single answer for them all. It should begin to become clearer very shortly."

On the end of the iron box nearest to them was a thick iron door a foot across. It was held in place by a hinged bolt locked into an iron claw, and screwed down against the end of the machine. Tom put his hand up against a large brass wing nut that held the bolt in place, and he gave it a hard turn.

Once it was free it spun smoothly and quietly, rotating quickly up along the bolt until it reached the end of the thread. He shifted the bolt to one side and opened the hatch.

Sarah attempted to peer into it, but there was a sheet of black rubber blocking the view. "What does it do?"

"Just a little more patience, my dear, and then I'll explain," Wickham replied.

Tom removed the lead cap from the key and placed his arm through the rubber curtain. When he withdrew his limb the key was gone. He closed the hatch and screwed the bolt back down.

The Sleuth took her hand and walked her over to the darkened windows on the machine's side. "Darby once said to me that he thought steam was what time was made from—the invisible hand of God that pushes man into the future. He believed that it was steam that allowed the angels to fly, and that one day, if harnessed properly, it would free men from all labor and war.

Wickham let out a sigh, and for a moment he looked very old. "He had visions beyond any man I've ever met. And he made so many of them come true. But I'm much more cynical than he was, I'm afraid. I told him that I thought steam was a demon born from fire, and that it will only work for mankind when caged behind iron walls. Even then, it's always trying to find a way to slip free from its prison and kill its master when his attention wanders. . . ."

Tom opened a panel on the side of the machine. There were a series of small levers inside, and he pulled them down, one by one.

"That's a dark view of something that gives us so much and asks for so little in return," Sarah said.

"Whether its intentions are good or evil, there are practical limits to what steam can do. It takes time to build pressure, and it must always be regulated. Too little gives you nothing, and too much can destroy the vessel that gives its power shape. And that energy is always an unstoppable force that must be balanced and tamed with gears and belts." Wickham looked over at Tom and nodded. "He's like that, you know."

Sarah wasn't sure exactly what Wickham was trying to imply, but she knew that sometimes it was better to say nothing, especially when men like Wickham were lost in a tale.

Or at least that's what she assumed Wickham was like. She had seen him often enough over the years, occasionally at the house, and at whatever Paragon functions her father had taken her to. She knew that he and Darby had been close friends as well, but she could only remember a handful of times she had actually seen them together.

But she had only spoken with him a few times, mostly when she was much younger. Wickham could always turn a phrase, and had always appeared to her to be the very definition of "grown-up." He was the kind of person who would squat down to make eye contact with a seven-year-old girl in order to say things like "How are you doing today, child?"

And no matter how she replied, even if it was something as simple as "We're going to get ice cream!" he would look at her seriously, as if she had said something profound. Then he would suddenly smile, look up at her father, and wink. "She's going to break hearts when she grows up, Alex. Her father's first, I'm afraid. No doubt about it." And Sarah would feel confused, proud, angry, and embarrassed—all at the same time. Some things never changed. . . .

The Automaton walked to the far end of the box and turned a wheel that stood in the middle of the tanks. The machine shuddered slightly, and through the darkened windows Sarah thought she could see a light beginning to glow. It was a simple pinpoint at first, gray and dim, like the moon coming out from behind a cloud.

"But Darby wasn't satisfied with just having a demon in a bottle," Wickham continued, and put up a finger up in the air to punctuate his point. "He wondered if you could *tame* it. Make steam now, but then use it whenever and wherever you wanted it, tapping however much, or little of it, that you needed."

The light quickly grew brighter, transitioning from moon to sun, and after a few seconds she found herself squinting. The glow seemed to almost be liquid, filling everything with a colorful glow, while darkness clung to the outline of everything it touched as if the world were an illustrated picture in a children's book. It lit up the machine like a relief, squeezing out from every portal, bright as day, even though the glass had been almost pitch black at the start.

Sarah held up her hand and stared at it in the strange light. "Steam without coal to heat it?"

"Steam that has the power of coal trapped within it, but thousands of times more powerful. The hand of God without the volatility of a demon controlling it. This is what Darby called 'fortified steam.'" He pointed to the Corliss engine. "Now, Tom, show Miss Stanton what it can do."

The metal man turned an ornate brass handle sticking out from one of the tanks. The box rattled for a moment, and then it let out a noise like a distant scream.

Across the room the metal arms of the Corliss engine began to move. The pistons turned slowly at first, like the legs of a horse laboring to pull a heavy carriage out of a muddy ditch.

The light from the box dimmed slightly, and the flywheel turned faster. Then, in a flash, the whole contraption was at full speed, chugging with the gallop of a steam engine, except that with each turn it expelled far less steam than would be expected, and without the oily wet hiss that usually accompanied it. The weights that had seemed so impossibly heavy before were now spinning at an almost dangerous pace. There was a vibration in the floor as it moved.

Sarah knew that what she was seeing was remarkable. "So quick . . ." was all she could say.

The machine continued to spin faster, and what had been a steady thump was quickly becoming a minor quake in the floor beneath them.

"Enough, Tom!" said Wickham.

The mechanical man slammed the handle back. Robbed of its incredible power, the engine began to slow immediately. As he pulled back on the levers, the light inside of it began to dim.

"That . . . was amazing," Sarah gasped. "Such power!"

"Just a practical example of fortified steam being applied directly. It can also be stored indefinitely at room temperature and released when needed. That's what those tanks at the end are for—the tamed demon."

"And it's totally safe?

Wickham shook his head. "Totally? No. There is an invisible vapor released by the element hidden in the key that can sicken anyone exposed to it for too long. The lead acts as shielding, and protects us from its rays. Sir Dennis theorized that too much exposure to the steam itself might have similar effects."

"Now I can see why someone might want to steal it."

"The truth be told, my dear, it is the source of almost all of the Paragon's miraculous powers."

"But neither Darby nor my father ever mentioned it."

"That's because it's a secret. Without it they would simply be mortal men dreaming of miracles. Even some of the Paragons are unaware of how the steam is produced, or how their own devices truly work." In the background the Corliss engine slowly ground to a stop, the last of the momentum draining away.

Sarah cocked her head in thought. "But the Bomb Lance knew what it was he wanted, and exactly where it was hidden. How did he find out?"

"More questions . . ." Wickham pulled out a silk handkerchief and quietly coughed into it. "*That* is a mystery that I still must solve—but not the only one."

"Before . . . you said that there were three keys. Where's the third?"

A smile spread across the old man's thin lips. "You've grown up to be a very clever girl. It's a shame that a mind such as yours must be trapped inside a female form."

Sarah found herself taken aback by his remark. "I may be limited in some ways, Mr. Wickham, but I assure you that in others I'm as capable as any man." Almost without thinking she thumped her fist against her chest as she'd seen Nathaniel do so often when he was angry. "More so in some cases!"

He let out a short laugh. "Ha! I have no doubt you will always let the world know what you're capable of, Miss Stanton, but it's more a question of attraction than equality." His gaze turned to look at something in the distance, and then his grin soured into sadness. A moment later the emotion vanished from his face, like a ripple fading away in a vast lake. "But no matter; I've already said too much."

He turned to the Automaton. "Come over here, Tom."

The metal man came toward them, moving with his slow, broken gait. Wickham pointed at the Automaton's heart, still visible inside his chest. "To answer your question, the third Alpha Element lives there. That key is what powers Tom's heart. He carries his own source of fortified steam."

Sarah looked up at Tom with new eyes. "But it's so powerful! It moved that huge machine like it was made of paper!"

"I am limited by this . . . body," Tom interjected. "But I am learning to go beyond my . . . limitations."

"Now Sarah, you are the third person in the world to know the truth about Tom." He coughed again into his handkerchief. "It's far too cold and damp in this place. I don't know how Dennis could stand it day in and day out."

"But then why tell me all of this? I'm not a detective. I just came down here to . . ." She let the words trail off.

The Sleuth widened his eyes. "Yes, Miss Stanton. That would be my next question for you. What exactly was it that you came down here *for*?"

"It was," she stared down at the ground, "Sir Dennis's final request. He wanted me to help Tom. There's another body—a new one, that he built for him. I was supposed to come here and help Tom use it."

The Sleuth turned to face the mechanical man. "And what happened to that body, Tom?"

"It is gone. Someone has taken it," Tom replied.

The Sleuth appeared concerned. "Do you know who took it, Tom, or where it went?"

"It disappeared the same day Sir Dennis died," he replied.

Sarah's eyes opened wide. "But who would have known?"

"And if the Bomb Lance had managed to successfully destroy Tom that morning on the bridge . . ."

Wickham finished her thought. ". . . Then whoever took it would have the only Automaton in existence."

"They still have everything they need to make another."

"No, they wouldn't," Tom interjected. "The . . . Alpha Element around . . . Sir Dennis's neck didn't work."

"I don't understand," said Sarah.

"Tom is right." Wickham turned to her. "Sir Dennis only wore that key as a reminder of the humility and the hard work he believed were necessary to succeed. The first prototype of the Alpha Element was a total failure."

"What was wrong with it?"

Tom answered. "Sir Dennis never discovered the reason. In every way it was the functional . . . twin of the two that came after it."

Wickham continued. "When it failed to create fortified steam, Dennis was devastated. Theoretically it was perfect—his math was impeccable—but it just didn't *do* anything. He thought there was a mistake in his theories. He spent several months searching through his equations, hoping to find the error, but it all worked out perfectly on the page."

"So what did he do?" Sarah asked.

"If at first you don't succeed . . . He tried again."

"And it worked?"

"Perfectly." Wickham nodded. "That second one lives inside Tom's heart now."

Sarah smiled. "Whoever wanted the key, and stole Tom's body, is going to be *very* disappointed when they discover it's useless."

"Even more disappointed than Dennis was, I'd gather." Wickham smiled slightly. "There are only three in the world. I've told the others that the main one, the one that I'm wearing, was hidden by Sir Dennis, and that we have yet to find it."

Sarah felt shocked and thrilled at the same time. "You lied to the Paragons? All of them?"

"Right now, no one but you and Tom knows that I have this key, and it needs to remain that way. So as I said before, I am trusting you with a great deal."

"But why lie to them? To my father?"

"Because if anyone still needs the Alpha Element, I want to make sure there's only one place they can find it." He looked over to the Automaton. "I'm sorry for making you a target, Tom."

"No need to apologize, . . . Mr. Wickham."

"But this news about your missing body is most distressing. I was reasonably sure you were safe down here. Now it has suddenly become very likely that whoever the thief was, he is also a member of the Paragons, and if that's true, we're all in a great deal more trouble than I thought."

Chapter 6

The Relationships of Paragons

Alexander Stanton listened to the dying echo of his own voice, the final syllables ringing off of the mirrored interior of the stepped ceiling that led up to the roof and projected light in the chamber. Waiting for just a moment, he solemnly flipped over the last sheet of Darby's final testament and placed it facedown onto the top of the rest.

Quietly he picked up the water glass in front of him, took a long sip, and then placed it down onto the granite tabletop before speaking. "My fellow Paragons, it should be obvious to all of us that Sir Dennis harbored a radically different vision for the future of our organization than we had thought possible. He was, as we know, a man of infinite vision and blinding intelligence." He looked at each of the other three men in the room in turn, holding his gaze on each of them until he was sure it was returned. "So rather than simply rejecting his request outright, I would suggest that we all take a moment to reflect on what he has asked of us, and organize our thoughts before moving forward together to decide on the future of the Society of Paragons."

The meeting table they all sat around was a massive stone ring carved from a single slab of polished white granite. It was four inches thick and twenty feet across from side to side at any point. Inlaid into the surface were copper lines radiating outward to form a sunburst. And circling the four-foot hole at the table's center in gold block type was the motto of the Paragons: "To Protect Those Who Cannot Protect Themselves."

Each of the men had been given a seat that reflected his chosen identity as a Paragon. Stanton sat at the head of the table on an ornate wooden chair covered in gold leaf. Carved smokestacks made up the arms and legs.

Alexander watched the faces of the other men in the room as they continued to work their thoughts around the full weight of what they had just heard. Even Grüsser, who had started out so eager to rush through the last words of their departed leader, now seemed at a loss. His jowls hung down from his gaping mouth, making him appear even more like a confused and hungry bulldog than he usually did.

Behind Alexander was a three-foot-tall marble dais built of three concentric rings of white stone. Bolted to the top of it was a chair constructed from wrought iron. It was black and skeletal, with a series of bronze spikes radiating in a semicircle out of the back of it like the rays of the sun.

Behind it, a metal rod rose straight up from the marble, ascending a few feet over the top of the chair before it bent at almost ninety degrees. At the end of it was a laurel wreath cast in pure gold. It hovered high enough above the chair that any man sitting in it would find the crown floating above his head like a halo. It was intended to define the leader's chair as a symbol of power that a man could occupy, but never own.

It had, since its construction, been Darby's seat, and it had remained empty since his death. The time had come to find someone else to fill it.

Stanton knew that Sir Dennis was prone to fits of idealism, but Darby had also been a man of wisdom and pragmatism. It had driven him to figure out the most practical way of achieving the impossible. How could the old fool have ever expected the rest of them to do anything but reject the choice of the Automaton for his successor?

The estate lawyer had delivered the will to him on the day after the funeral. When Alexander had finished reading it he had shaken the envelope it had been delivered in, hoping to find a secret message hidden inside.

He was convinced there was something else—perhaps a ruse to outwit his enemies. But if that were the case, and Darby had actually been one step ahead of whomever it was who wanted him dead, then the old man would still be alive, and there would have been no need for a will at all.

Stanton assumed that Wickham had read it previously as well. When the Sleuth had wandered off in the middle of his reading, he was sure of it.

It was possible he had even helped with the writing of it. The old Englishman had always been one of Sir Dennis's closest friends and greatest supporters, and there were rumors that what existed between them was more than just a platonic friendship. Neither of them had ever married, or really interacted with women in a serious manner outside of an ardent circle of older female admirers who would invite them around to tell their stories over tea and petit fours. He hoped it wouldn't come to it, but even the implication of impropriety was a useful tool, if it ever came to that.

"Ridiculous," Bill Hughes roared as he broke the silence. "He can't have been serious."

Stanton nodded in agreement. "It's no joke, Iron-Clad."

Hughes's seat was unlike the rest. The fingers of his right hand cupped a large brass knob that poked straight up from the arm of his massive oak chair. He pulled it toward him until it made a soft click, and an instant later the gears and springs housed around the axle jumped into life, turning the wheels on either side of him and rolling him away from the table with a wooden creak so sharp it almost sounded like a screech. "It's pure garbage. And it won't happen! Not while I'm here." He rose his left hand up in front of him and gave it a shake to drive home his point. But these days Hughes's hands shook most of the time, no matter what mood he was in.

Stanton couldn't help feeling sorry for the man. Ten years ago, when he had first become the Iron-Clad, he had been a veritable ox: six feet tall, broad shouldered, piercing gray eyes, his face completely framed by a mane of fiery red hair. A man who could practically knock someone over simply with the aura of strength he projected. And whatever his will couldn't move, the mighty Iron-Clad armor would clear out of the way.

As recently as a month ago he had still been able to gather together enough willpower to rise up from his chair and show the world that he was capable of being that stunning figure again, if only for a little while. He had managed to stand for almost the entire funeral.

But the days where he could still gain the upper hand against the disease that was wasting him away were almost gone now. His withering muscles were slowly, but irrevocably, turning his massive size against him.

Now it was almost impossible for him to even pretend that he was anything but a prisoner of his chair. Every single movement was obviously an agonizing effort, and he could only stand for a few minutes at a time before he slumped back down into the mechanized seat that Darby had constructed for him. The strain was rapidly aging him, and his fiery red hair and beard were streaked with lines of gray.

Stanton wondered if Hughes ever considered the cruel joke that it was the same man who had been responsible for creating the armor that gave him the power of ten men who had also built him a chair that allowed him to act with barely the power of one.

Out of the corner of his eye Alexander saw Nathaniel rise up from his slouch. "May I take a look at those papers, Industrialist?" Turbine's chair had been carved to make it look like he sat on four columns of rising smoke with an angel at the top of each one, their arms stretched toward the heavens.

"Of course, Turbine." Alexander picked up the pages, straightening the short stack by tapping it against the table a few times before he handed it over.

The nonfunctional "dress" version of the Turbine costume that Nathaniel wore was an off-white sweater with matching breeches. It was far more lightweight than the woolen body stocking that Darby had given him to wear when he was using his flying apparatus. It also lacked the interwoven metal threads that sparkled in the sunlight when the Turbine flew through the air, but the cut was definitely dashing.

Nathaniel's actual "flight jacket" hung heavily over a tall crossbar on the back of his chair. Cut from layers of asbestos and wool, there were dark streaks down the back of it where the column of fortified steam from his flying apparatus had soiled it. Stanton had told him that he would be glad to pay to have a similar-looking jacket constructed from lighter material, but Nathaniel had told him that he liked the authority he felt he gained from wearing the real thing.

Stanton rose up from his chair, the leather of his costume creaking slightly as it shifted around him. Perhaps his dresser was right—maybe he *had* started to gain a little weight recently. And grief could turn a man to skin and bones, or expand the waistline rapidly. If his sorrow had to choose a form he would rather it was the former, but it seemed the latter would be the outcome of the pain he felt from Darby's loss. All the responsibility that had been thrust upon his shoulders had driven him to consume more strong drink and rich food.

Less than a year ago he had still been the head of a major railroad. He couldn't begin to imagine how all this would have affected him if he had still had that to deal with.

It was obvious that selling off his shares in the company had been the right thing to do, but he missed the work terribly. As Alexander Stanton he had felt both comfortable and useful in his offices in Brooklyn. There were days when there seemed to be no problem he couldn't solve from that room. Crisis after crisis had reared their ugly heads, and he had smacked them all down. When he sold it, his railroad ran almost the length of Long Island.

But even before Darby's death the mantle of being the Industrialist had taken up a great deal of his time, and it was getting harder and harder to make excuses for his life as "The man whose gears grind for justice!"

And now, without a leader, the city was vulnerable to anyone who might decide to attack. And whoever it was who had killed Darby was still out there, waiting to strike again. Villains always had plans, and this plan was clearly far from over.

Nathaniel started to mumble out loud as he read the damning paragraphs over again. He spoke softly at first, but soon enough the mumbling gave way to coherent speech. "'After his heart has been fully installed into the new body that I have prepared for him, I request that the Automaton replace me as the leader of the Paragons.'" Nathaniel shook his head. "'This may seem like an outlandish request, but he will be a benign and logical authority, unswayed by the passions, jealousies, and other petty emotions that might cause weaker men to abuse the power that we have amassed here.'"

Hughes sneered. "If we made a damn machine the leader of the Paragons, we'd be a laughingstock." His voice was stronger than usual, although the progress of his disease had let some of the more uncivilized tones of his younger days creep back into his speech, undoing the work of half a lifetime of elocution lessons. "It just don't . . . doesn't make any sense."

"Ja ja." Grüsser harrumphed. "I zink ve can all agree zat ve will not be making der Automaton our new leader."

Nathaniel flipped back and forth between the pages of the speech, squinting at each word as if it might change to reveal its secrets. He looked up at Alexander. "Is this the original?"

Stanton shook his head. "A copy, made by my assistants."

"And you're sure this is what he wrote?" He held up the pages. "Word for word?"

He nodded. "Word for word." That was a lie, of course. "The people working for me never make more than a single mistake." And that *was* the truth. They always did exactly as they were told.

Stanton hoped that these events would finally force Nathaniel to grow up and shed what remained of the dewy righteousness of youth.

Like the naïve forthrightness that his daughter Sarah clung to so desperately, his stepson still held onto the hope that somewhere beyond the calculus of human greed and raw desire lay a simple truth—an ultimate good worth fighting and dying for without compromise. Stanton imagined that Darby's death, along with the thick scar forming on the boy's thigh, had been the first clear message that the world would never be that black and white.

Helmut Grüsser leaned back in his seat, stroking his waxed mustache between his thumb and forefinger. "So, Herr Stanton, ze matter of fact remains zat despite der most unusual vishes of our departed founder, vone of us must now be chosen as der new leader. Und I assume zat you sink dat der most qualified person for zat job ist you."

Stanton tried to hold back the sudden flush of anger that rose up like acid from his gut. Grüsser had plenty of bad habits, but blurting out things in inappropriately plain language at inopportune times was one of his worst, and most reliable. "I'd be happy, Submersible, to become the new leader of the Paragons—*if* that's what we decide . . . *together*." The man's brutal and impolitic directness was clearly a large part of the reason he was wearing a ridiculous costume at this table in Manhattan, rather than sitting as a powerful lord back in Prussia. Not a bad consolation, perhaps, but a step down nonetheless.

"I only say vat it is ve are all zinking." The little German popped up from his chair and then clicked his heels together. "You have my vote, Herr Stan . . . Industrialist. You vill be a fine leader." He collapsed back into his seat.

Nathaniel put the papers down and was opening his mouth to respond when he was cut off with a dull smack as the flat of Hughes's hand slapped down onto the polished white granite of the table. "Damn it, Submersible, we haven't called for a vote yet! And where the hell is Wickham?" The man could still make noise when he wanted to, despite his infirmities.

Now that both Grüsser and Hughes had mentioned the vote this matter needed to end quickly. "Off solving another mystery, no doubt," Alexander said.

The Sleuth's clear tones floated across the hall. "On the contrary, my dear Mr. Stanton, I'm afraid I'm discovering far more mysteries than I've even begun to solve."

"It's so very nice of you to take off some time from conjurin' up conspiracies to actually join us," Hughes grumbled. "After all, we're only about to figure out the future of the Society of Paragons."

The Englishman pulled out his chair and leaned his hands on the large eye that made up the back of it. "And am I correct in supposing you've decided that Sir Dennis Darby's last wishes are *not* to be respected?"

The moment of confrontation that Alexander had long been expecting had finally arrived. He didn't look forward to these power struggles; he never had. But as he had said numerous times to his staff, disagreement is always the *first* step in the art of negotiation. "And I suppose you've arrived just in time to tell us why we should make the Automaton our new leader?"

Wickham slid into his seat with a single smooth motion. "You may believe that he went mad in the end, but I think that we never went far wrong following Darby's vision while he lived."

Hughes jumped in. "If the old man went a little bit crazy, well, it happens to everyone, eventually. But that doesn't mean we're gonna hand over the Paragons to his favorite toy."

The Englishman dropped his cane onto the table, letting it clatter as it bounced across the polished stone. "I'm just wondering if it isn't worth actually having an honest discussion about what Darby's intent for us might have been, rather than just dismissing it outright."

Nathaniel's voice was low and sharp. "The Automaton is an object. A thing. Do you think it actually cares about us?"

A look of shock crossed the Sleuth's face. "You can't be serious, my boy. Tom saved your life up on that bridge. He's saved all our lives at one time or another."

"A gun or a knife would have saved me, too," Nathaniel said with a sneer, "but we're not talking about making a revolver our new leader. Men use machines, not the other way around."

"Now now, I—"

"Let me speak!" Nathaniel's voice grew louder. "That thing practically tore my leg off trying to 'free' me. It's lucky I can still walk at all!" He stared straight into Wickham's eyes for a moment. "And I'm not a 'boy' anymore, Wickham."

Wickham nodded sharply. His tone was more serious now. "I'm sorry, Nathaniel. . . ."

"Paragon names only at the table," Alexander said, cutting him off. It was time to start using the rules to his advantage.

"Of course. I'm sorry. But Darby clearly had something greater in mind when he suggested this."

Grüsser let out a forced guffaw. "Zen he should have said vat it vas along vis all ze other words zat ve just sat through."

Wickham ignored the German and looked straight at Hughes. "There's something about the Paragons that's changing. And not, I think, for the better. Perhaps with the Automaton in charge we could—"

Hughes cut him off. The full fury of his booming voice wiped away the Sleuth's proper English tones like a hurricane. "Could what, Peter? Send us back to the good old days? Face it, if we ever had any of those, they're long gone now."

Stanton nodded in agreement. "Despite England's great love of tradition and royalty, in the United States, we know that growth and change drive the engines of enterprise."

"So the Paragons are an enterprise now?" Wickham replied, a note of obvious sarcasm creeping into his voice. "I didn't realize that we're in the hero *business*. Is that what we've become since Darby died? Have we fallen so far so fast?" He grabbed his cane and pointed to the golden letters that circled the inner edge of the table. "'To Protect Those Who Cannot Protect Themselves.' Isn't *that* the real reason we're all here?"

Grüsser clicked his tongue. "Enough vit zese emotional displays. You know vat Stant . . . der Industrialist meant."

Wickham shook his head and frowned. "Are you sure about that, Sumbersible? Because it sounded to me like he just compared the Paragons to a bunch of money-driven robber-barons."

He turned to Nathaniel. "You know Tom would never intentionally hurt anyone. You believed in Darby. Tell me that you're willing to at least discuss this. You loved the old man almost as much as I did."

Nathaniel didn't look up as he spoke. "He's a *machine*, Sleuth. And he's hurt plenty of people when Darby ordered him to—that's why Darby always kept him on a short leash. Now that his master is gone, it's time for us to lock up the dog so that the world can move on."

The Englishman looked around the table for a moment, but no one returned even the slightest glimmer of sympathy. "And do you want to tie him down as well, Industrialist? Lock the goose that lays the golden eggs up in its coop?"

"Und vat does that mean?" asked Grüsser.

Stanton had wondered when Wickham would play that particular card. There were good reasons that he and Darby had decided to keep the true source of fortified steam secret from the German and the boy. In both cases it was a matter of trust, although he was beginning to think that Nathaniel was finally mature enough to keep that secret once the current crisis was past.

In Grüsser's case, he could never be sure where the Prussian's true loyalties lay. The man was an excellent Paragon when it came to the fight—utterly fearless in the heat of battle. And he had made a difference in the times when he needed to. But the crimes that had sent him here were almost unforgivable, and spoke to a moral failing that could never be fully erased.

And taking the secret of fortified steam would be more than enough of a prize to get him back into the good graces of his Prussian masters, no matter what he had done. "I'm not suggesting we lock him up forever. I only want the Automaton out of the way until we can figure out who is in charge. As Nathaniel pointed out, the Automaton is a weapon, and with Darby gone someone needs to take responsibility for using him."

He saw Wickham's eyes still glancing from person to person looking for an ally. Or perhaps the old man was still fishing for clues to his latest mystery. Maybe both.

Wickham cracked a smile. It was wide, but tight-lipped. "Then there's obviously nothing more important for us to do right now than choose our new leader."

Alexander Stanton leaned back into his chair. Had he really won this easily? "If we're done with this discussion, as acting leader I'd like to call for the official vote." He looked straight at Wickham. "If we *really* are done . . ."

Wickham sighed. "Yes, Industrialist. I've said my piece. Clearly your minds are all made up. But Darby saw something we didn't, and I think we'll all come to regret ignoring his advice."

"Time will tell." It was a flip remark, but Stanton was getting tired of ominous warnings from the deceased. He picked up the wooden gavel sitting on the table in front of him. It was a mahogany sphere with detailed carvings across the entire surface, featuring an ornate letter "P" on both sides. The bottom of it was flat, with a thin sheet of worn leather tacked on with a series of brass cobbler's nails. He banged it down against the granite three times. "Then this session will officially come to order! This meeting of the Society of Paragons is on Friday the sixth of February, 1880. The Industrialist, acting chairman, presiding."

He placed the gavel down and called the roll. "Turbine!"

Nathaniel stood up. "Here!"

"The Submersible!"

Grüsser rose and snapped to attention. "Here!"

"The Sleuth!"

Wickham simply nodded and tipped his hand.

"The Iron-Clad!"

Hughes lifted up one of his arms.

Stanton spoke the next part from memory. "Like the great Atlas, who held the weight of the Earth on his shoulders, so too must the Paragons carry the burden of all mankind upon theirs, for the world is a dangerous place, full of evil men bent on destroying the greatness and the potential of humanity." He had helped to write the words, after all.

"Gentlemen," he yelled out, "what is our purpose?"

The voices of almost all the Paragons rose up in unison. "To protect those who cannot protect themselves!"

Wickham said nothing.

"You may all be seated." Stanton finally felt himself relaxing as he sat down. After so much insanity in the month since Darby died, it seemed as if things were about to return to some sort of normalcy. There was a part of him that still wished Darby was up there, sitting in the leader's chair behind him, but he couldn't undo what had happened, and Alexander Stanton had never been a man to miss an opportunity.

Once again he banged the gavel onto the table. "We have gathered here today because according to the laws in the constitution of the Society of Paragons, if a leader should fall, then one of the existing members must be named as the new leader as soon as it is possible. Once chosen, it becomes the duty of that man to provide vision and direction to our organization, as well as be our true strength in times of trial."

He looked out across the table. "We will now select that man according to the laws of the Paragons. Nominations are open."

The gavel banged again, and instantly Grüsser's hand shot up into the air.

Stanton nodded. "The chair recognizes the Submersible."

"I nominate you, the Industrialist."

"The chair thanks you." No matter what his sins, it was hard to stay angry at Grüsser for long. He was a dangerous and unpredictable madman, but the Prussian's heart was in the right place, most of the time. "Is there a second?"

Nathaniel raised his hand.

"The chair recognizes Turbine."

"I second the nomination for Alexander Stanton."

"Paragon names only, please."

"I second the nomination for the Industrialist."

The gavel banged again. "The chair thanks you. Any other nominations?"

Wickham raised his hand up into the air.

Hughes's voice boomed again. "So help me God, Sleuth. If you nominate that machine of yours I'll walk over there and smack you straight in the mouth."

"Zat is unnecessary, Hughes," replied Grüsser. "If Wickham zinks zat he's going to find a second he can do vatever he likes."

"The chair recognizes the Sleuth." There seemed little harm the Englishman could do now.

"Point of order." Wickham turned and looked at Hughes. "I can't help but notice that the Automaton, even though he is a member in good standing of the Paragons, is not here to vote."

This time it was Nathaniel who spoke. "And without Darby here to tell him when to raise his hand, what would he do, exactly?"

Grüsser chuckled, and Stanton banged his gavel again, louder this time. "That's enough, gentlemen! Members will speak when recognized by the chair and not before!"

This was almost over; the last thing he needed was childish gloating. "The chair concedes the Sleuth's point. If his vote is needed, then he will be consulted."

"Then I'll abstain my vote as well." Wickham stood up. "I'm not in the mood today for pointless exercises with foregone conclusions." He pushed the chair back toward the table. "And I'm sure you can handle this theatrical event without any further help from me."

Alexander felt genuine anger rising up in him now. "Wickha—Sleuth! This is childish. You're a Paragon; it's your duty to stand with us until this meeting is concluded!"

The Englishman had almost reached the door when he turned on his heels. "Perhaps it's my grief speaking, but at this moment it's impossible for me to look up at that empty chair and not feel as if a terrible wrong is being done in this room today. I won't sit here and be a part of it." He stopped for a moment and then let out a heavy sigh. "I'm sure I'll come to my senses soon enough, gentlemen, but for now I must take my leave."

As he watched Wickham walk out of the room, Stanton swallowed hard and squeezed his eyes closed, shutting out the world for just a moment and trying to let his rage subside.

He genuinely respected Wickham's abilities. It was impossible to see such a fearsome intellect in action and not respect the greatness behind it. But the Sleuth had been the last obstacle to his becoming the leader of the Paragons, and now he was walking out the door.

Chapter 7

Places without Names

Although there was a time when the place had actually been called something, the sign that hung above the door had been torn down years ago, leaving only two rusting chains behind. The locals referred to it simply as "the Irish," and that was all they needed to know.

The bar sat on a street a few blocks in from the west-side piers—far enough away that you couldn't see a glimpse of the water, but close enough that the stink of rot and sewage that collected at the docks for decades still filled the air.

Over the course of a cold Friday morning the establishment had been bustling with thirsty men from the waterfront: rough-talking longshoremen, sad-eyed horse-cart drivers, fat and lazy merchants, and even a few brave accountants who had ventured out of the relative safety of their counting-houses to wrap ink-smeared fingers around a liquor glass, sneaking in a quick shot with the rougher elements between balancing their columns and rows.

But as the sun lurched toward the middle of the sky, only a dozen or so customers remained: lonely souls who were either momentarily caught betwixt and between, or utterly lost and forgotten. They were broken men, whether they knew it or not, and they spent their time in the Irish staring down into their cups as if a greater truth could be hidden at the bottom of a glass beyond the simple need for another drink.

The booths near the back were made from rough wood and lumpy plaster, and the man who occupied the one in the corner had concealed himself in the shadows, but his face was already obscured by his thick mutton-chops. They were a surprisingly cheerful shade of bright red considering that his lips were so tightly pressed together and the corners of his mouth were pushed down into a permanent frown.

In the dim light that managed to make the long journey from the grimy windows to the back corner it was almost impossible to tell if he was actually an old man, or had simply been bent into the shape of one far too early by years of backbreaking labor. His body was stout and cylindrical, with a thin neck and head sitting on the top and a pair of sticklike legs sprouting out the bottom.

Sitting in front of him was a totally empty shot glass along with a mostly empty mug of beer. The liquid that remained was flat and still, robbed of any sparkle by the course of the hour it had spent sitting in front of him.

The man had spent a great deal of the last half hour staring at that unfinished beer. His staring contest was only postponed every few minutes when he would look up and let his eyes dart around the room, giving everyone he could see a taste of his short, hard glare. It was as if his obvious disapproval of the sum total of his own life was something that he was willing to share with anyone who could have fallen so far as to end up in the same establishment that he had.

Clutched in his left hand were two glass spheres. As he rotated them around each other they made a low grinding noise, with an occasional clacking sound. Their surfaces were the color of milk, clouded with scratches from where he had been rubbing them together.

Letting out a wheezing exhale so long it almost seemed to be a sigh, he lifted the glass to his mouth and took another tiny sip. As he placed the glass back down, the remaining beer settled quietly to the bottom.

The barmaid strolled by, waiting until she had passed him completely before coming to a stop, then turning to face him as if she had just noticed him there. The girl had a hard look about her, and although there was something in her face that could still be considered attractive, it had been mostly chipped away in a rough approximation of the same process that had left the walls covered with graffiti and gouges. She grabbed the empty shot glass, then stared at him until he looked up at her. "Are ya gonna just sit there and nurse that beer all day?" She had an Irish accent that sounded almost like a continuous growl.

Although it would have seemed impossible, the man's scowl deepened a little bit, and he responded with a Celtic drawl that seemed a bit closer to the old country than hers. "I'm drinkin' and I'm payin', aren't I?"

"Slowly," she said with emphasis. "The lunch crowd'll be showin' up soon, so if ye plan ta be *stayin'* the barman asked me ta make sure you'll be makin' it worth our while."

He lifted up his glass to his lips and drank the remaining beer in a series of small gulps. When he placed the glass back onto the table, it wobbled slightly against the edge of a swear word that had been so deeply carved into the wood that it seemed to be on the verge of going all the way through. "Then I'll have another."

"Well, it's good ta know yer good for something."

The man in red whiskers responded with a sound that landed somewhere between a cough and a growl. "You're a cheeky bitch, ain't ye?"

She rolled her eyes. "I don't know whether you think yer flirtin' with me or puttin' me in my place, but I don't care. Either way, if you don't watch yer manners, I'll have my boy put yer arse out on the street, and then ya can find the rest of yerself another place ta go and not drink some beer."

She stuck her free hand on her hip, waiting to see whether he'd take her up on her offer, but his only response was a curt nod, which seemed to be what she had been waiting for. She grabbed his glass and sauntered back to the bar, giving him a full view of the unladylike swaying motion of her backside, a show that had been the singular most popular attraction for the visitors of the Irish over the course of the morning.

As she walked away, the man relaxed slightly, his eyes once again challenging the other patrons, melting away the few pairs of curious looks that had lingered after the scene that had just occurred.

He sat quietly for a minute and then jumped to attention as the front door cracked open, letting in a stinking gust of the crisp winter air. A large man in a tweed coat followed swiftly behind it. His upper lip held a large, heavily waxed mustache. It had been weighted down by ice and frost until it was no longer able to support its own weight and drooped down on either side of his mouth, giving him a pair of walrus tusks.

Still wrapped in a cloud of the outside air, the man huffed out a stream of frosty breath. "Damn cold out there!" he said loudly, announcing his presence to everyone in the bar. He followed his exclamation with a series of quick slaps to his arms and a few solid stamps of his feet.

Finishing his commotion, he unhooked the buttons of his coat one by one, peeling back his cloth jacket to reveal a frame so egg-shaped that it seemed like it would be more at home as an illustration in a children's book than something that might be inhabited by an actual person. The misshapen and slightly stained bowler cap pulled down to his bright red ears only managed to magnify his cartoonish appearance.

The scowling man looked up from his corner, along with everyone else in the bar. He raised an eyebrow in recognition, and thinking that he had caught the eye of the new arrival, lifted up his hand in a curt gesture, motioning him to come over to his table.

"Is anyone here named Tim?" the round man said with a shout.

Once again the man with red whiskers tried to get his attention, this time with an actual wave.

"Tim? I'm looking for a fellow named Tim." He craned his neck back and forth but seemed oblivious to the obvious gesture.

"Over here, ya idiot," the man in the muttonchops replied, with obvious exasperation in his voice.

The egg-shaped man looked at him with a grin so wide it seemed as if he might have found his long-lost brother. Then he lifted up a handful of pudgy fingers to give him a wave. "*Guten Tag!*"

Tim settled back into his chair, clearly attempting to conceal himself in the shadows, but it was useless. Every eye in the bar was now staring hard as the fat man waddled over to him.

"You are Tim, then?" His German accent was still strong, and he pronounced his words clearly enough under the guttural vowels and thick mustache, although his voice was surprisingly reedy and girlish. "My name is Brandon. Brandon Kurtz." From his demeanor he was a man of the working classes, and had obviously been through some rough times. His skin was pale and flushed, setting off a bulbous nose colored like a winter tomato, and yet he still managed to maintain at least a tiny hint of youth.

Deepening the scowl, the red-bearded man held out his hand. "Tim Hogan."

Brandon gave the offered appendage a quick shake and then rested his fingers in the stretched pockets of his wool vest. Finally he leaned back and cocked his head. "Hogan . . . So you're a corker, eh?"

Tim cocked an eyebrow. "Whatcha gettin' at?"

"Irish. County Cork, a corker? You have not heard this before?"

"Well, I'm not *from* Cork. I'm from Tyrone. Now if we can get down ta business."

"Oh, I'm sorry. I thought you were Irish . . . from the same place."

"We're only 'all from the same place' once we're living in this stinking city." Tim stood up and put on his hat. "Listen, I've no time ta tell ya my life story, nor do I care ta. I was lookin' for the Children of Eschaton and—"

"No, no, no." The ridiculous smile melted away from the round man's face as his voice dropped down to a conspiratorial whisper. "You've found them." The mustache had drooped down over the front of his lips, and Brandon pulled at the strands to move them back into place. "If you want to get to the business, I think perhaps we should do it somewhere else. . . ."

The German squinted hard and stuck his face closer in, giving Tim a good look up and down. "With that hat . . . It *is* amazing. Patrick said you were a ringer for him, but I would not have believed it until I saw for myself."

"What are ya talkin' about?"

"You could be Mr. Murphy's brother. . . ."

The red-bearded man pulled back, clearly annoyed. "Murphy?"

"A dead ringer," Brandon exclaimed, and nodded his head a few times as if he were convincing himself. "Don't worry. You may meet him sooner or later."

The waitress's arm slid between them, depositing a glass of beer on the table. The rough landing burst whatever slight mist of actual foam had been clinging to the surface of it. "The barman says it's time to pay up."

Tim shook his head. "And what if my friend here wants a drink?"

She turned to Brandon and looked him up and down with obvious disapproval. "Then he can ask fer one."

The German smiled. "Now Shea . . . is there a need to be like that with me? We are old friends."

She took a step back to consider the man. "I won't say you don't look familiar, but there are plenty of fat Germans who walked through that door at one time or another, and I don't consider most of them my friends." She tilted her head. "But ya can be a customer if ya like. That's always all right by me. Now, do ya want a drink or not?"

"Sadly, I have not time to—"

"Fine," she said, and walked away.

"You can have a sip of mine if ya want." Tim nodded in the direction of the glass. "I've had enough today already."

"Thank you kindly, Mr. Hogan!" Placing the index finger and thumb of his left hand under each side of his mustache, Brandon pushed the hair up and away from his mouth, moving with a practiced swipe. The hatchway now freed from obstruction, he grabbed up the glass with a single sweep of his hand and poured the entire thing into his throat, swallowing it down with a single gulp. He completed his show by banging the glass down onto the table and letting out a roaring belch.

"Well done," Tim said in a flat tone. "Wouldn't want ta let any go ta waste."

"It may not look it, but I read the Bible, Mr. Hogan. It says to 'waste not want not.'"

"It does at that," said Tim, taking a moment to slip the glass spheres into the safety of his left vest pocket. "Now where are we going ta go?"

The German smiled and nodded toward the door. "You follow me, and I will take you to the man to answer all your questions about the Children."

Tim stood up, turned around, and slid a cane out from the booth behind him. It was a stiff branch of white birch, although it was yellow now—well seasoned and stained with some ominous rusty patches. Brandon eyed him closely once again. "You're older than you first look."

"Old enough," he said, leaning down on his walking stick.

"Old enough to be my grandfather."

"Old enough to beat ya like a child."

"Maybe, but I don't think so," the German said with a shrug, and turned to the door.

As they stepped outside, the cold breeze and bright daylight slammed into the red-whiskered man like a fist, causing him to hunch over. He coughed as his nose rebelled from the full force of the stink from the docks. Even though the rich odor was diminished by the biting cold, it was still an overpowering sensation. "I can only imagine what this place smells like in the summertime."

"You are not a longshoreman, then?"

"I've done plenty of honest work, but not that."

The round man completed buttoning up his coat and flipped up his lapels. "You get used to it."

"It smells like God's own fart, but I suppose that ya can get used ta anything given time."

"Yes. Almost anything. Now we should walk." The fat man began striding forward, making a surprising amount of speed on a pair of spindly legs that seemed like they would be unable to motivate the ungainly bulk that sat on top of them. But the overloaded appendages scissored back and forth with a speedy gait that reminded Tim of a two-legged centipede.

Clamping a hand down on his cap and scrunching up his face as far as it would go, he leaned into the cold wind and began to follow him. "Is it far?"

"Not far, no. But nothing is very far away in this city, I think."

"Just honesty and truth," Tim grumbled.

The big man laughed in response. "I look for that only in what's in front of me, or in my Bible."

Except for the occasional dilapidated old building, the neighborhood was mostly made up of featureless brick and cast-iron fronts. High windows were open in vain hope that the only thing that would enter them was sunlight and fresh air.

Reaching the end of the block, the round man turned a sharp corner and entered into the shadows of an alley. Tim turned and followed him into the darkness. After a few steps the breeze disappeared, the roar of the wind replaced by an echoing howl that rang through the cold blue gloom that filled the alleyway.

"Is this a shortcut?"

"Oh no. This is the *way*."

At first it seemed like it must be a short path, but instead of finding its way out to another street the alley twisted and turned between tall buildings on either side. The red-bearded man dragged his hand along the wall and muttered to himself with each bend, clearly attempting to keep track of which way they were going, but after the six or seventh bend it would have been almost impossible for any man to remember the path they had taken.

The German laughed. "I wish you luck, Mr. Hogan. It took me many months to remember the path."

"I'll take that as a challenge."

They walked a few yards down a straight lane before taking a sharp right that took them out of the maze and put them at the entrance to a small courtyard formed from the windowless backsides of the buildings that surrounded it. Any windows that looked into the space had been papered over, and the loading docks had long ago been bricked up.

A trio of poorly constructed shacks leaned up against the walls. They were pieced together from mismatched scraps of wood and bricks, with each of them sporting a windowpane with impressively unbroken glass. Smoke rose up from their tin chimneys, floating toward the sky in dark columns until it reached the rooftops and was torn apart by the wind.

In front of them sat three men all dressed in tweed coats and silk ties. They were clearly part of a gang of sorts, and the leader was a tall figure in a top hat. His jacket reached down past his knees and was a finely tailored piece of clothing, free of the patches the rest of them wore. It had been cut to be worn long and tight, and it made him appear like a bent reed about to snap.

The leader leaned against a barrel, his long legs stretching out in front of him. In his hand he held an apple that he was peeling with a shiny pocketknife. He threw a chunk of rind into the cheerfully burning brazier in front of him, and it hissed as it landed in the flames.

He let out a quick whistle, and two more men came out from the shacks, one of them still young enough to be considered a boy.

"You've been asking a lot of questions about the Brotherhood," said the man on the barrel.

Tim stopped short, letting his escort waddle his way to the rest of the group. Brandon slid into the group as smoothly as a tool being put back into its case—although he clearly was designed for a different use than the others.

"Aye, and no one seemed ta know a damn thing."

"Not many people do. They're not supposed to." His voice was dramatic, with his long "O"s revealing the broken remains of an English accent.

"But I'm bettin' ya know *all* about them," Tim replied.

The tall man dragged his feet along the ground and then rose up from the barrel like a spider. Even without his top hat and boots he would have stood well over six feet tall, but taken altogether he was closer to seven. "I know that you've been asking about things you shouldn't even know exist. That makes it my job to find out how much you do know, and how you come to know it." It took a moment for the others to realize that they were expected to stand up behind their leader and act threatening.

"So, what's your name, old man?"

The fat German took a step forward and broke in breathlessly. "His name is Tim Ho—" His words were cut off by the wet smack of a half-peeled apple as it exploded in his face. Brandon's look of surprise was punctuated by a trickle of blood that rolled out from his nose.

"I didn't ask you, you fat idiot," the leader sighed.

The German wiped his face, taking a moment to stare at the crimson streak on his hand before replying. "Very sorry."

"Don't apologize! I should say thanks to you for managing to bring him back here without getting lost, or alerting the police."

Brandon pulled out a handkerchief so gray and tattered it was impossible to tell where the stains ended and the clean parts began. He pressed it up against his nose. "You're welcome, sir."

"I'm not a sir."

"Sorry, Jack."

The red-whiskered man raised up his cane. "My name is Tim Hogan, if ya still care ta know." With his left hand he reached down through a hole on the inside of his coat and slipped his hand, unseen, into his vest pocket, using his fingertips to grasp one of the glass spheres. "I figured that the Children of Eschaton was just a *name*, but I guess the 'children' part was right."

Jack turned in his direction and smiled. "Clever, Mr. Hogan." He took a single step toward him, but with his long legs it moved him a great deal closer. "But then, you would have to be, in order to uncover the name of a secret organization that only recruits members from men *it* chooses to invite." He began unbuttoning his black coat, flicking the buttons open one at a time with a snap of his fingers. The cloth draped heavily as it peeled apart, pulled downward by a row of small but nasty looking steel knives that had been sewn into the jacket lining on either side.

"I'm not that smart," Tim continued. "I simply heard two men talking about yer crew. It sounded interestin', so I thought I'd go ahead and ask around."

"Unlikely story." Ignoring the blades he had just revealed, Jack reached into the outside pocket and pulled out the knife he had been using to peel the apple. With a smooth snap of his wrist, he flicked it open.

"You say that, but now that I've met a few of yer men, I'm thinkin' they're not the sharpest tools in the box."

Jack chuckled. "Are you listening, boys? This man says he doesn't think you're very bright."

Somewhere under his walrus mustache Brandon smiled. "I may not be smart, but I am useful, aren't I, Jack?"

"You are indeed." The tall man smiled back as he spoke to Brandon. His grin managed to be warm and predatory at the same time. "You should know, Mr. Hogan, that Mr. Kurtz here is a medical marvel. He is not only twice as strong as he is stupid, but he was born entirely without a conscience. There is no act on God's green earth too despicable or debased for him to carry out if I order him to do it. If you want kittens drowned, of any size or species, then Brandon Kurtz is the man to do the job. It makes him tremendously useful for extracting information or inflicting punishment."

The German nodded and stammered, "Th-thanks, Jack."

Jack patted the German on the shoulder. "Now, hopefully Tim, you'll give me the answers I'm looking for, so I won't find it necessary to unleash him on you."

Tim put his cane on the ground and swayed forward slightly. "You know my name, and I already met Mr. Kurtz, back at the bar. But we still haven't been formally introduced."

Jack snapped shut the knife in his hand and opened his arms wide, letting the polished blades that lined his jacket glitter in the murky light. "The boys around here call me Jack Knife."

"Then I guess I'm pleased ta meet ya, Jack." Shoving his cane up under his left arm, Tim took a step forward, his hand outstretched. The other men immediately jumped up, thrusting their hands into their pockets.

"That's all right, boys. He's just an old man. He isn't going to do any harm." But instead of returning the gesture, he flicked the knife in his hand open again. "Now that you've found us, Mr. Hogan, what would you like to know? Ask me anything you like, anything at all."

"I heard you boys are working on a job. Something big."

"And you think you can help?"

"I may be old, but my hands are still good. There's not a safe built that I can't open up."

"A cracksman? Well that would be most useful to us, except for one small problem."

"And what would that be?" He let one of the balls drop down his pant leg. It rolled softly off his shoe and dropped to the pavement.

Jack lifted up his knife. "Your beard, it's peeling off. And honestly, that's the sort of thing can make you doubt a man's veracity."

Tim's hand reached up toward his face, stopping a foot away from his cheek. He looked into Jack's eyes, but they were giving nothing away.

"Now then, boys," Jack said, his grin widening. "What you see here is what the educated folks call a 'conundrum.'" He flipped his knife up in the air and caught it without a thought. "Because Mr. Hogan here is either sure that his beard is real, and stopped because the very idea of it peeling off his face is utterly ridiculous, or he is wearing a false beard, and he's afraid if it isn't peeling off he'll give the game away for sure if he checks it. Either way, we know something he doesn't."

Brandon opened his mouth to speak, and Jack jabbed his elbow into his chest. The German gasped as he doubled over, sputtering. "So don't give away the game, Brandon. I'd be very angry if you ruined my fun."

The red-whiskered man stood frozen and then slowly lowered his arm. "It's as real as the hair on your head."

"Unless, of course, it *is* peeling, in which case I *know* you're a liar."

"And why would I be wearing a pair of false whiskers?" He lifted his cane a few inches off the ground.

"I can think of a few, actually, but how about we try this one on for size?" Jack's smile grew. "Because you're actually Peter Wickham, the Sleuth, and you've come to try to find out who it was that killed Dennis Darby."

"Damn," he said in a most perfect and proper English accent, and smashed the tip of the cane down onto the glass sphere at his feet. It exploded violently, ripping the cane out of his hand and sending up a cloud of white smoke that enveloped him completely.

Wickham used the momentum of the explosion to throw himself backward, hoping the commotion and confusion could allow him to appear to vanish. It would have been no small feat to pull off the trick successfully at the best of times, and Jack was clearly a man to be reckoned with.

Two small steel blades ripped through the cloud. The first passed through empty air, traveling through the space that had been occupied by Wickham's head only a moment before.

The second blade struck directly into his chest.

"Damn and damn," he repeated as he fell.

Chapter 8

Awkward Situations

As a young girl Sarah had enjoyed sneaking around inside the Stanton mansion, imagining herself fighting bad people in faraway places. Grown-ups would not only play the role of whatever imaginary evil it was that she had dreamed up, but they were, more often than not, genuine foes of grand adventures and interesting secrets. And now, years later, she was fully grown, and still skulking around the halls of her house, hoping to avoid any other adults.

At least the servants were far less capable than Mr. Wickham. Yesterday, when one of the maids had caught Sarah riffling through the papers in the basement, it had been easy to convince the woman that Sarah was simply looking for something of her mother's, and the maid had let her be.

The only one of the house staff that she was genuinely afraid of was O'Rourke. The gray-haired butler had informed her father of every infraction she committed in the house, no matter how small, and he had done it for longer than she could remember. Any new bits of strange behavior by "the young miss" were simply fresh suspicion to be added to the mountain.

Not that his opinion actually mattered much. She had been given the free run of most of the mansion after her mother died, although there were still two places where her presence might arouse more than just a few casual questions. The first was the library, simply because it was somewhere that women weren't ever invited or welcomed.

She had been caught in there once, years ago, after having spent a most enjoyable hour unrolling the cigars in her father's humidor one after another in a naïve attempt to discover what it was at the center of the strange brown cylinders that made them able to produce so much smoke.

But eleven years later she wouldn't be able to get away with simply claiming ignorance and shedding a few tears, although she was sure that she could come up with *some* suitably convincing story that would keep the help from telling her father.

The other room was another matter entirely. The prohibition against being in her father's office was absolute, and had been enforced with the promise of a spanking (or worse) from the time Sarah had been old enough to know what the term "off-limits" truly meant. Not that it had been enough to keep her out the last time. . . .

And yet here she was, inside her father's inner sanctum, searching for clues that she hoped would help her to uncover something in her father's notes that might reveal who the thief actually was.

So far she had found nothing of interest beyond a few stacks of papers and certificates. From what she could tell, they seemed primarily to concern her father's business dealings and other investments. They were, she had to admit, neither interesting nor revealing of anything beyond the fact that Alexander Stanton, a man who found satisfaction charging into battle against monstrous villains with guns blazing, seemed to harbor an equal passion for the most minute and boring details of the business world.

She was sure that had he been given access to the same information, the Sleuth would already have discovered some curious notation, an out-of-place decimal point, or some other detail that would have allowed him to construct a conspiracy of people, places, and things that would have led to a clear answer as to who the thief must be.

But even if Sarah wasn't a master detective, that didn't mean she was completely unable to understand the numbers in front of her. Under the tutelage of Sir Dennis she had already learned far more about mathematics than was considered proper for a lady. And Sarah had shown more of a natural flair for numbers and mathematics than Nathaniel ever would. Even so, there was a difference between being able to understand the figures, and recognizing that the spreadsheet in front of her actually pointed to something nefarious. "If," she said out loud, to remind herself, "there actually is anything there to be found at all."

She began to organize the papers she had looked through back into a tidy stack. She had to admit to herself that she wasn't the Sleuth, and never would be. If there *was* something to find, then it would need to reveal itself to her in a far more obvious way.

When she had decided to raid her father's office, Sarah had made a promise to herself that she would only search what was open and available. But the thrill of being in here, of being surrounded by the forbidden, made her want to uncover more. "And who knows when I'll get another chance, or manage to find the courage to take it?"

She rattled the desk drawers again, just to see, but they remained locked.

Trying to decide what to do next, her eyes wandered to the safe standing on the sidewall by the window. It was an impressive-looking black box, with the requisite brass locks and hinges, and a large dial that sat in the claw of an eagle painted across the front of it—wings spread menacingly.

The safe was obviously the place where big secrets should be kept. But the few times she had been invited into the office, her father had left it open. It usually contained an impressive amount of money and stock certificates, but neither of those were valuable information.

What Sarah was looking to uncover were deep, dark secrets—the kind that would be kept in deep, dark places—and she had a very good idea where those would be hidden. It was somewhere she had been before.

When the Industrialist had first appeared to the world, wearing his smoking hat and holding an automated pistol in his hand, no one had known who the man behind the mask really was. The enigmatic "Capitalist of action" quickly became the talk of the town, with artist's renderings of him appearing on the front pages of all the newspapers, along with a torrent of fanciful novels that had imagined all sorts of lurid origins and ridiculous secret identities.

But despite all the attention, for the first few years of his career the flamboyant hero managed to maintain his anonymity. Politicians, newsmen, and other villains had all been unable to uncover who the man behind the mask really was. And it probably would have remained that way, if not for a curious nine-year-old girl stumbling onto her father's secret and revealing it to the wrong person at the wrong place at the wrong time.

It was a sequence of events that had begun with Sarah sneaking into the same room she was in now. They had ended, three years later, with the Industrialist, revealing his identity to the world, hoping to save the life of his wife and child from the dastardly villain who had kidnapped them. Only Sarah had escaped with her life.

As she pulled her thoughts back to the present, Sarah caught herself looking up from the desk and letting her gaze rest on the gas lamp coming out of the wall behind her. That was the exact spot where the trouble had begun, and looking at it now it was a wonder that such a little girl had ever managed to reach it at all, let alone manipulate it in exactly the proper way to cause the wall to open up.

She walked over to it and dragged her fingertips across the long brass tube. It was the first time she had touched it in eleven years, and it felt smooth and cool to the touch. She had often wondered if her father had modified the mechanism since she had opened it. He had had Darby help him remodel his sanctum a few years ago, and he certainly could have created something far more—

The familiar click surprised her. She had pushed it in without even thinking about it, or at least without thinking about thinking about it. She caught her distorted image in the clear blown glass of the lamp and saw that there was a trace of a knowing smile on her lips.

It dawned on Sarah that secretly this had been her plan all along. Her promise to herself that she would avoid coming back to the scene of the crime after all these years was a lie, and the curious nine-year-old girl who still lived inside of her was thrilled.

The adult, however, was not so sure, and she hesitated for just a moment before twisting the lamp to the side—but only for a moment.

There was a heavy "thunk" as the chained weight behind the wall was released, and the panel behind the desk started to rise. It was still exactly the same. Her father was nothing if not a traditionalist.

As she watched the oaken wall behind the desk disappear into the ceiling she realized that one thing *had* changed: there was a large portrait of Alexander Stanton dressed as the Industrialist hung on the wall that was rising up, and there was no place for it to go.

Sarah dove for the picture, tripping over her heels as she went. She bumped into the rising wall, managing to find just enough purchase to push her hands upward and slip the picture off its hook before the panel passed the point of no return.

Freed from its stable hook, the large portrait wobbled in her hands and then began to topple over. She managed to make a desperate twist to the right, driving her corset into her ribs. The top edge of the gold rococo frame banged into the track where the wall had lifted away, and stopped.

She breathed a sigh of relief as she slid the picture to the ground. She looked up and realized that there was a spring-loaded flap in the ceiling perfectly sized to let the painting slip through.

"Damn," she said. So far her attempts at being a master detective revealed that Sarah was far better at being clumsy and desperate than she was at being clever. She wondered if the Sleuth's true special powers were simply that he had the patience to consider all the possibilities *before* he acted.

Her mother, she was sure, would have reminded her that lack of attention was a weakness of her gender.

But Darby had never had any patience for those kinds of excuses. When he had first created the Turbine costume for Nathaniel, she had asked the old man why he couldn't make her into a Paragon as well. "My mother said it's because I'm a girl."

The scientist had laughed at that. "My dear child, it isn't your gender that makes you a hero," he had told her. "And it isn't a costume either. Any fool with a gun can already perform acts beyond those of an ordinary man. It's having the strength of will needed to overcome your own *inabilities* that makes you special." But in the end it had still been Nathaniel whom he had chosen to give the ability to fly.

Sarah stared into the open closet in front of her. The secret room had changed very little in the years since she had first peeked inside. Laid out on a large central table were multiple sets of the Industrialist's red-and-blue leather costume, each with its own version of the ridiculous steam-spewing hat that her father seemed convinced was the *pièce de résistance* of the entire suit.

A frame in back held up his shield along with the mechanical bandolier that allowed her father to feed a seemingly endless stream of bullets to his guns. Bolted to the back of it was the small metal bottle that acted as a reservoir for the fortified steam that propelled them with such terrifying power.

It was all far more advanced than it had been when she had first discovered her father's secret. Before Darby had gotten his hands on it, the weapon had simply been a mechanical device created by one of Alexander Stanton's brilliant young engineers using a series of clockworks and springs, along with a crude gunpowder mechanism. According to her father it had been bulky but effective, although it often froze at inopportune moments, a weakness that was almost fatal when it ignited during a battle with Dr. Phlogiston.

After that he had worked with Sir Dennis to reengineer the suit completely, and anyone familiar with the old man's style could see the inventor's handiwork in every element of the device. It was compact, streamlined, efficient, and beautiful in a way that revealed a true artistic skill.

Looking at it now, it felt as if a part of Dennis Darby were here in the room with her. She felt a pang of loss in the pit of her stomach stronger than anything she had felt since the funeral.

The other, less conspicuous element that had been "updated" since she had first stumbled onto the costume was that the waistline of the suit was larger than it had been a decade ago. Aging was something that her father had great difficulty accepting, although she had often assured him that he was still very fit for a man of his years.

Maybe next time he complained about getting older she could just tell him what Darby had told her. "You must remember, Father," she would say to him, "it is a person's ability to overcome their *inabilities* that makes them special."

She smiled at the thought of what his reaction might be to *that*, although the image was soured by the fact that his response would be something both withering and sarcastic.

She thought she could hear his stern tones now: "She must be in this house *somewhere*. I want you to find her and bring her down to my office right away."

Sarah gasped. The words, along with some very determined footsteps, were more than just in her imagination—they were echoing from the hallway outside of the door! And although the size of the house made it easy enough to hear conversation coming from almost any of the main halls, the fact that the words were so clear meant that it would only be a matter of seconds before Alexander Stanton burst into his office and discovered his fully grown daughter reenacting the exact event that had stolen away his secret identity and almost killed his family.

The panel, the lamp, the painting, the wall . . . Possibilities flashed through her mind, but each option seemed more useless than the last. *The door.*

Desperation gave wings to her feet as Sarah bolted across the room. But her constricting garments made her graceless, and her hip grazed the edge of the massive oaken table as she tried to clear it. Pain lanced through her, but she still managed to finish bolting across the carpet, landing on her bustle with a thump before she wedged the heel of her shoe against the lower corner of the door.

A moment later the lock shifted, and she felt her father's strength pushing against her foot. The pressure was ferocious, and she half expected the wood to flex, bulge, or crack.

She held her breath and prayed that she would be strong enough to hold him back. Even if the door only moved the tiniest bit he would be able to guess that it wasn't jammed. . . . Sarah shuddered to think what her father would do if he imagined that some intruder had invaded the security of his office.

But the quality of the door allowed it to remain as unmoved as an Englishman hearing a ribald remark.

"Damnation!" her father swore as he gave it a second mighty shove. She imagined that he would not have cursed so loudly if he knew that it was his daughter that was the obstacle on the other side of the door. But then again, Sarah thought to herself, if he knew *that* he would be doing a great deal more than simply attempting to shove his way in.

Even through the excitement, her hip was beginning to ache from where it had smashed into the desk. It was painful enough that she wondered if she might have broken the skin. Creating excuses to explain bruises to the housemaids was difficult enough, but at least they were used to her clumsy, boyish ways. But actual bloodstains were sure to give rise to questions that would be almost impossible to answer.

"Ungh!" her father exclaimed as he shoved against the frame one more time. "What is the matter with this blasted door?" Her foot was aching now, too, ready to give up in its war against Alexander Stanton's legendary stubbornness.

Then the pressure was gone.

"O'Rourke!" her father cried out, his voice fading as he turned away. If he was calling for the butler that might mean he was giving up. She waited for another moment, then heard his footsteps fading as he moved down the hall. "O'Rourke!" he shouted again, louder this time.

For a moment she considered opening the door and attempting to slip out. But with all the commotion going on in the house, there was no way that Sarah would be able to make it to the stairs without being caught and questioned. There was only one way out. . . .

Sarah scrambled across the rug, barely managing to get to her feet as she grabbed for the mechanism that controlled the secret panel. She turned it again, and the panel in the ceiling began to descend.

As Sarah prepared to duck inside the secret room, her eye caught the dropped painting that still sat on the floor.

A fresh wave of panic flooded through her, although with less force than it had a few minutes ago. *Perhaps it's the pain in my hip*, she thought to herself.

Sarah considered her options: she could drag the canvas with her into the secret closet—but that would only postpone her troubles. Her father would find the painting where it shouldn't be, and Sarah would be the only suspect.

Despite the fact that his daughter had revealed to the world that her father was a Paragon, the existence of the secret room was still known only to a few select members of the household. After he had saved her from danger, Alexander Stanton had sat his daughter down and made her promise to never again enter that room. "You are," he told her, "its special guardian. You must help me keep it safe from prying eyes, as well as the ever-hungry dusters wielded by the housemaids!" It had been a long time since they had shared a moment together like that.

The ceiling continued its relentless downward slide. There would be no way to get the painting back onto the wall and still sneak inside the room. She would need to quickly find a hiding place.

The painting was too tall to hide behind the couch, and neither the fern nor the globe was a genuine option.

"The safe!" she exclaimed with relief. Sarah wrestled the frame into her arms, trying not to notice the dent in the gilt where it had banged into the wall. She carried it over to the side of the cast-iron monstrosity and placed it on the floor next to the wall. She gave it a shove, sliding it behind the squat metal box. At least the safe was tall enough to hide it. As it disappeared from view, her father's painted eyes seemed to be giving her the most disapproving look in the history of pigment.

Once it was completely hidden, she ran for the back wall. She scrabbled underneath the falling panel just as it was about to reach the floor, her hip loudly reminding her of the indignity that it had already been subjected to. It was followed by a popping sound as some of the boning in her corset snapped from the pressure. "More questions from Jenny," she whispered to herself.

The wall closed behind her, and the clanking mechanism dwindled away into silence as it wound down. Sarah's sigh of relief was interrupted as it dawned on her that she was surrounded by utter darkness.

Through the wall she heard the sounds of her father entering the room.

Chapter 9

Things Askew

"Damnation!" The day had already been going badly by the time Alexander Stanton found himself vexed by the door to his office. He supposed he should have expected it. Since taking over the leadership of the Paragons it seemed that every time he turned around there was another bit of bad luck attracted by all the others. The feeling of having a dark cloud hanging over his head was, he had to admit, more than a bit ironic for a man that wore a chimney for a hat.

But superstition was nonsense for the weak, and Alexander Stanton had spent his entire life attempting to define himself through the power of rationalism, reason, and science. Whatever was going wrong had to have an explanation beyond being a curse. But reason also said that if the handle turned, the door must be unlocked.

Mumbo jumbo or not, it was an annoyance—every moment spent was a moment wasted. There were papers that needed to be signed and a million things that needed to be done—things that were not going to get done in the hallway. He gave the door another hard, sustained shove.

"Ungh," he exclaimed loudly as he enlisted his shoulder into the effort. The door didn't budge.

"O'Rourke!" he shouted as he turned and walked down the hall, trying to see where the old manservant had gotten too.

When it came to yelling, the acoustics in the house were spectacular, and most of the time he didn't need to bother with the bell. But lately, he had to admit, his butler had started to act as old as he *looked*, and his hearing clearly wasn't what it used to be. More and more often he would send the Irishman off on some specific errand only to find that O'Rourke had forgotten the task entirely and fallen into some old habit—plucking up balls of wayward dust from behind the settee or strapping on his apron in preparation for scrubbing away at a previously unnoticed bit of tarnish on the silver tea set. Although, Stanton supposed, finding out where his daughter had hidden herself was as much of an old habit around this household as anything else.

"O'Rourke!" he cried out again, louder this time. If he was being honest with himself, it was long past time to let the old man retire. And under normal circumstances he would have worked out some kind of acceptable pension and sent O'Rourke off to live out his remaining days in relative comfort. But he currently had neither the time nor the inclination to break in someone new. Just the thought of attempting to find someone who could anticipate his habits sent a chill down his spine.

Inside Alexander's head his businessman's voice chided him for being penny-wise and pound-foolish. Every day he waited would make the inevitable transition that much more difficult, and when the inevitable day came when he was *forced* to find someone new, O'Rourke might be in no condition to pass on any wisdom. It was, he told himself, one of the occasional poor investments a man must make during his lifetime. *Poor excuses for poor choices*, the businessman shot back. Unsurprisingly, it sounded just like something his mother would say.

Hoping that his call might yet be answered, Stanton looked up the stairwell, then peered down toward the kitchen. Considering the amount of money that went into employing a full-service staff, he was always amazed when it appeared as if there was no one in the house.

Like a rabbit bolting out of its burrow, he saw a figure in black and white scurrying across the hall, attempting to avoid detection. "Mrs. Farrows!" he yelled after her as she disappeared into the next room.

"Mrs. Farrows?" he repeated. For a moment there was no response, and then a woman's face peeked out at him, the rest of her matronly figure still hidden behind the doorframe. "Mr. Stanton, sir?"

"Could you please come here, Mrs. Farrows?"

She scurried toward him, her skirts rustling across the floor. "How may I help you, sir?"

"Mrs. Farrows, I seem to have lost Mr. O'Rourke."

"I'll go find him, sir!" she said, her body reorienting to head her off in a new direction.

"Hold a minute, please."

"Yes, sir." She twisted back again instantly, the skirts swirling around her feet as they worked to catch up.

Stanton considered himself committed to the idea that there should be no aristocracy in an American household, but he had to admit that the proper deference from a servant sometimes scratched an itch deep inside. "If you find *anyone* capable of helping, please tell them the door to my office has become jammed. And," he continued before she could find another opportunity to bolt, "I'd like you to find my daughter.

"Once you've succeeded, send her to my office." For a moment he wondered if Sarah and the locked door could somehow be connected. It was preposterous, but not, he noted sadly, completely outside of the realm of possibility.

He realized that Mrs. Farrows was still there staring at him, blinking like a confused forest animal. "Well?" he asked her, trying to make his impatience as plain as possible.

"Is that all, sir?"

"Yes," he snapped. "I'll meet whomever it is you find first right here."

He stomped back down the hall in a huff. With his luck they'd have to replace the door completely, or tear it free from its hinges. It had been carved from a solid slab of oak, and it would cost hundreds of dollars to replace it.

With nothing better to do he put his hand to the knob and gave it another twist. This time the door swung open effortlessly. "What in hell?" he muttered to himself as he stepped through.

He felt a bit wary as he traversed the Persian carpet in front of his desk. As he traveled around the edge of it, he threw down the envelopes that he'd held stuffed under his arm and finally plopped himself down into the chair. Both he and the springs let out a groan as he settled into it.

He tapped his fingers on the desktop a few times, hoping that it would help some of his tension dissipate. Darby had always said that calming the nerves was fundamental to preservation of health—although the old man had a saying for everything, and being calm had proved to be of little help when someone had fired a harpoon into his chest.

Alexander shook his head. No matter how difficult the old man could be from time to time, he had deserved to die with more dignity.

And perhaps he was right. In all likelihood Stanton *was* suffering from too much anxiety. How long had it been since he'd last left New York City? But the idea that the door to his office might simply have joined in the conspiracy against his nerves bothered him more than he liked to admit. And superstitious or not, he'd fought with more than one maniacal machine in the past. The days of the great mechanical villains seemed to be slipping behind them now, as even the best wind-up contraptions proved no match for fortified steam, but there had been a good, long while where there didn't seem to be a spring or latch in all of New York that hadn't been connected to some kind of deadly device or mantrap.

He still remembered the wave of terror that the Reformer had managed to create by installing his self-activating guillotines to the top of random wine bottles across the city. "Temperance or Death" had been the madman's motto, and the city had, for a short period of time, mostly chosen the former.

When they had finally reached his hideout, the Reformer's multibladed "morality machine" had almost been the death of the Industrialist. Even though he had seen the villain chopped to pieces by his own devices, Alexander still got chills whenever he lifted up a bottle and heard a clicking sound.

The thought made him thirsty. He glanced over to the liquor cabinet, considering that he might have a drink to take the edge off the day. But if he was being honest with himself, and lately it seemed he could be nothing but, an edge was exactly what he needed most right now.

Still, something in the room felt off, although for the life of him he couldn't put his finger on exactly what it was—something missing? But from where he was sitting, everything seemed to be right where it should be.

Grabbing one of the envelopes he'd carried in with him, Alexander pulled open the flap and slid the contents out onto the desk. Written at the top of the form was the name of a man who was hoping to bolster the ranks of the Paragons. They had received a flurry of applications after Darby's death, and with the Automaton relegated to the basement, Hughes clearly already beyond the rigors of active duty, and the Sleuth too old to truly be of use in a fight, it was time to bolster the ranks with some genuine firepower before they faced a threat that they were simply not prepared for.

As usual, the majority of the applicants had been easily dismissed. Some of them were outright jokes—fake applicants with rude names and ludicrous, impossible powers. He'd long passed the point where monikers such as "The Cocksman" or "Gas Pipe" were even remotely funny.

On the next tier were the would-be heroes who thought that the basic requirements for becoming a Paragon were nothing more than a good workout regimen, a costume, and a desire to fight.

Truth be told, it *had* been more like that in the early days. The hope had been to inspire others to follow their example, and to create a sort of costumed militia of heroes and do-gooders. But beyond the vigilantes who thought that wearing a costume was a license for violence, it had only taken two slit throats and a would-be daredevil blindly tumbling off a rooftop to make most people realize that putting on a costume and risking life and limb was a job better left to professionals and people who had more luck than sense.

Of course there was no way to completely avoid what Darby had referred to as "intense personalities." After all, it took a certain amount of insanity to put on a costume to begin with. But it wasn't like it used to be . . . in so many ways. Time had proven that being a Paragon was a dangerous business, and even the luckiest of them had ended up dying from something other than natural causes.

He picked up the application in front of him and read the name aloud: "Hydraulic-man." It was a good name—simple and direct. The attached daguerreotype showed that he was a strapping fellow in his thirties, clearly of aristocratic stock.

The provided sketches revealed that he had created a series of mechanical devices based around the principles of water pressure, primarily using them as a weapon. Grüsser would be very excited to have another damp hero around. . . .

But the machinery also looked suspiciously familiar. Most probably the basic designs had been purchased (or stolen) from the estate of an old villain, and then "modernized" by a well-paid engineer. Not that there was anything wrong with borrowing here and there, especially from the villains. The trick was being discreet enough to keep the source of your miraculous technology a secret.

At first glance Hydraulic-man didn't seem powerful enough for the Paragons, although a "high-pressure water gun" might allow them to more easily subdue an enemy without the need to resort to lethal force. And any half-decent invention could be radically improved by the judicious application of fortified steam. Without Darby around it would be more of an effort to implement the upgrades, and they probably wouldn't work half as well, but it could be done.

His fingers found the hidden latch without a thought, and he pulled open the desk's left drawer. From the jumble of objects inside he pulled out his self-inking pen. He stared at the device and frowned. Darby's legacy was still all around them, but they would need to find a way to move on, even if it meant going back to nibs and inkwells. Perhaps that was what Darby had had in mind all along when he tried to put the mechanical man in charge. But if it was, he should have said so. And he should have told Alexander about his decision *before* he died.

The old man must have known that Alexander wouldn't have obeyed his orders from beyond the grave.

This time the words in his head were in the stern tones of his mother's voice: *Idealism and daydreams are both equal enemies of success.* He often wished he could banish her from his mind, but it had been that old witch, with all her rules and homilies, who had given him the wherewithal and drive that had made him the man he was today. She'd never leave him completely.

He slid the next application out of its envelope. "The White Knight" was printed across the top of it, along with a sketch and the man's true name: Jordan Clements.

Stanton grimaced slightly as he read through the details. At first glance Mr. Clements seemed to have all the necessary qualifications; born and raised a Southern gentlemen, he had followed it with a distinguished record as a Confederate lieutenant in the last war. He also seemed to harbor little or no outward animosity for the North since it had ended, choosing instead to rebuild his family fortune in a postslavery world by taking advantage of the opportunities in the Reconstruction. And over the last decade it had all come together as a sizable fortune, allowing him to be welcomed back to polite society.

Clements had also recently purchased a sizable piece of property just above the fashionable end of northern Fifth Avenue, not far away from the Hall of Paragons.

But for all his success as a capitalist, the actual abilities of the White Knight seemed to be minimal: he claimed some degree of strength beyond that of the average man along with "exceptional reflexes" supposedly gained through some combination of chemicals and electricity that had bathed him in boiling liquid and given him some degree of superhuman powers.

Alexander flipped through to the notes attached at the back. The Sleuth's research stated that if there had been an "incident" behind his origin as a hero, then it was far more likely the outcome of a whiskey still explosion than a scientific experiment. Alexander chuckled out loud at Wickham's remark that they might consider renaming him "Mr. Moonshine."

And on closer examination there were a number of disturbing elements to his costume: a white cloth hood, a noose tied loosely around his neck, and two crosses on his chest. At best it was morbid, and at worst it smacked of the kind of association that could easily fuel charges of racism and elitism.

News of the white supremacy movement wasn't the kind of thing that Alexander had followed too closely after the war had ended. After the endless horrors of battle, he had, like most people, been content to concentrate on pulling the country back together and healing the wounds of a divided nation. He'd also been busy fighting crime and amassing his fortune.

But the Klan's crimes had been heinous enough that they had generated nationwide news and conversation in a postslavery world, and when the organization was finally shut down by the government almost everyone had breathed a sigh of relief.

Adding a Klansman into the mix would surely be a poor way to improve their standing in the popular imagination, not to mention how the newspapers might respond. The Paragons already had enough problems, with the working classes considering them to be an organization of elitists and upper-class snobs.

Altogether the White Knight seemed to be a rather dubious character, and had it not been for his heritage, and the fact that some upstanding members of the community had vouched for his abilities, he would have rejected the application without a second thought.

But now that he had made it this far, and the others seemed to think he was worthy of their attention, Alexander had to at least give the man a chance to state his case to them directly.

He considered his response for a moment, then pulled out a sheet of paper and wrote out a note to that effect, emphasizing that it would be necessary to see the man prove his claims of superhuman powers before they could even make a decision. He attached his note to the bottom of the stack and slid it back into the envelope.

The last application was simply marked "King Jupiter" on the outside. As he lifted the flap, a mechanical snap echoed through the room. Alexander leaped up from his chair.

Chapter 10

Sticks and Steel

As he fell, the Sleuth could feel the knife cutting into the left side of his chest. He had no idea how deeply it had penetrated, but it was clear that it had done some damage, and landing on it would certainly not improve the situation.

He twisted violently, managing to land flat on his back, and coughed out an involuntary "ungh" as the cobblestones smacked the air out of his lungs. He was dazed, but the thick padding of his disguise had absorbed some of the impact, and hopefully the majority of the damage from Jack Knife's blade as well.

The air around him was still cloudy with white smoke. The exploding glass balls had been Darby's concoction, based on the description Wickham had given of a device he'd seen a Japanese assassin use during his adventures in the Orient. The violent cloud of smoke hadn't managed to allow the Sleuth to make the spectacular escape he had intended, but it had given him a moment of surprise—and he was still alive.

He heard his cane clatter to the ground nearby, returning from its journey into the sky. From time to time Sir Dennis's attempts to "improve" something had been so effective that they were almost useless for their original purpose.

His ears were still ringing from the explosion, but he could hear the thumping of shoe leather against stone as the villain's lackeys jumped into action. If he had any hope of escape, he would need to get moving and find a weapon.

At least he knew the stick was close by, although it wouldn't be much use until it was in his hand.

Wickham rolled over onto his stomach and began to crawl toward where he thought the cane might have landed. He had only traveled a few feet before he ran into a pair of legs covered in threadbare herringbone cloth.

Looking up he saw the dirty face of the youngest henchmen. The scruffy lad was wielding a short length of chain and smiling down at him. He was quite young to be missing so many teeth. "He's over here—uhhh!"

Wickham had wrapped his hands behind the young man's calves and pulled. The boy crashed backward, arms flailing, his head making an unpleasant smacking sound as it bounced off the paving stones.

Wickham felt a twinge of guilt, but he had no time to check on the condition of his opponent. Instead he continued to grope his way forward, managing to grab the boy's chain as he rose to his feet. It was not a weapon he was as comfortable with as his stick, but it would be more effective than bare hands. "Five left to go," he thought to himself, but it didn't sound convincing.

The forms of the other henchmen were starting to swim out of the smoke as the cold winter air swept the smoke toward the sky. "He's got Donny!" one of them yelled.

Realizing that his cover was almost gone, he wrapped his left hand around the other smoke ball in his pocket.

"Give it up, old man." Jack's broken accent echoed off the brick walls that surrounded them. "I'd rather take you alive than dead, but I'll have you either way."

Wickham doubted that there was any hope of appealing to the villain's thin mercy. The man was terrifyingly accurate with a knife, and if the lethal intent of his previous attack was anything to judge by, the offer to spare him was a lie.

As final shreds of white mist cleared away he saw his cane—it sat directly in between him and Jack. The tip of it was somewhat scorched by the explosion, but otherwise it was little worse for wear. A couple of feet behind that, and slightly to the right, stood another henchman. The look of surprise on his grizzled face made it obvious that he hadn't realized just how close his prey was until the smoke was gone.

"Now watch, boys," Jack said, letting out a single barking laugh. "If you can get the blade to stick in deep between the eyes sometimes they'll dance a jig before they drop." He pulled his hand back toward his ear, ready to throw.

The plan that flashed into the Sleuth's mind in that moment was born of an instinct that had been trained through half a century of practice, fueled by a sense of desperation that was only a few seconds old. He dropped into a run, moving one step to the right so that he could put the henchman directly between himself and the lanky psychopath. With his second step he hurled the glass ball up into the air, sending it up with a prayer that Darby's tendency toward being dangerously overzealous when it came to explosives was consistent.

With his third step he dropped downward into a crouch. The last thing Wickham saw before he stared down at the ground was the look of annoyance on Jack's face as the marksman hesitated, unwilling to risk hurting his own man.

As he landed, Wickham's hand hit the ground, his palm perfectly centered over the cane. He tucked his head and let his momentum carry him forward, ramming into the henchman and grabbing his stick at the same time. The man tumbled over like a wooden skittle.

In the next instant there was a loud crack as the smoke bomb finished its arc and landed on the stones nearby. Now it was his enemies who were surrounded by a white cloud.

The Sleuth rolled into the smoke and began to rise up. There had been a time when his acrobatics would have been smooth and graceful, but his old bones protested at being put through such punishment, and Wickham needed the cane to steady himself; he gasped as his sense of balance began to give way.

Then his momentum overcame the instability of his roll, and he landed on his feet, although he wobbled slightly.

Unable to see anything but white, and knowing that the thin man would already be swinging his knife in front of him, hoping for a lucky hit, Wickham did the same. He swept the chain around him in an arc, hearing the satisfying slap as metal connected with flesh.

He gave it a downward yank and was pleased to feel that whatever appendage he had managed to wrap the chain around followed his motion. Clearly his opponent had some fighting skills, but the Sleuth had been trained in the art of using a man's skills against him.

Still clenching the chain, he spun to the right, following behind with a sweeping blow of his cane. The hard wood caught Jack square in the face, and Wickham could feel him collapsing to the ground.

Part of him was still shocked at how easy it all was once he was in motion. Even if the memories of those years of intense training in faraway lands had faded, the knowledge he had gained was permanently etched into his body and mind.

Seeing Jack's form in the clearing smoke, Wickham jumped onto the man's back and raised up his cane, intending to deliver a blow to Jack's head strong enough to knock the fight out of him for a good long while. "Now let's see *you* dance a jig."

As he began to bring his arm downward, he felt five meaty fingers wrapping themselves tightly around his wrist. They plucked him into the air like a feather while a second hand grabbed his cane and ripped it out of his fingers with what felt like an unstoppable force.

He was roughly spun around, the action causing him excruciating pain in his shoulder and neck. As he finished the rotation he found himself face-to-face with the Ruffian. "That," Brandon Kurtz huffed from beneath his ridiculous mustache, "is enough."

The round man peered down at his friend on the ground. "Are you all right, Jack?"

The thin man let out a muffled groan that sounded like it was supposed to be words, but made no actual sense.

"It's good you left him alive. I'd be very angry if he were dead. I am a man of the Bible, Mr. Hogan." The Ruffian let go of his hands and transferred his grip to the old man's neck. "'And if the revenger of blood find him without the borders of the city of his refuge, and if the revenger of blood *kill* the slayer; he shall not be guilty of blood.'"

Wickham felt as if his throat had been caught between iron gears. It was clear to Wickham that if he didn't escape in a matter of moments he would end up dead. "That's from Numbers," the large man said in a matter-of-fact tone.

The Sleuth reached up and boxed Brandon's ears, then slid his hands inside the other man's arms and pushed outward. It would have broken a normal man's grip easily. And although the tension around his throat loosened slightly, it was not significant. His vision was already starting to swim, blackness creeping in from around the edges and narrowing the world.

Wickham's bag of tricks was empty, and he could feel what little energy he had left draining out of him. A hissing roar began to fill his ears. He knew that it must mean that his body was preparing to die.

The thought of his own end filled him with a feeling of sadness, but something like relief welled up inside of him as well. He had spent decades fighting against death—never giving up, even when there was no hope. But perhaps now was a good time for him to go. He would see Dennis again. . . .

"Let him go." The booming voice was loud enough for Wickham to hear it even through the veil of darkness that was closing around him.

The grip relaxed. Although the unstoppable egg of a man still had his hands wrapped around the Sleuth's throat, they were loose enough that he could draw a breath, and the light of the world began to creep back into his vision.

Brandon seemed confused. "But Jack wanted him dead!"

"And I want you to *let him go*!"

The choking hand released him suddenly and completely, as if a spring had been disengaged. Wickham landed hard on his ankles and then collapsed onto his hands and knees, gasping for breath. Something felt out of place inside his neck, but it wouldn't kill him.

"Jack and the boss, they both want him dead. That's why I brought him here."

"No one told *me* that." The voice was coming from beside him now, and the Sleuth looked up to see where it was coming from.

What he saw made Wickham imagine that he must be hallucinating, or worse, had died without realizing it. Where a man's head would normally appear was the snarling face of a jackal. It was an image he recognized from mythology: "Anubis," he muttered to himself.

As his vision cleared he realized that the demonic vision was real, but shaped out of black leather. The mask was similar to the one he would be wearing if he had ventured out as the Sleuth instead of in this pathetic disguise—although in the end the padded shirt had managed to save his life. He patted his chest and found the knife still stuck into it. When he pulled it out there was a jolt of pain as the tip of the blade tore free from his flesh. The edges of the knife were barbed, and it dragged a good deal of blood-soaked padding out of his shirt as it went. He slipped the blade into his pocket.

"Jack is in charge here, not you, dog-man," Brandon said, sounding a bit confused.

"And neither are you," Anubis replied, following it up with a solid whack from the long metal rod he was holding in his hand.

Wickham couldn't help but be impressed by the costume, and he'd seen a few in his day. The man was dressed from head to toe in a bodysuit made from what appeared to be black kid-leather.

Strapped across his chest was a set of armor constructed from thick bands of boiled hide and steel. Bolted to the center was a large ankh that glittered like gold. For the Sleuth, whose powers relied on subterfuge, it seemed dangerous and impractical to wear such a large chunk of precious metal on the center of your chest, even if it was his most armored feature.

Bringing the costume together was a simple white loincloth held up with a silver belt. It was clearly more ornamental than practical, although the contrast was quite striking. The entire design brought together Egyptian and Roman elements to form something that recalled ancient times but provided practical protection as well.

A few feet away Jack was starting to wake up. As the thin man lifted his head up from the ground there were a number of oozing cuts and red bruises across his face.

The villain turned and looked directly at the Sleuth. His daze seemed to vanish as his gaze caught Wickham's. "I won't miss this time, old man!" His right hand slipped into his coat, and when he drew it back out again he held another one of the barbed knives from his bandolier. He flicked it straight at Wickham with a single snap of his wrist.

Wickham could see the knife coming toward him as if time had slowed down. He knew that he needed to move out of the way, and quickly, but he was still dazed from his brush with death, and the desire to move his head and the actual ability to do it were somehow disconnected.

Before the blade could impale him there was blur in front of his face, then a spark and a ping as the knife ricocheted off the metal rod and flew off in a new, harmless direction.

"Damn you, Anubis!" said Jack, grimacing as he used his hands to try to wipe away some of the blood from his face.

"I won't have the death of another Paragon on our hands. It will bring twice as much trouble down on our heads."

"Lord Eschaton said he was to die," the round man interjected. "Do *you* want to tell him we didn't do what he asked?"

Jack shook his head. "And what more trouble could he bring dead than alive? He's seen our faces; he knows where we're hiding. What's worse than bringing the rest of the Paragons down on us?"

Wickham started to back away. If there was any chance that he was going to get out of this alive, it wouldn't come from waiting for the mercy of Jack Knife or the Ruffian. And honestly, even he found the argument in favor of his death far more compelling than the meager defense his savior in black had put up so far.

Reaching a point where he figured he had at least a fair chance of escaping, the Sleuth leapt to his feet and bolted for the entrance to the alleyway.

The padding of his costume chafed and scratched him as he ran, and with every step his legs demanded that he stop sprinting and act his age. He had no doubt that he could outrun the potbellied strangler, but that wasn't who he was worried about. With his life on the line he could ignore the screaming pain in his knees for a little while. He'd pay for it later—if there was a later.

The safety of the alleyway was only a yard away when he heard one of the men shouting "Stop!" behind him. A second later a chunk of brick in the wall near his head shattered as it was struck by one of Jack Knife's blades.

He entered the maze at a full run, knowing that his pursuers must be only a few steps behind him. The shadows felt comforting, but this was their territory, not his, and the only advantage he had was the few yards he had gained with the element of surprise. But no matter how motivated Wickham was, he was too old to escape by vigor alone—he'd need to come up with a plan.

Chapter 11

Sitting in Judgment

The sound that had caused Alexander to bolt from his chair brought all his senses to full attention. Until he felt the tingling in his nerves he hadn't realized how deeply the mystery of the stuck door had set him on edge, but now he felt a bolt of excitement tear through him, transforming Alexander Stanton into the Industrialist.

He looked in every direction, trying to determine where the sound had come from. If there was going to be an attack, he would need to find the best possible position for his defense.

The next sound was more of a dull thump, and this time he was positive that it came from behind him. More than that, it had come from *inside* the hidden closet in the wall.

He turned to the lamp, determined to open up the panel on the wall behind him. Just as his hand reached up to activate the mechanism there were a series of quick raps on the door to his office. He spun around, his hand automatically reaching for the Industrialist's gun at his waist, but there was nothing there.

For a moment he felt totally vulnerable—an unarmed man, facing a threat that it would take a Paragon to defeat.

But it only took a moment more for him to realize that there was no real threat at the door.

"Sir?"

After three decades he had become infinitely familiar with the sound of his butler's voice. "Come in, O'Rourke!" he yelled out with irritation.

The old butler opened the door slowly and shuffled into the room. "I see, sir, that you somehow managed to unstick your door." Alexander had long given up trying to figure out whether the old man was mocking him, or simply had a gift for making everything he said seem sarcastic.

"Yes, thank you, O'Rourke. That isn't my problem anymore."

"And what would be your problem *now*, sir?"

Alexander sighed and sat back down heavily into the chair. "It's nothing," he said testily. "I thought I heard a noise."

"A *loud* noise, sir?"

The idea of explaining his anxieties to his butler made the whole thing seem ridiculous. "It's nothing. I was concerned that we might be being attacked." He paused and stared into the butler's emotionless face. "Because if something or someone were about to attack me, they would have taken advantage of the opportunity while I was distracted by my bumbling butler."

"Most likely, sir. I am hardly a strapping hero such as yourself."

"Your gift for understatement remains as strong as ever, O'Rourke."

"Thank you, sir," he said without a trace of audible irony. "It was probably simply vermin in the walls, sir." As always, the old man's face remained utterly unreadable and totally placid.

Alexander didn't know all the details of O'Rourke's life before he had arrived in the United States, but he had learned that his family had been utterly destroyed in some terrible misfortune: a wife and two children, O'Rourke's entire young life had all been wiped away by a catastrophe that the man had chosen never to discuss. "Would you like me to call the exterminators?"

"No," Alexander said, shaking his head. Try as he might to feel sympathy for the Irishman, he always found that it was quickly erased by the man's attitude, which seemed to travel back and forth from total disregard to utter condescension. "What I'd like to know is why it's taken half an hour to simply find my daughter and have her brought to me."

"I could go and find out, sir."

Stanton opened his mouth to yell at the man, and for the umpteen-thousandth time thought better of it. At first he had felt that the butler was too new to berated; then he had become too important to upset; and now he was simply too old. And for all his flaws he was an unswervingly loyal and damned efficient servant. For example, unlike the maid, O'Rourke knew better than to start a journey until he had been directed to do so.

"Then go do that." Stanton waved him away, picking up the remaining application from his desk and pretending to stare at it.

As the butler turned to close the door behind himself, Alexander looked up at him. "And leave the door open, O'Rourke."

"Open, sir?" Once again, his face refused to match the tone of surprise.

"Do as I say."

"*Just* as you say, sir." The old butler wandered off down the hallway, each footstep echoing with a dull snap followed by a scraping sound as his feet dragged against the marble floor.

Alexander pulled out the last application and tried to focus on it enough to read it, but the meaning kept sliding away. He had to admit that the fresh jolt of fear from the noise in the wall had once again set his mind wandering in search of excitement.

His eyes wandered back to the gas lamp on the wall. He could use it to open the gateway to his other life. Then all he would need to do is put on his costume and be on his way, free of any responsibility that didn't involve adventure.

He was also sure that the exact moment he placed the Industrialist's hat on his head would be the same one that his daughter would come skipping in through the office door.

He actually dreaded the thought of talking with her, but it was clear that she had been greatly affected by Darby's death. For the first few weeks he had hoped that it would pass over her without the need for his intervention, like a winter cough, but things were clearly not going to be that simple.

Sarah was, no matter how difficult it might be for the average person to see it, grieving. And he, having been so wrapped up in his plans to succeed Sir Dennis as the leader of the Paragons, hadn't even been able to see it until a few days ago.

She was a sensitive girl, like her mother, and instead of dealing with her sorrow with weeping and lethargy, Sarah had become even more charged than usual—racing through the house, sewing a small army of misshapen dolls to "be given away to the orphans," and disappearing into her room for hours on end.

She had also taken to long walks in the park in her mourning clothes, necessitating that one of the house staff go along with her as a chaperone, taking them away from duties that were far more pressing.

In the end it had been Jenny Farrows, the house maid, who had brought the issue of his daughter's suffering to Alexander's attention. She told him that if there were to be any chance for Sarah to get over it, then he would need to speak to his daughter, *specifically* on the subject of "the passing of her mentor."

He was already getting wound up simply at imagining their conversation, and she hadn't even entered the room yet. But Stanton promised himself that he would keep a cool head. What Sarah needed was guidance and wisdom, and neither of those things was delivered effectively at a loud volume.

Since the death of his wife, there had been many days when Alexander wished there were someone to comfort *him* with quiet words, but he had been alone long enough that he'd found he could replace that feeling with action.

But the work before him meant that he was denied even the simple pleasure of putting on his costume and running through the streets of the city as the Industrialist.

Truth be told, even before the Professor had been murdered, the number of times he could sneak out of the house in his costume with a gun strapped to his belt had been fewer and farther between with every passing year. There were dozens of reasons, all trumped by the fact that he was simply getting older. And these days he spent a good deal of the time simply wandering the streets in search of a little peace and quiet instead of hunting ruffians.

Sometimes he would stop and chat with a concerned citizen or one of the police. Dressed up in uniforms of their own, many of them were enamored with vigilante heroes. Technically the Paragons were outlaws—illegal under the same statutes that had been used to shut down the private police forces when the municipal constabulary had first been established. But the city and its heroes had come to an understanding, and when the mechanical villains had started their reign of terror even the newspapers had agreed it was good to have Paragons protecting them.

"The Paragons," he said with a sigh, and glanced down at the last application. He read the man's name out loud. "King Jupiter." It was an odd name, and like the White Knight, there wasn't much that made him stand out on paper except for the description of a few superhuman abilities that made his authenticity even more dubious. "Skin like that of a stone. Master of electricity. I am able to throw lightning bolts at will," he said, reading off the paper.

"Doubtful, unlikely, and poppycock," he muttered to himself.

He couldn't even really make out the man's costume from the supplied image. It was a strange affair that covered him from head to toe, like a union suit—although lacking the rear hatch. It had been sewn from a thick fabric, and from the glinting light that had been picked up by the camera in his portrait, there were clearly golden threads sewn into the material as well. Tied around his neck was a piece of ermine fur that, he did have to admit, gave the whole thing a slightly regal air, especially when you paired it with the scepter in his hand and his obvious physique.

Alexander let out a slight guffaw when he realized that points on the top of the man's helmet were actually supposed to make it appear as if a crown had been attached to the top of his head. In front of King Jupiter's face was a solid metal plate that had a blank visage except for the eyeholes, and a beard of stylized curls that turned into fine golden chain mail that covered his neck, making sure that his features were completely hidden.

The chain mail was another point against him. "I hope for his sake that his skin really is made of stone," he mumbled to himself. He had seen men try to dress in that kind of armor before, with unpredictable results.

Years ago, when he was just getting started, Alexander had spent some time fighting crime with a young hero who had called himself "Pendragon." The man's heart had certainly been in the right place, and he had carried an electrified sword that had managed to put a quick end to more than one dangerous situation.

But Pendragon's career as a Paragon had come to a sudden end when he went face-to-face against a maniac calling himself the Steel Woodsman. Failing to dodge in time, he had taken a nasty blow from the villain's axe. His armor had protected him from losing a limb, but the blade had driven the metal links of his chain mail deep into his skin. He had managed to use his sword to permanently chop down the Woodsman, but the "Arthurian Avenger" had limped away from the combat badly wounded, and was never seen again.

Half a decade later, Alexander had run into a man on lower Broadway who claimed that he had once been Pendragon. By this time the identity of the Industrialist was no longer a secret, and Stanton had put up with a number of people who tried to claim that they knew him as one masked hero or another.

The man's skin was flushed and red, his teeth yellow and crooked, and he was well out of shape—except for round. The strange fellow was a far cry from the lithe young swordsman who he had once partnered with. The only way he could prove that he had really once been the hero he claimed to be was by showing Alexander the rings of metal that were still lodged in his flesh. Alexander had warned anyone off of chain mail since that day.

Shaking away the cloud of nostalgia, he returned to the application on his desk. King Jupiter was claiming to be a genuine "Miracle Man," with powers that were more mystical than mechanical. As a Paragon Stanton had seen his fair share of unexplainable events, but discovering a person who had true superhuman abilities was very rare indeed.

Most heroes were simply people with one or two skills that, with training and focus, could undeniably put them in a better class than the average man.

But true superhuman abilities—whether they came from machines, chemicals, or even the supernatural—were no guarantee of survival. After all the wars, riots, and villains that Alexander had battled against, he had learned that what gave you the best odds of survival were a desire to fight for what you believed in, the ability to rely on the men who fought beside you, and a lot of damned good luck. "And sooner or later, luck always runs out," he heard himself say in a dark tone.

The idea that *both* the White Knight and King Jupiter would prove to be what they claimed was impossible. One of them had to be a fraud. He'd need to see them in action and find out which one it was before he'd take either seriously as a possible Paragon.

But why was he being so negative? He had wanted to be the leader of the Paragons, and now he was. If Alexander was upset by the responsibility of finding new heroes, he had no one to blame but himself.

Grabbing a pen, he wrote "to be considered" across the top of King

Jupiter's application and stuffed it back into the envelope. After all, if you were going to judge the measure of a hero simply by the cut of his costume, then the Industrialist would be the first to go.

Having finished his review, his eyes turned back to the gas lamp. Maybe he *could* sneak out after all, just for a little while. It wasn't like Sarah wouldn't be around when he got back—this was her home But there was something else that was bothering him—something was missing. . . .

"Mr. Stanton."

"What?" Caught off guard he snapped his head back to see that Jenny Farrows was standing just outside the open door, the deceptively sweet features of his daughter peering in just over her shoulder. "I'm here, Father," she said to him.

"Yes, all right. Come in then, Sarah." Adventuring and the solving of mysteries, would, it seemed, have to wait for another day.

Chapter 12

Escaping from the Darkness

Stuffed into a tiny little room, trapped in utter blackness, and flat on her back, every breath Sarah took sounded like the rumble of thunder in her ears.

She had been in pitch blackness before, but that didn't make this time any better. It wasn't so much the dark that scared her—it was the *consequences* of being discovered trapped in her father's most secret place.

But if she was going to escape her predicament without alerting anyone, the first thing that she would need to do is take stock of her situation: Currently, she was wedged into a small patch of wooden floor, crushed in between the lip of the wall, where the panel had dropped down, and the square wooden pillar that held up the central display table. Her shoulders fit in with only an inch to spare.

Testing how dark it actually was, Sarah held up her hand in front of her face. She wiggled her fingers to try to see something in the blackness, hoping that there might be some stray ray of light that would become perceptible as her eyes adjusted. But her vision played tricks on her instead, showing her streaks of white in some nonexistent distance, or making it *seem* as if she could see her fingers, only to be disappointed when the motions she made completely failed to match up with the luminous mirage.

And finally on her list of current problems was her throbbing hip. With nothing to distract her from the pain but desperation, the sensation of it began to bloom, growing in size and shape. For a moment it felt as if a monstrous creature had attached itself to her by its teeth and was breathing along with her. The sucking beast contracted slightly with each inhalation, then grew larger and hotter with every exhale, as if it were expanding like a balloon.

Trying to ignore the pain, Sarah now went through her options. The easiest way out was, as usually seemed to be the case, the one that she dreaded the most: a few short raps of her hand against the wall would alert her father to the fact that there was something more than simply his costume hiding behind the plaster wall.

And while giving up might quickly get her back into the daylight, she had already gone to so much trouble to stay hidden from him that it made no sense to alert him to her presence without at least *trying* to figure her way out of the trap. If he caught her it would hardly matter whether she had been captured on purpose or by accident—either way, she would receive equal amounts of both punishment and blame.

So if she wasn't giving up, her next option was to start exploring the possibilities. She had some idea of the layout of the costume closet, along with the knowledge of just how small the space was that she was trapped in. Sarah slowly lifted her hand. A few feet above her head her fingers reached the bottom of the table. She slid her palm against the rough wood until she found the polished edge.

She kept her hand moving through the air, slowly and steadily, until it touched the back of the secret panel. The distance between the end of the table and the front wall was twice the span of her hand, and when she spread out her fingers she was able to bridge the gap entirely. Even if she had been thin enough to pull herself through, and with some squeezing she might have been, there was no way that Sarah could hope to do it silently while she was wearing her bustle and corsetry.

If her adventures so far had taught her a single lesson, it was that the reason no woman had ever kept up with the Paragons was that they were all hobbled by their garments. Next time she went sneaking around perhaps she'd dress as a man. . . . The thought of her pulling on a shirt and pants put a smile on her face, although the sensation was cut short by another twinge of pain in her hip.

Given that there was no means of escape from where she was, she would need to move to somewhere else. And to do *that* she would have to get off her back.

Sarah used her right elbow to prop herself up and began to wiggle her hips in order to flip herself over. As she did so she could feel her bustle beginning to wrap itself tightly around her waist. She almost let out a curse, but along with whatever small sense of propriety her mother had given her before she died, a mental shout of "Quiet!" in her mother's voice kept the word on her tongue before she could open her mouth.

Sarah lay back down and then tried to bend down to reach her feet. Her head smacked against the immovable wooden table above her before her arms could assess the situation down by her ankles, and the pain forced her to stifle another very unladylike word.

Failing to reach down, she attempted to drag her legs up toward the rest of her. Even though the bustle resisted, this seemed to be a far more effective strategy. She could clearly feel a tugging of the hem.

She frowned in the darkness as she realized what had happened—the edge of her dress had become trapped underneath the panel when it had closed.

Sarah tried not to think about the logical conclusion, but it was obvious: if part of her dress was caught *inside* the room, then the other part was trapped *outside*. It was the second time today that she was praying that her father would be oblivious to the obvious.

As she lifted up her legs one more time to reach down for her skirts she felt the boning in her corsets digging deep into her skin. Grabbing a handful of the bustle, she gave it a tug, but the trapped hem refused to budge.

With a sheen of perspiration already gathering on her brow, and her knickers literally in a twist, Sarah was feeling more unladylike by the second. And it wasn't just the exertion that was causing her distress—the air was definitely much warmer in the closet than it had been just a few minutes before.

Lifting up her legs again, she pulled harder on the hem. She could feel the framing of the bustle twist as she slowly increased the pressure. Something would have to break, and in a few moments the fabric gave way, pulling free with a distinctive ripping sound.

This time she did curse out loud: "Damn!" The word had slipped free, although she had managed to catch herself before she could curse at herself for cursing. Even though she had limited it to a single slip, she doubted that her mother would have been very proud of her.

Freed from the wall, Sarah flipped herself over. Her hip let out a shout of pain as it made contact with the floor. It would be bruised; there was no doubt about that. But she seemed to have found the outer limits of the pain from the injury. It didn't feel any worse than it had a few minutes before, and there was no wet or sticky sensation that she would have associated with blood.

Dragging herself forward, she ignored the sound of the rest of the fabric pulling away. It was something that would demand her eventual attention, because no matter how often her father ignored the obvious, there was no way he would miss a two-foot strip of black taffeta on the floor of his secret wardrobe.

With a rustle of skirts and badly misaligned support clothing, Sarah grabbed the edge of the table and pulled herself over to the side of it. There was at least three feet between the table and the wall, and she stood up into it.

The moment she got to her feet, she unhooked her bustle and placed it on the table, on top of her father's costume.

Sarah felt somewhat pleased with her progress in spite of the fact that she was still lost in pitch blackness. She had managed to free her dress, stand up, and remove one item of constricting clothing, all in the dark.

Although, if her father raised the panel now, he would find that his daughter had descended halfway to savagery after simply having faced the challenge of getting up off the floor.

If she was going to escape she'd need to do more than disrobe—she'd need to find a way out.

Sarah closed her eyes and tried to conjure up a more detailed image of the room from her brief survey of it a few minutes before. She could see the table and the walls, but details eluded her, overshadowed by the image of her father's Industrialist costume.

She furrowed her brow, sternly telling herself that her future well-being, and her relationship with her father, was dependent on her escape, but her mind's eye offered up nothing new.

Out of ideas, Sarah leaned back against the side wall to give herself a moment to think. As she did so, something small and hard dug itself into her shoulder blades.

When she reached around behind herself, Sarah's hand grasped the familiar shape of one of Darby's gas lamp igniters. She was sure there had been no light at all inside the tiny room when she had explored it as a child. This was part of Darby's redesign.

She turned the dial and was rewarded with a soft hiss from somewhere nearby as the gas began to flow. Then there was a sharp snap as the gas ignited. A few seconds later a flickering light banished the darkness, turning everything a soft yellow color.

As Sarah hopped up from the wall with a renewed sense of purpose, she knocked her bustle to the floor. It landed with a thump. Even though she was no longer wearing it, the damnable thing had *still* betrayed her!

She stared at spitefully. It had been created to hobble and undermine women for the benefit of men, and it was managing to do its job admirably.

Her blood went cold as she heard her father's footsteps coming closer to the wall, and she realized he must have heard her. In a few seconds all her planning would be undone. But realizing that there was nothing she could do, her rising sense of panic was overwhelmed by a sense of calm—she could finally escape this nonsensical adventure and free herself from the stifling closet.

Closing her eyes, she waited to hear the inevitable sound of the mechanism starting up. Sarah tried to compose her face in an expression of innocent repentance that might somehow lessen her father's anger, even if just for a moment.

But instead of the telltale noise, she heard her father yelling out the name of the old butler. She had, once again, managed to escape detection. There would be no easy way out.

Sarah was most definitely perspiring now, and she felt a trickle of sweat break free and roll down the back of her neck. Darby had once told her that the skin leaked water in order to cool itself, which had led to a long conversation about how a wise creator might choose to implement more practical and efficient methods. At the end of it, though, Darby had assured her that God's choice was quite sufficient and that even if they could manage to come up with something better, it was far beyond his abilities to modify an actual human to use it, although he had outfitted Tom with a number of unique ways to vent excess heat.

Her feeling of suffocation was still with her, and the air inside the closet felt warmer and thicker with every passing minute. Sarah wondered if she was going to suffocate soon, and for a moment she could feel tightness in her throat as she wondered if the air was already running out. But one look at the healthy flame on the wall made her realize that there was a steady flow of—if not *fresh* air, then at least a waft of something breathable. And, she realized, it had to be *coming* from somewhere.

All the Paragons had a predilection for secret doors and panels, and she was seized with a certainty that her father's own obsession would mean that he would not have passed on the chance to have a secret exit to the outside, although she hadn't found it the last time she was in here.

And now that she thought more about it, there were many evenings that her father never seemed to leave his study, and yet somehow the Industrialist had still managed to find trouble and adventure.

Sarah took another look around the dimly lit room, trying to pay more attention to where such an escape route might be hidden. She walked around the desk to the back of the table and opened the top drawer in one of the cabinets that lined the right half of the back wall.

It contained two copies of the Industrialist's signature gun. She considered picking one up, just to hold it. The weapon needed fortified steam to fire, so there was no danger of it accidentally going off. Still, with her luck so far today, she was probably better off leaving them alone, and she closed the drawer.

In the drawers beneath it were incidentals, including some of the pieces to her father's earlier costumes. She picked up a pair of gloves. Embroidered into the top of the thick black leather was a pair of golden cogs.

The Industrialist had mostly abandoned the cog imagery except for his shield, but the sight of the old gloves threw her back to a forgotten moment in childhood, clinging tightly to her father's gigantic hands, tears in her eyes, as he explained to her that her mother had died.

Without even trying to come up with an excuse for doing so, Sarah slipped her hands into them.

They were large, but not too large. Did her father have ladylike fingers, or were her hands as mannish as Nathaniel had always claimed they were?

She made a fist and could feel strips of metal hidden underneath the leather pressing into her skin. She took a few jabs at the air, imagining what it might be like to smack her hand into the jaw of a villain.

She rolled open the top drawer and picked up one of the guns.

Taking up the other half of the back wall was a large mirror firmly set into an oaken frame. Sarah took a pose in front of it, with the gun in her hand. "The Industri-lass!" she said to herself with a whisper.

She suddenly felt quite foolish, and she turned to put the gun back into the drawer. As she rolled the cabinet closed she saw a sheet of paper sitting on top of the cabinet, a straight pin still stuck through it from where it had been attached to some other object. A note was scrawled across the front of it: "*Section 106 removed and reordered as requested.*"

A clue! she thought to herself with delight, and folded up the paper and put it into the pocket of her jacket. Then she stuffed the gloves into her pockets as well.

Realizing that she still needed to find the way out, Sarah began to slide her hand around the gilt edges of the mirror frame. The mirror was obviously about the same size as a door, but she could find nothing but polished wood and dust.

Sarah turned her head to look for any other object that might conceal a secret entrance when she saw that on the right wall was a large wooden button in the center of a brass ring. The word "Exeunt" had been painted underneath it in precise letters. Perhaps there was no need to have a hidden switch inside of a hidden closet. . . .

The button depressed easily, reaching its end with a satisfying click. A moment later the mirror quietly swung open. A cool breeze flowed in, bringing a moist, earthy scent, and the gas lamp grew a little brighter as it devoured the fresh air.

There was only one more task she needed to complete before she could escape: Grabbing up the dreaded bustle, she slid herself around to the other side of the table and kneeled down. She could see the long strip of black material that had been torn away when she pulled herself free, and she grabbed it close to where it had been trapped under the door.

From this angle it came away easily, and she shoved the cloth down into her already-stuffed pocket.

When she grabbed the mirror it swung open easily, and beyond it another gas lamp was already illuminating the way down the corridor.

"The light," she said to herself with a gasp. She had almost forgotten to put it out. She turned around to head back in the room and then stopped herself. A second control, placed just outside the exit, would be just the kind of detail that the old professor would think of.

Sarah stepped into the corridor. The floor was packed earth, and the heels of her shoes sank slightly into the damp soil. Yet another clue to her presence she'd have to hope her father wouldn't find.

When they had been children, she and Nathaniel had always been convinced that any self-respecting mansion should be riddled with secret passages and hidden doors. They had spent years trying to uncover them, but never seemed to manage to actually find anything.

Nathaniel had convinced her to give up their search after years of failing to find the slightest clue. It was both exhilarating and disappointing to discover that she had been right all along. "Nathaniel," she said with a small amount of disgust, and shook her head. Once he'd left childhood behind he always seemed to desire a world that was less amazing than it appeared. In contrast, for all his reliance on rigorous science, Darby had constantly shown her that the world was more magical than even she had been capable of imagining.

Sarah smiled when she found the switch exactly where she had expected it to be. Even after death, Sir Dennis was providing an occasional miracle. She twisted the dial around the outside of the igniter, and when she looked back into the secret closet it had gone dark.

Grabbing the brass handle on the back of the door she pulled it shut behind her. There was a familiar clicking sound as the mechanism that held it tightly in place reengaged.

The dank corridor was only a few feet wide, and she was barely able to drag her bustle behind her as she moved through it. She considered leaving the beastly thing behind, but it would hardly do to have come this far only to have her father discover her treacherous garment abandoned in a secret hallway.

After a few feet she reached a short set of unpainted wooden stairs, where the corridor made a T. If Sarah's sense of direction was working properly, then the way to the right clearly led to some secret exit out to the grounds. As excited as she was by the idea of uncovering a new way to escape the house, she was hardly dressed for another adventure.

She turned left, and as she reached the end of the tunnel she saw a small viewport built into a secret door at the end of the corridor. Peeking through it she was given an almost completely unhindered view of the basement. Sarah wondered if her father had ever surreptitiously watched her while she had been down here going through her mother's moldering belongings.

But whether he had ever spied on her or not, the truth was that as long as she was in this house she would never truly be her own woman in any way that really mattered. And giving in to her father's constant and growing pressure for her to find a husband would, she imagined, only be trading one kind of imprisonment for another. Another bustle to tie her up and slow her down, while the men in her life traveled down secret corridors to unknown destinations.

Sarah could feel a rising sense of self-pity. Perhaps it was her proximity to the basement, always her favorite place to engage in a bout of melancholy. "Back to it," she said, banishing her negative thoughts, and opened the door. The gas lamps in the secret corridor extinguished themselves behind her, and Sarah felt like Alice traveling through the mirror as she stepped back into the house, once again leaving the world of the Paragons behind.

She held out her hand and let it brush against the boxes of her mother's things as she walked to the stairs. She'd need to get back up to her room before anyone found her missing.

Climbing up to the cellar door, she opened it and gave her eyes a moment to adjust to the daylight. She winced as she heard Jenny Farrow's voice calling out to her, "*There* you are! Your father has been looking for you for *hours*. He's got the whole staff in a panic wondering where you are."

Sarah opened her mouth to protest, but the maid cut her off before she could even say a word. "I've got no time for your nonsense today, Sarah." She grabbed the bustle out of her hand and instantly discovered the place where Sarah had ripped away the fabric. "And what did you do to *this*? I've told you that you shouldn't be mucking around down in the basement in your day clothes. Your father is already close to being in one of his moods without you playing around in the dirt."

Sarah tried to get a word in edgewise. "Jenny, I . . ."

"Well, there's no time for that now," Jenny said, giving her no chance to plead her case. Before she could protest Jenny's hands were fluttering to and fro across her clothes, flicking away stray bits of dust and smoothing down ruffled bits of her garment in an attempt to make her presentable.

Then the maid's wandering arms were in her pockets, pulling out the strip of torn cloth. "At least you had the good sense to keep this. I'll see what Mary can do about repairing the damage."

"And what's this?" Jenny said, pulling out the gloves. She stared at them, clearly having a moment of recognition, and then looked directly into Sarah's eyes. They had known each other long enough that Jenny didn't need to say a word—her disappointed frown did all the speaking for her.

Sarah expected Jenny to reach back into her pockets again and pull out the folded paper. Instead Jenny shook her head twice and stuffed the gloves down into the front pocket of her apron. "I'll put these up in your room, and we can talk about it later."

She spun Sarah around and shoved her forward. "You're still a mess, but you need to get to your father's office right away—before he gets any angrier than he already is, if that's possible."

"Thank you, Jenny," she managed to blurt out. The discovery of the pilfered items, along with the fussing, had completely robbed Sarah of all the feelings of self-pity and righteous anger that she been wallowing in just a minute before. Instead she traveled down the corridor in a daze as the maid pulled her along to the entrance of the very same room that she had just worked so hard to escape from.

The door was open, and she saw her father sitting at his desk as Jenny reached the entrance. "Mr. Stanton." The housemaid's voice was practically a whisper.

"What?" he replied, obviously annoyed.

Sarah saw his head rise up over Jenny's shoulder. "I'm here, Father," she said to him.

He waved her in with a broad gesture. "Yes, all right. Come in and take a seat." He gathered up the papers and daguerreotypes on his desk into a pile, clearly trying to hide Paragon business from his daughter's eyes.

While normally Sarah would have been hungry to catch any scrap of information regarding the heroes, it now took every ounce of willpower that she could muster to not let her eyes lock onto the iron safe as she walked past it. Instead, she forced herself to stare at the blank spot on the wall where she had removed her father's portrait and put on the warmest, widest smile that she could possibly muster. Hopefully her father would think it was him that she was staring at, but she couldn't bear to meet his eyes.

Reaching the chair on the nearest side of the desk, she put her hands solidly on its back, digging her fingers into the soft padding under the red leather as if she were clutching onto a log in the middle of a raging river.

Her father looked up at her with a frown on his face, but it wasn't her he was scowling at. "Is there anything *else* I can do for you, Mrs. Farrows?"

When she turned her head, Sarah saw the maid staring wide-eyed at the safe. "I just wanted to . . ."

"What did you want to see me about?" Sarah said to her father, then turned to glare back at the maid. She put every ounce of her will into getting Jenny to look at her.

"What did you say?" Jenny turned to face Sarah and Alexander, withering instantly under the combined stares of the Stanton family. "Nothing, sir."

"Then that will be all, Jenny." He tapped twice on the pile of papers in front of him. "And if you could please close the door behind you?"

"Certainly, sir." She shuffled quickly across the floor and swung the door shut behind her with a heavy thud.

The whole tenor of the room changed as the outside world vanished behind the solid oak. When she had been here without her father the office had been a place of mystery and adventure, but with him sitting there in front of her she felt like Theseus, attempting to escape but ending up back at the center of the minotaur's maze.

"The door was acting in a most peculiar way a little while ago. You wouldn't know anything about that, would you, Sarah?"

She turned her head slightly to the side. "Peculiar how, Father?"

He shook his head. "No, of course you wouldn't. From the look of you, you've been far too busy playing around in the mud."

She bristled. "I've been going through some of Mother's things in the basement."

"Again," he huffed. "You spend far too much time digging through those relics. I'm starting to think it would be better for both of us if they weren't around anymore."

Among all the emotions she had been manufacturing to try to create a sense of realism she suddenly felt a genuine pang of fear rise to the top. "You wouldn't, Father!"

He looked up at her. "Sarah, I . . ." Stopping, he shook his head. "Let's start again. This isn't the conversation I want to have with you—not at all."

She sat quietly for a moment and watched him deflate. For an instant it seemed as if all his usual bluster and bravado had deserted him. It made him look a bit sad and old. "I'm sorry, Father. I didn't mean to make you angry. What is it you wanted to discuss?"

After a moment he looked up into her eyes. "I know that the last few weeks have been very difficult for you, and I know you must be angry at me for the way I've been acting."

There were a million things she could say, but she had no idea what particular bit of behavior it was that he was about to apologize *for*, and it seemed that her best course of action would be to sit there quietly and find out what he was going to say next.

"Having a man die in your arms . . ." he continued. "Although why he brought you up there in the first place I'll never know."

"Because I was curious, and because he thought I was intelligent."

"I don't doubt that he did. And here you stand, smart as a whip, educated beyond reason, and still unmarried."

Sarah opened her mouth to reply when her father lifted up a hand and shook his head. "No. I'm sorry. I don't mean that, either."

"Then what did you want to tell me, Father?"

"I don't know, exactly, but I don't want to fight with you. Having someone you care about die in your arms is a terrible thing." He paused for a second. Sarah didn't know the exact details of her mother's death, but she knew he had been by her mother's side when her mother had taken her final breath.

"And," he continued, clearly trying to push back the emotions that were welling up inside of him, "it's something I wouldn't wish on my worst enemy, let alone have it happen to my own daughter."

"You don't have to worry about me, Father. I'm not as fragile as you think I am."

He smirked. "Nor are you quite as tough as you believe yourself to be."

Sarah folded her hands and stared at the floor. She could feel a blush rising up in her cheeks. "What's past is past."

"Death is never that easy, I'm afraid. And as you grow older you'll discover that the past has a way of catching up with you."

He was attempting to reach out to her, and yet every word that came to mind had a stinger hidden in it. She struggled to find something neutral to say. "If you say so" was the phrase she chose. As she said it Sarah realized her contempt was right out in the open.

"I do say so!" he replied with a bit of thunder in his voice, although he was obviously trying to keep it under control. "I know that you must be angry with me about keeping you away from the Paragons since Darby died, but it's clear to me now that allowing you any relationship with that part of my life has brought this family nothing but tragedy."

"Sir Dennis was my friend!" she blurted out.

He nodded. "I know. He loved you very much, almost as much as if you were his own daughter. But that didn't stop you from nearly being killed on the bridge, and it didn't save his life. I should have never let you go!"

Sarah felt a tightness across her chest even beyond the corset. She stared straight into his eyes, and he turned away before he started to speak. "If you had died up there . . ."

Alexander shook his head, obviously trying to halt his tears, but Sarah already knew that he would never let them fall. "If that maniac had killed you I would have lost both you *and* your mother to enemies of the Paragons, and that simply can't happen. I won't let it!" His face was red now, and he had let anger wipe away the sadness.

"You can't protect me forever, Father."

"No, you're right. Keeping you safe is something your husband should be doing."

"My husband?" she said with a laugh.

They both sat there in silence for a moment, and Sarah continued to wrestle with her own tongue. She wanted to shout at him and tell him that she was her own woman. She certainly didn't need a husband to protect her! But her mind betrayed her, playing back images of that horrible morning: the spear, the screams, her hands covered in the blood of Sir Dennis and Nathaniel. It had been everywhere, and there was so much of it. The wetness, and the smell of it . . .

She didn't realize she was crying until she heard the sound of her tears landing on the fabric of her dress.

"Oh, Sarah," her father said. He stood up and crossed the distance between them, easily rounding the edge of the table that had done such an effective job of smashing into her hip.

His arms enfolded her, along with a familiar scent of tobacco and wool. Once again he had succeeded in reducing her to the state of a child, although at least this time it genuinely did make her feel a bit better.

The moment was interrupted by a series of sharp knocks at the door. Alexander Stanton stood up. "Not now, O'Rourke!"

"I'm sorry, sir," came the muffled reply through the wood, "but a gentleman has delivered a note. He said it was urgent that you give him your response at once."

He leaned back down to her and whispered, "I'm sorry, Sarah. It will only be a moment."

She looked up at her father and tried to give him a brave smile. At least the tears had stopped. "Don't worry. I'll be all right."

He nodded and headed toward the exit.

"And Father?" she continued, catching his attention just as his hand settled on the doorknob. "If you could close the door behind you . . . I'll need a minute to compose myself."

"Of course, Sarah," he said with a warmth in his voice that she had rarely heard since her mother had died. "Take all the time you need."

He opened the door and marched into the corridor.

"All right, O'Rourke," he said, slamming the door shut behind him. His voice melted away into muffled sounds.

Sarah sat alone for a moment. Through all the other emotions there was a sense of glee that she had managed to escape from the closet without being detected.

Feeling the itch of the tears on her face, she reached into her pocket to try to find a handkerchief, but it was gone—probably confiscated by accident when Jenny took the cloth.

She wiped her sleeve across her cheeks, leaving a shiny slick along the dark silk. She rubbed away what remained of her tears as best she could with her hands, then wiped her damp palms against her skirts.

"All right, Sarah Stanton," she said to herself, "one, two, and up!" She rose from the chair and sprinted over to the safe. Sarah grabbed the frame and gave the portrait a hard tug, expecting it to pull out as easily as it had gone in. Instead there was a loud "tunk" as wood struck metal.

"What?" Sarah pulled again, but the painting was, against all logic, stuck. She spent a few moments trying to manipulate the image back and forth, but somehow it had grabbed hold of the metal box.

Sarah felt panic rising up in her throat. She had no idea how long her father would be gone, but it seemed likely that after such a rare moment of genuine emotion between them he'd be eager to come back and see his daughter. If he found her fighting with his portrait . . .

Letting go of the painting she walked around to the other side of the safe. From this angle it was obvious what had gone wrong. A particularly ornate rococo flourish had entangled itself on the safe's back leg. She freed the painting by shoving it with her foot and tilting it forward, clearing space in front of the frame.

Running back to the other side of the iron box she slid the image out as easily as she had initially expected to. There was another small bit of damage where the gilt had been mashed into the leg, but it was a small-enough blemish that he might still not notice it.

Jenny would certainly see it, but it was obvious that she was already well aware that the picture had been moved, and by whom. Sarah would need to make the maid promise her silence, although she believed that their friendship might be enough that she'd at least ask Sarah before giving her up to her father.

She dragged the picture along the floor to the back wall, then rotated it so that it was facing the right way up underneath the picture hook.

As she slid it up the wall she cursed herself again for bothering to take it down in the first place. "But there's nothing for it." She felt the seams on her jacket complain as she lifted her arms up to try to get it back in position.

"Drat!" Not only was the frame refusing to hang, but she couldn't even feel the hook pressing up against the wire.

Lifting it up over her head she peered underneath to see why it hadn't caught. The wire was long and slack, hanging down to the midway point. There was no way she'd be able to lift the portrait high enough for the wire to reach the hook.

The pump was already primed from her conversation with her father a few minutes before, and she felt tears of frustration about to flow again. The picture, her bustle, the hook, Jenny . . . everything—"*Everything!*"—seemed to be conspiring against her in an attempt to betray her to her father.

Sarah let the painting sink to the floor and took a moment to collect her thoughts. If her father could hold back his tears with nothing more than sheer force of will, then she could do the same!

From somewhere outside in the hall she heard the sound of her father's voice. Sarah froze. For an instant she was sure he was on his way back, and that she had finally lost.

But as the volume rose she realized that it was simply him shouting at someone. She could only hope that whoever it was who had the misfortune of being the target of her father's temper, he or she had committed a great enough sin that Sarah would have the time she needed to finish hanging the image.

She pushed her father's chair away from the desk until the back of it was up against the wall. The contraption didn't look too stable, and it was not something that she would consider using as a stepladder under normal circumstances, but it would have to do.

Sliding the picture upward, she tilted the frame back and stepped onto the chair. The springs gave a mighty creak as they took her weight, but it all seemed relatively stable as long as she kept her weight forward.

As she lifted the painting into place she realized that she was staring nose-to-nose with the image of her father. Ignoring his disapproving gaze, she gave the painting a final nudge, hopping the edge up and over the dreaded hook. Then, lifting her arms up as high as they could go, she slowly lowered it back down, letting out a sigh of relief as she felt the weight lifting off her hands.

Her modest celebration was interrupted by the sound of shoes tapping back down the corridor. She felt herself tipping backward, and she hopped off the chair, scooting it into position behind the desk place.

Realizing that she would never make it back to her side of the desk in time, she grabbed a book randomly from a nearby shelf. Just as she read the title her father burst through the door. His face was red and shining with perspiration.

She closed the cover of the volume in her hand and slid it back into its place. "Is everything all right?"

He looked over at her and scowled. "I didn't know you cared for war histories."

Sarah frowned back at him. "If you left me in here much longer who knows what I might have decided to learn about next." Both of their eyes went to the gas lamp on the wall.

"Sarah, I don't have to tell you . . ."

Sarah gave a slight smile. "Don't worry, Father. I won't go uncovering any more of your secrets."

He pulled out her chair and pushed it forward as she sat down. "You know I only want to keep you safe."

"I know."

He began to walk around the edge of the table, and then glanced up at the image on the wall. "That's odd . . ."

"What?" Sarah asked, her voice catching in her throat for a second. "Is something wrong?"

He grabbed the edge of the frame and gave the picture a slight nudge. "It's crooked. I could have sworn it was perfectly straight when I walked out of here."

Sarah suppressed a grin. "Well, it's perfect now."

"That's the problem with having help around the house. Nothing is ever exactly where you want it to be." He sat in his chair and leaned back. "Now where were we?"

Sarah could think of a dozen other topics that she'd rather discuss than her looming spinsterhood. "What was the message?"

He looked up at her, any attempt at finding continuity with their previous conversation totally wiped away. "What? You mean just now?"

Sarah nodded.

"Nothing you need concern yourself with. Peter Wickham—"

"You mean the Sleuth?" she said innocently.

"Exactly right." He tapped the table and moved his lips back and forth, clearly deciding whether this was something he should share with his daughter. "Well, it seems the old man has reactivated the Automaton, against my express wishes."

"That's beastly!" she replied.

"Well, I think he had a soft spot for the machine since he and Darby were such . . . close friends, and I—"

"No, I mean you *deactivated* the Automaton? He's one of you—a Paragon!"

He let out a sigh. "I knew I shouldn't have said anything. I'd forgotten that you were friendly with it as well."

"Him." Sarah said, trying to calm herself down. Her fake outrage felt all too real, and having just escaped from the frying pan, she realized that she didn't need to be playing with fire.

There was no telling which tiny mistake it might be that would alert her father to the fact that she'd helped to revive the mechanical man. But Sarah was a Stanton just as much as her father was, and sometimes her temper seemed to get the better of her, *especially* where her father was concerned.

"*It*, Sarah—just an infernal machine and nothing more. Not a man in any of the ways that truly count."

Her face went red as she realized what he meant. "Father!"

"Sarah, you're not a child anymore, and the world I live in has become far too dangerous for you to be around. You have your whole life ahead of you, and it won't be filled with decrepit inventors and clockwork men."

"Father, I can—"

He stood up from his chair. "I should have mentioned this before now, but it's what I brought you in here to tell you: I've taken over Darby's place. I'm the leader of the Paragons now."

"Oh!" she said, genuinely surprised. Dark thoughts raced through her head as she realized how he had profited from Darby's demise.

She pushed down her suspicions and forced herself to pay attention to her father. "But it also means that whatever danger this family was in before is doubled now. Darby's murderer is still out there somewhere, and I wouldn't be surprised to discover that he's coming for me next."

Sarah considered it very unlikely. After all, they already had the Alpha Element. But . . . "The Children of Eschaton are coming," she mumbled to herself.

"What was that?" her father asked.

She said it louder this time. "The Children of Eschaton are coming. That's what the Bomb Lance told me to tell you. He said there was nothing you could do to stop them."

He smiled. It was both paternal and patronizing at the same time, but maybe that was part of being a father. "Sarah, villains always say that. Well, the madmen do, at least.

"They all think they have a master plan that will be the end of us. But in the end, so far at least, they make the mistake of thinking that anger and greed alone can defeat righteous and honorable men."

"I understand, Father. I'll try not to worry, then." She stood up. "And congratulations. I'm sure you'll be a great leader."

He came around the table toward her. "I know it hasn't been easy for you, Sarah, being raised by me. It hasn't been easy for either of us since your mother died, but I do care about you." He stepped forward and wrapped his arms around her a second time.

This time, with her father's arms holding her to his chest, she didn't feel like a child at all anymore. Sarah felt as if she were very old indeed.

"I love you, Sarah," he said to her, and tightened his hold, but after all the ups and downs of the last few hours she realized that she had no more emotions to be squeezed out of her. She put her arms around him anyway.

"I love you too, Father," she replied. Right now all she could do was hug her father hard enough to make him feel better.

Chapter 13

Filled with Twists and Turns

Wickham furrowed his brow as he ran, trying to gather his thoughts. His lungs were burning from the exertion and the large quantities of the frosty air that he was pulling in through his nose.

While his body might not be as strong or reliable as it once had been, his mind was as sharp as ever. There was a slight concern, however, as he reviewed the path of the maze in his mind, that Brandon had taken them in a complete circle before he had brought him back into the cul-de-sac where the ambush had taken place. And that meant that even if he went the right way, they'd still be waiting for him before he could escape. But would the Ruffian even be able to pull off a scheme like that? He prayed the German was truly as big a buffoon as he appeared to be.

He made a sharp left and relaxed when he saw the street a few yards ahead of him. Once he escaped the maze he would be relatively safe. They could chase him, but assaulting him in public would mean police, or at the very least witnesses.

As he burst into daylight, Wickham's feeling of triumph instantly evaporated. He hadn't managed to reach the street at all. Instead it was another cul-de-sac—this one even smaller than the one he had just escaped from, and no more useful.

From behind him he heard gleeful shouts from Jack and his thugs. "We've got him now, boys!" The tone of the man's voice was truly the most atrocious blend of London and New York accents he had ever heard. Wickham would at least tell him that before he died.

He turned around to face his pursuers, holding up his stick as menacingly as he could manage. If he was doomed, then he'd go down fighting.

He hoped it would be Jack who came through first. He'd taken down big men like the Ruffian before, but it was the ability of the marksman to attack him at range that put him at the biggest disadvantage.

As he steeled himself for the final confrontation he felt something slip around his shoulders. Before he could react it yanked tight, pinning his arms to his sides. He gasped when he realized that he'd been roped and was rising up into the air.

It was painful and awkward, and by the time he had devised a plan to struggle free, he was already too far off the ground to avoid plummeting to his death. And even if he could survive the fall, he'd end up face-to-face with his pursuers.

With the next jerk of the rope the cane fell from his hand and dropped to the ground below. It bounced back into the air a single time before clattering across the cobblestones and finally rolling to a stop next to a pile of rubbish in the gutter.

Wickham looked up to the rooftops to try to see who it was who had captured him, wondering if it was friend or foe. But what he discovered was not an answer to that question. Though the details were hidden by the glare of the sun, the distinctive shape of the mask above made it obvious that he had once again been rescued by Anubis.

The enigmatic figure in black made no noise as he pulled the Sleuth up to the rooftop. He simply, and steadily, lifted the rope up hand over hand, as if he were pulling up an anchor from the bottom of the sea.

A few feet before he came to the ledge, Wickham heard a commotion beneath him and looked down to see three figures entering the courtyard below. "No use hiding, Sleuth," Jack yelled out. His voice was filled with anger and anticipation. "But if you come out without making us look for you then I'll promise to kill you quickly." At least his promises were getting more believable.

When Anubis finally grabbed him, the hands that dragged him up and over the edge of the roof were impressively powerful—close to, if not stronger than, the ones that had so recently been wrapped around his neck. But they also had a surprisingly gentle quality to them, and they placed the Sleuth softly onto the rooftop, standing upright on his feet.

Wickham began to ask "Why?" but found a gloved hand placed over his mouth. The masked figure shook his head and then pointed downward. They would need to remain silent until the others had left.

Wickham exhaled as softly as he could and leaned back against a brick chimney. Robbed of the urgency that had given him his strength, it seemed as if there was no longer a single joint in his body that hadn't joined the screaming choir that was telling him that he had pushed himself far too much for a man his age.

But even through the pain, he could hear the angry shouts from his pursuers as they went from taunting their cornered prey to the slow realization that he had somehow managed to escape them.

"I know you're in here somewhere, old man!" Jack yelled, but the tone of his voice made it obvious that he wasn't *actually* so sure.

The Sleuth let go of the chimney and took a long breath. He was rewarded with a series of popping sounds as his joints tried to settle back into place. If he actually was safe, and Anubis didn't end their meeting by dropping him off the roof, it would take him days to recover and realign himself. And even then he would need to find some pills and powders to dull the pain.

Peering over the edge he saw the round German using his massive arms to dismember a pile of trash. The round man paused for a second and then reached down to pick up the grubby walking stick. "I found something," he said, holding it up.

Jack stalked over and grabbed it out of his hand.

"I think this belonged to him," Brandon said.

Jack raised it up over his head menacingly, and the fat man cowered. "I know that, you jackass." It was an amusing sight, like a fox threatening a bear. He lowered it without striking him. "But where the hell did he go? He can't fly, can he?"

Jack's head turned upward to make sure that he was wrong. Wickham realized that the sun was at his back, and if the villain turned his way he'd see him perfectly outlined against the clear blue sky.

A voice boomed out from the alleyway, and every head turned to look toward it, including the Sleuth's. "No, he can't fly, but they call him the 'cleverest man in the world' for a reason."

Jack nodded. "Anubis. I was just wondering where you'd got to."

"I was searching the rooftops. As far as I can tell he figured out where the false wall was and escaped the maze."

"You're sure?" Brandon took off his top hat and wiped the sweat out of his brow. "He didn't see it as he came in."

Anubis turned to face him. "No one doubts you *think* he didn't see it. But you can keep digging through garbage if you like."

Jack stood frozen for a moment and then let out a shout. "This is your fault!" He pulled out a knife and flicked it at the man in black.

Anubis deflected the blade casually, almost as if this were a common occurrence between them, but his next words made it clear that it wasn't. "Try that again, and I'll knock the next one back into your throat."

Jack sniggered. "Impossible."

"Let's find out."

Jack pointed a finger at him instead. "This is still your fault, mystery man. I don't care why you did it, but *you're* going to be the one to tell Lord Eschaton what happened and why, not me." He began walking back into the maze. "C'mon Brandon. We're going to need to strip everything out of here before the Paragons come."

Brandon bumbled after him, as did the other lackeys. "But I like it there," he said with the tone of a petulant child. The echoing sound of footsteps vanished quickly.

Wickham looked around to see where Anubis had gone, but there was no trace. He'd been abandoned, and as tired and beaten as he was, he'd still need to find some way down from the rooftop. There were no obvious fire escapes, and he didn't have any idea what was actually inside the building he was standing on.

The sun was completely hidden by clouds now, and even though the wind had died down, it felt much colder. "It'll snow soon," he remarked to no one in particular. It would be just his luck to escape from a cadre of villains only to freeze to death on a random rooftop somewhere on the West Side. "Sleuth found frozen in his tracks!" the paperboys would yell. It was the kind of sensational headline that editors killed for.

Shaking off his morbid thoughts, he took a step back from the edge of the roof and felt something poking his back. As he jumped forward with surprise, Wickham stumbled over a seam in the tin roof and tumbled toward the edge until a steady hand grabbed him by the back of his collar. When he turned around Anubis was standing there like a mysterious statue.

Wickham held out his hand. "We seem to have gotten into a very bad habit of having you save my life."

Anubis grasped it and gave a single, firm shake. "Consider it repayment for everything you've done for this city over the years."

"So, you've heard of me." Now that he was no longer fighting for his life, Wickham noticed how flat the man managed to keep the tone of his voice at all times. Anubis had let no hint of emotion creep into his words, and his neutral cadence revealed nothing of his origin. He was, for all practical purposes, invisible to the Sleuth's methods of deduction. But there were other ways. . . . "I thought you worked for that Eschaton fellow?"

"They found me. I said yes."

"But you're not his man?"

Wickham could see the outline of his jaw as it clenched under his mask. It was good to see that beneath his leather covering Anubis was at least a bit more human than the Automaton. "I'm not *anyone's* man but my own, Mr. Wickham. There are, I'm sure you'll agree, many methods of disguise and infiltration. Some are simply more effective in particular cases."

The Sleuth let his response sink in and then smiled. "Ahh, I see. Touché."

Wickham reached up and felt his whiskers. They hadn't been peeling off at all; he had simply been outsmarted. "But for all the indignities I've suffered today, I'm still no closer to finding out who it was who killed Dennis Darby."

"I can give you the name of his killer. The Bomb Lance is a man named Martin Murphy. He lives on the top floor of a tenement building on Allen and Grand.

"But you must have already deduced that there is more going on here than simple revenge. If you want to find out the reasons behind the assassination of your friend, then you'll need to know more than the name of the thug who pulled the trigger."

"Like the whys and wherefores behind the Children of Eschaton . . ." The Sleuth reached his hands high up into the air and felt some satisfying pops run down his spine as some of the bones and muscles fell back into place. Perhaps it would only take a couple of days to recover. . . . Even so, there was a painful catch in his back that spoke of pains to come. Perhaps he would treat himself to a massage when he got home.

Anubis watched him quietly for a moment before replying."I need your help. There are things I can't find out by myself. I'm already under suspicion." The Sleuth thought he could sense a note of annoyance in the man's voice.

"I can only imagine what they'll do to you for rescuing me."

"I can handle Jack Knife and his crew. Jack may like to pretend that I'm an errand boy, but Lord Eschaton trusts me more."

"And how do I know I can trust *you*?"

The Sleuth noticed that Anubis's gloved hand tightened around the metal pole. "Because I am going to tell you something that is absolutely true. It is asomething that you may have, up until now, only suspected."

"And what is that?"

"One of"—As the second word came out of Anubis's mouth, the pieces that had been so jumbled inside of Wickham's mind slid into place. He knew the rest of what Anubis was going to say to him, even before he said it. "—the Paragons is a traitor."

"So I was right. . . ." It came out in a whispered croak. "But who is it?"

"I don't know, but I'm trying to find out."

Wickham shrugged off his coat. The cold bit into him, even through the padding of his disguise. He needed to know more from his friend in black than words alone would tell him. "Don't know, or won't tell me?"

The Sleuth took a quick, aggressive step toward Anubis, and his motion was matched almost exactly by a step back. Wickham was impressed. The man's reflexes were lightning fast, totally smooth, and utterly practiced.

He took another step forward, and this time found himself chest-to-chest with the other man.

"I don't know," Anubis replied. He was almost a foot taller than the Sleuth, and tilted his head down to look at him.

From this close vantage point there was nothing more disconcerting to Wickham than the way Anubis's mask completely hid his eyes from view. He could only see darkness and shadow behind the holes in the mask. "Is it worth it?" he asked.

"I am not lying to you!" Anubis replied with obvious anger in his voice. The intensity had put something into his words—a trace of something identifiable.

"And I'm not accusing you of lying," he replied. "I'm simply wondering if you think it's worth obscuring your vision to hide your identity."

The jackal mask leaned closer to him. "You won't find the answers you're looking for that way."

"Fine," replied Wickham. "Then let's try this." He kicked the rod out of Anubis's hand, sending it clattering across the tin rooftop.

The figure in black reacted immediately to the attack, dropping backward and crouching defensively.

Wickham wasted no time in pressing his assault. He pushed forward, his hands chopping the air in front of him in short, hard arcs. He no longer had the reflexes it would take to defeat Anubis, if he ever had, but that wasn't what he was after. He'd unlock this enigma one way or another, even if it meant that his joints would scream at him for the rest of his days.

After easily deflecting a few blows, Anubis shot back with a series of punches. The old man danced away, his fists held high. Even with the difference in their ages entirely to his advantage, Anubis could not seem to find his target.

He tilted his head to one side, the snarling black jackal in his mask giving him the appearance of a curious, if still demonic, puppy. "Are you testing me?"

Wickham laughed and danced closer. "In a manner of speaking. I'm sparring with you, old chap." Slipping underneath the clenched fists, he reached up and smacked his opponent on the silver ankh on his chest before slipping away. "And it appears that I'm winning."

The man in black let out a short laugh. It was a strange sound to hear coming out from underneath his grim visage. "All right, old man, if that's what you want, it seems you've given me no choice but to teach you a lesson." But under the serious words there was a clear loosening in his posture. Realizing he was no longer in genuine danger, Anubis had settled into a sparring pose.

"Have at!" the Sleuth yelled, and danced toward his opponent. In a matter of seconds they had traded a flurry of blows, each attempting to find an opening and being immediately batted away. Their feet blurred as they stepped in and out of each other's way.

Simultaneously, as if the entire thing had been choreographed, they both backed off, sinking into similar stances.

Wickham smiled and nodded at him respectfully. "You've studied the martial arts."

"If you say so," Anubis replied.

"Gung-foo . . . from northern China . . . I'd say." He was wheezing slightly with each breath. "I hope you won't take offense when . . . I say that I find it . . . very doubtful that you have actually . . . visited the Orient."

Without another word, Anubis jumped forward, pressing the attack for another round.

For a few moments it appeared as if they were equally matched, trading blow for blow. But after a minute of dancing with his opponent, Wickham's breathing was far more ragged, his feints sloppy and slow, and his counters coming fewer and farther between.

"Kai ya!" Wickham shouted as punched. But the blow went wild, sending him off balance, and his wrist ended up caught in Anubis's grasp.

He waved him off with his free hand. "I . . . yield," he said, gasping for air. "I yield!"

Anubis nodded and let him go. "That's very impressive, Mr. Wickham—doubly so for a man your age."

Wickham leaned back against the chimney, pulling in air through his nose. "You should . . . have seen me . . . when I was . . . in my prime." He paused for a long inhalation. "I might have . . . even beaten you!" He felt nauseous. He'd pushed himself beyond his limits for the third time today, and once again his reward was that he'd landed on his backside instead of his face. Still, it was nice to see that he could hold his own for a few seconds, even if it was only play-fighting.

Wickham felt the sweat trickling down his skin underneath the padding. Anubis was breathing heavily under his leather mask, and Wickham could only imagine how hot it must be inside his black leather skin. "I'd love to meet the man who trained you how to fight like that."

“He’s dead,” the man in black replied, his voice once again disturbingly neutral.

“I’m sorry to hear it.”

“Perhaps by working together we can still save some lives.”

“Did Lord Eschaton kill the man who trained you?”

“No . . .” He paused and stared away for a moment. “But someone very much like him did. Lord Eschaton’s intention is in his name. The word is Latin; it means—”

“‘The end of the world.’”

“He’s a madman, and a genius—smart enough not to challenge the Paragons directly until the time is right.”

Wickham frowned. “What would you call killing Darby on top of the Brooklyn Bridge?”

“A diversion.” Anubis walked toward his metal staff, pointing at Wickham’s jacket as he went. “Do you have a pencil and paper in there somewhere?”

“I should.” The Sleuth followed him and picked up his coat, trying to ignore the twinges and shudders of pain shooting up and down his back. He pulled at a frayed edge of his jacket, tearing away threads specifically designed for that purpose. From a hidden pocket inside the lining he removed a notebook bound in embossed black leather. He pulled out a pencil from its loop.

Anubis took the objects from him, opened the notebook to the first blank page, and began to scribble something inside. “This is the address to a warehouse. It is one of Lord Eschaton’s secret factories. What you will find inside will disturb you, and it is only part of his plan.” He finished writing and held the page out for Wickham to look at. “Can you read it?”

Wickham stared at the string of numbers and letters. “Yes. But your handwriting is poor. You didn’t go to a very good school.” He squinted and looked closer, bringing the book up almost to his nose. “In fact, I’d say that you might not have gone to school at all, although you’re educated enough. . . .”

“Mr. Wickham.”

“Since you’re wearing a mask, you can call me the Sleuth.”

"Sleuth, if we are going to work together I need to ask that you please stop trying to uncover my secrets."

He felt a blush rising to his cheeks. His insatiable curiosity was his greatest gift, but it had also cost him numerous friends and lovers over the years. At least Anubis was willing to give him a second chance. "No, I'm sorry—it's me. . . . It's the way my brain works. I'm sorry."

"We all have secrets, Mr. Wickham."

"Yes, we do." There was something in that voice, even under the emotionless tone. If he could just place it . . .

He tried to stop it from happening, but the pieces simply fell into place. He gasped with the realization. "Of course! You're—"

"Nothing!" Anubis bellowed back, wiping out his next words before the old man could even say them. "I asked you to leave my secrets alone!" There was a touch of desperation in his voice.

He turned and walked toward the building's edge with unsteady steps, his confidence clearly shaken by the Sleuth's realization.

Holding up his staff he fired the tip into the chimney, a wire rope trailing behind it. "Uncover what's inside that building, and we'll meet again. But whatever it is you think you know . . ."

"I'll take it to my grave," Wickham replied, still shocked by his discovery.

Anubis jumped over the edge, slipping off into the shadows. A few seconds later there was a metallic click as the tip of the rod retracted its metal spines and then fell away.

Wickham had been standing there thinking to himself for almost five minutes when he realized that he still had no earthly idea how he was going to get himself down from the roof.

Chapter 14

Masters of the House

The idea that it would take only thirty-five years for the full urban force of New York to roar northward and completely envelop Darby Park would have been laughable to anyone present at the mansion's groundbreaking. But during those three short decades the city had grown relentlessly northward, and over that time the park had been transformed from a proud estate to a defiant oasis, and finally to its current status as a curious anachronism in uptown Manhattan.

But if the estate was going to war with progress, at least it was well defended. The mansion itself was placed well back from Fourth Avenue, sitting on three-quarters of a city block, kept out of sight from the street traffic by a tall stone fence, trees, and rows of manicured bushes.

Soon after arriving in New York, Dennis Darby's father had purchased the entire block. The area was, at the time, well beyond "uptown" in the city.

Clinging to the righteous naïveté that had driven him across the Atlantic, Christopher Darby had intended to build an estate that would be a part of his family's future for generations to come. He had even involved young Dennis in the home's design in an attempt to bridge the growing divide between father and son.

But whatever legacy it was that Christopher Darby had hoped for, it was certainly not to be found in the city that New York had become in the fifteen years since he'd passed away. Although there were still a few other stately homes that survived in the neighborhood, none of them inhabited such a vast, unspoiled swath of land. And with the endless amount of wealth and investment that were flooding northward as the city grew, few owners remained who could resist the vast sums of money that were being offered for their homes. But even if the old world was crumbling under the weight of a wrecking ball, for now at least, Darby Park still stood on this snowy February night.

It was already well past ten, but the gas lamps in the gardens were still lit. Their yellow lights flickered bravely against the cold, tinting the snowflakes gold as they fluttered toward the ground. A few inches had fallen already, enough to smooth over the world in a soft cover of solid white. The corners of the windows were painted with swooping patterns of frost as the moisture settled into the glass panes and froze where it touched the cold glass.

Inside the house the Automaton reached down and picked up an abandoned top hat from one of the stairs on the main staircase. The mechanical man brushed off the lint from the rim with a series of quick and efficient back-and-forth swipes. He climbed the stairs slowly, and when he was almost at the top, he found a pair of white gloves that had been hastily dropped on the floor. He grabbed them and placed them into the hat.

On the landing, flung over the polished wood of the banister, was a fine black wool coat with fur lapels. It was slowly slumping downward, and clearly would have jumped from the balcony to the floor below if Tom hadn't rescued it.

Coat over his arm, he entered one of the upstairs bedrooms, placed the hat on the dresser, and hung the coat on a rack by the door.

On the other side of the small space Nathaniel Winthorp lay unconscious and sprawled out across his bed. His eyes were closed, a soft snore rising up from his loosely parted lips.

One foot lay on the floor next to a puddle of congealed wax that had dribbled down from a burning candle onto the floor. His other leg was still on the mattress, the boot still on, sitting in the middle of a damp, brown ring that had formed when the slush had melted and soaked into the sheets. The tail of his white shirt was half tucked into his underpants, and all the buttons were undone except for the top two, still hidden under a yellow silk cravat that was twisted around the heavily starched collar.

The Automaton reached down again, this time retrieving a dinner jacket that sat perilously close to the candle while doding Nathienl's right arm. The limb was stretched out over the floor, his hand resting loosely around the neck of a bottle of Kentucky Club whiskey that was a bit more than half empty.

The young man cracked one eye and used it to glare at Tom. "Get the hell out."

"I am sorry . . . Nathaniel. I was simply trying to assist you."

The young man's other eyelid opened, and he rotated his head to stare straight at the ceiling. "I feel like hell."

"I'll get you a packet of . . . headache powders." He gave the jacket a good shake, getting it mostly back into shape. "You have consumed a great deal of alcohol."

The young man rolled his head to the right, then groaned. "Yes, I still have the bottle right here, in my *hand*. So thank you for stating the mostly obvious." He lifted it up, balanced it on his chest, and pulled out the cork. "Now if you could be so kind as to follow my previous order and close the damn door we can both get on with our business." Lifting up his head slightly he poured a good portion of the brown liquor into his mouth and then swallowed, managing to dribble only a small bit down his chin. "Although, in your case, I have no idea what that would be, nor do I care."

"As I understand it, it is now my business to take care of this house and also to help you." He walked a few more steps into the room. "Perhaps I can help to remove your . . . boots."

Nathaniel sat up on his elbows and waved the bottle at Tom. "What would help me the most from you is your absence. Get out." The bottle slipped from his hand, slid down his chest, caught the edge of the bed, and flipped over as it dropped to the floor with a thud and a bounce. Landing on its side, splashes of whisky gurgled onto the rug until the level in the bottle slipped below that of the mouth. "Damn."

Tom stopped moving. "Please . . . Nathaniel, I . . ."

"And damn you too, machine! Do what I ordered you to!" The words came out in a slurred shout. "Get the hell *out!*"

He swung his left leg onto the floor, sat up, and shoved the flat of his hand into Tom's chest. "*Now!*"

Tom nodded. "I apologize . . . Nathaniel. I was told that my new . . . task was to take care of the . . . mansion. I simply wish to do that in the most effective way."

Nathaniel laughed. It was a throaty, sarcastic sound, punctuated by a drunken rasp at the end of it. "You're thick, aren't you? No one *cares* what you do anymore, Tom. They just want you out of the Paragons. Out of the way!

Locked in the basement where you can't cause problems, or do any more harm. They just lacked the will to turn you off, and it turns out you're cheaper than hiring real help.

"I told them they should have sold you for scrap." He picked up the bottle from the floor and shook the mouth of it at the Automaton menacingly. "So what do you think would happen to you if I drowned you in whiskey?"

Tom paused for a moment before speaking. "It could, given enough time, jam my gears and impair my efficiency. No doubt that would be similar to what has happened to you, although the damage to me would be more permanent."

His cheeks flushed red. "Are you making fun of me?" He flung the bottle at Tom's head.

"I heard shout—" The Automaton's left arm jumped up and snatched the bottle out of the air just as Sarah Stanton's shocked face appeared in the doorway it was heading toward.

Her eyes went wide. "Nathaniel Winthorp!" she said in a tone of anger and shock. "What in the name of God do you think you're doing?" She had taken off her hat and coat, but her long white gloves were still on her hands. "Is this more of your childish abuse?"

The blush rose even higher into his cheeks. "You weren't my intended target." He made a noise that landed somewhere between a mumble and a chuckle. "But you'll do."

"You're drunk!"

"What of it?"

She crossed her arms and stared at him. "Again."

"And when everyone leaves me alone, I become sober again in the morning."

Sarah was staring down at the lit candle in a holder on the floor. "But will the house still be standing by then?"

"I'm sure the tin toy will put out any fires I might start."

"Tom isn't your manservant, Nathaniel." She took a step closer to the bed. "In fact, as I understand it, you were allowed to stay in this house with the understanding that *you* were to be the caretaker."

"Is that what your father told you, Sarah?"

"Yes, it is. He said that Sir Dennis willed Tom the mansion."

He looked up at her and sneered. "And that's true, as far as it goes."

Sarah narrowed her gaze. "If you ever want to be the master of anything, then you should get off your drunken rear end and start acting like a gentleman."

"I thought you just said the Automaton is the master of the mansion?" He let out a wry chuckle. "And if, my dearest Sarah, Queen Victoria herself were to decree that the royal carriage were destined to become the true son and heir to the throne of England, it doesn't mean that the people would be willing to actually have the coronation for King Coach once she died." He stepped up from the bed and pulled the bottle back out of Tom's hand.

Sarah stepped forward. "What are you saying, Nathaniel?"

He put the bottle up to his lips and drank the remains. "No matter what fantasies you, Darby, or that perverted old detective have in your heads, this machine is no more capable of being a 'master' of anything than a doorknob is the 'master' of a door." He thrust the empty bottle back into the Automaton's hand. "It's just a device. Machines don't have servants, own houses, or care about people. And they definitely don't love Sarah Stanton, patron saint of contraptions."

She looked down at her shoes and shook her head. "You have no idea what you're talking about."

"I'm trying to explain that stuffing a man-shaped dressmaker's dummy with wires and gears does not magically make it a human being. And that means I," he said, sticking his thumb into his chest, "*am* the master of this mansion now, so I expect to be treated with respect." He tugged his cravat off his neck and threw it at Tom so that it landed on the Automaton's shoulder. "And I expect you to ring the damn front bell before you come barging in."

Sarah pushed past Tom and stood at the side of the bed shaking a kid-gloved finger down at Nathaniel. "You really are a complete ass. If there's any of Sir Dennis left in this world, it lives inside Tom's heart. And I can only imagine how hurt Darby would be to see you tonight, drunk and sprawling in your own filth like a spoiled gutter rat." She whipped her hand behind her to point at Tom. "*He's* more honest and human than you'll ever be."

"Then leave me alone, Sarah. You can't fix me, and I don't need a mother hen."

"What?" She sounded genuinely shocked.

"Pardon me," said Tom.

"We're not children any longer," Nathaniel continued. I don't need a mommy anymore—especially not one whose own mother is long dead. You won't save me with temperance and clucking."

"Nathaniel, I know you wish that you and I were . . . But we've known each other since we were children. That must mean something to you."

"Excuse me," Tom repeated.

"It means I can ask you to leave." Nathaniel looked down at the floor and sighed. "I may have to live here with him, but I didn't invite *you*." He put his hand up over his eyes. "I just need some peace and quiet so I can enjoy my state of inebriation."

Sarah took the bottle out of Tom's hand. "And I didn't come here to see you either, Nathaniel. I was supposed to meet Mr. Wickham."

"Why does everyone have a key to this place?" He slumped forward. "I suppose you're planning on trading late-night makeup tips with your lavender uncle."

Sarah crossed her arms in front of her. "If you want me out of your life so badly, then I'll do the best I can to grant you your wish."

". . . Mr. Winthorp."

"Yes, damn you. What is it?" he shouted. "What is it I can do for the steam shovel that walks and talks like a man?"

"I wish to stay in . . . the mansion. I will do what I can to regain your . . . trust. I am sorry for whatever I've done to make you . . . angry at me and will do my best to convince you of my . . . good intentions."

Without looking at him Nathaniel flopped back onto his bed. "You can start by going: g-o-i-n-g. Do you *understand*?"

"Yes, sir." Tom turned and left the room.

"I hope you're pleased with yourself, Nathaniel Winthorp."

"I'll be pleased once you're gone as well, Sarah Stanton. Feel free to see yourself out once you've finished your tryst with the sodomite."

Sarah pursed her lips tightly for a moment, holding in something that she dearly wanted to say but clearly thought she had better not.

Spinning on her heels she shut the door behind her with a solid slam.

She passed Tom still moving across the upper landing. He was walking with a hobble—perhaps slightly more smoothly than he had when she'd seen him in the laboratory underneath the Hall of Paragons, but still obviously damaged.

Too angry to stop, she trotted past him and then clambered down the stairs as fast as her legs could go. Her shoes clacked across the marble of the entry hall as she stormed into the main corridor and turned right into the darkened parlor.

The glass panes in the double doors rattled as she slammed them shut behind her. She shouted into the darkness, "Gaaaaraaah! You're a damnable, beastly, frustrating child!"

And another voice answered her. It came from a chair in the darkest corner of the room. "Sir Dennis used to say that it was only worthwhile judging the character of a man in a crisis."

Sarah gasped. "Mr. Wickham!"

"Indeed, my dear." He unfolded slowly out of the chair and stood up. Sarah could almost feel the aches in his bones as he stretched with a series of audible cracks and pops. "Although I can't think why you should be surprised. This is where I told you we should meet, and at about this time." He was wearing his full costume; although this time he was carrying a cane with him as well. The top end was a hollow sphere of brass with a magnifying glass mounted into the center of it. As he walked toward her he leaned on the cane heavily. He seemed frailer than the last time she had seen him. "Where else would I be?"

"Nathaniel has me all wound up." Sarah tried to force herself to smile, then gave up the effort. "But if you'll pardon me for saying so, sir, you don't look well."

The grin that the Englishman flashed back at her was less than convincing. "No . . . I suppose I don't." He pulled off his long black coat and threw it on the settee. "So far it has been a grueling investigation, both physically and mentally."

"Sit down, then. I'm sure we can find you something to drink."

He swayed slightly as he leaned against the sofa. "No, no liquor my dear, thank you. I find that it dulls the mind, and at my age there are enough natural impairments to my reasoning that I would rather not pile on any artificial ones." He pointed at the couch and Sarah took a seat.

"I did some searching around my house."

His eyes grew wide. "I never told you too—"

"I know you didn't, but I wanted to see if there was something there that could help you."

"You're a very silly girl. There was no need."

She pulled out the folded piece of paper and pressed it into his hand. "I don't know what it means, but I found it in my father's closet."

He unfolded it and read it out loud: "'Section 106 removed and reordered as requested.'"

"Does that mean anything to you?"

He pondered it for a moment and then looked up at her. "Not particularly," he said as he refolded the page and slipped it into his pocket. "But I'll look into it.

"Now, Tom will be along any second, and there's something I must tell you before he arrives."

"Surely there's no need for us to keep any secrets from him?"

Wickham stood hunched above her. "He has many admirable qualities, but his grasp of guile is a bit . . . unreliable. It might be better if we only told him what he needs to know."

The irregular clump of Tom's footsteps could be heard from the corridor outside.

Wickham reached into his collar. Pulling out the necklace, he slipped the lead key over his head. "Take this," he said, grabbing her hand and pressing it into her palm.

"Your element?" She wrapped her hand around it, pulled it to her chest for an instant, and then held it back out to him. "What am I supposed to do with it?"

He shook his head and used his hand to wrap hers back around it. "Keep it safe, of course."

"But . . ."

"There's no time to argue. No one must know you have it." Standing above her he looked her straight in the eyes with a serious expression. "Not even your father. Do you understand?"

"Yes. I mean, I don't understand why, but—"

Tom came into view behind the glass. "And you must only ever use it if something should happen to me."

"Use it? How would I use it? And is something going to happen?"

"Hush, now put it away!"

Sarah stuffed it into a pocket just as the doorknob turned and the tall French doors to the room opened wide. Tom hobbled in.

"Close the door behind you. And you may drop the act in front of Sarah, Tom."

"Yes . . . Mr. Wickham." Tom straightened up as he pulled the doors closed, any trace of his hobbled gait vanishing as he glided toward them, as graceful as he had ever been.

Sarah clapped her gloved hands together. "But you're fine!"

"I have repaired myself, Miss . . . Stanton."

Wickham whispered to her conspiratorially. "But the others mustn't know, my dear. It was done quite without their permission."

She stood up and put her hand on his shoulder. "It's abominable the way you're being treated, Tom. This is your house, and you're one of the Paragons!" She stood up and looked him over. "They're selfish, foolish men."

"Foolishness, I've discovered, is an unavoidable human trait," Wickham sighed. "But they're far worse than that, I'm afraid—they're weak and afraid."

Sarah let out a sardonic laugh. "All my life all I've ever heard them talk about is how powerful they are. What could they be afraid of?"

Wickham looked her in the eye. "Progress, disease, old age—all the things that eventually rob every man of his power and glory." He stood up, a touch of the old gleam back in his eye. "But only one of them is afraid that the Sleuth will uncover his secret."

Sarah rolled her head slightly to one side. "Please, Mr. Wickham, I'm in no mood for riddles. What do you mean? What secret?"

"The seeds of my investigation have borne bitter fruit. I'm now sure that there is indeed a traitor amongst the Paragons."

"A spy perhaps, or a new villain, but—"

"Only a Paragon could have removed Tom's replacement body from the hall the morning of Sir Dennis's death. Only the Paragons knew where Darby was going to be the morning that he was killed. He hadn't even told you where you were going before you left for the bridge."

"That's true." Sarah sat back down. "But then who was it?" She thought of the paper she had given him, and of her father's ascension. She stared straight into the Englishman's eyes. "You think it's my father."

"What?" The Sleuth sat next to her. "No, I don't. . . . I'm sorry, my dear. I didn't think about how that might affect you. . . ." He took her hand. "I'm not sure who it is, not yet, although I have my suspicions. But I'm almost positive your father is innocent. Alexander Stanton is one of the founders of the Paragons, and if he has one great failing it's that he's too loyal to this group. He may care too much about costumes and not enough about actual people, but he's no turncoat."

"But if it did turn out to be him . . . you'd have to stop him, wouldn't you?"

"Sarah, if the new leader of the Paragons turned out to be a traitor, I'm not sure what stopping him would even mean. I can only promise that I'll follow every clue wherever it goes."

"I understand, Mr. Wickham."

"And I'll tell you what I've discovered the very moment I have something worth telling. But right now I need you to be brave and to do what it is I ask of you, no matter what happens. I think that many lives may soon depend on that, not the least of them your own."

He stood. "But it seems to me that you've already been through more than enough for one night." He pulled a silk rope by the door, and a bell rang in the distance. "My footman is in the pantry. He'll get you home. Tell him I'll be spending the night here."

He had her moving through the door before she could find a moment to object. "Now I have things I need to discuss with Tom, privately."

Sarah resisted Wickham's attempts to sweep her along, but it was almost as if he was dancing her out of the room. "But I can still help!"

"Of course you can, my dear. But the best help you can be right now is to not be here." He leaned forward and kissed her on her forehead. It seemed like his ability to send women on their way was a move that had been well practiced. "You're a brave, beautiful girl, Sarah Stanton. It's obvious to me why Dennis held you in such high regard."

Sarah kissed him on the cheek. "You'll take care of yourself?"

His eyes turned to Tom and then glanced back at her. "Of course I will."

"And we'll talk soon?"

"Yes, my dear. But it's getting late, and your father will be worried, I'm sure."

She pursed her lips together for a moment, deciding just how obstinate she wanted to be. Then she stuck out her hand. "Good night, Mr. Wickham."

He put out his own, and they shook. "Good night, Sarah."

She walked down the hallway toward the entrance, leather soles clicking as they struck the marble floor. When she reached the main entrance she turned and looked back. Reflected in the lamplight she saw the Automaton's hand as it . . . as *he*, closed the door to the study.

Chapter 15

The Omega Engine

The silence inside the warehouse was only broken by an occasional tapping as the howling wind outside knocked the door against its frame. Each rattle was followed by a long, strained tone as the air was sucked out through the cracks, moaning like a demented oboe.

The back-and-forth of rattle and moan had been going on uninterrupted for hours when the calm was broken by a violent thump against the door that made it shudder, sending small crumbs of dust and brick raining down.

The second attack quickly followed, even more violent than the first. The third thundering blow was more than the lock could take, and the thick bolts snapped free, followed, an instant later, by a series of pings as pieces of broken metal landed on the floor.

A gust of wind blew the door open wide, slamming it up against the side wall. Behind it came a blast of light and snow from the street, revealing—had anyone actually been there to see it—a shadowed figure standing ominously in the doorway.

Snow had stopped falling from the sky hours before, but the temperature had dropped precipitously as the clouds were blown away. In this crisp and gusty winter's night, the cold had tempered the snow that had already fallen, and the north wind was now blowing the brittle flakes around the streets in swirling drifts.

The Automaton stepped into the building. He attempted to shut the door behind him, but without the lock there was nothing to hold it in place, and it began to fly back toward him the moment he relaxed his grip.

Tom removed his right glove, revealing a palm sliced from a bronze cylinder, a squared section along the bottom acting as his wrist. He wedged his hand against the edge of the heavy iron door and pushed hard against it until the frame bent inward slightly, forming a small pucker in the metal. He grabbed the edge of the door and heaved it closed. The wood ground into the iron with a rough squeal, wedging it tight. The wind could no longer make it rattle at all.

With the winter wind sealed away, the moist warmth of the warehouse's interior settled around him, dew instantly forming on his exposed metal surfaces. The snow that clung to his clothes melted to liquid, then vanished into the fibers of his jacket and pants.

The interior of the building seemed oddly immune to the weather outside. The concrete floors still held enough heat from whatever had gone on here during the day to keep the temperature inside tolerable, if not actually warm.

Except for a two-story office that had been built along the far wall, the building was a single open space. Every window on the floor level had been blacked out with brown butcher paper covered over with a thick coating of pitch, and the whole space was dark and quiet. Whoever had decided to seal the room off clearly had no desire for anything from the outside to peer in, nor any need to see out.

The thick gloom was broken only by the glow coming from the pilot lights in the gas lamps, as well as pinpricks of light leaking in though the wooden slats that made up the front of the building where the walls no longer fit together tightly.

Tom lifted up his faceplate. It slid up on little rails that lifted it up and back over the top of his head until it clicked into place. Locked into the front of his brass skull was a large lens set in a brass tube.

He held up his right hand and wrapped the fingers of his left around his steel wrist and pushed downward. A collar slid free and revealed a circular frame that held a small piece of quartz crystal surrounded by wires. He reached up and pulled back his thumb until it almost touched the back of his hand. There was a popping sound, and a bright spark appeared in the middle of the quartz. In the light the shape of the entire room was revealed. At the same instant the lens in his head clicked open, taking a photograph.

The building wasn't huge, considering its original purpose—four thousand square feet with a forty-foot roof. But its current occupants didn't seem interested in using it for storage. There were a few crates around, but they were empty and open. The rest of the room was occupied by large pieces of machinery bolted to the floor, including a huge black metal tube that stood near the entrance.

But the most notable feature was the long row of dismembered metal limbs hung carefully along the far wall.

There was a whir as the photographic material in the back of Tom's head shifted the next slide into position. He rotated his head and fired another spark.

After he had finished with his photographs the Automaton lowered his mask back into place, pushed his hand back into its normal position, and walked into the room.

He weaved his way through the bulky machines. The first one was clearly designed for hand milling and rolling metal plates. Next to it sat a strange iron box with a series of metal wands sticking out from the side of it. Tom grabbed one by the tip and pulled. It came free, with the other end connected to a cloth-wrapped cord that ran back into the box.

On closer inspection the tip of the metal stick was scorched. Near the base of the wand was a switch, but when Tom moved it nothing happened.

He let go of the object, and the cord retracted. The stick slithered back to its metal home like a snake sliding into a hole.

Tom walked on, reaching the row of arms and legs that hung on the far wall. They were all fit for a giant, and if they had been put together into the relative shape of a man he would have stood over twenty feet tall.

Tom tapped one of them, and it sang out with a distinct metallic note.

The limb was squat and heavy and lacked a hand, ending instead in an empty hole encircled with a wide metal ring. As the ringing faded he pulled down an arm from its hook. It was made from four rounded plates of dark iron, each with a long, flanged edge pressed together so that they formed a tube. Tom ran a finger along one of the joins, but there were no bolts of any kind holding it together. Instead the seam held thick beads of steel, and it appeared that they had somehow been glued together using the metal itself.

Tom slipped his right arm down into it. The interior was empty, and his arm was easily able to travel all the way up its length until his hand found a crossbar that was placed just below the wrist.

He grabbed the bar and rotated his own hand. As it moved, a series of metal pins fanned up from the end of it. He quickly realized that he could move the bar in multiple directions, sending out a different combination of pins each time, reaching out to send information to whatever weapon or hand this device had been built to interact with.

Pulling his arm out, he hung the limb back onto its hook and examined one of the legs. It was as tall as a man, and the locking ring at the ankle was much thicker, with a second, reinforcing circle of metal above it. Wires poked out of the end. The interior was lined with a thick fabric, and a series of long wires travelled up and down the length of the limb, leaving just enough room for a human limb to fit inside. He stood the leg on the floor and lifted his face mask. He pointed the lens in his head directly at it and pulled back his thumb to let off another spark.

Leaving the leg standing on the floor, Tom walked back across the warehouse, heading toward the giant tube that sat near the blacked-out windows.

It was lumpy and ugly, covered with bands of steel and painted over with a thick layer of pitch that was flaking off in some places, oozing in others. The cylinder was the size of a steam locomotive but stood vertically, rising up toward the ceiling. Rather than the usual patchwork of brazed metal plates, the body had been constructed from a single rolled sheet of metal, formed into a perfect tube and sealed up the center with the same kind of boltless seam that had been used on the limbs.

A large symbol had been drawn across its surface in white. The paint had bubbled and dripped, but it was still legible. Tom ran his hand across the side of it, letting his fingers trace out the image, a perfectly drawn Greek symbol: Ω.

A ladder ran up the side, bolted to metal straps that encircled the tube every few feet. Tom grabbed the rungs and moved quickly and quietly to the top, his legs and arms making only a light tapping sound as they touched each one.

Reaching the top, he pulled himself up through a hole cut into a wooden platform surrounding the broad slab of metal that capped the cylinder. In the center of it was a hinged door with a glass viewing portal and a brass handle sticking straight up into the air.

Tom walked over to it and gave it a tug. The hinged door opened smoothly until it moved past the tipping point and fell against the iron plug with a slam that echoed through the room.

He pulled his thumb, and the light sparked brightly, illuminating the hole.

A second later another light flickered out from an unexplored corner of the room. Tom's attempt to spin around and locate its source was interrupted as he was struck by the bullets rising from the warehouse floor. They exploded as they hit him, throwing him onto the wooden platform. His desperate scramble for balance was lost as his feet snagged against the edges of the hole he had climbed through.

Tom tumbled over the edge, bouncing against the ladder once before he crashed to the floor, and lay there motionless as a cloud of steam rose up through his clothes.

The gas lamps around the walls flared up, melting away the darkness in the warehouse as their fire burned brighter.

A man stood next to the wall, his hand leaning on the gas control handle. He was just a few inches shy of five feet tall, covered in a long white smock made from thick quilted cotton smudged with long gray streaks, with a thick leather apron strapped tightly over the top of it. A pair of large brass goggles hung down from a heavy collar wrapped around his neck

Like the rest of him, his face was lean and pointed, and there was something about his features that gave him the look of a perpetually angry insect, his face framed by curls of hair that spilled out from all sides underneath a dirty bowler hat.

But none of these things was his most noticeable or striking feature. That distinction was reserved for the object that sat where the right arm of a normal man would have been—a small Gatling gun, black smoke still rising up from the brass barrels that had just been fired. The back of the gun was set flush against a squat metal box above his shoulder that was clearly designed to feed ammo into the device.

The contraption was held in place by the collar, along with a brace that traveled down to a metal belt strapped around his waist and upper thighs.

His pulled his left hand free from the gas control and held it out in front of him. The barrel of the gun swiveled around to meet it, and he grabbed the end of the brass handle sticking out of the side of the weapon.

"I gotcha," he said. The voice was surprisingly deep considering his lanky frame, and layered over with a thick Yiddish accent.

Tom lay in a heap, unmoving on the floor. Wisps of dark smoke curled up from where the bullets had struck his body.

The man took a few steps closer to him, the gun held pointed down at him. "All right. What kind of schmuck would be stupid enough to come breaking into *my* lab so late at night?"

He kneeled down and tried to shove the body over, but he could barely move it. "You're heavier than you look, my dead friend." Bracing the top of his gun arm on the floor the man tried again, managing to roll Tom over completely this time.

His face mask had somehow survived the fall intact, although it had come loose from the top of his head and was sliding around on its hinges. The photographic lens had been smashed in the fall.

The gunman jumped back in surprise. "You! I know you! You're the Automaton!" A broad grin split his almost-lipless face. "I shot the Automaton! Oy, I don't believe it!"

"Oh, Eli, so much bad luck, and now a little good!" he said to himself as he nudged the unmoving figure with the gun barrel, "Maybe today is your lucky day!"

In a single movement the Automaton's hand swept out and swept the man's legs out from under him. "Today is not over yet."

There was a loud crack as the gunman's back brace smacked against the floor. A moment later it was followed by an involuntary groan.

Tom rolled up and over, then attempted to leap back onto his feet. Instead he stumbled and almost crashed to the floor. Using his momentum he tried again, managing to rise up to his knees before Eli was able to crank his gun.

The weapon fired wildly, a thick puff of black smoke blowing out of the end of the barrel after each shot. Wherever the bullets collided with various metal objects inside the room, they exploded with a flash. Others smacked into the wall, sending out chips of brick in all directions.

Tom attempted to get out of the way by dropping to the ground, but an exploding bullet caught his right side, sending him spinning across the floor.

Eli scrambled to his feet and pointed the gun at the sprawling Automaton. "There's nitroglycerin in these bullets, machine-man. You try that again and I'll shoot so many of them into you, the only thing you'll be good for is a sieve." He moved a step closer. "I'd rather have you working, but if not, then not."

Tom said nothing. Instead he grabbed his thumb and pulled, sending out a blinding flash from the exposed crystal in his wrist.

Eli turned the crank, blindly spraying bullets in Tom's direction. Two of them smacked into the Automaton's chest armor, tearing apart his shirt, with a third ripping through his right arm and exploding inside of it. Everything below the elbow shattered, leaving only gears and wire dangling from the damaged end.

"I've had enough of your tricks," said Eli. The Automaton leapt straight at him, covering the ten feet between them in an instant.

Eli tried to turn the crank, but it wouldn't move. He looked up to see the fingers of Tom's left hand closed around the barrel. "Get off me, golem!"

"No." Tom turned in a circle, taking Eli with him. The moment he had reached exactly 160 degrees he let go, sending his opponent flying against the black tube. The gunman's hat flew off his head as he sailed through the air, and there was an audible clang as the brass back brace slammed into the iron cylinder.

Tom closed the gap and once again grabbed the barrels of the gun. "What is your full name . . . Eli?"

The man shook his head, as if something had been lodged in it. "Rapid Fire."

"Your real name."

He smiled as he looked up at him. "You can go to hell."

Tom took a step back, lifting up his opponent by his gun arm. He rotated slowly to the left and then shifted quickly to the right. The iron cylinder thrummed like a muffled bell as the man was slammed back into it. Eli let out a choked gasp of pain.

"Tell me your name." There was no reply. Tom repeated the slam, harder this time.

"Okay, okay. Eli Schmidt."

The Automaton was silent for a few seconds, and the iron continued to softly ring behind them. "Now tell me what this machine does . . . Eli Schmidt, or I will throw you into it again."

"Do your worst, golem. If I tell you, then what I get is worse than death."

Tom pinned the gun and Eli up against the cylinder. He held the remains of his right arm straight up in the air and then rotated the jagged stump ninety degrees so it hovered above the man's neck.

Eli winced and looked away. "What do you think you'll learn if you kill me?"

Tom rammed his stump down into the space where the gun-arm attached to the collar. He wedged his arm to the left, and the sound of grinding gears rose out of his chest.

"What the hell are you doing?"

"Disarming you." The sound of gears stopped for a moment, and Tom wiggled his arm deeper in. The grinding began again.

After a few seconds there was an audible "clank," and the gun assembly cleanly separated from Eli's shoulder, leaving only the wiggling pink stump of his arm poking out of the harness. It was a foot long, with a withered hand squirming on the end of it

Tom stepped back, and the gun-arm came with him, the base of it now attached to the remains of Tom's right arm. As Eli watched, his eyes wide, it retracted back into Tom's body, drawing up tightly against his shoulder.

"My mother always said that good people shouldn't steal nice things."

"I never had a mother." There was a series of clicks, and then the barrel jerked around in a series of spasms. "I have modified your weapon," Tom said, "so that I do not need to use my free hand to fire it."

In a smooth motion the barrel rotated 180 degrees to point directly at Eli's face. "Now, tell me what the machine is for . . . Eli Schmidt."

"All right, all right." He slumped down and exhaled, almost as if he were relaxing. "It's the Omega engine."

"And what is the purpose of it?"

"Not so smart as you look, are you? And no offense, but you don't look that smart." He turned his head upward and glanced up to the platform above them. "I mean, you went up there and you still haven't figured it out?"

". . . Fortified steam?"

"Fortified *smoke*! Ten times more powerful than that weak shvitz Darby invented."

The gun on Tom's arm twitched threateningly. "Darby created me."

"So he did, my mechanical friend. And you are a very amazing golem—truly a marvelous machine—but the world doesn't so much need you anymore."

"And why would you say that?"

"I've read all of Darby's books." A little grin appeared on Eli's face. "He wanted you to fill men's hearts with hope. Show them a better future, and maybe they'd follow the angels, he thought. Prove tomorrow can be better than today. But some of us know better."

Eli slowly moved his hand toward a pocket in his leather apron, never taking his eyes off the gun. "Darby was wrong. It isn't hope that makes people change, it's fear. *Fear* is the Omega." Pulling out his hand, he flicked his index finger away from his thumb, launching a tiny object toward Tom. It was a round black lump, no bigger than a currant, and when it hit the ammunition box it stuck fast. "People must fear the darkness before they can see the light."

Eli dove to one side and rolled himself underneath the metal cylinder.

Tom had just begun to spring into action when the black speck exploded, igniting the nitroglycerin in the magazine. The blast blew apart the weapon and tossed the Automaton into the air. He flipped over the steel rolling machine and into the rack of arms and legs on the far wall. Tom disappeared underneath a pile of metal limbs.

Eli jumped onto the ladder and began to climb up to the top of the Omega engine. "I'm glad I got the chance to meet you, golem." He was surprisingly agile despite his handicap. "Lord Eschaton, about you, he would never stop talking. 'His masterpiece,' he said. 'Darby's masterpiece.' I used to think it was the steam that was his greatest achievement, but now that I've met you, I think maybe he was right."

Reaching the top he stepped up onto the steel cap and reached down into the open hatch. "But now? It's time for you to go. You, mechanical marvel you may be, are also, I'm afraid, a false hope." He drew out a metal tube, six inches long and an inch across. It gleamed dull and gray in the gaslight. "But first, we need one more thing." He lifted a flap on his apron, slid the tube down into a slim leather pocket, and buttoned the cover in place with a practiced hand. He grabbed the brass handle and shoved it forward, bracing his feet in order to shut the door on top of the cylinder.

Then he clambered quickly down the ladder, almost bouncing as he landed on the floor.

"If I thought you had a soul, golem, I'd tell you to say hello to Darby in the afterlife for me." Eli grabbed a valve wheel sticking out near the bottom of the cylinder. He gave it a spin, then pulled a flat handle next to it and ran.

A hiss rose from the cylinder and became a squeal, followed by something that almost sounded like a sigh. A black cloud billowed out from the bottom of the Omega engine. At first it rose upward, the smoke piling up on itself as if it were something solid. The mass would have been indistinguishable from black mud except for a smoky haze around its edges. Bright flickers of light began moving around inside the darkness—thin white veins of lighting shooting up from the mountain of smoke.

After it climbed up for a few feet, the cloud spilled forward, toppling over itself and spreading out across the floor.

Tom rose up from underneath the tangle of lifeless metal limbs. The explosion had completely destroyed the Gatling gun, along with most of his jacket and shirt, and had scorched and pitted the brass chest plates underneath. His head was twisted around at an odd angle, and some of the struts holding it in place had been torn away, although it was still mostly connected to his neck.

The Automaton grabbed one of the metal arms from the pile that surrounded him and pushed it up against the ragged hole in his shoulder. The sound of grinding gears began again, this time with a rhythmic pinging that emanated from inside the empty limb, its pitch rising higher every time, like a piano string being wound tighter and tighter.

Eli jerked to a stop in front of the door. His hand moved toward the lock, only to find a hole in the door where it been broken off. For a moment he simply stood there, wide-eyed, staring down at the broken metal on the floor. His left hand clawed at the wood, and he slipped his fingers into the hole where the lock had been. Putting his foot up against the frame, he tugged until his hand slipped free. The door hadn't budged. It was as solid as a wall. "No, no, no!" The pool of black smoke from the cylinder was moving out in all directions with hazy black tendrils reaching out in front of it, followed by the ever-increasing mass of the central cloud as it hissed out of the Omega tank.

Tom pushed away the metal limbs that surrounded him, stood up, and walked toward the middle of the room. His new arm, squat and oversized, hung rigidly at his side, unmoving as he walked. The pinging had stopped, although the grinding continued as he walked, and his head slowly moved back into place.

Reaching the edge of the smoke, he held out his left hand. Tiny arcs of white lightning struck at his glove as one of the tentacles moved closer. There was a sizzling hiss when it came into contact with the leather. Tom pulled his hand back quickly, but some of the oily gas still clung to the tip of his finger. The leather blistered and hissed as the smoke ate into it, revealing his metal hand underneath.

Tom shuffled backward before it could reach his shoes.

Eli was not so lucky. "Not like this. Not like this." He was still tugging helplessly at the door, franticly attempting to escape, when the electric arcs jumped at him. "Not like this!" When the first black tentacle touched him he screamed and tried to run, but there was nowhere to go. His movements served only to disturb the smoke further, sending new tendrils shooting up toward his face. The shouting continued for a few seconds as he tried to beat the smoke back. White lightning danced across his skin.

After a few seconds of this his knees buckled, and he dropped into the smoke. Everything was quiet.

His back up against the wall, Tom stretched his new arm out in front of him. It responded smartly, as if it had always been a part of him, although it was ridiculously oversized for his frame and lacked a hand. The limb's weight made Tom wobble slightly as it moved.

He rammed the arm straight out and into the brick wall that stood in the back of the building. The old mortar crumbled easily, and after he had slammed the iron into it a few more times, he managed to tear open a small hole.

The smoke reached his feet and began to rise up as it ate away his shoes. Tom turned around and shoved his new arm through the hole. It took three tries before he was able to move enough of the bricks out of his way that he could pull himself through.

The neighboring space was a large factory floor with rows of mechanical looms spread out across it. Skeins of threads came down from the huge spools attached to each one.

Tom turned toward the hole, facing back into the other warehouse. The smoke had now covered the entire floor and was rising upward. A sharp sound, like cracking ice, came from the far wall as the windows shattered in their frames, the pitch holding the splintered glass in place.

The front door disintegrated under the pressure, the wood exploding from the hinges, and then all the gas lamps blew out at once.

The interior of the building creaked as the load-bearing beams were eaten away; then everything started to rumble.

Tom turned and ran as the building collapsed behind him and sent a combination of smoke, dust, and debris shooting out through the hole he had been looking through a moment before.

After a few seconds the entire warehouse collapsed in on itself, pulling down the neighboring structure as it went.

Chapter 16

A Strange Angel

Dennis Darby's office was large and sternly appointed, with only a single lamp providing illumination on the massive oaken desk that sat near the center of the room.

Wickham sat hunched over the wood, sitting on the edge of a large leather chair, his mask hanging loosely around his neck. His eyes were red rimmed and tired. Sitting to his left was a stack of papers almost an inch tall. The envelope next to them was labeled "The Last Will and Testament of Sir Dennis Darby," and a ribbon sat in a pile on the edge of the desk.

To Darby's credit it had taken the Sleuth the better part of an hour to find the secret cabinet where the documents had been hidden in the study wall, and half again that long to figure out how to get it to open.

To his right was a battered leather notebook, and Wickham was deftly taking notes using a self-inking pen that Darby had designed for him. The headline on the page in front of him read "Section 106." The metal nib made quiet scratching noises as his hand traveled across the paper. "Damn you, old man," he muttered as he wrote. "How could you have been so clever and still be so naïve? What did you think Stanton was going to do? She's his daughter, after all."

Finishing his notes with a flourish he slammed the cover of his notebook closed and leaned back in the chair. The old hinges and springs squealed.

The last few weeks had been some of the hardest of his life. The feelings of sorrow at the death of Darby, the funeral, his disappointment at the behavior of his fellow Paragons, and the physical pain from his battle in the alleyways—they had all been traumatic events. But death, pain, and betrayal were all things that he had experienced many times in his life, and they would pass in time.

But there was a nagging feeling that had been bothering him since the confrontation with Stanton, and after Anubis had confirmed the existence of a traitor it had only continued to grow. He couldn't put a word to it at first, yet it was familiar. And this morning, just as he placed his empty teacup back on the saucer and a bolt of pain shot up his arm, the word for it hit him like a bolt of lightning; he was feeling *old*.

At sixty-three years of age he had long been subject to the limitations and pains that came with maturity. But frequent trips to the Orient and India during his youth to study with a variety of different martial artists had endowed him with some techniques that had managed to stave off many of the most crippling effects that he'd seen plague people of similar years. They also did quite a good job of enhancing your experience in the boudoir, if you were partial to partaking of that sort of thing, which he had been from time to time.

But the truth of it was that Darby's death had finally given him cause to relinquish his hopes. Not all hope, certainly, but the dream that he would somehow leave behind a world that was fundamentally better than the one that he had been born into. And a great sadness had struck him when it became clear that it was now far too late in life for him to do anything about it. "So much wisdom and no time left to use it," he whispered out loud to no one. The world as it is now would be the way that it would stay for the rest of his time on the planet.

When Darby had created the Paragons they had believed they could make a difference, and perhaps they had. Or perhaps it would have all turned out the same except for some costumed fools, their steam-powered toys, and the insane villains they battled against.

"Still," he said with a laugh, "it's been a jolly good run."

He slid the papers back into the envelope and walked them over to the cabinet in the wall. So far no one else had thought to search for any notes hidden outside of the laboratory besides Wickham, and the pages would certainly remain secret and safe in the office for one more night.

Tomorrow he would show them to Stanton, and things would change again. And Alexander would begin to understand that Darby wasn't quite the madman that he had appeared to be in the will.

But once he knew the truth behind Darby's last wishes, it would only make the chance of him ever seating the Automaton as their leader even less likely than it was before. And things would be different, but not better.

Stanton had always been a clever man, with a quick, insightful mind and a passion for justice. But he wasn't without his flaws, the most glaring of which was his habit of using every bit of information he received as a tool to manipulate people into reaching the conclusion that would benefit him the most. As a younger man the Industrialist had been careful to make sure that the results had a positive benefit for everyone. But the death of his wife had changed him, and Wickham wasn't sure that Alexander cared much about anyone but himself anymore, with the single exception of Sarah.

He pulled open the cabinet door and looked into the rows of pigeonholes and the envelopes they contained. He wondered what other secrets were hidden in here. For the next few hours, until Tom returned from his mission, he'd have nothing better to do than to find out.

Wickham's planning was interrupted by a loud banging at the front door.

Shoving the doors closed, he held them in place until a mechanical mechanism inside snapped shut. A second later a panel slid across the wall, covering the doors and rendering the cabinet behind it invisible.

He picked up the chimney lamp from the desk and walked out into the main foyer. Whoever it was clearly had a key to the gates, or had somehow managed to avoid them entirely.

The banging came again, louder this time. "All right, all right," he said loudly, hoping that he could avoid waking the boy, no matter who it turned out to be. Nathaniel had been less than helpful over the last few days, and the last thing the Sleuth needed now was more of the young man's "youthful bravado" interfering with his investigations. So far Nathaniel had been too righteous to be dangerous, but it was obvious the boy would go running to Stanton the moment he discovered anything he thought could garner him favor.

Wickham peered out the window and was surprised to see a face peering up at him from chest height. "Bill," he said as he opened the door. "What are you doing here at this time of night?"

The large man pushed forward on his control. The chair bounced as it rolled across the lintel. "Peter. I'm glad you're still here. We need to talk."

"*Still* here? How did you know I was here in the first place?"

"Sarah stopped by the Hall to tell her father to come home, and she told us what had happened with Nathaniel." His eyes scanned the room. "Is the machine around?"

"I've sent him on an errand."

"He's allowed out?"

He had to be more careful. He was already tired, and the last thing he needed was to get caught in a sloppy mistake. "I sent him out."

"Of course." Hughes nodded. "That's good. This is partially about Tom."

Wickham realized the opportunity for further investigation of Sir Dennis's files was draining away. But the idea that there was a sudden need for him and the Iron-Clad to have a conversation was enticing enough to diminish his regret. "Why don't we go to the parlor?" he said, pointing the way.

"Good idea," Hughes replied. "And Nathaniel is still passed out upstairs, I assume."

"I believe so. You can check on him first if you'd like"

"I won't bother," he replied, missing Wickham's sarcasm as usual. "He drinks too much—especially for someone his age. Nothing good is going to come of it."

"I suppose not. But sometimes a man can discover temperance as he matures."

"Not the rich ones," Hughes said, followed by a guttural harrumph. "They just get better at covering it up."

"Here we go," said Wickham. He opened the parlor door for Hughes and waited for him to roll through.

"Thanks, Peter, but you don't have to baby me. I can still get around when I have to." The chair wheeled him into the room.

"I can see that," Wickham said as he grabbed the handles and pulled the doors firmly closed behind him. "Now how can I help you?"

Hughes spun the chair around to face the old man. "I'm worried."

"Understandable, as there seems to be a great deal to be worried about these days. But what fear in particular is it that has you coming here to visit me?"

"I believe that one of the Paragons is a traitor."

Wickham did his best not to let his surprise show on his face. "Really, Bill . . . Well, that *is* something to be worried about. . . ." He had no way of knowing how good a job he'd done.

"Darby wasn't impaled by accident. Someone knew about the secret of fortified steam."

"Obviously, since they stole the Alpha Element from around his neck before they killed him."

"A secret that even most of the Paragons are unaware of. Or at least we assumed they were unaware of. . . ."

"What are you suggesting?" Wickham lowered himself onto the couch and crossed his legs "That Nathaniel is . . . ?"

"Possibly. Although I think that Grüsser is a far more likely candidate—especially given his past."

"And you seem completely convinced of *my* innocence."

He drummed his fingers on the arm of his chair. "No, Peter, not entirely, but there's no one else I can turn to right now who wouldn't try to solve the problem using his fists first, instead of his brain."

"Well thank—"

"And besides, you and the Professor were . . . close. I figure you had nothing to gain by selling the old man out."

Wickham was already getting his fill of Hughes's gruff manner. Still, if the man was innocent he could be useful as an ally. "I appreciate that. Especially coming from someone who threatened to smack me in the mouth a few days ago."

"Yeah, well, I'm sorry about that."

The Sleuth watched as the large man's right hand played a nervous game with the chair's control knob, twisting it around just enough to avoid activating the seat's mechanisms.

"Things have been difficult for me lately," Bill continued. "I'm having a hard time controlling my temper."

"Not the best character trait for a man who wears a two-ton suit with cannons attached."

Hughes's hand jerked into a fist and then relaxed. "I get your point."

Wickham stood up, figuring that he might as well use his height to his advantage. "No, sir, I rather think you don't." He walked around the chair as he spoke. "Even if I believed that one of the Paragons was a traitor, I'd need to know that I could trust *you* before I was willing to join you on your crusade."

Hughes looked hurt. "Trust *me*? I'm one of the damn founding members, not some foreign freak who joined up once the going got good."

The Sleuth stopped behind him, forcing the other man to crane his neck around to see him. "Are you referring to me or Grüsser?"

He snorted out a laugh. "Take your pick."

"And yet you came to me with your secrets."

Bill spun the chair to face the Sleuth. "I guess everyone makes mistakes."

"Do they?" Wickham stopped and stared into the large man's face. There was a fire smoldering behind Bill Hughes's gray eyes that never seemed to completely go out, and it was burning very brightly at the moment. "And if I were to decide that we should work together on this, would you answer one question for me?"

"What's that?"

"I want to know the exact moment you decided to betray the Paragons."

"Don't be an idiot Wickham. I'm not—"

"When you've been uncovering mysteries as long as I have you'll discover that motive is the most important of clues." He needed to be careful. Hughes was an invalid, but hardly incapacitated—at least not yet. "The traitor had to be either you or Grüsser. But the Prussian wouldn't, I think, be so comfortable with murdering Darby to reach his ends."

"You've gone soft in the head."

"Given the state of the rest of me, perhaps that was only a matter of time. But I'm sound of mind enough to know for a fact that you asked Darby to make you a new suit of armor—one that would allow you to continue to fight, even in your diminished state." He dropped his tone down and spoke in a loud whisper, "And Sir Dennis refused."

"Darby said that my condition made any kind of new armor unsafe." He could see Hughes's anger starting to ignite. "He said that I no longer had the skills that it would take to control something so powerful safely."

The Sleuth was playing with fire now, and he'd need to be careful.

"So he built me this goddamned *chair*!" Bill flicked the control knob forward, thrusting the seat toward Wickham.

Smoothly stepping out of the way, the Sleuth continued. "And you went and found someone else. Someone who would give you what you wanted."

"Shut up, Wickham. You don't know what you're talking about!" The chair spun to the left. Hughes's face was a mask of anger surrounded by a mane of red and white hair.

"Don't I? I'm sure whoever it was, they promised you a great deal of power in return for giving them the Automaton's new body. And of course, the information needed to kill Darby."

"Stop talking before you make me do something that we're both not gonna like."

Wickham shifted his tone. "It wasn't your fault, Bill. I know you didn't want him to *die*." Hughes was trembling. There were tears in his eyes.

Without warning he exploded out of the chair, closing the distance between them before Wickham could react. There was something in Hughes's hand, and he held it out in front of him as he grabbed the old man.

Wickham felt as if he'd been punched, but it was worse than that.

"You're wrong about that, Peter. I wanted Darby dead. If Lord Eschaton hadn't sent the Bomb Lance to do it, it would have been me."

Wickham's vision was swimming, and when Hughes let go of him, he realized that he had no strength left. He tumbled to the ground, unable to feel his legs.

Hughes was still talking, tears rolling down his cheeks as he admitted to terrible things, but Peter Wickham could no longer make out the words.

The world was vanishing into a blast of pure white light. A figure emerged from the brightness, and he expected it would be Darby. Instead it was Tom who appeared before him, surrounded by a halo, his hand outstretched to lead him to the other side.

"Ironic," he said to the figure. "It's all up to you now, you know."

Tom said nothing, his face as impassive and immobile as always. Peter let out a little chuckle as he took his metal hand and rose up into the sky.

Chapter 17

His Last Mystery

Whether Nathaniel liked it or not—and the way things seemed to be headed, he most assuredly didn't—he was starting to wake up. And as he drifted toward wakefulness there were new and unpleasant sensations, each one of them overwhelming the one that came before.

First was a rhythmic throbbing pain in his head, as if someone were squeezing it from the inside.

Then came a raging thirst. It was a feeling so strong it was like the opposite of drowning, a desperate need for water made even more palpable by the actual, physical dryness of his throat and tongue. He tried to swallow, but couldn't.

Next was the chill. He had slept the entire night above the blankets in his bed, while the house had cooled down considerably. Not below freezing, but cold enough that his exposed skin was prickling and complaining, with a most noticeable ache rising up from his feet. And his left foot, he could now tell, was still most decidedly damp, making it uncomfortable in two unique ways.

The awareness of his state caused a shiver to spasm up and down his body, with his teeth chattering together every time it rolled past them.

It was a wonder that he wasn't suffering from hypothermia. Or perhaps he was, and it simply *felt* perilously close to a disastrous hangover.

He lay still for a few more moments, trying to wish himself out of consciousness and back into the gloriously unfeeling state of nonexistence that he had inhabited so blissfully just a minute before.

Then a new feeling appeared—one so strong that it drowned out all the others. It was a rushing sensation that rose up from his stomach like a locomotive.

Nathaniel's eyes popped open and he rolled over, his hands clawing desperately for the rubbish tin. It was a cloudy day, but still bright enough in the room that he could make out the form of the can in the gloom and pull it to his side an instant before the contents of his stomach ejected themselves into it.

When the first round of sickness subsided he leaned back and moaned softly to himself. An image popped into his head, a vague memory of forcefully challenging one of his friends to a raw quail-egg eating contest at the club the night before. He couldn't remember where the small, speckled eggs had come from exactly, or even who had won the contest, but clearly he was the loser now. Nathaniel heaved again.

Breathing heavily, he instinctually reached down to his trouser pockets for a handkerchief, but discovered that although he was still wearing his starched shirt, he definitely had no pants on.

He shivered again, which led to another series of involuntary heaving. The wretched excess of the previous evening passed before his eyes as it headed into the tin.

After the nausea passed away again, the front of his face felt as if it had been lit on fire from the inside, and everything was making the headache worse. "It is not," he thought to himself, "a good day to be me."

"Tomba!" he cried out. The word came out horribly slurred. His sinuses were stuffed with things he didn't want to begin to imagine. "Tomba!" he said again, trying to make that one word as clear as he could. Nathaniel wanted towels and water, but he certainly did not want to move. Certainly he could yell loudly enough to make the machine aware of his suffering.

And after the next round of sickness was done, he felt slightly better. The actual act of being sick seemed to take some of the headache with it, or perhaps he'd simply reached his maximum misery and the only possible next step was to feel better.

He yelled out Tom's name a few more times. He unbuttoned his shirt, then pulled off his undershirt and blew his nose into it. He gasped and moaned again as things not meant to pass through his nose did.

He waited for another minute to see if he would suffer any more illness. When it seemed clear that his stomach had ceased its rebellions, he rolled away from the tin.

Settling back onto the bed, Nathaniel turned his head and stared at the wallpaper to his left. Between the long lines of velvet were thousands of colorful curlicues and other flourishes. They started to swim in front of him, and just as the fleur-de-lis pattern transformed into a marching army, he slammed his eyes shut before they could complete their assault on his constitution.

With the world shut out, the forgotten events of the previous evening played out in his mind's eye. He saw flashes of the dinner party at the club in honor of his friend Alfred, who was *finally* taking that trip to Europe he had been going on about for so long. The memory was followed by a montage of what appeared to be a series of engravings, each one toppling over to reveal the next behind it. They all showed him with another drink in his hand, finally giving way to the quail eggs being broken over his mouth, his head tipped back to receive each one.

After that was the barely conscious trip home in the hansom cab, the long crawl up the stairs as he tried to disrobe with a bottle of bourbon in his hand. Then yet another argument with the damnable machine, and finally, "Sarah . . ."

He let out a sigh. Perhaps the words they'd exchanged last night were irrevocable, perhaps not. Maybe this would convince whatever part of him it was that made him such a fool for her that it was time to put her behind him. There were certainly eligible women who were actually interested in a wealthy young man of good breeding. "And none of you will ever be Sarah," he said out loud. Followed by, "No! No, no, no."

Opening his eyes, Nathaniel pulled himself upright, then swung both feet onto the floor. After a few seconds, once he felt he had managed to gain his equilibrium, he stood up.

As he rose from the bed it dawned on him that one foot was still covered by a boot while the other was not. The traitorous footwear threw him off balance, and he tumbled forward to his hands and knees, landing perilously close to the unspeakable steaming bin nearby.

Kneeling there like a dog, various aches and pains dancing through his body, an image rose up in his head of a packet of headache powder. He could see it lying there, his salvation waiting for him in the bathroom closet.

This was a very motivating vision, even more so as he had managed to do *something* painful to the palm of his right hand when he fell that the medicine might also help with. He rolled over, came up to a sitting position, and grabbed his booted foot.

The boot was attempting to resist his desire to get it off of him, and when it finally did come free, it did so all at once. Nathaniel rolled backward, and there was a "thunk" as the dreaded tin tipped over, leaking its horribleness out onto the floor.

He moved faster than he would have thought possible only a few seconds before, successfully managing to rise up and head away from the oozing mess. He grabbed the blanket, stripping it off the bed and wrapping it around his shoulders as he stepped out into the hallway.

He cried out for Tom a few more times as he wandered down the upstairs hall toward the water closet, but if the machine was in the house then it either couldn't hear him or it was simply being obstinate about doing what it was supposed to, like a stuck lever on an old boiler.

Reaching the bathroom, he stepped onto the tile floor. His already-frozen feet complained to him even more bitterly as he padded across the cold white ceramic to the medicine cabinet. By the time he reached it and pulled it open he was no longer sure if he could feel his toes. He dug through the shelves, shoving aside various tonics, tinctures, and grooming products until he pulled out a packet of Dr. Hansen's headache powder and a clean glass.

He traveled back to the sink and filled his cup. Opening the paper parcel he poured in the contents and stirred it for a moment with his finger to encourage its dissolving before knocking it all back into his throat in a single shot, leaving a white trail of undissolved medicine inside the glass.

As he bent down to fill the cup for a second drink he caught his reflection in the mirror in front of him. "Good Lord, Nathaniel, you look like hell," he said to himself, and smiled.

His eyes were red rimmed and puffy, and the deep red of the blanket thrown around his shoulders only managed to heighten how pasty and white his skin appeared to be. His dark brown hair, usually well coiffed, was sticking out at all angles.

He grabbed a brush and ran it through the tangled bush a few times, but his hair seemed to be actively resisting any attempts to get it under control.

Unscrewing the taps again he splashed ice-cold water on his face. It stung, but at least it managed to bring some color into his cheeks.

As he scraped his teeth clean with a rag Nathaniel tried to decide what he would do next. "A bath, definitely a bath," he said to his reflection.

With Tom missing and none of the regular house staff due to be in until later in the day, Nathaniel would need to go downstairs and light the water heater himself if he fancied actual hot water to bathe in.

He didn't relish the idea of journeying all the way down to the kitchen on a cold morning, but if he could actually survive down there he might well do with something to eat. "Something simple," he said to his stomach's rumbling reproach. "And a drink," he mumbled to himself. "A hair of the dog to get me back on my feet."

Taking a deep breath to fortify himself for the journey ahead, he plodded into the hallway and navigated the main staircase in a series of slow, woozy steps.

Taking a moment to steady himself at the bottom, he took a left turn across the marble floor of the entryway into the main hallway, gaining momentum as he went.

It was still mostly dark down on the main floor. The only daylight in the hallway was what came through the glass of the French parlor doors. When he reached them he glanced over to his right, took a look into the room, and stopped.

It was Tom. He was bent over above . . . *something*.

He narrowed his eyes. He knew what it was, but couldn't quite be sure. . . . Then it suddenly came into shocking focus—a body, prone on the floor. And the Automaton's hands were searching through the unconscious (*dead?*) man's coat.

What remained of Tom's clothes were completely ripped and burned. His pants were shredded, and his jacket hung on him in tatters. Almost all the exposed metal on his body was blackened and scorched.

There was the remnants of a leather glove over his left hand, but the right limb had been replaced entirely with some sort of misshapen, metal bludgeon.

Whether it was the powder finally starting to work, or the terror of seeing the metal man in this bestial state, the pain in his head seemed to vanish completely.

As his eyes adjusted to the light, even more details began to emerge. Blood was pooled underneath the figure on floor, and the dead man had a mask dangling around his neck and a long leather jacket. It was Wickham. "The Sleuth," Nathaniel gasped. The man was clearly dead.

The Automaton's head swiveled up to face Nathaniel. His face was mostly gone, and whatever had burned the rest of him had also done its work on the porcelain, leaving none of its features visible except for a single, badly scorched eye.

Nathaniel jumped back. "No!" he yelled without thinking. Clearly having heard him, the Automaton rose up smoothly and turned toward him. Despite what appeared to be grave damage, any traces of the limp that he had had over the last few weeks were completely gone, and he took a long step toward the doors. Tom was trying to say something to him, but it was muffled by the glass and the pounding roar that had filled Nathaniel's ears.

Looking to slow down the Automaton, he grabbed the tall bookcase standing next to the parlor doors. It wobbled as if it was ready to come toppling over, as so many of the shelves in the mansion seemed to be constantly threatening to do, but actually getting it to fall was taking more effort than he had imagined it would.

He clearly heard Tom call out his name. Realizing that the machine would be on him in an instant filled Nathaniel with a surge of energy, and the shelf went over, spilling Sir Dennis's precious books down onto the floor in a satisfying cascade.

He just hoped it would at least slow down the mechanical monster long enough to give him a chance to reach the study.

Nathaniel was sprinting now. When he reached the end of the hallway he turned right and ran into the rear study. It was a small writing room, no more than twelve feet in either direction, with a massive desk up against the window and built-in shelves on the other three walls. They were filled with the knickknacks and curios that Sir Dennis had gathered together from his adventures around the world, including a number of weapons taken from villains that the Paragons had defeated. None of them, unfortunately, were still in working order. Darby had always taken great pleasure, as he had described it, in "taking the tools of villainy and stripping them of their power."

"Always too damn clever," Nathaniel muttered to himself as he slid his index finger under the second shelf from the top. He drew it across the wood until he felt the familiar bump of the hidden switch. When he pressed it, a section of the shelving swung open in response, revealing a secret passage.

Nathaniel pulled the wall shut behind him, throwing a bolt into place on the inside. It might give him a moment's respite, but the Automaton knew where the entrance was, and was certainly strong enough to force it open. There wasn't a place in the entire Darby mansion that the damn machine couldn't reach.

As he entered the workshop at the end of the short corridor, the gas lamps ignited and brightened automatically, responding to the pressure plate hidden in the floor. The room was a pleasant little brick chamber thirty feet square, stuffed with workbenches and machinery.

The room was built underneath a false chimney, and Nathaniel could see the shafts of morning light coming down through it.

He pulled a large metal switch on the wall. There was a hiss and a thunk, followed by a hum, as hidden machinery activated beneath his feet and two metal plates on the floor began to swing apart, revealing a hole underneath them.

This room had been built by Sir Dennis to be the secret lair of the Turbine. "Your personal Aereodrome," was how Darby had described it when he first showed it to him. But Nathaniel hadn't been inside it for more than six months, having moved into the Hall of Paragons the same day that he had become a member.

When the plates were perfectly vertical the humming stopped for a moment, then began again as they sank straight down into the ground. When the frame began to rise up from the storage silo, Nathaniel fully expected to see the original Turbine suit resting on it—the one that Darby had given to him when he was sixteen years old.

Although it seemed crude compared to what he wore now, the first Turbine costume had still been an amazing piece of technology. With it a man could leap over incredible distances, taking off like a rocket and then floating safely back to earth like a feather.

It wasn't truly flying, but with it he had learned to take to the air, and he had surprised his fair share of villains.

But what was hanging on the frame wasn't his original prototype at all. It was something entirely new—the new Turbine outfit that Darby had been promising for so long. Despite his fear, and the hangover, a smile lit up his face. "Darby, you old bastard, you finished it. You actually finished it!"

Up until now the main flying engine had been a bulky box with the apparatus encased inside of it. That had been replaced by four small engines, each attached directly to a large wedge-shaped wing. Metal tubes coming out of the top of each engine joined together and plugged into the center of the wing. Curved steel pods covered in ornate etchings of birds in flight were attached to the thighs. Clearly they were the main source of the fortified steam used by the thrusters.

The harness was made of silk rope, webbing, and wire, with control stirrups at each extremity. A series of switches and dials sat on a belt around the waist.

Nathaniel's wonder at seeing his new costume was shattered by a heavy pounding from the hallway behind him. "Master . . . Winthorp, I know you're in there."

Nathaniel searched around desperately. "Tom, I need you to leave me alone right now." He had come here with the intention of finding his old suit and using it to escape through the skylight hatch. But as beautiful as this new outfit was, without Darby here to explain how it actually worked, Nathaniel was trapped.

Tom's singsong tones were closer now. "I can't do that until we've had a chance to talk. I think you've misunderstood the situation."

Nathaniel balled his hands into fists and pounded them softly against his still-aching head. He needed a plan. "I'm happy to talk with you later, Tom, but for right now I'd feel safer if you stayed on the other side of that door."

"I didn't kill . . . Mr. Wickham . . . Nathaniel."

"Of course you didn't, Tom." As he circled the suit he saw that there was a holster on the right side of the harness at around chest height, with what appeared to be a gun sitting inside of it. It was designed to be drawn with the left hand.

Nathaniel pulled it out and took a closer look. A thick rubber tube came out of the side of it and plugged directly into one of the fortified steam containers. It looked like a standard Colt six-shooter, but the firing cylinder had been replaced with a large bronze dial. He pushed against it with his thumb and it clicked as it rotated, clearly defining different levels of . . . something. Considering Darby's personality, the low level was probably used for heating tea while the next one would be useful if you were looking to demolish a mountaintop—and there were six levels on the dial

He stuck the weapon back into its holster.

Tom's voice rang out again. "Sir, the . . . Paragons are in great danger. I believe that one of them is a traitor, and that he was responsible for the murder of . . . the Sleuth."

"That's important information, Tom." His words sounded patronizing as he spoke them, but his stepfather had cautioned him that lies always sounded more obvious to the liar. "And we must tell them as soon as possible."

Nathaniel needed to call for help, and he needed to do it quickly. Pressing a button above the switch that controlled the frame elevator caused a long metal rod to drop out from a slot in the brick wall of the chimney. When it was fully extended it snapped into place at the back of the frame, and the skylight at the top of the chimney popped open.

Icy snowflakes glinted in the morning sunlight as the wind blew them down from the roof. A groggy thought in the back of Nathaniel's head pointed out to him that at some point in the last few minutes the morning clouds had cleared completely, revealing a sunny blue sky.

"I'm going to come in now, sir," Tom said, followed by a crash of splintering wood.

Finding a familiar-looking button on the belt, Nathaniel pressed it. A hatch popped open on the top of the wing, followed by a hiss as the propellant ignited, and a flare shot straight up into the air, missing the lip of the skylight by less than an inch.

When he brought his arms down he saw Tom standing in front of him. "Please, sir. I need to talk with you, alone."

The Automaton's burnt and broken appearance was even more horrific in the daylight. Something had melted in whatever conflagration it was that had consumed his clothes. The colored material had burned as it dripped down over his metal parts, and it looked almost like charred meat on his metal bones. Nathaniel could see the cracked lens of Tom's camera peeking from behind the broken mask of Tom's face.

The flare ignited above them in the cloudy morning sky. Its phosphor glow would send out a clear message, as long as there was still someone in the Hall to see it.

"I wish you hadn't done that," Tom said.

Nathaniel backed away from him until he felt himself pressing up against a worktable. "You don't want to hurt me as well, do you?"

"As I told you before . . . Mr. Wickham was deceased when I found him."

Nathaniel's temper managed to overcome his fear. "I'm not a fool, Tom. I was in the house all night. I would have heard it if someone had come in and shot a man."

"No. I don't believe you would have. Mr. Wickham was stabbed to death." Tom took another step toward him, but Nathaniel had nowhere to go. "You were also heavily . . . inebriated, and you never reactivated the . . . alarms after you returned. Did you even know that . . . Mr. Wickham had reentered the house?"

"No . . . I . . ." Nathaniel suddenly felt himself desperately wanting the drink that he had promised himself when he first headed downstairs. "I saw you trying to take something out of his pocket."

"I wish to find his . . . notebook. I am hoping that it contains some information I can use to determine the identity of the person who is betraying . . . the Paragons."

"Betrayal?" He spat out a laugh. "The only traitor is you, Tom. If you weren't a machine I'd call you a madman and a murderer as well."

Standing behind the new Turbine outfit, Nathaniel caught a glint of something that he recognized along the belt-line of the suit. He moved toward it, and Tom closed the gap.

"You are incorrect, sir. . . . Darby's, and now . . . Mr. Wickham's deaths were, I believe, engineered by the same party."

"That makes perfect sense." He reached out and flicked the switch at the waist, and the machine let out a hiss, then a hum. Some of the rubber tubing jumped to life, stiffened by whatever pressures were building up inside. "I'm guessing that person would be you." He hoped it would do what he expected.

The Automaton lifted up his hand. "I won't hurt you, sir, but I will . . . restrain you if you do not willingly cease your actions." Tom leaned toward the harness, clearly intent on turning off the suit.

Nathaniel stepped around to the other side and pulled the gun out of its holster. Without hesitation he aimed and pulled the trigger.

It simply clicked, and for an instant it seemed as if the weapon wasn't going to fire at all. There was just a rising whine coming from the suit's engines, and a loud "clack" as all four turbines on the wing shifted to the same direction simultaneously.

The report that followed was short and sharp, somewhere between a roar and a loud cough. Nathaniel found himself flying backward in a whirlwind of tools and papers that were exploding out in every direction. As he traveled through the air he wondered what setting this was, and then he landed hard against the edge of the workbench and returned to the state of oblivion he had longed for when he first woke up.

Chapter 18

The Fall of Darby House

Tom lay sprawled faceup on the snow-covered lawn of the Darby house. The already-tattered remains of his clothes had been completely torn away by the blast, exposing the scorched and battered metal of his body. His arms and legs were pointing off in different directions, and any stranger appearing on the scene would have been hard-pressed not to imagine that Tom was a giant puppet whose strings had been cut. The only hint that he was anything more than a discarded marionette was a thick jet of steam that was hissing out the right side of his chest into the winter air. Scattered around him were broken bricks and chunks of wood.

After a series of loud clicks, a whirring sound rose up from inside of him. His arms and legs began to move, spinning and turning in decidedly inhuman ways until all his limbs had returned straight to his sides.

A moment later he sat up. Water dripped down his back and landed in the puddle that had formed from the warmth of his metal body melting the snow underneath him.

He bent his right leg, but the left limb remained straight and unmoving, a loud series of clunks an obvious protest against his attempts to bend it at the knee. Tom tried once more, and the limb gave out a plunk, then a "plink" as a cog ejected from his knee and flew through air.

The Automaton lay back down. His only visible movement was a series of small twitches in his limbs, although all manner of noises rose up from inside of him, and a two-foot-long loop of stiff wire began to uncoil from his neck, looping out three feet of cable before it drew itself back into his body.

Tom's second try at standing was more successful, and he managed to rise up onto his feet in a single smooth motion. He reached down and tore away the trouser cuffs that had settled around his ankles, but ignored the leather belt hanging from the plates around his waist.

He walked back toward the house, pausing for a moment to examine the gaping hole he had created when the weapon flung him through the side of the house. Then he climbed back through it into the devastated workshop and walked over to Nathaniel's unconscious body. The young man had been smashed into one of benches, gaining a gash on the back of his head from the journey. "I'm sorry you didn't believe me, sir."

Tom lifted the young man up into his arms in what appeared to be a tender embrace. Nathaniel's head rolled back and forth as the Automaton walked toward the corridor. "I'll need to confine you until I can prove my innocence to you."

As he passed the Turbine suit, still hanging on its stand, he stopped in front of the pneumatic weapon. It lay on the floor, still attached by its tube.

Gently placing Nathaniel back down onto the ground he picked up the gun. Tucking the weapon into his belt, he tugged on the other end of the tubing until it snapped free. He shoved the broken end of the cloth-covered rubber into the empty hole at end of his right arm. After he had fed a few feet into himself, something grabbed it and reeled it up.

When it grew taut the tubing pulled the gun free of his belt, dragging it up until it was hanging flush against his wrist. Bent metal rods extended themselves around the weapon like skinny fingers. Each one of them had a crook on the end, and when they retracted they looped around the weapon, pulling the gun firmly into place.

Tom lifted up his new limb and pointed it back at the hole in the wall. The metal rod around the trigger twitched, and the gun fired. It was a far less devastating shot than the one that had been directed at him, but it still managed to further dislodge some of the loose bricks in the wall and send them tumbling out across the lawn.

Clearly satisfied with his jerry-built device, he reached down and took Nathaniel back into his arms. As he did so, a voice boomed out at him from the yard. "Attention, Automaton!"

It was being loudly amplified in some crude manner. The words were loud but broken and distorted by whatever process was being used to increase their volume. Even so, they were still clear enough to be comprehensible. "Attention, Automaton! Put down the boy, turn around, and walk toward me!"

Tom rotated his torso as the Iron-Clad rolled into view. It was a tower of metal, and although it was often referred to as "the modern colossus," the actual armor was squat and round with a sharp line of metal down the center of it. It was as similar to the Civil War battleship that had given the suit its name as it was to the human form that inhabited it.

The chest itself was constructed from a metal cylinder five feet across and equally tall. Big enough for a man to sit in, even a man confined to a wheelchair. The locomotion system was hidden under a flexible skirt constructed from layers of springs and steel. The layered metal was an innovation that Darby had incorporated into all his designs after coming back from a trip to Nippon, having seen how effective it was in the armor of the Japanese samurai.

But while this outfit did share many things in common with the original Iron-Clad armor, it was also clearly not the same suit that Hughes had been wearing when the Automaton fought alongside him the year before. This outfit was bigger, and far more menacing. An evolution of Darby's work, perhaps, but certainly not created by his hand.

And the Iron-Clad now had a face, staring down from a circular metal disk sitting high enough up on the chest that the crown of it was over a foot above the shoulders. It scowled with a grim visage of Ares, the Greek god of war. Two large cannons were mounted menacingly along its waist, giving it the appearance of a pair of deadly arms, and they were both pointed straight at Tom.

"I am afraid, sir, that I cannot comply," Tom said as loudly as he could.

There followed a moment of quiet, punctuated only by a sudden gust of wind and the hiss of snow being blown across the icy ground.

"I need you to step away from the boy."

"I assure you that I have not hurt him. He tried to use a . . . weapon against me with unfortunate results to his own person." Tom lifted Nathaniel's unconscious form slightly higher, so that it could better be seen through the hole in the wall. "The longer he remains . . . exposed to this cold, the more likely it is that he will require medical attention."

"We'll determine what happened here once you've turned yourself in. The other Paragons have been notified, and they are on their way."

"I'm afraid, Mr. Hughes, that current circumstances would be far too . . .

hard for me to explain to the other Paragons satisfactorily. I can only . . . assure you that what I'm about to do is for the . . . benefit of everyone concerned."

Tom's legs, still pointed in the opposite direction, began to run away. He ducked his head as he sprinted down the corridor and back into the house, being careful to shield his unconscious cargo as well.

From outside the projected voice of the Iron-Clad was loud enough to rattle the walls. "Automaton! Please come out now. I'll come and get you if I have to. You have one minute to get back out here, or things will get very bad for you."

Leaping over the splintered remains of the bookshelf that Nathaniel had used to block his way, Tom reached the door to the basement. He kicked it open, shards of wood flying as the lock tore free.

Tom moved down the stairs as swiftly as he could, landing in a small workshop that Darby had constructed in the cellar. It had been built as a compromise with his friends that allowed him to avoid his tendency to work in his lab at the Hall of Paragons well beyond the point of exhaustion, while fulfilling his need to be able to explore any new idea the moment it appeared in his head. The idea was good, but Darby had rarely bothered to use it for its intended purpose.

Since Darby's passing, Tom had made some minimal changes to the lab so that it could function as a place for him to spend his off-time. Nathaniel had told him that he found Tom's tendency to simply stand silently in different corners at night "horrifying."

But he had avoided moving any of the half-completed concepts that Darby had been working on at the time of his death, and the projects still lingered on the worktable, covered in dust. He leaned Nathaniel's limp form in a broken chair in the corner of the room; the boy's rump stuck out through the torn wicker seat, holding him in place.

Tom leaned his head down toward the tabletop and pressed a button on the side of his forehead. The broken camera lens came sliding out of his face, smashing away the last piece of his porcelain mask as it fell.

He opened the doors of a wooden cabinet standing above the table and pulled another cartridge of a similar shape down off one of the shelves. He tipped it up into his head, pushing it back until a latch caught it with a snap.

The new head-package had two green glass eyes in the front of it. They were suspended on wires so that they floated in front of his face. Tom rolled them around experimentally, looking up and down, then left and right.

He reached into the cabinet a second time and pulled out a new mask. This had been his first face, and it was much less realistic than his porcelain features. It was formed from a single hammered sheet of metal, with some simple features painted onto the steel. They were crude in comparison to the intricate details and subtle tones of his previous face.

He pulled off the remaining pieces of his current mask and locked the older one into place using the metal clips placed where a normal man's ears would have been.

Behind the new visage he moved his eyes again. Rather than making him appear "normal," it gave the illusion that a living person was trapped somewhere inside of him, desperately trying to escape. And it was that disturbing appearance that had originally caused Darby to relegate this version of Tom's face to the basement. Now it was all he had.

There was a rumbling from above as the Iron-Clad's amplified voice filtered down through the floor of the house, but the words were too muffled and distorted to make any sense, although it was clear enough that whatever deadline Tom had been given had now passed.

A circular brass plate, almost like the one that might be found on a pocket watch, popped open just above Tom's right leg, revealing a metal tube underneath. He grabbed a series of paper-wrapped bundles that were sitting on the shelf. Each one of them had been carefully tied up with butcher's twine, like a small parcel. One by one he placed each of them down into the hole; each one slid in perfectly.

The first was a package of short metal rods, followed by three stacks of cogs, each a different size. Finally he stuffed in two skeins of thin metal wire. Once they all had been placed inside Tom closed the lid, and froze for a moment.

If anyone had been watching him it would have been a very strange sight indeed. Bits of metal moved underneath him as if he were some kind of clockwork anthill. The strips of steel could be seen in his joints and other exposed areas, subtle hints that he was rebuilding himself.

His reverie was broken by the sound of a horrendous crash that literally shook the foundations of the building all around him. Dust spilled out from the ceiling and the walls, and there was a terrible groaning from the floorboards up above, followed by a series of cracking and popping noises as the frame of the house protested the demands that were being made of it. The Iron-Clad had entered the mansion.

Tom didn't react for a moment, waiting as the new materials distributed themselves throughout his frame, and then he ran back up the stairs into the main hallway.

A cold wind whipped down the corridor. Picture frames thumped against the wall, and the pages of the books that Nathaniel had toppled to the floor flapped noisily in the breeze, like hundreds of stranded fish in desperate search of water.

When he reached the entrance, the source of the wind was obvious: the large oaken double doors on the far side of the stairs had been blown half off their hinges and were now wobbling in the wind.

The library had originally been constructed as a ballroom, although there had only ever been one actual ball—an event where only four of the one hundred invited guests actually showed up. After that debacle Dennis Darby's father had decided that any further attempts to enter New York society would only serve to make him a laughingstock, and the room quickly became a storeroom, as well as a refuge that Dennis had run to when he needed to escape from the family and be alone with his thoughts.

After his father's death, Darby had decided that it would be far better to keep his large collection of esoteric journals in the space rather than simply using it as a large closet. As a memorial to the room's original purpose he had kept the original chandelier, along with a corner square of the corked floor and a grand piano, which were all now covered in grit and debris.

As Tom crossed the threshold he was surrounded by pages from Darby's beloved collection that fluttered in the wind. They mingled with blowing snow to create a strange blizzard in the room.

Just beyond them was a large hole created by the Iron-Clad's cannons. The Paragon had attempted to shove his way in through the breach he had opened, but the metal suit had not been able to find the purchase it needed to completely tear down the wall. Debris rained down as it tried to push through, and the floor beneath it was starting to sag and bow underneath the weight of it.

Tom looked up. "I do not think the . . . floor will hold you. Perhaps you should wait outside."

"You had your chance." A pair of metal doors in the shoulders to either side of the metal giant's face mask popped open. Gatling guns rolled out of the holes and locked into place with a menacing clank. The weapons appeared to be very similar in design to the ones that had been used against Tom by the man who had called himself Rapid Fire. They were clearly aimed directly at him.

"Mr. Hughes!" Tom said as loudly as he could. "Mr. Hughes!"

The distorted voice thundered out again. "Give yourself up!"

"Please, sir, I don't think you should come any closer." He held the brass palm of his hand out toward the Iron-Clad. "Also, it seems that your . . . flamboyant entrance has managed to rupture some of the . . . gas lines. Using your weapons is very likely to—"

"If you wish to save Darby's house, then give yourself up."

Tom shook his head. "It is not *my* . . . welfare that I am most concerned with."

"I'll take care of myself," the booming voice replied.

"It is . . . Mr. Hughes inside of the suit, isn't it? I don't recognize the armor that you're wearing. . . . It does not appear to be . . . Darby's design—although it is clearly based on his discoveries. May I ask . . . who created it for you?"

The planks under the floor let out a disconcerting squeal as the suit lurched forward another foot. "We've all had to become a little more self-sufficient since Sir Dennis was taken from us."

Tom nodded. "A most excellent job . . . Mr. Hughes." Tom swiveled up his new arm and held it up high so that the Iron-Clad could see it, the gun at the end pointed straight at the face of the Ares. "However, the workmanship does appear somewhat familiar. Would I be . . . mistaken to suggest that it was forged within the same . . . foundry where this arm was built?"

For a few long seconds there was no reply, and in the pause both machines faced each other completely motionless. The wind blew more gusts of snow in through the space between the Iron-Clad and the hole in the wall. The only other noises were a low hissing that came from the shattered pipes and the rustling of paper.

A sharp click pierced the air.

"No, sir!" said Tom. He threw himself out of the way, diving to the left, looking for cover behind a freestanding bookshelf. The first bullets were still ripping through the air when the gas ignited.

Flame filled the room instantly, loose paper bursting into fire in bright yellow flashes. The flame gathered together in a fireball and rose up toward the ceiling, flowing out across the frescos painted on it. The scene of dancing satyrs, nymphs, and other fantastic creatures had been commissioned by Christopher Darby, based on the beloved fairy stories that had been read to him as a child. The cheerful celebration of fantasy turned black and burned away in an instant.

An amplified scream came from inside the Iron-Clad as the fire washed back over the armor. The Gatling guns continued to churn blindly, pumping out bullets that ripped huge holes into the walls.

As the initial conflagration burned away, what remained of the room was smothered in smoke and flame. Yellow fire billowed from the ends of the broken gas mains, with a jet of flame blowing directly onto the left shoulder of the Iron-Clad's armor.

It only took a moment before the magazine inside cooked off, vaporizing the shoulder as it exploded. The scream that Hughes made this time had a tone of genuine suffering that the previous one had lacked.

Looking to escape from the fire that was broiling him alive, the Iron-Clad jerked forward, finally pulling himself free of the wall and moving out into the room. Air rushed in through the hole he had created, the flames burning brighter as they fed on the fresh oxygen.

The suit only managed to move a few feet forward before the floor began to disintegrate under the weight of the metal. Bullets were still firing from the remaining gun, splintering the floor as the suit topped toward the ground. The amplification system was also still in working order, and every word Hughes spoke inside as he toppled over boomed through the room. "No! Damn it, no!"

There was a second loud crash as flaming bookcases tumbled over, and Tom managed to keep out of their way. So far he had managed to remain relatively unscathed by the Armageddon that had engulfed the rest of the room. "Please . . . Mr. Hughes, stop firing!"

But it was only when the Iron-Clad had completely fallen over and the front of the Gatling gun was jammed into the floor that it ceased to shoot. Another scream rose up from inside the armor, both weaker and more desperate than before.

The ceiling was fully ablaze now, and the books all around them were igniting as well. Steam rose up from the floor as the moisture in the cork was boiled away by the heat.

Then the floor of the library gave way entirely, sending up a swirl of smoke and glowing embers as the burning timbers collapsed.

It was impossible to tell if the lack of any noise coming from inside the Iron-Clad as it crashed through into the basement below was due to shock, surprise, injury, or simply the amplification system finally giving up.

Tom tried to move toward the Iron-Clad, but there was no way to reach the suit that wasn't blocked by flame. He began to slowly squat downward, ratcheting up tension in his legs. He let go in a burst, flinging himself into the air, letting his momentum thrust him toward the hole like a demented mechanical frog.

The Iron-Clad armor had toppled over during the fall, and Tom landed sprawling on the front of the suit's metal chest.

The massive chandelier broke free from the ceiling above them and began its descent, heading straight down toward the hole and the Automaton. As it fell it tore out the gas piping from the ceiling behind it and traveled along a graceful arc that took it a few feet to the left of the hole. It impacted with the floor and exploded into a rain of hot glass beads and metal rods that clattered as they struck the metal bodies of the Iron-Clad and the Automaton.

When the crystal shower subsided, Tom rapped his hand hard against the Iron-Clad. "Mr. Hughes?" There was no answer from inside.

Bracing his feet on either side, Tom slipped the fingers of his left hand underneath the edge of the metal face of Ares and began to tug with all his strength. At first nothing moved. The only visible clue to his exertion was the steam rising up from his wrist. It was a small wisp at first, barely noticeable in the smoke and heat, but after a few moments it was a continuous stream jetting out of him.

His right foot slipped out from underneath him, and he crashed chest-to-chest with the soot-covered suit. Taking a moment to find firmer footing, he started again.

If there had been anyone able to hear the sound of Tom's heart above the roar of the fire they would have noticed that it was beating faster and faster every second.

There wasn't a single grunt or moan from the Automaton as he bore down, putting more and more energy into the effort to pry off the Iron-Clad's face. Then the metal face began to shriek as Tom's strength overwhelmed it. Rivets popped, one after another, and the entire disk came free, flipping over and away from him, taking the ring finger of his left hand along with it.

Underneath was a four-inch-wide hole in the metal. "At least that part of your armor's . . . design remains unchanged," said Tom, reaching his hand into it and finding a handle a few inches down. He tried to turn it, but it wouldn't budge, the heat having wedged it into place. The seond time he applied more force, and this time the sound of suffering metal came from inside of him.

Pulling out his left hand he shoved the end of the pneumatic gun on his right arm straight into the hole, rotating the barrel with his other hand. There were four sharp snaps one after another as he fired, and when Tom reached back into the hole the dial turned easily.

The Automaton took a few steps back as the lip of a triangular plate in the front of the suit popped open. He levered it forward, and as it opened William Hughes rose out of the armor, lifted up on a mechanical arm.

His body had been strapped to a thick pole covered in shaped padding and leather. It was a new version of the saddle that Darby had designed to keep him in place if the machine was upended, and it had worked as designed. Hughes dangled in the air, unconscious and upside down, his thick red and white mane tied tightly back and away from his face.

This new version of the machine had been designed with Hughes's infirmities in mind. His legs, once an integral part of the machine's control functions, were bound into a tube of thick white canvas that braced them to the pole while keeping them tucked in and out of the way. There were bloodstains on it now, although Tom couldn't immediately make out just how much damage the man's body had taken.

The flames above them were raging higher, getting closer and hotter with each passing second. As they licked over the edges of the hole stray wisps of Hughes's hair began to curl and burn from the heat. Tom reached his arms around the pole beneath the saddle and yanked. From somewhere deep inside the armor there was a protest as a mechanism shattered, and then the entire seat tore free from the machine.

Cradling the entire harness in his arms, Tom slid down the Iron-Clad's torso.

It was much cooler down near the foundations, although the flames were on the march now, burning through the ballroom floor, flickering across the basement ceiling as they ignited the wood.

Tom turned to face the broken wicker chair where he had placed Nathaniel, but it was empty now.

Tom braced the saddle across his shoulders, steadying it with his left hand, and started toward the stairs. In order to keep his movements steady with the weight of a man hanging off the back of his shoulders he needed to lean forward at an almost comically steep angle, as if he were walking into a stiff wind. He lifted his right arm and used the pneumatic gun to blow open the basement door.

When he reached the main hallway smoke was everywhere, although the main part of the mansion had only begun to be engulfed by the fire.

Tom used the blunt surface of his right forearm to smash open the doors to the parlor. Wickham's body still lay there, unmoved from where it had been when he first discovered it.

He propped the pole carrying Hughes up against the wall and with his hand free, Tom reached down into Wickham's coat.

After rummaging around for a moment, he pulled out a battered leather notebook with a black leather cover embossed with the image of a magnifying glass.

Tom began to rise, then stopped. Reaching down again he pulled

Wickham's mask up and over the dead man's head. Underneath it the man's eyes were still open, his lips pulled back as if he were about to deliver one of his stern admonitions.

Tom lifted up his right chest plate slightly, shoving the book underneath it, and then snapped the bronze slab back into place. He picked up the leather mask and tied it around his neck.

The flames had traveled quickly up the hallway, and the fire was licking up against the glass doors of the parlor. Tom grabbed one of the velvet-covered seats and spun in a complete circle, then let it go in a graceful arc.

The bay window at the far end of the room had been a gorgeous piece of work, with multicolored diamond-shaped panes and an intricate stained-glass pattern along the top that had spelled out the phrase "Insight is the truth behind knowledge" in Latin. The chair smashed it all into nonsense, turning the glass into a shower of fireworks that scattered across the snow.

Tom grabbed a blanket from the back of the divan and used it to swaddle Hughes's unconscious body. Heaving the pole back over his shoulder, he jumped through the shattered window and stepped out into the yard.

Nathaniel, dressed as Turbine, was waiting there to meet him.

Chapter 19

Out of Fashion

Since finding herself trapped by her clothing in her father's closet, Sarah found that she had lost what little interest she had for the sumptuous materials and finely tailored jackets and skirts that fascinated her friends. She resented the clothing she was forced to bind herself in every time she stepped out of the house, and the tight skirts and corsets left her feeling as vulnerable as a child.

But as an eligible lady of society, it was expected that she be a model of feminine couture. Being fashionable meant not only wearing the latest and best but also being well versed in the hows, whys, and wherefores of the way that two sets of clothing that appeared almost identical at first glance could actually sit at opposite ends of the fashion universe, with one being the height of envy and the other little more than a hopeless rag, all due to the placement of a few ribbons.

Knowing the difference required a tremendous amount of time and thought, including the need to fill your head with volumes of trivial information gleaned from the pages of *Harper's Bazar.*

Meanwhile, she was also supposed to be aware of all the latest gossip about who had said what to whom, what kisses had been stolen in the corridor, and who was in or out, with a fine coating of scandal on top. At least having a widower father who wore a leather costume with a smokestack hat and carried a steam-powered pistol made you immune to *some* of the day-to-day fripperies.

Even so, it was all considered so desperately *important*, right up until the moment you needed to forget it all in order to start on the next round of ephemera and idle chatter.

Sarah found it exhausting at the best of times. But since the incident on the bridge she had become more and more aware of how sad and fragile the world she lived in truly was—at any moment it could all come crashing down in a heap of death, violence, and secrets.

And now she had been tainted by the conspiracy. She had secrets that could cost men their lives. Since she had put the burning weight of Wickham's key around her neck, it had become impossible for her to focus on any of the hundreds of unwritten rules and rituals that were the foundation of New York society.

But needs must, and spring would soon be upon them. So this Saturday Sarah had headed out with a few friends to visit a new downtown hat store that "everyone was raving about," and possibly pick up some colorful frocks to wear when the winter finally broke and her period of mourning had come to an end.

And for the first few hours she had enjoyed spending time with Sally Norbitt and Penny Seals. It reminded her of simpler days, although she was painfully aware how few women her age still remained unmarried. And it was clear from the way she spoke that even homely Penny would soon be engaged to the dashing Hamilton Brooks.

But as the other two girls had nattered on about who would (and wouldn't) be coming to the wedding, Sarah's mood had grown progressively darker. She had realized that no matter what she did, no matter how hard she tried to escape the vortex of her life, the destiny of Sarah Stanton would always be to become just like them.

The breaking point had come when Sally asked her what she thought of a hat festooned with tiny ribbons. Seeing the ridiculous chapeau strapped to the side of her friend's head made her lose her ability to hold back her frustration. "It's utterly pointless and stupid!" she had snapped, and stormed out of the store.

Sarah had traveled half a block before she realized that the chaperones were nowhere to be seen. She slipped into the crowd and started walking north. There would, of course, be hell to pay. There always was when she broke the rules.

Disappointing her father was never fun, but if she returned home before her carriage did then no one could accuse her of deliberately causing anyone emotional distress. Except, perhaps, for Sally and Penny, and at that moment she didn't much care about their feelings.

Sarah couldn't remember the last time, if ever, she had strolled through the streets of New York all by herself, but at the moment she enjoyed it immensely, even if she was receiving occasional hard stares from the passersby. It was a cold February day, but the sun had started to come out, and she hugged the daylight on the west side of Fifth Avenue.

After twenty blocks her feet started to hurt. Her leather boots, although well made, were hardly designed for hiking, and Sarah was sure that her feet would end up covered in blisters. The rest of her outfit was similarly ill suited for the trek. Under her skirts things were shifting and binding in ways that would demand some clearly unladylike behavior to fix.

She decided that her best refuge for some badly needed sartorial repairs would be found at the Darby mansion. And while she didn't relish seeing Nathaniel, especially after his boorish behavior the night before, she could at least count on Tom to allow her to rest peacefully until a cab could be called to see her safely home.

When she was within five blocks of the mansion Sarah saw a large cloud of black smoke rising into the sky, as if someone were burning a large bonfire somewhere in the vicinity. And as she walked closer the acrid scent that reached her nose clearly spoke of something beyond just burning wood or leaves.

By the time she reached the entrance to Darby Park, it was clear that fire was coming from the mansion, and something was very, very wrong. She listened for the ringing of the fireboxes, hoping that someone had already reported the emergency, but she heard nothing.

Looking around the street she saw a tall man in a bowler hat and a black greatcoat taking long strides across the snow-covered sidewalk, his gaze fixed firmly on the ground, as if there couldn't possibly be a huge fire burning only a few hundred feet away.

She ran toward him as fast as she could in her ladylike skirts and boots. "Sir! Sir!" At first it seemed as if the man might simply ignore her, so she tried again. "Excuse me, sir!"

When the man finally stopped and looked up at her, he seemed very upset at having his stride interrupted. She almost found herself smiling in spite of the emergency. *New Yorkers never change, do they?* she thought to herself.

"Madam," he replied in a clipped tone from underneath his bushy black mustache.

The sound of urgency in Sarah's voice surprised her. "I need to report a fire!" She pointed to the sky.

His gaze followed her hand up and over to the column of smoke. His eyes widened slightly. "My God," he muttered. "But I'm sure that someone has reported that by now."

She pointed at the metal firebox standing on a pole nearby. "Wouldn't the alarm be ringing if they had?"

It was clear from the grimace on his face that he was most unhappy about having his day interrupted in order to play the Good Samaritan. "You're probably right."

"My friends live in there, sir! There's no 'probably' about it."

When he saw the look of anger on her face something in his demeanor changed instantly. "Of course, you're right! A most dreadful event! I'm sorry, madam," he said with a tone of contrition and a hint of a French accent. "I'll get help. You just wait here."

The man begun to run, and Sarah waved after him. "Thank you, sir! Thank you so much."

She had no intention of waiting, of course. Men seemed to believe that it was the natural order of things that once a male was in motion the nearby women must remain at rest, rooted to the ground until a figure of masculine authority could evaluate the situation and start barking orders.

Sarah had no patience for such nonsense. While she might not be as strong as most men, there were precious few emergencies where another set of hands couldn't be put to better use than simply fluttering around in the air, no matter what their sex.

Using a copy of the key that Darby had given to her, Sarah unlocked the gate. It was a simple padlock, and as she spun the key in the lock a bank of ominous clouds rolled over the sun, turning the burnt orange sky to a dull metal gray. She pushed the gate open just far enough to slip inside, then left it unlocked behind her. It would be necessary for the fire engines to be able to get inside when they arrived.

As she walked down the driveway she felt a pang of guilt for having left Nathaniel. She had no wish to see him hurt.

But he wasn't alone—Mr. Wickham and Tom were there with him.

They'd make sure that he wouldn't sleep through a conflagration, no matter how much he'd had to drink.

When she got close enough to actually see the mansion she realized that she had underestimated the size of the disaster. Flames were shooting twenty feet into the air above the roof of the main hall, and it was clear that they were spreading quickly. The entire northern end of the house had collapsed, and smoke was pouring out from it in a thick column, barreling up toward the sky. It was almost ridiculous to think that there was enough fuel in the house to support so much flame.

Sarah ran as quickly as she could, but the rough cobblestones seemed to be attacking the heels of her boots, and her fashionable clothes constricted her legs so badly that she could barely go at any rate faster than a limping trot.

The yard outside was empty, although there were two fresh ruts dug into the dirt to the right of her. The tracks were massive, and they were heading toward the southern wing of the house.

The main entrance was already engulfed with flames, and Sarah stepped off the cobblestones and onto the lawn. The ground was sodden with melting snow, and her boots sank deep into the mud. The ruffled edges of her petticoats hung down limply as they became sodden with water.

As she followed the tracks to the side of the house she was shocked to see that a large section of the wall was simply gone. Paper, glass, wood, and tools were strewn out across the yard. There was a large wound in the grass where something had landed roughly in the snow. The parallel gashes continued on around to the back. They had torn up the ground as if a madman had decided to attack it with a plow, but images of a more likely scenario were beginning to appear in her head, and she didn't like what her imagination had to show her.

As she rounded the back of the house she let out a sigh of relief. Tom was standing a few yards away from her. He looked a mess, and all his clothes had been stripped away except for a belt hanging loosely around his waist. She had never seen his unclothed form in motion before, and was fascinated by the movement of the steel plates that covered his body as they slid over one another. It was as if she were seeing a new kind of painting by da Vinci. . . .

Sarah turned her eyes away for a moment, feeling an involuntary flush of embarrassment when she realized she had been staring at a "nude" mechanical man.

When she looked back Tom was facing something that was still hidden from her view, and he lifted his right arm and pointed it straight out in front of him. The limb was completely mismatched to the rest of his body—a thick tube of iron with a hand that had a single long finger at the end of it.

She stepped closer, moving past the trunk of the large willow tree that had sat in the backyard for more years than she had been alive. Sarah had spent a great deal of time in its branches during her youth, and with a tinge of fear and regret she wondered if it would survive the fire. But the fate of a single tree was hardly worth considering now that she could finally see what it was that Tom was pointing toward. Nathaniel was dressed in his Turbine costume, although it was a version of it that she had never seen before.

Both of the young man's arms were outstretched. The turbines locked onto the end of each wrist faced threateningly toward Tom, although knowing what she did about his abilities, she doubted that the small fans could really be any threat to a machine that weighed as much as the mechanical man.

The breeze shifted unexpectedly, blowing acrid smoke directly into her face. It blinded her and filled her lungs, and Sarah began to cough violently. She stepped back from the increasing heat that radiated out from the house. It was growing more intense every second, and she felt an unladylike prickle of sweat breaking out underneath her hat.

The roaring of the flames was accompanied by a crash and a tinkle of glass as a section of the library roof collapsed inward, taking down another section of the wall after it. When a wave of smoke rolled out in all directions Sarah buried her face into her arm.

She heard Tom's voice first. "If I had intended to kill you, or . . . Mr. Hughes, why would I have let you live while you were unconscious?"

Nathaniel seemed to genuinely consider the point for a moment, then shook his head. "I don't know. You're an inhuman monster. Perhaps you had darker plans for me later." Then he started to shout. "Anyway, I don't need to know what your *motivations* are! I just want you to stay here long enough for—"

When he saw her a look of shock crossed Nathaniel's face. "Sarah! Run!"

She didn't move.

"You need to run! The Automaton tried to kill me and the Iron-Clad, and he burned down the mansion. Run! Run and get help!"

Sarah had almost forgotten the corollary to the "women must never move rule," and that is that when ordered to by a man, they were then supposed to run as fast as they possibly could, which wasn't actually very fast at all.

She frowned and walked toward them, although the intensity of the heat and smoke made her skin prickle as if it were covered with a horde of tiny insects.

"Didn't you hear me, Sarah? The Automaton's gone mad!"

"Are you still drunk, or have you finally gone totally round the bend? That's the biggest load of nonsense I've heard come out of your mouth in the ten years I've known you."

"Twelve years," Nathaniel replied, correcting her.

Sarah stepped in between the man and the machine, her feet disappearing into a growing mud puddle. She could feel the ice-cold water seeping in through the leather of her boots. "Now both of you, it's time to put a stop to this nonsense."

Nathaniel lowered his arms an inch and then shuffled a few steps sideways, clearly looking to find a line of sight to his opponent that didn't have a girl standing in the middle of it. "Sarah, this isn't a good time for another one of your hysterical tirades." He pointed to the side of the nearby willow tree. "Look what he's done to Mr. Hughes."

Sarah turned to see what Nathaniel was pointing at and let out an embarrassing shriek. Somehow she had missed it before, but William Hughes, wearing nothing more than a body stocking, was trussed up to a padded metal pole sticking straight up out of the ground. Blood stained the canvas sling holding his legs, and the whole contraption had been thrust into the earth deeply enough to allow it to stand upright next to the tree trunk. He was completely limp, his eyes closed, either unconscious or dead.

"Tom," she said sharply, "what is going on here?"

"I was attempting to bring . . . Mr. Hughes to safety when . . . Mr. Winthorp appeared in his . . . costume and told me to put him down. I tried to do so in a way that would not cause him to freeze to death before we had finished our . . . confrontation."

"Af-af-af," Nathaniel spluttered. "After you almost killed me in the Aereodrome!"

"Mr. Winthorp attempted to attack me using the very same . . . pneumatic weapon that is now attached to my arm, and managed to knock himself . . . unconscious in the process."

"He's lying to you, Sarah. Tom killed the Sleuth." He lifted up his gauntlets and aimed them back at the Automaton.

Sarah needed a moment to fully understand the words that had just been said to her. "Wickham is dead?" she said in a tone so calm it almost surprised her.

Tom gave her a quick mechanical nod. "I found his body in the . . . parlor when I returned to the . . . mansion this morning. I was attempting to examine his . . . corpse for clues when . . . Mr. Winthorp found me."

Despite all her attempts to avoid the clichés that came along with being the weaker sex, the sheer volume and impact of the information that had just been given to her, along with the growing heat of the fire, made her feel as if she was going to swoon. And truth be told, the thought of falling into the icy waters of the puddle seemed like it would come as a relief. Instead she summoned her Stanton wherewithal and mopped her brow with the sleeve of her overcoat.

"Are you all right, Sarah?" Nathaniel said with alarm. "I need you to move out of the way so I can take care of this menace to humanity."

Wickham was dead? How could that even be possible? She had seen the old man hale and hearty just a few hours before.

Sarah took a breath to rally herself and grimaced as the smoke bit into her lungs. Perhaps she would have been better off taking the Frenchman's advice and waiting for the fire brigade in the street. But there was no time for that now. "Clearly you've both had a traumatic—"

Nathaniel rose up into the air in front of her, the turbines on his back spitting out a plume of white steam as he rose toward the sky. He let out an almost-comical yelp as the improperly tightened harness dragged him up by his arms and crotch.

With Sarah no longer in his way he aimed both hands out in front of him and activated the turbines on his wrists. Streams of compressed air and steam shot out toward the empty space where Tom had been a moment before. The focused pulse of pressure smashed through the fire-weakened walls of the house so perfectly it left two holes behind.

Nathaniel, unable to exert any genuine control over his new suit, found himself at the merciless hands of the immutable laws of physics. He was flung backward, trying to regain control before he crashed into the ground.

There was a sucking sound as the fire inhaled the fresh air through the new holes. And from somewhere inside the mansion there was a heavy vibration, followed a moment later by a dull thump.

The nearby wall and window disintegrated completely as a fireball ripped through them and enveloped Tom and Sarah. She shrieked as it hit her. From somewhere far way she heard Nathaniel scream out her name.

For a moment Sarah was weightless, then she plunged into darkness. Time and all feeling seemed to slip away into a comforting feeling of floating, as if she had simply been cast out of the world—free of all feeling, lost in a moment of pure nothingness. Everything in her world was now cool, quiet, and peaceful, like a tranquil cave.

Sarah's moment of calm lasted until she tried to take a breath. The dirty water that entered into her lungs threw her out of her reverie and into a reality defined by darkness and terror.

Her hands were icy cold, trapped in a thick ooze. And as she tried to find some kind of purchase to escape from the darkness, her lungs attempted to expel the water, each shuddering convulsion only managing to drag in another drowning breath.

When she finally managed to rise upward, and air flooded back into her, she coughed violently—water expelling itself from her lungs in a series of rasping barks. Her vision was blurry, and she couldn't make out anything but a vague sea of brown and green.

After a few seconds the world began to come back to her, and her first realization was that she was down on all fours, hands sunk deep into the freezing mud. There was also a new sensation: a tingling down her entire left side, as if she had been simultaneously smacked and pulled by hundreds of hands.

As her vision cleared in her right eye, she could see the remains of her winter hat. It slowly disappeared underneath the muddy water in front of her, far too singed and misshapen to ever be fashionable again.

A bony hand grabbed her shoulders and tugged her upward. Sarah turned to look up at Tom, and she realized that she couldn't make out the words he was saying. Something about a fire . . .

Then the Automaton grabbed her around the waist and lifted her up as if she were nothing more than a child's toy doll. She felt her left boot slide away from her foot as she was pulled out of the mud.

Tom took her and ran away from the house, but she could still feel the heat on her neck and back as a long tongue of fire licked out toward them.

A few yards away Nathaniel sat up. He had landed on his back, and the suit had been badly dented by the impact of what had clearly been a very ungraceful landing.

Tom set her down on a snowy patch of grass, and Sarah coughed again. She encouraged it this time, hoping to clear out the remaining dregs of mud in her lungs. Her throat felt constricted and raw.

The tingling along her left side was now being replaced by genuine pain, with a fresh new area of rawness that seemed mostly centered around her left eye, and a reminder that her hip had only just begun to heal. As she reached up to touch her face Tom's left arm stopped hers. "No . . . Miss Stanton. You have some . . . glass in your . . . face. Let me help."

The fingers of Tom's left hand reached up and delicately plucked at something just above her sight.

"I . . . I can't see out of my left eye, Tom."

"There is no obvious damage to your eyes, but there is a great deal of . . . blood. I should get you to a . . . hospital as quickly as possible."

From the street beyond came the distant sound of clanging bells. The fire brigade was finally on the way, although it was clearly coming too late to save any significant portion of the Darby mansion. The flames burned even more voraciously after the explosion and were clearly blazing through Darby's collection of rare books. She found it hard to care, although she was sure the world would one day miss the secrets hidden in that house. "I'll be fine, but you need to go."

An angry voice came from up above them. "Get off of her, you monster."

Sarah looked up and saw Nathaniel through her unblurred right eye. Even to her he didn't seem very much of a threat.

"Don't be—" Her response came out as nothing more than a croak. She swallowed and tried again. "Don't be an idiot, Nathaniel. Tom just saved my life."

"He's tricked you, Sarah. He's been fooling all of us for a very long time, but he won't fool *me* anymore."

From her position on the ground it almost appeared as if there was a jet of steam shooting from Nathaniel's head. His rush to get into this new costume had clearly been one of a string of bad ideas. The body stocking was bunched up underneath the straps of the main harness, and a long shock of his hair was dangling down from underneath the helmet. The turbines that had been attached to the wing along the back were either broken off or hanging loosely at odd angles. He looked simultaneously ridiculous and pathetic, and she couldn't help but laugh at him. "You're right. I'm a fool, Nathaniel. But it isn't because I believed Tom. It was for thinking that you would actually be able to grow up."

Nathaniel twitched as if he'd been physically struck. "Sarah, you're still in shock." He held out his hand, as if to comfort her.

"For the longest time I couldn't understand why you act the way you do. Every time someone says something you don't want to be true you tell them that they're sadly mistaken. But I'm not. The world isn't always black and white, Nathaniel." She could feel blood trickling down into her collar. "And there are more flavors to people than just good and evil." At that moment she realized she must have looked something like a harpy from hell, but she wasn't going to be afraid to use it to her advantage. "You're not a Paragon. Not really. You're just a little boy playing dress-up, thinking you can make the world be the way you want it to be by acting like the pathetic old men you've watched play at being heroes for your entire life."

"Please Sarah, I . . ." He stopped and took a step back, holding up his one working gauntlet. "You need to step away from Tom now."

"No, Nathaniel, I don't. I'm not going to do what you say. I trust Tom, and I don't trust you." Sarah turned around and faced the Automaton. "Take me to the hospital, Tom." The bells of the fire carts were getting closer.

"Yes . . . Miss Stanton." She felt herself being lifted up. Tom's metal arms were still warm from the fire.

Nathaniel still stood ready to fire, but the look on his face made it plain that he was clearly at a loss for what to do next. "Don't do this, Sarah. You'll regret it."

She smiled at him, then winced from the pain in her face. Whatever it was that had kept that pain from overwhelming her was starting to fade. "Somehow you've managed to let Darby and Wickham die, burn down this house, and almost kill me, Mr. Hughes, and yourself in the process. I can't imagine what you'd do to the poor woman foolish enough to love you."

She pointed toward the wall. "Let's go, Tom."

Chapter 20

Saying Good-bye

It took Tom a dozen strides to reach the high stone wall that surrounded the house. Moving at speed, he launched himself into the air, reaching the ramparts of the stone fence in a single bound, stepping onto the top of it as if he were walking up a flight of stairs.

Outside the park the streets weren't busy, but a number of residents had come out of their houses to watch as one of the last grand mansions in the neighborhood burned to the ground.

The onlookers reacted with shock when Tom and Sarah appeared, smashing onto the sidewalk. "It's the Automaton!" one man yelled out, and the rest cheered. The people of New York still remembered Tom as a hero.

Sarah had expected to feel a shuddering jolt as she landed, but somehow Tom absorbed most of the shock. As he began to run down the street the buildings turned to a blur even in her good eye. Sarah felt as if she were floating down the street. If not for the growing awareness that she was wet, cold, and blind in one eye, it would have seemed like a magical ride. Then she felt an unpleasant shock of realization. "Stop!"

Tom tried to respond, but his feet struck a patch of ice and started to skid. They spun around, careening across the road, until Tom slammed up against a brick wall. "Miss . . . Stanton. What's the matter? Are you hurt?"

She looked up at his metal face. "You're taking me to the Hall of Paragons?"

"You said you needed . . . medical help. That is the closest place to receive it."

She shook her head violently. "No! They confined you to the house. If you go there now, looking like this . . . They won't let you leave, and after Nathaniel tells his version of the story they'll destroy you."

His face turned toward hers. She had never seen him wearing his "human" eyes before. The effect of it was far more unsettling than she could imagine. There was something about them being not-quite human that made them even more monstrous than his artfully painted features ever had been. "You're hurt. Getting you some . . . help is my first priority."

"But not at the cost of your life, Tom."

"Then where should I take you?"

She pointed southward. "Our family doctor. He has his office on Thirty-fifth and Seventh."

"That is quite a bit . . . farther away."

"I won't have you disassembled on my account. Nothing is worth that. Anyway, I don't think I'm hurt that badly." The actual sensations of pain seemed to be growing more intense, and appearing in more places. "Some scratches, mostly. I'm guessing that Nathaniel's pride was wounded more than I was." But her sight was starting to return in the left eye. Perhaps it had been more shock than anything else. She just hoped that the frost creeping up her dress didn't mean her exposed foot would be frostbitten before they arrived.

They had only been standing still for half a minute, but already a small crowd of onlookers had begun to form down the block. "All right . . . Miss Stanton. I will take you to your . . . doctor." He began to move again.

"And then what?"

Tom's shoes, or what was left of them, made a loud rhythmic slapping as they pounded against the sidewalk. "I'm not sure I understand your question."

"After you've delivered me to safety, what will you do?"

"I have retrieved . . . Mr. Wickham's notebook from his corpse. He had made some . . . inquiries in his attempt to discover which member of the Paragons it is that has turned traitor. I shall endeavor to continue that investigation."

"To what end?"

"The Sleuth sent me out last night to investigate a . . . warehouse where he believed I would find evidence of the . . . conspiracy. I was attacked, but I also discovered evidence that someone has stolen . . . Sir Dennis's inventions for their own ends.

"And that was where you were when . . ."

". . . Mr. Wickham was killed," Tom replied.

"But you can take the other Paragons to the warehouse!"

"Unfortunately it was completely destroyed."

Sarah frowned. "Why is it that the Paragons seem unable to enter a building without demolishing it?"

"I could not . . . answer that question."

Sarah barked out a laugh. "Nor should you! But if that's the case, then who is the traitor?"

"I still cannot be certain."

"I'm not trying to play twenty questions with you, Tom. Who do you *think* it is?"

There was a long pause before his reply. "I don't think it is wise for you to become any more . . . involved in this . . . affair than you already are . . . Miss Stanton.

"As you said earlier, the fact that . . . Nathaniel will report this . . . encounter between us will already make things far too dangerous for you once the traitor . . . realizes he has been found out."

"Don't patronize me, Tom. Just because I'm a woman doesn't mean that I'm unable to think."

"Of course not . . . Miss Stanton. I have no bias toward your gender. But I am no longer in a position to . . . protect you."

"Protect me? From whom?"

"The . . . Paragons, or anyone else who would wish you harm."

"My father is the *leader* of the Paragons!"

"As was . . . Sir Dennis."

She gripped his arm more tightly. "Do you think he could be next?"

"No. At least there is no . . . reason to believe so as of yet."

She relaxed slightly, although she was unsure whether she could believe him. "That's some good news, at least."

Tom came to a sudden halt. He spun around sharply, then quickly traversed a small set of stairs. "We are here . . . Miss Stanton."

"Perhaps it's time you started calling me by my first name."

"If you wish . . . Sarah." Tom lowered her gently to the ground. Even after the journey through the winter wind, the bricks were shockingly cold against the exposed skin of her foot.

"I do." She wrapped her arms around him and gave him a hug. His slightly inhuman shape made it awkward, but she held him close against her for a moment, feeling the thousands of vibrations as the machinery inside of him churned. Sarah wondered for a moment if this was how Tom sensed the world, feeling the movements of everything around him. "Thank you, Tom. I know things have been hard recently, but I've grown rather fond of you over the last few years."

"I appreciate your trust in me . . . Sarah." He put his left arm around her gently and squeezed back. Sarah was surprised. She hadn't expected it. "I will do everything in my power to . . . prove that your faith in me is not misplaced."

"Pish. You have nothing to prove to me, Tom. Or to anyone." The cold was starting to get to her now. She could feel the shivers rising up, sapping what remained of her strength. Another minute and she'd collapse to the ground.

"The others may not be able to see it, Tom, but you're more like Darby than any of them care to admit."

He let go of her and took her hand. "I found our time together . . . pleasurable."

"Don't give up hope," she said quietly. "We'll find a way to save you."

"I am afraid that after today there are not many . . . outcomes in which I will continue to exist for long."

Sarah let go of his hand and pointed a finger at him. "Don't say that!" She was surprised to feel tears welling up in her eyes.

"But if I am destroyed, I will endeavor to leave whatever . . . information I gather where you can find it."

"I thought you said I shouldn't get involved."

"When I am . . . gone you will be the only one who still knows that the . . . Paragons are compromised. Your honesty and . . . forthrightness will be needed." He pulled the pneumatic gun free from his iron arm and held it out to her. A length of tubing trailed after it back into his arm. "You may need this."

Sarah waved it away. "A gun? I can't—"

Tom moved it closer to her. "It is an air-powered weapon. It was created by . . . Sir Dennis for . . . Nathaniel."

She took it and cradled it between her hands. "It won't kill?"

"It does not have to. Now please hold the base of the . . . weapon toward me."

Sarah did so, and Tom twisted something into it with his left hand. The tubing dangled free and then retracted into his arm.

"It uses fortified steam. I have modified it so that it is weaker and safer than it once was, but still powerful enough to protect you." Reaching under his chest plate he pulled out a small metal sphere. "You will need to find your own supply of . . . fortified steam once you have used this." It had a brass nozzle with a grooved fitting along the top of it. He snapped it into place along the bottom of the weapon. With the brass ball underneath the barrel, the weapon had a gangly, otherworldly appearance. "But it will shoot at least . . . ten times before then." He flipped it over before placing the weapon back into her hand, grip first. Then he reached out and rapped on the door behind her.

Sarah lifted up her bustle and shoved the gun in between the hoops. When she dropped it back into place the weapon was invisible. Sarah was pleased to discover that the garment was good for something. "I want one more thing from you, Tom."

"What is it . . . Sarah?"

She stood up on her tiptoes and then reached her hand up behind his neck. Their faces moved closer together.

Sarah grabbed the Sleuth's mask and began to tug it up and over his head. "This."

He realized what she wanted and used his hand to untie the cord. Once that was done it came away easily. "I think . . . Mr. Wickham would be happy to know you have it."

The sound of someone clambering down the stairs could be heard from inside the house. "But you should be . . . careful. Sir . . . Dennis said that when a man puts on a mask he discovers his greatest . . . confidence and his darkest desire at the same moment."

She looked up at him and smiled, her hand tightly clutching her prize. "It's lucky for me that I'm not a man, then."

"Stay safe . . . Sarah Stanton."

"You too, Tom." She gave him a kiss on the side of his face. It was cold against her lips.

Tom turned and moved down the stairs. "Good-bye."

Sarah watched him as he began to run down the street. It was a loping, almost animal movement, like a rabbit or a deer. The mechanical man turned a corner and vanished into the streets of Manhattan just as the door behind her opened.

She turned to see the doctor's assistant looking down at her with shock and horror. "What in the name of heaven has happened to you?"

Seeing herself in the woman's terrified eyes she realized just how frightful she must look. "I've been in a fight, I'm afraid." Then her legs gave out, and Sarah heard the woman scream out her name as she collapsed to the ground, the world turning mercifully black.

Chapter 21

Family Matters

When Jenny Foxbrush had arrived in the Stanton household she had only been nineteen, but already had the stern temperament of a woman in her forties. She could silence a man at ten paces with a single withering look—a useful skill for a girl who rarely actually spoke to anyone unless she was forced to.

Gossip had ran rampant among the household staff that she had spent her youth as a child of the streets, left homeless after her father was sent to jail for slaughtering her mother in front of her eyes.

Whether or not the story was completely true, Sarah did know that Jenny had lived with an aunt—a housemaid who had instilled in her niece the most amazing skills at cleaning clothes—for most of her teenage years. Jenny could find and remove almost any stain known to man. She also had the useful ability to recall the location of any object in the house, even if she had only glimpsed it out of the corner of her eye. This was a talent often put to use by the other members of the household staff, who used the girl to track down things that they had lost or misplaced, when they dared to speak to her.

But her plans to remain quietly hidden from the attention of the Stanton family had been undone when the four-year-old Sarah had decided she would follow the young maid everywhere she went. It was certainly not conversation she was after, and the young girl was quite content to sit quietly and watch the maid do her washing work for hours at a time. Considering that the young Sarah had gained a reputation for her epic tantrums, it was considered something of a miracle when a few stern words of reprimand from Miss Foxbrush had put a stop to her unpleasant displays once and for all. The two of them had maintained their odd friendship ever since.

But fifteen years later Jenny was no longer simply the quiet little housekeeper with a gift for laundry. She had filled out and turned into the head of the maid staff, managing to find her voice, as well as the time to also become the bride of Mr. Jonathon Farrows, the handsome footman from the house next door. And Sarah was now a young woman, older than Jenny was when they had first met.

The two of them were together in the kitchen of the Stanton house. Sarah leaned back on a stool, her neck resting against a towel on the edge of one of the large porcelain sinks, her ruined hair dangling over a pool of warm, soapy water.

Mrs. Farrows's fingers were shoved deep into the tangle of young Miss Stanton's locks. She scrubbed furiously, a large white bar of soap at her side, stopping only to pick out the occasional shard of glass. "Look at your *face*! You're supposed to be a young *lady*, not a hooligan! What were you thinking, getting into a fight?"

"I got into the middle of *someone else's* fight," Sarah replied with a sniff. "Which is a very different thing."

"Don't try and squirm out of it—there are six stitches in your forehead! And the doctor said that you were lucky not to have lost your foot to frostbite."

"Dr. William thinks every cut and bruise is either fatal or can only be cured by having something sawn off."

"Well, this is more than that." The matron pulled her hand out of the mass of soapy hair, pulling a clump of long blonde strands with it. "I'm not sure if we're going to be able to save much. You may need to wear a wig for a while."

"Maybe I'll just chop it all off and wear a hat."

"Sarah, getting hurt may seem funny to you, but—"

The smile melted away from her face. "No, Jen, it isn't funny. I know that."

"I was going to say," she said with a stern note of anger in her voice, "that your father isn't going to see any humor in it."

"I'm already sure of that." And while there might be tears, there would certainly be no hugs.

"And they say the Darby mansion is gone—burned to the ground. And young master Winthorp was badly hurt."

Sarah's eyes flared. "Badly hurt? Who said that? I saw Nathaniel when I left. His only real wounds were a raging hangover and a badly bruised ego."

Jenny put one soap-covered hand on an ample hip and wagged the finger of the other hand at Sarah. "I *know* that you're not telling me that you don't care what happened to your stepbrother."

Sarah jerked her head up, sending out a spray of soap and warm water. "You didn't see him, Jen! He was a self-righteous monster, accusing Tom of everything! It was *his* foolishness that caused me to get hurt!"

The maid frowned and lifted up a corner of her apron to wipe a foamy blob of soap from the corner of Sarah's eye. Then she gently pushed her back down toward the water. "Well, that's not what they're saying upstairs. The word is that the mechanical man attacked you."

Sarah pursed her lips, and a wave of red spread across her face. "Of course that's what they're saying. People always seem to find a way to blame Tom for everything that's gone wrong since Sir Dennis was killed."

Jenny pushed Sarah's head back into the water and resumed her work. "Young lady, you need to get ahold of yourself. Your father was extremely unhappy when he discovered you were involved in this mess." Mrs. Farrows grabbed the tap and swung it wide, sending a fresh deluge of steaming water into the tub. "Greeting him with an attitude is only going to make it worse."

"I'll try to keep my mouth closed, then." Sarah let out a sigh. "But it's never going to work. How angry is he?"

"I don't really know." She fanned out Sarah's hair, checking for any hidden pockets of soap or glass. "He locked himself in his study this afternoon."

"That's not good."

"No, it isn't. You don't remember what day it is, do you, Sarah?"

"Day? It's the sixth of February. . . ."

Mrs. Farrows squeezed out what water she could, then helped Sarah up. "Maybe that explosion rattled your brains more than you realize. It's the seventh."

Sarah's eyes widened. "Their anniversary . . ." Ever since her mother's death seven years ago, Alexander Stanton had honored the memory of his wife on the day of their marriage rather than the day of her death. He had explained to Sarah, "It is far more fitting that I celebrate our life together rather than the miserable existence I have had to endure without her."

Sarah was pulled out of the sink and found herself smothered under a stiff white towel. A feeling of nostalgic calm settled over her as the maid used it to blot the water out of her hair.

Jenny wrapped the linen around her head, carefully avoiding the stitches, and then twisted it until it gripped Sarah's skull like a vise. "Seven years may seem like a long time, but to your father it's still a fresh wound."

"I loved her, too!"

"Of course you did, but you're old enough now to understand the difference between the bond shared by a mother and her children, and that of a husband and wife."

Sarah realized that she understood the idea of that *kind* relationship, although the practicality of it still escaped her for the most part. Still, it was clearly the wrong time to explore philosophical questions of love with her housemaid, no matter how close of a confidante she might be.

After a bit more twisting, Jennifer unwound the towel and let Sarah's hair fall in a damp, stringy mess all around her head.

Sarah looked up with a hopeful smile. "How is it? Do I still need to get out the clippers and a hat?"

Mrs. Farrows tilted her head and clucked her tongue. "It looks like someone has set fire to a rat's nest, and then left it in the street." She reached into the pocket of her apron and pulled out a small handful of hairpins. "But perhaps you won't need a wig."

They sat in silence for a few minutes as Jenny pulled and pinned her wet locks.

At first Sarah tried to relax, but in the quiet, thoughts swirled around in her head. When she spoke again the words seemed to almost burst out of her. "What would you do if you found out that someone you loved wasn't actually the person you thought they were at all?"

The maid stopped her work and pulled out the remaining pins she had been holding in her mouth. "Whatever do you mean?"

"If it turned out that your entire life had been a lie, and that someone you thought had been honorable was actually despicable—what would you do?"

"Oh, Sarah, such melodrama," Mrs. Farrows said, stepping in front of her former charge and looking her straight in the eye. "I know you're a forward-thinking girl, but up until now you've lived in a world of privilege and wealth that's kept you apart from a lot of the cra . . . bad things in this world." She put her hand up to Sarah's face in a compassionate gesture. "I've told you this before, but you need to know that life can be dangerous no matter what your station, especially for a pretty young girl like yourself. And you can only be as willful as the people around you are willing to put up with, especially if you're a woman."

"What about right and wrong?"

"Nice luxuries when you can afford them."

Sarah rolled her eyes. "You're saying I should apologize to my father."

"I'm saying that despite any misgivings you have about Master Stanton, he has given everyone in this house a very good life. Perhaps not always an easy one, but no one who lives under his roof, no matter *who* they are, should take him for granted."

"He'd never throw me out."

Jenny lifted up some hair hanging in front of Sarah's face, pulled it outward, and then pinned it back roughly. "Never say 'never,' girl. Nathaniel was once a second son to that man, and he hasn't been allowed to set foot in this house for the last two years."

"Allowed? Nathaniel chose to move out."

"So everyone told you." She held out her hand and helped Sarah up from the stool. "But what you *don't* know can fill volumes."

Before Sarah could ask another question there was a knock at the door. "Come in," Jenny said, looking up. "She's ready."

The kitchen door swung in to reveal the house butler, O'Rourke. He always spoke in a metered and deliberate tone, as if he were announcing a funeral. "If the mistress would come with me . . ."

"We'll talk more later," Mrs. Farrows said, giving her a kiss on the cheek. "And just remember that he's still your father no matter what."

"Thank you, Jenny."

She followed behind the old Irishman as he trundled down the wood-paneled corridor, the gas lamps doing their usual futile job of effectively lighting anything but the ceiling. Sarah thought back to the marvelous electric lights from Darby's laboratory and imagined how much less ominous everything would appear in their full and friendly glow.

Her father's office was at the end of the hall, behind a massive oaken door. It seemed like a different place now. No longer a room full of forbidden secrets, but a cave with a terrible monster at its core.

The hinges gave an ominous creak as O'Rourke pulled it open. "The butler's bones," she thought to herself. It was a childhood joke that she and Nathaniel had shared, and the smile it brought to her lips quickly faded.

The room beyond was mostly dark. The curtains were drawn, and the light inside came from an oil lamp sitting on her father's massive wooden desk, and from a roaring fire on the side wall, its crackling flames sending out a glow that seemed to dance around the room.

"Come in, Sarah." The voice was cool and even.

"Will that be all, sir?" said O'Rourke.

Her father lifted his arm and waved his hand as a response.

The butler didn't say a word this time. He simply nodded and melted back into the darkened hall with practiced grace. The door shut behind her, and the room became darker, and quite possibly colder.

Sarah didn't wait to be ordered in before she stepped forward. "Father, I—"

He cut her off. "Don't bother to try and give me one of your 'explanations,' Sarah. I've heard all I need to know." She recognized the timbre of his voice immediately—the familiar note of disappointment she'd been hearing from him almost constantly for the last few years. This was a different man than she had seen the other day, and she would need to be careful.

She took a few steps forward, trying to stop at the edge of the carpet. Instead she tripped slightly, her foot coming down onto the wooden floor with a sharp snap. "All you need to know without actually bothering to speak with me, you mean."

He sighed and leaned back in his chair. "I've indulged you too much. I'm realizing now that that may have been the cause of all this."

He looked up at her. There was a tense quivering around his eyes that made her feel a deep sense of unease. "But I'm sure you have something to say for yourself."

"I don't know what Nathaniel told you happened out there, but it—"

"Did you know that they've had to amputate Bill Hughes's legs?" He moved his lips as if he were chewing on an invisible cigar. "The poor man could barely stand by himself anyway, and now his damn legs are gone."

"Father, I—"

"Your precious machine man did that." His voice was still low, but somehow he made it sound like a shout.

"Tom? That's not—" Sarah tottered back a step, feeling the force of her father's anger. "I—"

"I've tried with you, Sarah. I have. And you've always had a tender heart." He looked away from her. "You're very like your mother in that regard. It's a good trait in and of itself, but in your case it's become one of far too many weaknesses."

"What are you saying, Father? Are you going to cast me out?"

"Cast you . . . ?" He made a face at her, followed by a grim laugh. "I love you, Sarah. You're my only daughter. Do you believe that I would turn you into a ruined woman of the streets? You really think so little of me"—he took a deep breath—"or of this *family* and our good name, that you think I might be willing to do that out of anger?"

Sarah felt her resolve wilting in spite of itself. Her father seemed capable of turning her back into a child at a moment's notice under the best of circumstances, and these were far from the best. "What happened at the Darby mansion . . . I was only trying to help."

"Why were you even *there*, Sarah? I told you I wanted you to stay away from the Paragons. What possible good did you think you were going to do by getting involved with that ridiculous machine?"

"Darby trusted him."

"Darby *made* him. But even a trained dog can become a feral animal when its master isn't around to hold the leash."

Sarah leaned forward and spoke softly. "If you just stopped and thought about things for a minute you might realize that you've never given Tom a chance."

He slammed both hands down onto the oaken surface of the desk. "Don't be such a child!" The ink and blotters jumped as he did so, sending the pen rolling off onto the floor. "I've fought by his side. I've seen him kill men with those metal hands. He isn't a person, Sarah, or a china doll. He's a machine, a weapon." Her father stood up, sending the chair behind him crashing down. "He's as emotionless and deadly as a Colt revolver."

"Guns don't speak. They don't think."

"Enough!" her father thundered. "I'm not going to debate with you about things that you had no business being involved with in the first place." He pointed to the chair next to her. "Now I want you to take a seat, Sarah, while I explain to you how things are going to be from here on out."

Sarah looked over at the padded office chair sitting next to her. When she looked back she saw that her father was picking his own chair back up off the ground.

He turned his head and looked up at her. "Can you no longer simply obey the simplest request I make?"

She stood there in silence, her brain trying to wrap itself around what was happening, but failing to find any context for it.

"I said *sit*!"

Sarah grabbed the chair and dropped herself into it. Even as the springs sagged underneath her she could feel herself moving into a petulant and angry pose—the classic position of a child being scolded by an angry parent.

Having finished pulling his chair upright her father sat back down and faced her across his desk. "Now then . . ." His face was red with a slight sheen of moisture across it, although it clearly wasn't the exertion from picking up a chair that had made him sweat.

He grabbed up a sheet of paper that had a short list of items drawn on it. She could see that it was numbered, but she could not read the rest of it from her position.

"First, you're already long past a reasonable age by which you should at least have found a suitable prospect for a husband. Instead, at the age of nineteen, your only genuine suitor is the boy who was raised as your brother—one you seem quite content to let burn alive in a fire."

"I didn't!" she gasped.

"*Not*," he said firmly, "another *word* until I'm finished." He gave the paper in front of him a terse little shake. "I will do whatever it takes to see you engaged by the end of the social season."

Sarah pursed her lips, but didn't respond.

"Second, you are no longer allowed to leave this house without my permission, and even then you must be in the company of an approved chaperone. For some reason you believe it is perfectly acceptable for a girl of your age and station to roam the streets of New York alone. I can assure you that it is not. You may not care about this family's good name, but the last thing I need is for my daughter, the daughter of the leader of the Paragons for God's sakes, to be hurt, killed, or worse in some random street crime. So far you've managed to keep yourself out of the papers, but not for lack of trying, it seems.

"Finally, you are, from now on, absolutely banned from having anything to do with that machine, or any Paragon business of any sort. I've somehow been unable to convince you that your life is no longer a part of that world. Bad enough that I have to deal with your stepbrother gallivanting around in that ridiculous flying suit of his.

"Darby tried to convince me that allowing you some freedom would make you a well-rounded girl. But it made you rebellious and willful."

Sarah felt a ball of growing dread rising up in her.

"And if, for some reason, you come into contact with the Automaton again, I expect you to treat that machine like the deadly menace that it is and report it to the Paragons immediately."

Sarah sat there in silence, and as the words faded she realized that her hands were wrapped so tightly around the arms of her chair that her fingers had turned white.

Her father crossed his arms and leaned back into his seat. "I know you sometimes find this hard to believe, but I love you, and I'm doing all of this for you."

She found herself so filled with rage that she was almost unable to move. Responses bubbled through her head, but she couldn't possibly vocalize the words. Not only would they make things worse, they'd open up a gap between her and her father that would never be closed.

He did love her; she knew that. Maybe differently than she hoped, not unconditionally and not with the same respect that he had given her mother. . . . She tried to tell herself that this was the only way he knew how to show it.

She opened her mouth to say "I understand." The words that came out were entirely different. What she said was, "There's a traitor in the Paragons." It surprised her when she heard it coming from her own lips. More so because there was a part of her that still thought that it might be him.

Alexander Stanton sat up in his chair, his face reddening.

Sarah wanted to stop herself from saying any more, but the words were out there. It was as if she had dropped an anchor from her mouth and the chain was dragging everything else out of her as it fell. "Someone had to have told the killer when we'd be on the bridge," she continued. "He couldn't just have been waiting for us there by coincidence."

Her father closed his eyes. She could hear the breath flooding in and out through his nose. It was like a bull getting ready to charge, or a locomotive gathering speed. He said her name slowly out loud, and she could hear the strain in his voice as he did it. "Sarah . . ."

"Someone killed Mr. Wickham."

"Sarah!" Once again his hands slammed down onto the desk, harder than before. "Your tin toy killed Wickham!" he roared. "I've already told you once: *You are done with the Paragons!*"

He stood up and pulled a thick gold rope that hung from the ceiling next to him. From outside in the hallway there was the sound of a ringing bell. "And you are obviously incapable of reason right now. Sterner methods are required."

Her eyes flew open wide. "What are you saying?"

"You are absolutely forbidden to leave this house until such time as I believe that I can trust you again."

Sarah laughed nervously. "That's ridiculous! I'm trying to help you. . . . Help everyone."

"You've been mesmerized by Darby and his sodomite friend. Hopefully this will help undo that influence." He pulled the bell rope harder this time, but instead of having the intended effect, the bell made a single, strangled "gonk" as it was pinned inside of its box. "If I find out that you've left this house without my authorization, then I'll have you sent far away from New York to a convent where you can learn to be a proper lady."

The door swung open, and Daniel O'Rourke was standing behind it. To

Sarah's eyes it appeared as if he was eager to take part in whatever hysteria it was that had brought him here. "Yes, sir?"

"I want Sarah taken to her room immediately. She is to remain there until such time as I have determined that she should be able to leave it."

"I'm an adult! You can't just—!"

She felt the Irishman's hand close around her forearm. "Please come with me, Miss Stanton." She had an instinct to spin round and punch the man, but she held it in check.

"Father, if you truly do love me, you have to listen to me. Tom wasn't lying to me. I know it!" She knew the outbreak would only serve to make things worse, but she had to get the words out. She felt desperate and alone, but maybe she could at least say something that might let her father realize the truth—if not today, then soon enough to do something about it . . . if he wasn't the traitor himself.

"Get her out of here."

Gripping her arm tightly, and with surprising strength, the old butler steered her out through the door and into the hallway. She looked back just as it closed, and in that instant saw Alexander Stanton glaring at her through narrowed eyes.

Chapter 22

Deathbeds

In the two days since the Darby house had burned to the ground the snow hadn't stopped falling. Sometimes it dropped in a heavy white curtain; other times it was simply a few flakes blowing to and fro in the wind before reaching the ground. But across the city only the stone and brick sides of the buildings were still visible, while the roofs and streets were an endless vista of white.

It was still New York, but somehow a quieter, gentler version of the place. On the Lower East Side the wide-eyed faces of children peered out onto the streets from inside the front-room windows of candle-lit tenements, drinking in the magic of the city transformed.

Along Allen Street their vigilance had been rewarded with the sight of a mysterious man who had been standing in the middle of the road, unmoving, for half an hour. He wore a badly torn cloth coat, with thick woolen gloves covering his hands. The boots on his feet were old and scuffed, and the hood over his head kept his face mostly in shadow.

The children weren't the only ones who had noticed the man, and one of the tenants stepped out the door of his dilapidated tenement to face the stranger. He stood threateningly on the top of the stairs with a long wooden club in one hand and a lantern in the other. The chimney glass had a large crack in it, and the cheap oil smoked badly as it burned, smothering the light so that it could only let out a grimy yellow glow. Snowflakes hissed as they landed on it and vaporized.

"Whatcha want?" the man said, holding the polished branch up above his head. He was dressed in breeches and a buttoned-up shirt that was so worn it was only a step above rags. The paper jammed into his shoes was sticking out through the holes in the leather, and the misshapen hat on his head had once been a simple Irish cap—now it was just a wedge of cloth pulled tightly over his head, the brim threadbare and misshapen.

"There is no need to . . . threaten me. I simply wish to talk with one of the . . . residents inside."

"Ye can go to hell for all I care, but yer not gettin' in here." The man's accent was thick already, but he was clearly drunk, and it made him slur the words even more. "Go 'way." He took a swipe at the air with his stick.

The Automaton did not move. "I can wait."

His face was unshaven, and when he opened his mouth to speak it was clear that the time he could have been helped by any kind of dental surgery was long past. "Ye been waitin' here fer 'aff an hour already. Don't need some bastard in a mask freezin' ta death on our stoop, bringin' cops and rats and God knows what else."

Tom tilted his head upward slightly, letting the light reflect off the flesh-colored paint on his face. Two glassy, lidless eyes looked out from behind the eye holes. They moved away, and then back at the man again.

"Jaysus! What the hell's wrong with yer face?"

"I had a very bad . . . accident. This covers my burned . . . flesh." He reached up toward his mask with a gloved hand, as if he was about to lift it away and reveal what lay underneath. "It keeps the . . . children from screaming."

The man held up his arm to cover his eyes and turned away. "What are ye doin' man? I din't ask ta see it."

Tom dropped his hand. "I mean no one any . . . harm. I only wish to speak with a person named . . . Murphy McAuliffe. Does he live here?"

The man walked down the snow-covered steps to the street and shoved his lamp forward, looking the Automaton up and down. "There's over one hundred souls in here, and so maybe he does and maybe he doesn't. But if ya don' leave now yer sure enough gonna get a taste of me shillelagh." He brandished the knotted branch at him threateningly.

Tom took a stride forward, and the man swung the club at him. It was an expert blow, and even if the man's addled state had taken some of the precision out of it, it still was aimed directly at his head.

Tom caught it with his left hand and plucked the stick away. "I told you that I mean no harm."

The man tried to back away and slipped on the snow. Tom dropped the weapon and grabbed his wrist, pulling him up to his feet before he could fall.

"What the hell?" the drunken man replied, and slammed Tom's head with his fist.

"You are obviously unwilling to help." Extending the arm that was holding the man's wrist, he swung around and then let go. The man went flying out into the street, tripping on a hidden piece of rutted ice and collapsing onto the snow, his hands digging into the filth and mud hidden beneath its pristine white surface. "Please stay out of my way."

There were ten steps from the street up to the door. As Tom neared the top the door swung open and a woman stepped forward onto the stoop. She was clearly in her later years, and time had been decidedly unkind to her. Her face was puffy and blotched, with a shiny sheen, as if she had been waxed too many times. Her back was stooped, and she walked with a shuffling gait. "So, you want from this man you're going to see, what?" Her accent spoke of a very different world from the Irishman's.

"I believe he killed some . . . friends of mine."

"And you're telling me you mean him no harm?"

"Only if he . . . attacks first."

"I suppose you don't think what might happen to the rest of us when you fight." She pulled her shawl tighter around her shoulders. It was clearly only of limited use against the cold.

Tom's glass eyes danced around hard enough to make a metallic click. "I will do my best to . . . protect you if I can."

"Because you think you're a hero. Like one of them high-and-mighty Paragons?"

"Much like that, yes."

"Feh," she said. "Heroes don't care. All *they* do is make sure their rich friends, they don't get hurt. But do you think they ever come down here and protect us?"

"If they knew . . ."

"You think they *don't* know? You think they couldn't come down here and clean up Five Points, or that fancy dead scientist couldn't make an army of metal men to come down here and be a police for this place?" Her righteousness had brought back a touch of youth to her cheeks, and for a moment, as her rage grew, she seemed to stand a few inches taller. "Nobody cares about anybody. Everyone just wants: wants to get out, wants to get rich, wants that little bit of food their neighbor has. All that wanting, down here, you ain't getting none of it." Suddenly a look of shock grew on her face. "Look out!"

The drunk man had slowly snuck up on Tom from behind, raising his shillelagh. The Automaton wheeled his massive right arm up and behind him, landing it firmly against the man's chin.

Struck hard by the blow, the man flailed his arms as he tumbled back down the stairs, dropping his weapon but managing to grab the stone railing on his way down. His momentum was stronger than his grasp, and as he wheeled sideways his feet slid out from underneath him.

Losing his grip, he tumbled down the rest of the stairs and landed head-first on the sidewalk. He sat there unmoving, and if the snow had cushioned the fall it was impossible to tell from the way he had fallen.

Tom's eyes clicked again, then popped and jiggled around in an inhuman manner. "I didn't mean to hurt him." Something had become stuck in the cold. "I am . . . sorry."

"That one? That one you can kill." She closed her eyes and nodded. "He's a stupid drunk, so maybe you are a hero after all."

"I . . . assure you that I'm—"

She nodded. "Murphy's apartment is on the top. Him and his no-good took over the whole floor." Her shoulders sank as she continued. "Stole it. Wouldn't let nobody in and kicked all the tenants out, even the nice lady whose husband ran away on her."

Tom started to move past her when she continued. "But you won't find McAuliffe in there."

"Where is he?"

"Gone."

"I'll wait." He took a single step upward and then turned back.

"You can wait all winter. He's not coming back."

"Where did he go?"

"Left his friend to die up there. Like a dog." Her foot scuffed the snow. "Such a thing, Eli so sick now and all . . ."

". . . Elli?"

She tried to make the name clearer through her accent, "E-li. Eisenshmidt. Smart boy, like a whip. He was going to be a rabbi, but once his mother passed away he stopped talking to God. . . ." Her voice trailed off for a moment, and she waved away something invisible. "That Irishman, the good-for-nothing, he said he was his friend, and then left him. No friend would leave you alone to die."

"I am told every . . . person dies alone, in the end."

She wiped away a tear that had gathered at the corner of her eye and then looked at the Automaton more closely. "Not you I think, golem."

Tom nodded. "I appreciate your . . . help." He reached into his pocket, pulled out a coin, and pressed it into her hand.

At first she looked at it as if she was going to protest. But when she saw the golden dollar he had placed there, the woman closed her mouth and shuffled out of the way.

The Automaton opened the door and entered into the darkness of the front hallway. Flickering yellow stripes of light appeared as the ground-floor residents peered out through thinly opened doors, looking to find out more about the commotion outside.

The wooden floorboards creaked under the weight of Tom's steps as he mounted the stairs and moved slowly and steadily upward, stopping only to turn and head up the next flight of steps. Besides the groans of the wood, the only sounds were muffled whispers behind the walls.

When he reached the bottom of the third stairwell Tom stopped in front of a thick wooden timber that barred the way. The beam had been painted red and was bolted to a hinge so that it could be easily lifted to provide access. The word "STOP!" had been crudely painted across it in large white letters, with an omega symbol drawn to the right of it.

Tom lifted the gate out of the way and went up the stairs to the landing. A huge omega symbol had been painted on the wall, with "The Brotherhood of Eschaton" lettered underneath in neat block print. Tom quietly ran his hand across it.

There was a door to the right, and although it was locked, the wood splintered easily enough when he shoved it with his massive right arm.

The inside of the apartment was dark and cold. All the walls had been ripped out, turning the space into a long tunnel with a single window at the far end that had been plastered over. Wooden workbenches of different sizes and shapes were pushed up against the wall. They looked similar to the ones Darby had kept in his basement, with tools and metal objects strewn across them.

Pausing in front of one of them, Tom reached down and picked a large metal box out of a pile of parts. It was the barrel of a Gatling gun, and the harness and handle of Rapid Fire's weapon sat nearby.

Tom put it down and left the workshop by the door he had entered. He walked back into the corridor, and as he began to explore a loud groan came from an open door on the far end.

"Murphy? Is that you?" The voice was familiar, but sounded weaker than the last time Tom had heard it. "Did the boss make you come back for me, you sorry Irish bastard?"

Tom opened the door and stepped into the apartment. "I told you Lord Eschaton wouldn't abandon me!" the man yelled. It was followed by a burst of coughing, and then a series of short gasps, as if Eli were being choked.

Most of the apartment was taken up by a large coal stove. A few clothes hung above it along a thick piece of rope that had been stretched across the room, but the iron was cold and the interior was dark, any embers having burned out a long time ago.

The coughing subsided. "Murphy? Why aren't you answering me?"

Tom opened the door to the back room and stepped inside. "Because I am not . . . Murphy."

Eli was lying in a small bed, covered in a swath of sheets and blankets that he had tucked around his frame to ward off the cold.

Shaking as he moved, the man reached over to the small table at the side of the bed and slid open a box of wooden matches. He pulled out one and struck it against the bed frame. It exploded violently into flame. "Ah. The golem." He held the fire up against the edge of a candle until it lit. "I should have guessed you would find me."

"Hello . . . Eli."

"How do I look?" As the candle guttered into full brightness the extent of the man's sickness became more clearly visible. Despite the cold the covers were thrown back, and he lay stretched out on the bed, naked except for a pair of dirty white cotton briefs that were tied around his waist. His withered arm was folded tight against his side, as if there were a child hidden underneath him.

"I cannot 'see' you, but my . . . senses tell me that you're not well." Every inch of the man's exposed flesh was mottled and gray except for marbled lines of pure white that streaked across his body. Occasional blisters had formed on his skin, filled with a translucent pink liquid.

But it was his head that had clearly borne the brunt of his illness. It was swollen and misshapen, with weeping sores everywhere. His hair was mostly gone. Only a few clumps remained. "What do you think of the new me—the monster that a golem created?"

Tom took a step forward. "I have no . . . opinion."

"That's nice of you."

"This was from the . . . fortified smoke?"

"You got it." He let out another series of long, unhealthy-sounding coughs.

"'A miracle,' I thought! The building collapses, but somehow I'm still alive. The smoke makes me tough, I think, so I looked for you, hoping to take you back to him. But you'd escaped somehow."

"I broke through the back wall."

"Through the wall. Why didn't I think of that?" Eli lifted his hand weakly and waved a finger at the side of the bed. "Can you get me a glass of water? I can't stop sweating."

Tom obliged, grabbing the badly chipped pitcher that stood on the wooden table and pouring out a full glass. He held it out to him.

Eli tried to lift his good arm, but it was clear from his wildly shaking hands that he no longer had the meager motor skills needed to hold anything. "I'm afraid I can't move so much anymore. My body keeps getting harder. I'm stiff like a thousand-year-old man. . . . It's not so easy to talk, too, but for you I'll spare a few words before I go."

Tom lowered himself down next to the sick man, slipping his left arm underneath the pillow to lift up Eli's head.

Eli groaned, and then grunted as he stiffly and slowly rose. "How do you like your new arm?"

"I liked the old one better." Tom helped him up. When he was high enough Tom tipped the glass into his mouth. As the water touched his lips the gray coloring on his skin started to swirl and move, as if it were being repelled. The smoke parted for an instant, making a visible path on the surface of his skin as the liquid slid down the entire length of his throat. It stopped when it reached his stomach, and then closed up behind it. Eli looked down. "Can you see that, golem? It's some kind of miracle, all right—just not the good kind."

"I can't see it, but I can sense it."

"Strange, no? The smoke reacts to the water, even though it's in my skin. It's like a coat, but there's no way to take it off."

Tom lowered Eli back onto the bed. The white lines along Eli's body twisted and flashed as he did so, like cracks opening and closing in his skin.

Eli glanced up at the Automaton's iron right limb. "How did you do that, with the arm?"

"I can repair myself."

"But a whole new arm . . ."

"Since Darby died I have had to learn how to take care of myself." Tom lifted up his borrowed limb and waved it around. "Given the . . . events since I last encountered you, this has turned out to be a useful . . . tool."

"I heard about you beating up the Iron-Clad."

"Did you build his . . . armor as well?"

Eli closed his eyes and rolled his head to the side. "Is this going to be an interrogation now? Because if you came here to get my secrets, golem, I can promise you that most of them—" The coughing started again. "Most of them, I'm taking to the grave." He managed a smile.

Tom put down his arm. "I came here to find . . . Murphy."

"That miserable Mick is long gone. When he figured I was going to die, he ran away. Then I thought, maybe the boss, he would save me. I mean he's been through the same thing. Maybe he knew . . ."

"Who is the . . . boss?"

It was intended as a chuckle, but the sound that actually came out of Eli's throat was a deep, rusty rasp, followed by a series of wheezes. "You still don't know, you poor sap? The mighty, mighty Paragons, greatest goyim in the history of the world, and altogether you know less than nothing. Lord Eschaton has your friends wrapped all the way around his little finger, and none of you even know a damn thing." He started to laugh again.

"Murphy mentioned the . . . Children of Eschaton that morning when he killed . . . Darby."

The horrifying wheezing stopped. "That's because he was *supposed* to tell you that. Give you a message."

"Where is he?"

Eli began coughing again. It was the same as before, but a note lower. The intensity seemed to double with each exhalation, until finally it caught somewhere between a rumble and the smothered screams of a man being strangled to death. The white streaks began to move again, shaking and jumping across Eli's entire body.

Tom stood up and pointed his right arm at Eli. Steam began to pour out through the hole. He waved it back and forth, spreading the mist across the sick man's body. The instant it touched his skin the gray disappeared. At first it simply parted, and then it spread out, rolling back the darkness that covered his flesh like the sun burning through a morning fog. After a minute the taint had disappeared entirely, and Tom dropped his arm back down to his side.

The coughing slowly passed, and Eli gulped in the air, drawing it down deep into his lungs. He lifted up his left hand to look at it, and his eyes widened at what he saw. "You've cured me!"

Tom shook his head. "Doubtful. Even if the . . . poison is gone, your . . . brain is still dangerously enlarged, and the . . . sores on your skin may become infected."

Eli ignored the words. "It's a miracle. A miracle is what it is!"

"Perhaps. If it is, will you revise your opinion of . . . fortified steam?"

Eli laughed. It was a very different sound than the rasping chuckle he'd made only a few minutes before. "Maybe that Darby was onto something after all."

Tom reached over and grabbed the pitcher from the table next to him. He tilted his head backward, farther and farther until it almost leaned against his back. He poured the remaining water down into a tube in his neck.

Eli sat up. When he tried to move Tom placed his left hand on the man's bare chest, his fingers spread wide. It took only a small amount of effort to push Eli back down onto the bed and hold him there. He placed the pitcher back down, and his head slowly lifted itself back into place.

The little man struck out with his fist. It made a loud crack when it connected with Tom's mask, which was followed by a very human yelp of pain. "Damn it, golem. What's the matter with you?"

"Flesh versus metal usually has a clear winner." The Automaton's arm didn't move or flinch as Eli tried to pull it away from his chest. "Now tell me about . . . Lord Eschaton."

"Do you even know what Eschaton is?"

"Yes. It is a . . . Greek word. It means 'last.'"

"Close. It means 'the end.' The end of everything. You, me—the world! Everything you know!" He grunted as he tried again to pull the metal arm away. Tom pushed harder, sinking the man deeper into the straw mattress.

"And why would you want that? Wouldn't the end of the . . . world be the end of you as well?"

"Maybe? Maybe we're reborn in this new world. Giving up fighting the metal arm he reached over and rubbed the stunted limb on his right side. "And what did I have to live for, golem? I'm not like your fancy rich friends in their uptown apartments. For a freak like me this world has not very much. What *I* wanted, I wanted to be left alone and to build stuff. But instead I got grief."

"The woman . . . downstairs said you were once close to becoming a rabbi."

"Hattie? So she wishes. . . . I've got nothing to say to God anymore." He rose up a fist and shook it toward the ceiling. "You hear that, Yahweh? You're a children's story! People should tear down your churches and burn all your books!"

"But you don't . . . wish to die."

"Lord Eschaton has a plan for after the world ends. What's next is something better."

"I need you to tell me how to find him."

"Go to hell."

Tiny black dots started to grow on Eli's skin. "Just a name or a . . . location. Give me one of those and I will be . . . lenient."

"I don't need your pity, or your mercy."

"I helped you after you tried to . . . destroy me."

The dots were growing larger and faster—joining together to create dark patches across his skin. Eli coughed and held up his arm. A look of horror grew on his face as the gray returned. "What's happening to me?"

"I told you that it was . . . doubtful I had cured you. You are still dying . . . Eli."

Eli reached up and grabbed the back of Tom's metal arm. "No! You're a Paragon. You've gotto help me! I can't go through this again. I don't want to die!" He let out a moan, then a scream.

"I'll try . . . Eli. But I need you to tell me how to find . . . Lord Eschaton."

Things were progressing rapidly now. The gray had covered Eli completely, and the white lines once again danced like living things across his flesh. One of them twitched across his chest, pulsing brightly. The smell of burnt skin rose into the air on a puff of smoke. Eli screamed. "You've got to help me, golem! In the name of God!"

Tom poured more steam out from his arm. The gray parted, but this time it didn't recede. "It's no use. Please tell me what I need to . . . know before it's too late."

Every word Eli spoke came out of him as a croak. He jerked and twisted as his muscles began to violently spasm and constrict. "Tomorrow . . . The arm."

Tom held up his borrowed right limb. "This arm?"

"Schmuck! No! Arm . . . at the square!"

"I don't understand."

There was a wet snap as one of Eli's ribs gave way under the pressure of his own contracting muscles. He screamed, and his mouth stayed open, pulled wide as every tendon in his neck contracted and refused to relax. Smoke-colored tears pooled in the corners of his eyes and then rolled down across his face.

"I need more! . . . Eli!"

“Garden . . . Liberty . . .” he said, and then froze. His muscles locked into rictus, freezing him as a screaming statue. Tom placed his hand on Eli’s chest. The heart beat once more with a thunderous boom—then froze.

After a minute the white lines faded and turned to black.

Chapter 23

Liberty's Arm

The sun had dropped below the horizon an hour before, and the clouds that had blanketed the city for the last few days had finally parted. For anyone who cared to look, the glowing remnants of the day were still visible, outlining the western edge of the city skyline in a rusty orange. Smoke and steam billowed up from the buildings, filling the night air with twisting columns of white. Frosted hotel windows all around glowed with yellow lights from the people who huddled inside them.

But this was still New York City, and despite the treacherous roads and the cold, traffic continued to move up and down Broadway. As the final few wagons headed back downtown after a day of deliveries in treacherous weather, the tired iron-shod hooves of the draft horses clip-clopped against the icy cobblestones.

The temperature was already well below freezing, but it still had farther to go. The bitter cold was gripping the city, refreezing the snow that hadn't melted during the day, leaving behind patches of ice that temporarily memorialized the remnants of the human activity that had passed through it. Full of frozen ruts and footprints, the sidewalks were now treacherous terrain.

Madison Garden was empty now, free from the constant activity of the shoppers and tourists that filled it during the daytime.

Only a single pathetic figure, dressed in rags, sat on the benches in Madison Square, rocking slowly back and forth.

Only an occasional cheer—a muffled roar that rose from inside the arena at the north end of the park—could be heard punctuating the silence. Nearby, the flickering light of the gas lamps reflected dimly in the copper surface of the Torch of Liberty. The gigantic disembodied arm stood in the middle of the promenade, its hand holding the flame up just high enough to reach above the leafless, snow-covered trees. A sign at the base of it explained that it would be a gift to the people of America and that one day the torch would be raised high above the New York Harbor, but that there was a great deal of money still needed in order to begin the work to assemble the massive statue.

Underneath it stood two men. "Not really a gift if they're asking for other folks ta pay for it," said the shorter man. He was dressed in a worn tweed greatcoat, his misshapen kepi cap pulled down tightly to protect him against the cold. Sitting on the frozen ground next to him was a large carpet bag, held shut by a brass latch.

The other man was much taller, pushing past six feet by a good few inches, raised up even higher by the heels of his polished black boots. His clothes spoke of wealth and power, the brocade patterns in his long black coat tracing out the Greek omega symbol over and over again in a fine gold thread. His face was hidden—wrapped up with a scarf so that only his eyes were visible between his coat and his hat. "You shouldn't mock their goals, Murphy. It's no small thing to plan a great endeavor."

"As you know, Lord, nothing ever happens without a solid plan." He rubbed his gloved hands together. "I don't think Eli will be meeting us here tonight."

"No, perhaps not. I was hoping . . ." He nodded. "I was hoping that Eli might have survived."

Murphy scanned the park again. "It was an accident."

"Death by Automaton. . . . It was an accident that took years to perfect." He clapped his hands together. "I would have called it providence had it turned out differently. To discover some proof that I'm not the only man able to survive the process would have been a great relief."

"Maybe if you'd gone back to help him . . ."

"There is no cure, no medicine that would have saved him. Live or die—that is all there is."

"Then it is what it is."

A few yards away from them the ragged figure stood up from his bench. A liquor bottle dangled from his left hand and he stumbled toward the street with a weaving gait. His back was hunched, with a severe hump poking up from his right side. His wandering motion made it appear as if he was heavily inebriated, but he took another pull from the bottle.

The Irishman nodded in the vagabond's direction. "Maybe we should ask that one if he's seen anybody?"

The tall figure turned his head to look. "He appears fairly close to death himself. But go ahead and ask him if it will settle your conscience."

"Aye!" Murphy yelled out. "You! Come over here."

The figure stopped, looked up at them for a moment, and then began to sway in their direction. The bottle slipped free and landed on a clear patch of concrete. It shattered into glass fragments, instantly indistinguishable from the ice all around it.

As the vagabond moved closer it became clear that he was also well bundled up against the cold. He had a large piece of cloth wound around his head, but it was not nearly as stylish as what the tall man wore. He stopped a few feet away and held out his hand. "Coin for a war veteran?" The voice that rose up from the pitiable figure was horse and ragged, but each word was spoken slowly and deliberately.

"My master and I are looking for a friend of mine. I'm wondering if you might have seen him."

"What did he look like?"

The Irishman stepped forward. "Oh, you'd notice him. His skin would be black. Not brown like a negroid's, but gray."

The figure shuffled for a moment. "No. Ain't seen no one like that around here."

"You're sure?"

"Yah."

Murphy dug into his pocket and pulled out a coin. "All right, old man. Go find yourself someplace warm to sleep."

The vagabond's gloved hand reached out and grabbed the man's wrist. The coin clattered to the ground. "What the hell?" He tried to pull his arm back, but it was held fast. "Let go of me!"

The ragged man lifted his head and let the Irishman look into his false eyes. "Hello . . . Murphy. I've been . . . looking for you." He swung the man around him, letting him go after he'd completed three-quarters of a circle. The Irishman retained his balance long enough to stumble backward a few paces before his feet lost purchase on a strip of ice. The air was forced out of his lungs with a tremendous grunt as he landed flat on his back.

The force of the maneuver dislodged the cloth from the Vagabond's face. His metal mask was now clearly visible. "Your friend . . . Eli is dead."

The tall man smiled when he saw Tom's face. "The Automaton? But this is too perfect. I've been trying to figure out how I was going to track you down. With you being on the run from your friends I had assumed you'd *stay* in hiding until I at least threatened the Stanton girl. This makes everything so much easier."

Tom reached up and pulled away the rest of the cloth. The material fluttered down to land on the snow. "You are . . . Lord Eschaton." His voice had returned to its usual musical timbre.

"Yes, Tom. And it's good to hear you call me by that name." He held out his right hand. "And even better to see you again."

Tom didn't respond to the gesture. "Again? Do I know you?"

"No reason you should remember me. But I was there at your birth—the midwife at the beginning of your marvelous life."

Lord Eschaton reached out with a gloved hand and lifted up the right side of the Automaton's jacket until it slid off his shoulder, revealing the bulky iron arm hiding underneath. "Eli mentioned that you had figured out a way to incorporate new materials directly into your body. That's a most impressive trick—far from your creator's original design."

"I am able to reason beyond my basic functions." Tom shrugged the coat off and let it drop. "I can learn new things."

"Remarkable . . ." Lord Eschaton began to walk around him. "But *how* do you manage to do that, Tom? *Where* exactly do you remember it?"

Tom continued to turn so that he could face the taller man at all times. "It does not need to be explained. . . . I just . . . am."

"*Cogito ergo sum*, Tom? By all accounts you've bridged the great gap between thought and machine. No wonder the Paragons are terrified of you—something greater than they can comprehend."

Lord Eschaton began unwinding the scarf from around his head. "But I know your real secret. I know what it is that truly separates you from humanity, beyond even your clockwork body."

Tom cocked his head to the side. "And what is that?"

Underneath the silk, Lord Eschaton's skin was gray—darker in shade than Eli's had been, and completely free of any white streaks. The top of his head down to his nose was covered by a form-fitting leather mask. "You don't think with your head; you think with your heart." His words spilled out into the cold with his steaming breath.

The mask's features were blank and smooth, painted with a black gloss so thick that it almost seemed to gleam in the gaslight. Painted onto the center of it in gleaming white, in the same broad strokes that had been used on the fortified smoke cylinder and the tenement wall, was the Omega symbol.

Tom took a step backward. "You've been tainted by the . . . smoke."

"You said you visited Eli."

"He died in . . . agony."

"That's a shame." Eschaton pushed his face closer to Tom's. He smiled broadly, his lips pulling back to reveal the whiteness of his teeth shining out in stark contrast against his darkened gums. "I'm sure you were a great comfort to him in the end."

"He told me where to find you. What do you want with the . . . Paragons?"

"Always straight to the point, when it's what you want. A trait you've taken from your creator."

Lord Eschaton took a step back and continued. "All right, let's get to it, then. What I want from them is exactly what they want for you: destruction. They are an obstacle to my plans."

"Plans for the end of the . . . world."

"Indeed." He swept his arms out to his sides, holding his palms up in a grand, theatrical gesture. "This great city, this industrial era of man—it's all reaching its end. With or without me, it's just a matter of time."

"There is a great deal left for us to . . . discover."

"Us?" Lord Eschaton let out a chuckle. "How long do you think it will be before mankind has managed to infest every corner of this planet and squander all its precious resources? Five decades? Ten?" His voice gained volume with every word. "By the end of the year this park will be lit by electric light from a steam engine powered by coal. Then it will be the city, and one day the world. It will burn brighter and brighter until we have squeezed out the world's last drop of fuel."

"It is called . . . progress. Humans discover to survive."

"More Darby nonsense. I thought you said you were capable of learning, but it turns out you may not be much more than a fancy telegraph machine tapping out the words of a dead man."

Lord Eschaton drew in a deep breath of the cold night air. "Yes, progress, but where is it leading us? This is a broken world, already overflowing with humanity—armies of poor and starving wretches are allowed to live and breed based on the needs of keeping a few rich men satisfied."

Tom shook his head. "Sir Dennis said that the greatest success of . . . technology is that ultimately it . . . eases the lives of all men."

Eschaton furrowed his brow. A single white line snapped into existence straight down the center of his face. "And yet thousands more are born into poverty every day." He took a moment and smiled. "I only want what Darby wanted. It was the proper *solution* that he was always afraid to grasp.

"I don't just want a more efficient world, or a faster one. Those are meaningless dreams. We ride trolley cars across the city, and steamships over the ocean, but none of these things truly make our lives *better*. And there are so many more of us now."

He reached up and pulled the glove off of his left hand. "I want a future for the human race where we can make scientific pursuits that lead not just to quantity, but to quality."

"And to do that, you believe you must . . . destroy."

Lord Eschaton clapped his hands together, the leather smacking against his smoke-black palm. "Just so! We must immanetize the Eschaton! The time has come to destroy this world so that the better one may be born."

When he opened them, his hands contained nothing, but he pantomimed a small planet cradled above them. "The new world will no longer be built on fear and war, or any of the products of man's hatred and the rising tide of humanity. It is a world that will be built on nobler pursuits, and it will have room for more than just humans. It could be a place where an entire race of intelligent machines might find a home."

From a few feet away Murphy stirred and moaned.

Tom cocked his head to the side. "Tell your . . . man to stay down. I will have no problem finishing what we started at the . . . bridge."

Eschaton nodded. "Do as he says, Murphy, at least for a little while longer. Tom and I need to finish our conversation."

Murphy groaned out his reply.

Tom turned his head so that his glass eyes were facing Lord Eschaton again. "What you are . . . proposing is wrong."

"And what does the concept of right and wrong mean to a machine? What ethics lesson about the fundamental nature of humanity should I take away from something that isn't even human? What can I learn about life and death from something that has never been alive?"

"I am what . . . Sir Dennis made me."

"Cast in the image of his god."

"Just so."

Eschaton stood silent. His eyes traveled across Tom, following his outline up and down. "This has been a most enlightening conversation." Lord Eschaton shrugged off his coat and threw it in the direction of Murphy. "But now I know your position, and I don't think words change anyone's minds." The Irishman had managed to get to his hands and knees, and the coat landed on his back.

"But I'll be sure to keep your ethical dilemmas in mind after I've activated your brother. He will be a being created in *my* image. I'm sure he'll want to know something about you." Underneath his jacket Eschaton was wearing a clean white shirt stuffed sharply into a pair of tweed pants. Suspenders held them high up on his broad frame. The Omega symbol had been stitched into the hem in yellow thread.

Pulling down the suspenders he began to unbutton the shirt. The body underneath of it wasn't defined as much as chiseled. The flesh almost seemed to be a stone relief, except for the occasional twitches that rippled through the muscles. It was as if his every fiber were held on the verge of contraction, and only sheer force of will kept him from rolling up into a ball.

"You were the one who stole my replacement body, then."

The tall man let his shirt drop to the ground. "Not all by myself, no. I had some help—from more than one person in the end." He flexed his muscles. They moved like steel plates scraping across each other.

There was a sound of ripping fabric as the hatch in Tom's left shoulder tore through his shirt. With a hiss, a rocket ignited inside of him and flew into the night on a column of smoke. It was quiet for an instant, and then the firework exploded, bathing the park in a shower of bright light. After the pattern faded, a bright flare floated slowly to the ground, illuminating everything around them in a shimmer of green.

The look on Eschaton's face instantly turned from amusement to anger. "But why tell them you're here? You're still a fugitive."

"I am still a . . . Paragon." Tom clenched his left hand into a fist. "You and . . . Murphy McAuliffe will remain here until the . . . authorities arrive."

"No. We'll be gone long before then." He folded his hands into fists and raised his arms. "But you still have something I need, and I'm curious to find out the limits of your power."

Tom's left arm shot out in a blur and latched onto Lord Eschaton's left wrist. "I would ask you to listen to reason."

Lord Eschaton smiled. "We've tried that." White bolts raced down across his skin and gathered together at his hands. "But we simply lack common ground." He smacked Tom with his right fist, sending electricity crackling through the air.

Tom was thrown backward, the force of the blow wrenching him away from Lord Eschaton.

"You see, Automaton? I'm more than just a man now."

Tom had managed to stay on his feet. "Eli had the same reaction in his skin."

The sparks were gathering around Eschaton's hands again as he stepped forward. "Because we were both bathed in fortified smoke." This time the left fist crashed into Tom's face, denting his mask and throwing him sideways.

He followed his attack with an uppercut, and Tom stumbled backward a few steps before crashing into the park fence.

"The . . . smoke killed him."

"A just punishment. He failed to capture you, and your destruction of my warehouse set my plans back by months."

Using the gate as a brace, Tom launched himself toward his opponent. As he got close he swept out with the iron broadside of his massive right arm. It caught Eschaton along the side of his chest and swept him around. He landed on his knees in the snow.

"I *felt* that!" He rose up to his knees and clapped his hands together twice, each smack sending out a small cascade of sparks from his palms. "I actually felt it!" He clapped them together a third time, and tiny arcs of energy leapt into the air. After the fourth time, he opened them up wide to release a lightning bolt that arced across the gap between them.

The electricity sizzled and danced around Tom for an instant, and then faded away. Steam rose up from Tom's exposed metal parts, condensation dripping down onto the ground, the hot water poking small holes into the fragile crust that had formed over the surface of the snow.

Tom held up his left arm. "Is it my turn now?"

Eschaton smiled, the split of his grin revealing his dazzlingly white teeth. "We don't take turns." He charged at Tom directly, jumping into the air, and kicked his right leg into the Automaton's torso.

There was a solid thud, but the grunt that rose up didn't come out of Tom.

Lord Eschaton tried to use his momentum to step back, but Tom grabbed the tall man's left arm. He pulled up his knee and punched it into Lord Eschaton's stomach.

The gray man staggered backward from the blow but managed to find his balance after a few short steps. "Tom, you are a most surprising and outstanding piece of machinery." As he rose up his hands started to glow again, brighter this time. "Darby's crowning achievement." White streaks had started to coalesce around his fingers, snaking up from the rest of his body. The streaks of energy continued to gather until his arms were solid white all the way up to his shoulders. "I'm almost sad that I'm going to have to defile his memory."

Tom brought up an arm to block the glowing forearm that smashed down toward him. "How is it that . . . Eli died and you survived?"

"I don't actually know." A massive electric arc snapped out as their limbs pressed against each other. The crackling energy forked up to a nearby tree branch. It ripped through the wood and left it burning. "If I live for another hundred years, there may be no reliable way to rid myself of this curse, or share it."

For a moment, neither man nor machine moved. They were locked together like a single statue, connected arm to arm. Then, almost imperceptibly, Eschaton faltered.

The gray giant crossed his right arm over the left and redoubled his efforts. "I only wish you could see the body that Darby made for you, Tom. It surpasses the one you have now in every way."

And then it was Tom who was slowly being pushed back. "If only you weren't so much like your creator—so sure of your rightness about the future—I could have used you."

There was a high-noted "tink," the sound of metal snapping, and Tom dropped a few inches toward his knees. "It is not a . . . moral issue—it is what I was created for." He lifted up his right arm and pointed the handless wrist at Eschaton. Pressurized white steam poured out of it.

Everywhere it touched Lord Eschaton's skin he turned from gray to pink. Tiny electrical arcs flew into the air, leaving dark welts behind. He let out a scream and fell to his knees.

Holding the arm out in front of him, Tom continued to let the steam pour out of him until the cloud had enveloped them both.

When the vapor slid toward the ground, Eschaton's skin was white, with a slightly golden hue. It was clear from his features that he had at least some Asian heritage. The tall man looked down at his own hands, shocked. "What have you done to me?"

"Something you thought would take more than your lifetime." Tom whacked him expertly, almost surgically, with his left arm. "I cured you." He bashed Lord Eschaton repeatedly about the head and shoulders, driving him to the ground. With each blow the skin turned red, but didn't break. After a few strikes the tall man landed in the snow with a crunch. "Unfortunately it won't last long."

A wire extruded itself from the end of Tom's right arm. "Hopefully a few of these will hold you." It curled into a circular shape as it came out of him.

As Tom bent down to apply the impromptu restraint there was a nearby clank, and before he could respond a harpoon smashed into him, throwing him backward. The lance failed to penetrate the iron armor of his right shoulder, shattering as it struck. Metal shards flew in every direction.

"You forgot about me, didn't you?" the Bomb Lance said, as he stood in front of Tom and smiled.

Tom rose up, snow falling off of him. "I misjudged how long it would take for you to regain your . . . bearings and load your weapon."

"None of us are perfect." As Murphy moved his left arm upward there was a quiet whistle. A four-inch metal rod was now sticking out of his shoulder, appearing out of nowhere. The Irishman turned to look at it with disbelief. "What in hell?"

Tom was aiming his right arm directly at Murphy. "A new trick that I learned from you."

"Damn you!" He tried to aim and fire, but two more metal rods appeared next to the first. Murphy fired wildly, his harpoon making a ringing sound as it pierced the copper skin of the arm of Liberty.

Tom fired two more of the tiny spears into the Irishman's legs. Murphy dropped to the ground, screaming in agony. "You're a monster! A damned monster!"

Tom got to his feet. "I'm a . . . machine. Something you should be very . . . glad of, since I do not have an urge to take . . . revenge on you for killing my creator." He fired another rod into the fallen man, pinning his shoulder to the ground. "Not . . . much of one, anyway."

Lord Eschaton's voice boomed up from behind him. "So you do have emotions—the ability to hate, perhaps?" The gray had rolled back over him, covering him completely except for two small spots in his chest where it seemed unable to retake its hold. White lines pulsed around the place where shards of iron—broken splinters of the Bomb Lance's harpoon—were still sticking out of his body. He grinned his black grin and then pulled one of the shards out of his skin. The blood on it was white.

Tom held out his right arm again. He fired off a stream of rods, each one pinging as it bounced off of the huge man.

Lord Eschaton smiled. "It's over now." Moving around to the side of the Automaton, Eschaton grabbed the iron arm and twisted. "Eli made that for *me*. I'm going to take this back." There was a terrible sound of wrenching metal as the iron arm tore free. A cloud of steam hissed out from Tom's shoulder. Where it touched Eschaton's skin the darkness thinned, but didn't disappear.

"You had me, but you failed to finish me." He raised the arm up above his head. "I'm afraid that was your only chance." He brought the freed limb down in a vicious arc. It connected with Tom's head and spun him around.

Without missing a beat, Eschaton reversed his motion and smashed it back up again. Stumbling backward, Tom collapsed against the arm of Liberty. The copper let out a hollow ring. "Stop." After the next blow Tom's head lolled to one side, torn free from the mechanisms that had controlled it. Water gurgled up from the tube in his neck.

Tom lifted up his remaining arm to defend himself. Lord Eschaton smacked it away, then pinned it against the copper arm with his foot. He raised the iron arm up like a club and rained down blow after blow. The Automaton's metal face was torn away, then the eyes, the glass orbs shattering on the ground as the wires holding them in place ripped free.

"I am sorry about this, Tom. You were something very special." With the next blow the head came away entirely, tumbling toward Murphy, who was still attempting to pull one of the rods out of his shoulder.

"Stay dead, you monster," the Irishman said as the battered brass skull rolled to a stop.

Eschaton reached down and ripped open the front of Tom's shirt. The Automaton's legs were drumming against the arm of Liberty. A heavy grinding started to rise up from his chest. "I'm not sure if you can still hear me, Tom." He wrapped his fingers around the brass chest plates and pulled. They came away with a series of pops, and when he threw them to the ground they landed in a patch of snow with a dull thud. "But I want you to know that you did the best you possibly could." The cogs inside of Tom were still moving, metal rods and wires sliding around toward his shoulder, trying to form some kind of rudimentary arm. "It wasn't your fault. It was too late from the moment it began."

Throwing the iron limb aside, Lord Eschaton reached in and wrapped his hand around Tom's heart. "There has always been corruption in the Paragons." The first tug pulled up the whole torso with it. "The seeds were planted when Darby founded that ridiculous organization, and it has taken root in the years that followed." Then he let Tom slide down onto the ground. "All I did was water it a little bit."

Holding Tom by the cage around his heart, Eschaton smashed the

Automaton against the arm. Cogs flew out in every direction. "They think they're civilized men, but just under the surface lives their vanity and anger." After a first few blows the legs stopped moving, simply dangling in the air. "Darby's desire to see the best in humanity blinded him to it."

He threw Tom to the ground and stepped onto his waist. Reaching down he ripped the brass cage free from the center of Tom's chest. Cogs and springs spilled out onto the concrete.

Removed from the body, the heart was little more than a large metal sphere held in a brass cage. Spinning rods jutted out of it at different angles, a circular cog at the end of each one. The toothed wheels spun back and forth, seeming almost desperate to find something to latch onto. A small jet of steam sprayed out from it in a regular beat.

On the bottom of the brass sphere was a large bolt with a wing nut on top. "Can you still hear me now, Automaton? I wonder." He began to unscrew the bolt. "Where does your body end and your thoughts begin?" There was a metallic squeal as metal threads twisted against each other. "We may never know.

"Darby thought his Alpha Element would save the world—a source of clean, limitless energy that would power a new Utopia." After a few more turns the bolt came free. "But it's a lie. Technology alone won't save humanity. We aren't such noble creatures." Eschaton slipped the bolt out with his gloved hand, and the instant he did so the heart stopped.

"Here it is." Held in the other end of the bolt was a small, shining metal shaft. It cast a wavering, glowing light that glimmered off the copper arm standing above him. "Here is the alpha to my omega."

Murphy's voice rose up from nearby. "Did you find it, Lord?"

Eschaton nodded without taking his gaze off the object. "I did." He handed the empty heart to the other man, and the smile on Lord Eschaton's face grew wider.

"Finally, I have everything I need." He slipped the element into a lead case and dropped it into his pocket. "Now we can—"

There was a sound like a thunderous belch, and Eschaton flew off the ground like a leaf the wind. He landed five yards away, falling hard as momentum abandoned him back into the brutal hands of gravity.

The wind struck Murphy, as well, but only indirectly. As he slid across the ground the heart was torn from his hands, and it landed heavily on the concrete.

Standing next to Liberty's arm was a female figure wrapped in a man's leather coat that was clearly far too big for her. It was held in place by a thick belt strapped around her waist. A black leather mask covered her face, while the rest of her features were hidden by a curtain of leather that dropped down below her nose.

She looked down at the Automaton's body. "You killed him," she said in a threatening tone as she pointed the gun in her hand directly at the fallen form of Lord Eschaton. "I'll tear you apart!"

Chapter 24

Seen and Not Heard

After the argument with her father, Sarah had spent two days mostly in her room, and mostly alone.

For all her father's bluster, she was hardly a prisoner in the house. There had been an invitation to tea with Lady Mardens, and she had even received messages from two of her old school friends offering to come by and commiserate with her. At first she felt a little guilty for being so antisocial, especially considering that she had been completely absent from any events since the death of Darby almost two months before.

But her face was still marked from the glass. And while she would have appreciated the company, the last thing she needed to be doing was trying to explain her cuts and bruises to women who thought that having too much salt in their fricassee was a terrible act of violence.

At least the physical wounds she had incurred at the Darby house had begun to close up and scab over. Now it was the emotional pain that caused her the most discomfort.

She had spent most the night after the confrontation crying. Yesterday, after managing to gain some composure, she had admitted to herself that the girl she had been only a few short years before was dead and gone. Then Sarah had cried all the more when she realized how utterly maudlin and self-absorbed she was being, considering the real loss that had been going on around her. Later that day she decided that it had really been more about Sir Dennis than it had been about herself.

But Sarah had found herself unable to genuinely weep for Darby's death. The feelings of rage and frustration could open up the taps, but the tears wouldn't flow when she thought of the old man himself. She wondered what was wrong with her, that she could be so unfeeling. But perhaps she just wasn't ready to truly grieve for him yet.

Sarah peered out of her frosted window, staring down the street at the flickering gas lamps. Things were happening out there right now—millions of people living their lives, in a million different ways. But, she wondered to herself, how many of them carried the Paragon's greatest secret around their necks?

Somewhere down the hall a door was violently flung open, sending out a booming sound that rattled the walls of her room. It was followed by a flurry of footsteps—her father's stocking feet pounding the floor as he ran.

Sarah jumped up and pressed her ear to the door. Her father was calling for the footman, demanding that someone flag down a carriage, the horses having already been put to bed for the evening.

She cracked the door open to better be able to hear what it was that was going on.

"When did you get this? Why wasn't I told?" Her father's voice was loud and agitated. "Get on the telegraph and let the others know! If this is true . . . Damn that metal man!"

Sarah leaned back and gasped. "Tom!"

She opened the door wider this time. Her father was screaming out requests followed by mumbled, inaudible replies. "Where the hell are my boots! I'll need to go by the Hall first, and there's no damn time! Who's on duty now?"

It wasn't the first time such an emergency had swept over the Stanton household. Nor was it even the tenth. But it was one of the first times she could remember since her mother died that she had not been a part of the commotion. Her father would charge out of his office, screaming that there was an emergency at the Hall, and the staff would call the continued screaming. Up until now she had always been a part of preparing him to "head out into the action" as he liked to put it.

She closed the door and leaned back against it. Sarah hadn't just spent the last few days crying. She had been considering plans of her own. What she would do if the Automaton needed her. . . . Her eyes glanced over to the bed.

But what if it wasn't really Tom? Perhaps it was just Nathaniel, or any one of the others, caught up in another nonsensical battle, fighting some trumped-up gang leader and an army of dandies. . . .

"What other mechanical man could he have been talking about?" And if it was Tom, and if he needed her help, she had promised to come help him. But her previous attempt to protect the Automaton had resulted in her nearly losing one of her feet to frostbite. People who stood in the way of the Paragons got hurt in the most surprising ways.

And even if she could escape, there was no way that she could figure out where Tom was. . . . Sneaking into the Hall of Paragons on a Saturday morning was one thing, but in an emergency it would be buzzing with preparations for battle, with both heroes and servants preparing.

Perhaps she could hide out nearby, and follow them when they headed out. . . .

She shook her head and spoke sternly to herself. "You're being ridiculous, Sarah. You're just a girl—not an adventurer." She was standing on thin ice as it was. If her father discovered her chasing the Paragons, there was no telling how much trouble she would be in.

And she didn't want things to get any worse. She had already decided that she wouldn't let her father force her into some loveless society marriage. But waging that war would have to be done with guile and patience. If she tried something now he'd have her wed in a month, just to get her out of his hair.

She closed her eyes and tried to order her thoughts. The anxiety inside of her only seemed to grow.

Throwing caution to the wind, she fell to the floor and pulled the box out from underneath the bed. She lifted it up and tumbled the contents out onto the mattress.

Sarah reached down and picked up the pneumatic gun. It had taken some work to keep the weapon a secret from Jennifer and her father when she had gotten back to Stanton House, but she had managed to use the commotion to sneak it up into her bedroom. And after she had been stripped of her mud-covered petticoats it had only taken a moment's distraction to kick it under the vanity.

The pistol felt heavy and cold in her hand, leaching away the warmth from her skin. It was, she thought to herself, in every way the opposite of Tom—a machine without grace, thought, or mercy. "But you're mine," she said to herself, "and you'll do just what I tell you to."

She placed the gun back on the bed, stripped off her clothes, and picked up the thick riding breeches and black boots she had selected. They were the only actual pants that she owned, and for what she had in mind layers of petticoats would be absolutely the wrong thing to wear.

She had also stolen one of her father's white dress shirts. It was much too large for her, and she needed a pair of garters to hold up the sleeves.

Once it was somewhat fitted she pulled one of her black winter corsets over the top of it. She laced it up as best as she could without the help of any of her servants. It might not look right, but at least she was able to breathe.

There was a reverberating slam from downstairs that signaled her father's departure. The commotion in the house died down instantly. She ran to the door, hoping to lean her ear up against it and find out just how much time she had.

"Miss Stanton?" She gasped with surprise and stepped back as it swung open. Jennifer Farrows's voice rang out. "Your father told me to . . . What *is* going on in here?"

Sarah lost her balance and fell to the floor, her bottom landing with a solid thump on the carpet.

"I was trying to hear something." She looked up at the maid with a ridiculous grin on her face.

Mrs. Farrows looked around the room, giving herself a moment to grasp what was going on. "What are you wearing?" The look of surprise on her face melted into one of outright horror. "This! This is . . ."

Before things went too far Sarah jumped to her feet, swept around the flustered maid, and shut the door behind her. "I need your help."

"My h-help . . . ? What you *need* is a good spanking from someone with a firm hand!"

"I'm not a child anymore, Jennifer." Sarah turned around and presented the strings of the corset. "But if you do still have a firm hand, then I could use your help in cinching this up properly."

The older woman's trained fingers reached out and grabbed the strings automatically, tugged them tight, and then dropped them. "Sarah, you're wearing your corset on the outside of your father's shirt."

The maid looked over her shoulder and saw the rest of the objects spread out on the bed. "No, I won't help you with this. I know I'm just the maid, but I'd like to think that I'm also your friend."

Sarah turned around. "It must seem like madness. It seems that way to me as well." She took the other woman's hands into hers. "But let's be honest with each other. Can you truly imagine me sitting up here, rotting away until the summertime comes so I can be married to some rich idiot who'll stuff me into some other mansion? I'd go mad in a week." She clutched her hands to her chest, taking Mrs. Farrows's with them.

Neither one spoke for seconds as they looked at each other. Then a tear fell out of Mrs. Farrows's eye, and Sarah sniffled, breaking the silence.

Jennifer took back her hands. "Turn around." Sarah tried to reply, but her words caught in her chest. "Turn around," Mrs. Farrows repeated.

Sarah did as she was told to, and the older woman grabbed the corset strings and pulled them tight. "You'll never be able to manage this ridiculous costume on your own."

"It's the best I could come up with, given the circumstances."

The older woman took a second look at the jumble of items still lying on the bed. "Look at that mess." She frowned. "You're definitely your father's daughter, there's no doubt about that."

"I only wish that he could see that."

"You're both too stubborn for each other's good." She spun Sarah around. "And you both dress like French perverts."

Sarah giggled. "Mrs. Farrows! I had no idea."

"Well, it's true. And if you're going to Madison Square dressed like a tart, you'll end up getting unwanted attention from more than just the villains."

"Madison Square?"

Jenny clucked her tongue. "Damn it."

"Such language! What do you know, Jenny Farrows?"

"I overheard your father saying that the Paragons had received a note that they were to meet the Automaton."

"When and where?"

"I shouldn't say."

Sarah spoke more slowly and directly. "You know you'll tell me, so save me the trouble."

Jenny rolled her eyes. "Madison Square Garden at seven p.m."

Sarah glanced at the clock on her dresser. "But it's nearly seven now!"

"It seems that O'Rourke didn't take it seriously." She rolled her eyes. "Anyone who's been in your father's employ for as long as he has should know that the more outlandish something is, the more likely it is to be true."

Jenny regarded Sarah for a moment, then pressed her hand to her face and tapped her index finger to the apple of her cheeks. "You're going to need a coat. Meanwhile take a look in the bottom drawer in your closet. There should be some old costume pieces along with some other bits of junk that might help you with your suicidal journey.

"Now wait here, and I'll be right back." Mrs. Farrows bustled backward out the door.

When Sarah pulled open the drawer she felt her heart drop. Jenny had taken the gloves she'd stolen from her father's closet and placed them on top. Sarah could only wonder at how angry and disappointed Alexander Stanton would be if he knew that she had stolen them from his closet. Still, it felt like wearing something of her father's could bring her good luck, and the steel-reinforced fingers might come in handy. She threw them onto the bed.

Rummaging a bit deeper she grabbed an old tricorn hat. It was battered and worn, an actual hand-me-down from her revolutionary grandfather that had managed to make it into her hands. She pulled it over her head and looked in the mirror. It certainly made her appear less feminine. "That could be useful."

She walked back to the bed, reached down into the pile, and lifted up the Sleuth's mask. While the front of it was clean and polished, the interior looked well used, and she wondered how many adventures it had been on with Mr. Wickham. She pressed it against her skin and looked into the mirror above her vanity. Her face was gone, replaced by a black veil, her green eyes masked by a thin scrap of black muslin tightly stretched across the eye-holes. Tom's words rang in her ears: "When a man puts on a mask, he discovers his greatest confidence and his darkest desire at the same moment."

The door snapped open and then shut again. Sarah turned to see Mrs. Farrows entering the room, a black leather coat hanging off her arm. She stepped behind Sarah and held up the jacket. "Now try it on."

Sarah slipped her arms into the sleeves. "No smart comments."

"I've already told you this is ridiculous, and you've already ignored me." Jenny reached around Sarah's waist and began to tie the belt.

The coat was oversized, but not too big. There was a layer of thick wool inside to keep her warm, and a row of heavy buttons down the front. With the right tailoring it could seem quite dashing. "Where did you get this?"

"Jean-Tom, the cook. It's from when he lived in Paris. He asked me to take it out for him, but he's grown far more stomach than this coat will ever give."

Sarah scooped up the hat and gloves, and slipped them on. Then she stepped in front of the mirror and sighed. "I do look ridiculous." Although there was something about it that was thrilling as well—she hadn't dared to imagine it, but she was a Paragon. "Or at least I'm pieces of Paragons. . . ."

"You're a fool is what you are, Sarah Stanton." Jenny smothered her with a hug. "And if you're going to be a fool, then I think you'll need this." She held out a battered book. The words "National City Bank of New York" were stamped in faded gold leaf on the cover.

"My bank book?"

A tear rolled down Mrs. Farrows's face. "In case you can't come back."

"Don't be silly, Jen. I'll be back."

"I've known your father as long as I've known you . . ." She slipped it into her coat pocket. "You may need it."

Sarah held the other woman's hand and looked into her eyes. What had seemed to have existed for years as a flight of fancy now felt dangerously real. She had fantasized about becoming a hero, but she had been told over and over again how truly dangerous it was.

Something rose up in her, a moment of desperate realization—this was the point of no return.

"Are you okay, Sarah?" Mrs. Farrows asked her.

She realized that the mask was hiding her face. "Thank you, Jen."

"Do what you have to do. Save your metal friend if you can. Just promise you won't get killed. I couldn't bear it." Jenny ran to the door, opened it, and stepped into the hallway. "Now get going."

Sarah was almost out of the room when she turned back and grabbed the gun off of the bed. It slipped easily into the inside pocket of the coat.

As she ran quietly down the circular staircase to the front door she heard Mrs. Farrows's voice behind her. "You've become exactly what you promised your father you wouldn't be."

"The Adventuress," she said to herself, and smiled.

Chapter 25
A Traitor

It began to dawn on Sarah that many of the problems facing a costumed hero in a city the size of New York were logistical; how did you get from where you were to where you were so desperately needed, and do it in time to be of any real help?

The Paragons had developed a series of fireworks and flares, along with plans to minimize the time between almost any two points on Manhattan.

But Sarah was without those resources. Desperate for a solution, she reverted to something she had seen Nathaniel do as a child—a game that he had called "double dare."

Reaching the corner Sarah waited, and then grabbed hold of a passing delivery wagon. The undercarriage was almost four feet off the ground, and it took every bit of her strength to lift herself up using the chain that held the rear doors shut.

With some maneuvering she managed to stand on the thin wooden lip sticking out from the back of the cart, her feet splayed out parallel to the edge. The cart lurched forward and she felt a jolt of pain shooting up through her arms and feet. The trick had worked, but Nathaniel had ridden the back of a cart for more than a city block.

The streets were blissfully empty, and they seemed to be heading in the right direction, turning onto Broadway a few blocks north of Columbus Circle.

As they rolled southward she expected someone to call her out to the driver, but the few people who did seem to notice her seemed content to point or wave. Certainly no one cared enough to interrupt her ride. She had never appreciated the average New Yorker's ability to ignore the unusual as much as she did right now.

Thirty-five blocks later she arrived at the park exhausted and half frozen. The burning sensation in her arms from hanging onto the carriage was excruciating—magnified by the cold along with the constant vibration of wooden wheels against the cobblestones. It conspired to make her feet feel numb and her hands feel like claws made from wire and pain.

And then a green flare exploded into the sky. She heard the carriage driver in front of her muttering to himself, "It's them Paragons again." He snapped the reins and veered the carriage left at the next intersection. "I'll be damned if we're going near that kind of trouble," he said to the horses.

Sarah dropped off the back of the cart and took a few wobbling steps to slow herself down. Her feet were somehow both aching and half asleep simultaneously, but she forced herself to march forward. Her boots were already chafing, adding yet another layer of pain to her suffering feet. Sarah made a mental note that comfortable shoes were clearly a key part of being a successful costumed heroine.

A metallic crack ripped through the air, and Sarah instantly turned to see where the sound had come from.

A figure was sprawled against the Arm of Liberty, a tall man standing above him, hammering away with what appeared to be a very large club.

For a moment she was too shocked to do anything but stare. She had never seen one man attack another with such violence before.

When the sprawling figure's head flew through the air she almost screamed. And when the arms and legs of the fallen figure continued to thrash even after the decapitation it was obvious who the victim was.

There was a pause, and the Automaton's body collapsed to the ground. Then the attack began again, with the giant man picking Tom up bodily by his chest and smashing him back down.

Sarah slipped the gun out of her jacket pocket. Where the cold, heavy weapon had seemed dangerous in her room, it felt comforting to her now.

Sarah had lived her entire life around fighting men. Her father had fought on the Southern battlefields, and after her mother died he had been liberal about allowing her to spend the occasional evening curled up in the corner of the sitting room, listening in as her father told the other Paragons stories of the battle of Gettysburg. He had, of course, toned down the violence and ribald humor that she had heard her mother complain about (and that she would have desperately liked to hear for herself). But she had learned a few lessons from these war stories, one of which was the importance of the element of surprise. It was, as her father always said when discussing it, "an advantage you only get to use once." The other Paragons had always heartily agreed.

Remaining hidden while Tom was literally being torn to pieces was no easy task, not only because there was so little for her to hide behind in the lamp-lit park but because her anger was threatening to get the best of her.

She had seen the Automaton repair himself before, but she didn't recognize the object that the gray man had ripped out as his clockwork heart until she saw the glow of the Alpha Element as he slid it free.

Creeping up closer to the man, she could see that there was something deeply wrong with his skin. His body was a dark gray, speckled with spots of black, almost as if he had been covered in soot.

He handed the heart over to another figure. When she realized it was the Bomb Lance her eyes narrowed and her resolve grew.

The gray man held the silvery cylinder up in front of him. "Finally, I have everything I need." He slipped it into a metal case and put it into his pocket. "Now we can—"

Sarah pulled the trigger, and the gun let out a loud burp, then a hiss. The effect was immediate: it flung the tall man into the air, and he landed with a crash onto a strip of sidewalk fifteen feet away.

The Bomb Lance vanished as well, and Tom's heart crashed to the ground almost exactly where he had stood.

Sarah was thrown in the opposite direction, managing to stop herself by grabbing onto the side of Liberty's arm. She would need to find a way to brace herself more solidly the next time she fired.

Tom's body lay nearby—a headless mess of scattered cogs and broken metal, almost unrecognizable as the elegant living machine he had been only a few minutes before. After all of this—the loss, the suffering, the grief—she had not been in time to save him.

She let out a scream of helplessness, frustration, and anger and then turned to look, as he attempted to rise, at the man she had just shot. "You killed him!" she snarled. The words came out from deep within her throat, and the low tones made it sound like the voice of a stranger. "I'll tear you apart!"

Lord Eschaton was dazed, trying hard to come to his senses as Sarah walked toward him. He shook his head and then ran a hand over his face. His mask had been torn away. "Who are you?" he muttered. He pulled away his hand to reveal glowing white blood smeared across it.

Sarah lifted up the pneumatic gun and pointed it directly at him. A small voice told her that this was not the way—not the way the Paragons would do things, and certainly not the way a lady should conduct herself. She laughed under her mask at the thought of it. "A lady," she said out loud. The words came out sounding cruel and uncaring. The gun was pure power in her hands.

As she began to press down on the trigger, she heard a familiar sound coming from her left—the mechanical thunk of a harpoon being readied to fire. She spun around and pointed the gun at the source of the noise. She and the Bomb Lance fired simultaneously.

The harpoon went wide, missing her entirely and tangling itself in an iron gate a few feet beyond. Sarah's weapon relied far less on accuracy, and it knocked the Bomb Lance flat on his back, the momentum and wind sending him skidding across the cement until he reached the edge of a patch of snow-covered grass. His frame caught in the mud, and he jerked to a halt.

Her element of surprise was utterly gone now, if she had ever had it It had been the Irishman who had almost impaled *her*.

"Dear God," she said as waves of panic rolled over her. How close to death had she come? Then it dawned on her that the Irishman might not be her only hidden opponent. How many of them were there? What had she been thinking?

She turned to see the tall man running toward her, his hand outstretched and glowing white. He lunged at her as she jumped out of the way.

There was an explosion of energy as the gray man's hands made contact with the ground. The sparks reached out to Sarah, sending a tingle through her body that caused all her muscles to twitch, including quite a few she'd never felt before. She could only imagine what would have happened if he had been able to make contact.

The air stank of burned metal. The odor was similar to toasted bread, and it was oddly comforting, reminding her of the time she had spent in Professor Darby's lab. But her lingering moment of calm evaporated when Sarah realized that she had dropped the gun.

She glanced around for it desperately. When she saw it glinting in the gaslight, Sarah dived for it.

As she wrapped her hand around the barrel she felt something grabbing onto her ankle. The gray giant had grabbed onto her foot.

He looked up at her and smiled. It was a wicked grin, made even more shocking by his shining white teeth. "I don't know who you are, girl, but I'm impressed with that weapon." She felt herself being dragged toward him. "If you tell me where you got it, I won't kill you right away."

Sarah picked up the gun and placed the grip in her left hand as the gray man dragged her closer.

The pneumatic blast threw him backward, but he managed to hold onto her long enough to send them both tumbling painfully across the ground. All she could think about as she spun head over heels was maintaining her grip on the weapon.

The moment she came to a stop she tried to find her enemy. Lord Eschaton let out a moan, revealing to her that he had been smashed hard against one of the park's thick, black, wrought-iron fences.

Sarah winced as she stood up. The skin of her calf where he had grabbed her felt raw underneath her riding breeches.

She held up the gun and walked toward the gray man. She wondered how she could stop him. Even if she had a temporary advantage, there was no way she could subdue him without at least knocking him unconscious. And what then? She had no rope or handcuffs. It hadn't even occurred to her that she would need them. There would be no way to "win" this fight that didn't involve someone getting badly hurt.

And she needed to find Tom's heart. If she could get back to the Hall of Paragons, perhaps she could use her copy of the Alpha Element to—

There was a loud pop, a smack, and then a hiss, like a mechanical sigh. It repeated itself, the smack coming much closer this time. A small chunk of sidewalk flew into the air in the space between her and the gray man.

"Turn around." The voice was shockingly familiar. Any hopes she'd had of something positive coming out of this confrontation had now completely evaporated. "Tell me what's going on here."

She turned to face her father and tell him what had happened, but the other man spoke first. "She used that gun to destroy the Automaton, and then she almost killed me. Shoot her before she can shoot you."

The Industrialist—*her father*—was pointing his gun straight at her. "Drop the weapon. I don't want to shoot a lady, but I will if I must."

She had never seen him like this before. Certainly she had witnessed him dressed up as the Industrialist a number of times—his gun, the shield, that ridiculous steaming hat. But what she faced now was what his enemies saw: a smoking monster, full of anger and menace.

He screamed at her. "I said *drop it!*"

And for just an instant she actually considered trying to outshoot him. Some part of her wanted to know if her trigger finger was faster than his—to test herself against this supposed legend, a man she knew as an aging blowhard.

The bravado was a trick of the adrenaline that was coursing through her. She knew that. Her mother had always said that what her father did was madness, and now she could feel the truth of it. She let the weapon drop from her fingers. "I'm sorry, Father."

Sarah closed her eyes and felt the sweat rolling down her face, or was it a tear? Underneath the leather mask even she couldn't tell.

When she brought the glove up to her face, her father's eyes widened in recognition. "A cog? My gloves? Sarah? Is that you?"

And then, like someone jerking out of bed only to discover that they are still trapped in the nightmare they thought they'd escaped, a harpoon slammed into her father's arm, just below the shoulder. It severed the connector for his gun, and red steam spewed out from the wound.

"Thar she blows!" cackled Murphy as he raised his arm into the air and reloaded his frame.

Sarah dropped to the ground, desperately grasping to get her weapon back into her hands, and when she stood up she heard a roar coming from up above. Looking up into the moonlit sky, she saw a small figure soaring above the rooftops, a trail of steam behind him. "Nathaniel," she said softly.

The gray man was already grabbing his coat and shirt from the ground. He looked at her and smiled, his teeth flashing. "So kind of you to join us for the evening, *Lady Stanton.* My name is Lord Eschaton." He tipped his head as a greeting. "I only hope that every one of us got what we came for."

Her eyes glanced toward Tom's body, and the gray man smiled. "Feel free to loot whatever you want from the mechanical man's corpse, my dear. I already have everything I need." He turned and ran in the other direction, the Bomb Lance hobbling after him.

She raised the gun and aimed it at the fleeing figures, fully intending to stop them both by whatever means necessary. "Sarah!"

"What?" she shouted angrily, then turned and looked at her father. Blood had soaked the snow where he landed.

"What the hell are you doing here?"

She looked at him, then at Tom's shattered body, and finally at Nathaniel descending from the sky toward the park. This time she was sure that what she felt on her face were tears.

"Tell me it isn't you," she said, turning toward him.

"What are you talking about? And why are you wearing Wickham's mask?" He seemed confused, and Sarah realized that her face was hidden from him.

"Promise me that you aren't the traitor," she pleaded, her voice raw with emotion. Once again it was a stranger's voice that was coming out of her.

"Sarah, it's time to stop this nonsense. There is no traitor." He tried to sit up, but only managed to groan as the harpoon shifted in his arm. He reminded her of Nathan on that morning on the bridge—children, playing with toys, until they got hurt. . . .

"There is. I'm sure of it, and I hope and pray it isn't you." She shoved the pistol into the pocket of her coat and walked past Tom's corpse. "Wickham told me that he didn't think you were involved, and if that's the case then it must be either the Submersible or the Iron-Clad." She was talking to herself as much as him, letting the words flow out of her. "I know that Nathaniel isn't capable of doing anything like this. He loves you too much." She did what was almost a curtsey as she reached down to pick up Tom's empty heart. It was solid and heavy, but somehow still lighter than she had imagined it would be. The surface was scratched, and it made an unpleasant sound that spoke of broken metal inside of it.

"I told you to stay away from this! Now look at me! Look at us. . . ."

Something else was sticking out from Tom's broken body—a battered notebook with a black leather cover.

"No, Father." She reached out, tugged the book free, and then stuffed it into the pocket of her coat. "Not until I know for sure." Across the park she could see that Nathan had landed and was sprinting toward them.

Clutching Tom's heart to her chest, she turned and ran away into the night.

ABOUT THE AUTHOR

ANDREW MAYER has been creating video games for almost two decades, including designing the original Dogz and Catz digital pets. He currently lives in Portland, Oregon, and posts his musings on writing and media at www.andrewpmayer.com.

This is his first novel.